STO[NE]

Graham Edwards wa[s] [born] and grew up in Bou[rnemouth. He went to] school in London and now works in a special effects design studio. He lives in Nottingham with his wife Helen and their two children. *Stone & Sun* is his sixth novel.

Voyager

GRAHAM EDWARDS

STONE & SUN

HarperCollins*Publishers*

Voyager
An Imprint of HarperCollins*Publishers*
77–85 Fulham Palace Road,
Hammersmith, London W6 8JB

www.voyager-books.com

A Paperback Original 2001
1 3 5 7 9 8 6 4 2

Extract from 'The Peaches' by Dylan Thomas from *Collected Stories*,
published by JM Dent, quoted by permission of David Higham
Associates.

A catalogue record for this book
is available from the British Library

ISBN 0 00 651072 8

Typeset in Meridien by Palimpsest Book Production Limited,
Polmont, Stirlingshire

Printed and bound in Great Britain by
Omnia Books Limited, Glasgow

this one's for Anne

There, playing Indians in the evening, I was aware of me myself in the exact middle of a living story, and my body was my adventure and my name. I sprang with excitement and scrambled up through the scratching brambles again.

'The Peaches'
Dylan Thomas

Come with me now
Hold on tight
Trust me
I won't let go

Prologue

My name is Areken.

Isn't it?

Suddenly her name seemed wrong, as if it did not belong to her at all. As if something had reached into her mind and changed its inner architecture. Changed her sense of self, moved things around.

Made space for something new.

Areken. Areken.

It didn't sound right at all.

But if she wasn't Areken then who was she?

I am a dragon, *she began. That was good, that was fine. She knew that was true, knew it right through her very soul. Nothing could ever change that one, elemental truth.*

I am a dragon.

Good. Now, what else?

Long ago, in the age of charm, I tried to steal the secret of immortality. I succeeded. I became immortal, but in becoming immortal I was robbed of my physical form. I became a deathless dragon ghost, trapped in the deep ice at the crest of the world.

A million years passed by. Both charm and dragons were swept from the world.

Slowly I gained power until at last I found myself a new

body, a temporary host in which I rode on a quest for a new dragon form. This host was one of those flimsy, mortal creatures known as men, but which I knew as faeries.

This particular faery was a female, a woman. Her name was Annie.

In Annie's body I rode between worlds, crossing over to the strange, upturned realm of Stone, where dragons still lived.

And across Stone I journey now, still trapped in this charmless faery husk, still seeking the dragon form I am surely destined to inhabit.

Except now I come to doubt myself, my identity. Something is probing my mind, an intruder. I can feel it touching me, trying to take hold.

What is it? Who is it?

And who am I?

Areken.

Can it truly be my name? Can it?

Areken turned her attention from within and looked out through her borrowed faery eyes.

The ledge on which she stood was built from broad wooden planks projecting from the world-sized wall of Stone. Beyond the ledge the sky was a vast blue tapestry striped with falling clouds. Stone: a world tipped uncompromisingly on its side.

Other faeries were clustered on the ledge: her companions. Jonah and Gerent and Malya. A fourth faery – a winged one – was flying towards them.

The flying faery's body was caked with mud and a blue star was painted on his belly. The wings were not his own – they had been fabricated from stolen dragon scales and attached to his shoulders with a makeshift harness. Beads of magic were gathered in the small of his back, shed by the flight-charm he had also thieved.

Areken knew this abominable creature. His name was Frey

2

and before committing his crimes he had tortured the dragon to whom the scales had belonged.

You will pay for that, faery! *she thought. The anger cut through, clean and welcome. Oh, how you will all pay!*

For a moment she forgot her confusion over her name and knew only the anger.

There came a whisper. She looked back into the cave-like interior of Annie's skull, the living chamber in which her soul was being carried. It was huge and there was only her anger to fill it.

Into the empty space a voice screamed her name.

'AREKEN!'

Everything else came to a halt.

The clouds tumbling down through the vertical sky slowed and then stopped, curlicues of vapour held motionless against the pull of gravity. On the ledge the faeries froze; the flying faery froze too, every part of his body locking in place: wings, arms, the expressive muscles of his furious face. Yet, like the clouds, he did not fall.

All around her the great river of time was coming to a standstill.

Areken knew a lot about time but not, it seemed, as much as she thought she did. She sensed something massive in the distance, approaching at dizzying speed from a direction that was not here, *not* there . . .

Something exploded into her mind.

'AREKEN!' it screamed again, raping its way in, wrecking its way into her world. The intruder was a constant scream bullying inwards, as irresistible as an avalanche. Then, abruptly, the avalanche stopped. Areken stared across the cave of Annie's skull. Something else was in here with her, something from another world. Something icy cold that floated and shone like a sun.

The intruder spoke.

'Do you not know me?' it said. The voice was Areken's own.

Areken said nothing. She tried to think nothing too, aware

3

that her thoughts must be naked before this . . . this monster. *But her anger betrayed her, spilling over the mental barrier she was trying hastily to erect.*

'Such fury!' *remarked the intruder.* 'I had quite forgotten. Still it may be useful on the journey ahead.'

Areken's defences collapsed even before she had completed them, withering beneath the icy glare of the intruder. She squinted into its blazing presence, trying to make it out.

'Who are you?' *she said.*

The intruder shone brighter for a second, then the light dimmed to reveal a dragon just like her.

'Who am I?' *the intruder laughed.* 'That's easy – I am you!'

Areken's anger licked through the skull-cave like fire. Cast aside, the pitiful remains of Annie's own faery consciousness cowered in the shadows it cast.

'Since we are sisters,' *the intruder went on,* 'I intend to be scrupulously honest with you.'

The voice, so like Areken's own. Yet a cold voice, filled with ice, devoid of emotion. Therefore terrifying.

'Then speak,' *growled Areken.* 'But be quick – I have little patience.'

'I bring you a great gift: the chance to learn patience. Now listen to me. I am a dragon, just as you are. Indeed I am, as I have already said, you. My name is Archan.

'Our stories are almost identical, Areken, yours and mine. I too travelled to Stone inside the body of a faery called Annie. I too was accompanied by a second faery called Jonah Lightfoot. Jonah and I journeyed together, for a while at least. A little later Jonah did something very interesting with the rods.'

'Rods? What rods?' *interrupted Areken. She felt hot and dazed. And angry, so angry!*

'Ah yes, I forget – you have not yet encountered the rods. Well, there will be time enough to describe them in detail later.

4

Suffice it to say they contain memories. All the memories of the world. Stone is a storage place, you see, and the memory rods are the means by which it contains history.

'Jonah . . . he is an unusual being. An adept, able to explore the memory rods: using Stone, he can travel through time – more than that, in fact, he is able actually to alter *the memories it contains. In short, he can change history, Areken – past, present or future.*

'In my version of Stone, Jonah travelled back into his own past to prevent one of his faery companions – Malya – from being killed. He succeeded, but in doing so he altered the natural flow of the river of time, splitting it into two separate streams. He created a paradox, and in creating a paradox he created an entire world.

'You belong to the world he made. I am the Archan from the original Stone. You are the Areken from a version of Stone created by Jonah Lightfoot's interference. And now I need your help.'

Areken assimilated the flood of information without question. Archan's authority was beyond doubt; listening to her was like looking into the clearest crystal mirror. Indeed, she scarcely heard the words; it was the truth she was absorbing, unfettered by vocabulary or grammar.

But believing it did not mean she had to like it.

The instant Archan had finished she raged, 'How dare you storm into my mind and make it your own?' Her fury was an expanding sphere of fire. Archan deflected it casually and grasped her twin with talons of pure ice.

'I dare because I am stronger than you.' Archan's voice remained cold and calm. 'I am older than you. I am your future self. Never forget that. I have battled with Jonah. I have swallowed Stone's memories and they have brought me strength. I control you. You cannot resist me. You are entirely within my power. You are, in fact, my slave.'

Areken lost control. She lashed out, spilling her wrath into

Annie's mind. The remains of the faery whimpered incoherently in the sun-bright glare. Archan sat back, the ice by which she was surrounded taming the fires before they could catch. Soon Annie's entire mind was Arctic cold.

Sullen and defeated, Areken ceased her attack and glowered at her sister. Archan was the merest sketch of a dragon: a red skeleton perched atop an icy pedestal, leering at her twin through eyes of perfect, blank chrome.

Sister or not, Areken resolved there and then to kill her.

'If you're that powerful, Archan, why do you need me so badly?'

Archan's craggy skull did not so much as move. Her mirror-eyes blinked once.

'I am . . . in my world, my Stone, Jonah Lightfoot has found a way to . . . well, let us just say I am temporarily incapacitated. The time has come to rid the world – all the worlds – of Jonah Lightfoot once and for all. The time has come for the final confrontation. After that the future can at last begin.'

Areken grinned fiercely. 'He's locked you away somewhere, hasn't he? He's found a prison for you. You're trapped and you can't get free!'

'The details are not important. What matters is that I have found my way here. And now I need you to take me somewhere.'

'Where?'

At first Archan did not reply. Instead she tilted Annie's head until it was facing straight up. Areken gazed at clouds frozen in the sky. A near-vertical cliff face rising into distant haze, spiralling up into the future.

'There,' whispered Archan at last. 'Up there.'

Time flowed smoothly forwards again.

On the ledge the faeries battled. The flier with the stolen dragon wings brandished a miniature skull at his assailants. Beams of focused charm streamed from both its eye sockets and its gaping mouth. The raw magic splashed across the bodies of the faeries, setting their soft skin alight. The hair on their heads

6

ignited instantly, crowning them with fire. Howling, they died, Jonah and Malya and Gerent. When they fell from the ledge and into the abyss they were clinging to each other like children.

Frey, the winged faery, frowned at the one remaining female, the one he knew as Annie but who was really Areken. He was aware that something was wrong. Very wrong.

Then Archan took control.

Charm swirled through the skull-cave, sucking Areken's spirit entirely free of Annie's body. She felt her disembodied consciousness hauled through the air to where Frey was hovering. She entered the flying faery's mind through his eyes, which barely had time to widen before they both rolled back and turned to chrome.

A new host, a new prison.

Looking out through this new set of eyes Areken found herself looking for the first time on Annie's face.

Female. Dark hair, dark leather garments. Dark and haunted eyes. Briefly, beneath the fear and fatigue, hope.

Annie swayed, teetering on the very brink of the wooden ledge. The abyss yawned, hungry beneath her.

Something else was moving inside Frey's faery skull. It was Archan, of course. She had come too.

Archan raised Frey's hand, the one holding the magical skull, and sent a spear of charm through Annie's throat. Annie died, and then she fell.

Areken watched, powerless, as Archan flexed Frey's stolen dragon wings and took them up into Stone's endless sky.

Behind them both, pale and tiny in the combined light of the fire and the ice, Frey's subjugated soul retreated to the furthest, darkest corner of the cave of his skull, where he curled up and waited.

The wings continued to beat, taking them up.

1

Gauntlet

With his eyes closed, Jonah could almost imagine he was standing on a flying carpet.

In fact he was cradled in the cupped hand of the Goddess of the ocean: Ruane, who was also known as Rata Kadul. Measuring a good half-mile from head to toe, Ruane was big enough to hold Jonah in Her hand as he might hold a spider found behind the wainscoting.

Ruane's ocean was very different to the Earthly seas over which Jonah had once voyaged. It, like everything else on Stone, was tipped up at an angle ten degrees short of vertical. It was literally a wall of water. The miraculous power of charm kept the ocean from crashing down Stone's precipitous face, while the ever-falling wind maintained a steady pattern of waves across its ever-shifting surface.

If Jonah tipped his head over, the sideways ocean of Stone was not so very different from the Pacific, the greatest sea on the world of his birth.

These days it rarely occurred to him to do such a thing; he was a denizen of Stone now. The Earth, with its flat horizons and high-domed skies, sometimes seemed no more real to him than a dream.

'A little to the right, Ruane!' he shouted, knowing She could not hear him.

Her fingertips drifted to within a few yards of the Bark's hull. The Bark was pitching violently in the swell, but Ruane had a delicate touch for one so large and moved Her hand in perfect synchrony.

Confident She would not let him fall, Jonah marched along Her inclined index finger and lightly jumped the gap to the platform jutting from the Bark's hull. He landed with a thump on damp wood, slipped and grabbed a gnarled handrail before turning to wave to the Goddess. Already the hand was withdrawing. Ruane's face, a quarter of a mile distant, was lost behind the waves and the gigantic swell of Her breast.

Jonah could feel the difference at once. Standing on Ruane's gargantuan form he might just as well have been standing on a rock. But the Bark was a different matter. Though this spherical, living ship had grown considerably bigger in recent days (it was now as large as one of the tea-carrying clippers Jonah had seen on his passage to the East Indies) it was still essentially a ship, and therefore a platform on which even the most strong-stomached of Englishmen might readily become sea-sick.

Gripping the handrail, Jonah lurched forward and leaned over the side, struggling to hold down his breakfast (Gerent's delicious version of kedgeree). Spray crashed across him and within a few seconds he was soaked through. Water trailed through his long red hair and the itching in his waterlogged beard was maddening; he wondered if it was time to borrow one of Malya's razor-like knives and start shaving again.

A face appeared in the hull behind him, embossed into wood that had momentarily become as soft as wax. It was eight feet high, an old and elfin face, and it was smiling sympathetically.

'It's soft you're getting, Jonah,' it said. Its voice was deep and bristly; brambles quivered in the corners of its mouth. 'Time you spent some time at sea.'

'I suppose you can arrange that, Grandfather Tree,' groaned Jonah, bending down to splash his face with the sea water pooling around his feet. The platform reared up then fell back and wallowed for a while, heaving in a way that was somehow worse for being more gentle.

'You'd like to sail somewhere?'

'Not exactly. We may indeed be about to undertake another voyage, but you know as well as I that it will probably not be by way of the ocean. In fact, I hope that is why you have summoned me here today. Is the Bark ready?'

The face, still smiling, melted back into the wood without answering. In its place a round aperture spiralled open with a noise uncommonly like a creaking door. Relieved at the promise of shelter from the constant spray and the roar of the waves, Jonah ducked inside; the aperture closed behind him with the same eerie sound. Wiping the water from his face he looked around.

He was standing in a small vestibule; as near as he could determine the room was a perfect cube. The wood from which it was made looked like oak so dark it was nearly black. The ceiling glowed, a square of warm light. Directly in front of him, etched into the wall, was a Mah Jongg symbol: the domino pattern of Five Circle. He glanced round and saw the rice-bird of One Bamboo marked on the door through which he had just come.

He was about to call out when Grandfather Tree's face emerged from the floor. Able to manifest himself at any point within the Bark's wooden structure, the ancient Russian tree spirit was the pilot of the magical vessel, the ghost in the machine.

'Another door it is,' he rumbled. 'Just push!'

Jonah touched his hand against the Five Circle symbol. The door whispered aside; as he passed through the opening he could see no seam in the frame at all.

Beyond the vestibule was a round room, fractionally

bigger than the small parlour Jonah had left behind in Kent, an entire world away. Grandfather Tree was waiting for him, his broad face spread around one full third of the room's circumference. A perfect replica of a Queen Anne chair extruded itself from the timber deck; Jonah sat down and clasped his hands in his lap.

'Welcome! The news: it's good,' said the lesky. 'I've been rebuilding the Bark. Now, complete is the work. At last he is what he was. At last he is as he was when the basilisks, the makers of Stone, used him to journey across their creation.'

Grandfather Tree was more at home here than he had ever been in the forest that had been his natural habitat. That forest – Stone's version of the great taiga in which he had once lived on Earth – was now burned and abandoned. Of all the changes the lesky had experienced since leaving the trees, the greatest was his new-found enthusiasm for *freedom*.

Jonah nodded. 'The vessel certainly looks ship-shape, Grandfather Tree, from what little I have seen of it. Only so much of it is visible to mere landlubbers such as myself, you understand.'

'Like an iceberg, he is,' agreed the lesky, 'with his greater part hidden behind the waves. But no longer! Already you have seen the Bark crawl over the land, but always has he returned to the water. Now the Bark is fully restored. Now he can go anywhere!'

Grandfather Tree's face slipped around the wall behind Jonah. In its place opened up a panoramic view of the ocean, as though seen through a window with soft, blurred edges.

Beyond the massive superstructure of the Bark, all timber curves and knots of bramble, was the uncompromising geometry of Stone and sea: the far line of the ocean tipped almost to the vertical, the zebra stripes of cloud coursing down through the sky.

'The Bark looks very much as it always has, Grand-father Tree: like a wood-carver's fantasy of a sub-marine vessel.' Though he was trying to maintain his decorum, Jonah found his heart was beating a veritable tattoo. The lesky's excitement was infectious.

Do we truly have the power to make this journey?

'Wood-carver! Oh ye, that's me all right.' Grandfather Tree's laughter echoed around the small room like a gale through a forest. 'Now watch!'

The Bark juddered. Then it was moving, emerging side-ways from the waves as it headed out towards the sky.

Water sluiced down its decks and through the hap-hazard lattice of branches. As the Bark left the grip of the ocean an array of vanes and probes deployed themselves, countless strange fixtures unfolding from recesses in the hull. Some of these were articulated, swivelling in complex arcs as they tested the air like the insect antennae they resembled; others turned slowly, blades adjusting themselves to direct the flow of air across the Bark's outer skin; still more sat motionless, their functions unguessable.

Then the window closed.

'Is there something you do not wish me to see?' asked Jonah.

'On the contrary. You must see it all. Come!'

The door behind him opened again. Beyond it, across the vestibule, the outside door was already open. Jonah stepped through it and out on to the deck that hugged the spherical hull like a crumpled version of Saturn's mighty ring.

'We are flying!' he exclaimed.

Sure enough, as the last of the pitching and rolling died away the Bark broke clear of the waves.

All around Jonah jostled the blades and spears of the Bark's new array of devices. This close he could see that they looked not so much made as grown. The feelers were really more like branches than antennae, and the air-deflecting vanes reminded him of nothing so much as sycamore seeds. Their texture resembled tree-bark, but when he looked closely he could see elaborate decorative patterns engraved into their surfaces.

'It is beautiful!'

'Ah ye,' agreed Grandfather Tree, 'beautiful he is.'

Jonah took a deep breath. He had seen the Bark float and he had seen it grow legs and walk. This was the first time he had seen it airborne. Inclining his head, he gazed upwards, letting Stone's falling wind splash his face with spice.

'Annie says we must go up there,' he said. 'Can you take us all the way to the top, Grandfather Tree?'

'Never have we moved against the grain.' Grandfather Tree grinned. 'But now . . . let's try!'

Ten days had passed since Archan had made contact with Annie.

Jonah had been with her – they were lying together in the hollow of Ruane's flank, basking in the noon heat – when Annie suddenly sat up. Her whole body was shaking, as though galvanized by an electric current.

'Annie!' he said. 'My darling, whatever is the matter?'

She stopped shaking at once and turned to look at him.

For an instant, Jonah thought he saw a sheen of chrome covering her eyes. They had looked like that once before, when he and Annie had first crossed over to Stone, when Archan had been riding inside Annie's mind. In that dreadful instant he believed the dragon was back.

Then Annie blinked, and when her eyelids opened he was looking into the eyes not of the dragon but of the woman he loved. She started to tremble again, an honest, human trembling this time. Behind it was nothing more supernatural than simple fear.

14

As he wrapped his arms around her she said, 'Oh shit, Jonah – it was her. It was her! She came into my mind. Goddamn it I thought I was rid of her for good!'

'There now, calm yourself.' He felt anything but calm. By stroking her back he managed to slow the frantic beating of her heart but not the wild run of her thoughts.

'Shit, Jonah, what if she can find her way back into my mind again, I mean right back into my mind? I just got a glimpse of her, kind of a glancing blow. It was like, I don't know, like a face at the window, you know, when you're in your home in the dark and this face just appears but it's gone before you can really make it out. Except I knew it was her, dear God yes it was her all right.'

Her eyes were fretful, darting from side to side, but already supplanting her fear was anger. Tearing herself free from Jonah's embrace she stood up and railed at the sky.

'Come on then, if you want me! Come and get me, you cold-hearted bitch! You locked me up once but you won't do it a second time. My mind's my own – if you do find your way in again you sure as hell won't find your way out.'

She stopped suddenly, one hand poised as though she were about to conduct an orchestra. It looked for all the world as though she were listening to something, a voice perhaps, although Jonah could hear nothing but the distant surf.

'Wait,' she said, 'wait, I think . . . she's still far away, Jonah! Thank God, I don't think she can reach me, not really. But . . . I think she's got something to say.'

When Annie turned to face him her eyes were still her own. They were shining with excitement.

'She's still trapped, Jonah! Right where we left her. And she can't get herself free, leastwise not without one hell of an effort. She's trying of course, but she's also making a whole mess of mistakes. And do you know what the biggest mistake is so far?'

Jonah shook his head, simultaneously enthralled and horrified.

'Coming back to haunt me!'

The Bark floated between the opposing walls of stone and sea. Every so often it bobbed upwards like a hot-air balloon straining against its guy ropes. It was silent as an owl; beneath its hull was a very slight vibration, the restrained power of the night hunter.

Grandfather Tree had directed Jonah to an open cockpit near the top of the Bark; from here he could see the entire upper half of the ship.

The Bark began to turn. Then the sea was moving downwards, a huge curtain of water detached from its rails. Acceleration pressed him into the wooden bowl of the cockpit. Clouds fell past like rain.

It was exhilarating. After a time he lay flat on his back in the cockpit, arms and legs spread wide, allowing the wind to pin him like a captured butterfly. Vapour streamed past, an ever-expanding kaleidoscope. The sensation of speed first thrilled him, then lulled him. Islands drifted down, dots of green and yellow set like jewels in the vast tapestry of the hanging ocean.

They journeyed on past wave and water. A continent dropped towards them, fell away, a vertiginous land from which plumed streamers of smoke. Volcanoes? Or a magical race of fire-makers? No way to tell, nor any time to stop. Jonah dozed; he might even have slept.

Gradually the clouds thickened. The kaleidoscope of vapour began to spin, falling fog that twisted round and became a whirlpool. Jonah's eyes seemed to spin in their sockets; at the same time a vast pressure forced its way into his ears. A layer of turbulence was approaching with sickening speed. Something roared.

'Grandfather Tree!'

Jonah could hardly hear the sound of his own voice, though he was yelling with all his might. He tried to sit up, but the irresistible wind kept him flat.

'Fear not!' The lesky's voice was like thunder beside his head. 'Trust the Bark.'

'But . . . the Helix! You have yet to tell me if we can cross the Helix!'

A fat fist of cloud crashed against his body, briefly erasing the world. When the air cleared again all sense of direction had gone – all he could see was a billowing blueness, a sky that was not a sky. Dark cracks began to trace their way across it like breaks in a frozen sea. Still there was the roaring.

'We must at least slow down!'

He remembered the day he had fallen from the citadel of the dragon giant Torus, fallen through Stone's endless sky. Before that fall had been safely broken he had felt his mind begin to unravel, had known the truth of Stone's fundamental law.

Ascent is forbidden, to fall is to die.

Like a woodscrew, Stone took the shape of a slender cone pointing straight up; like a woodscrew it was encircled by a helical thread. While travel was permitted along the line of this thread, or *Helix*, the thread itself was impenetrable. Any attempt to cross it met first with insanity, then with death.

Grandfather Tree believed the refurbished Bark had rewritten the law.

The wind strengthened.

The cracks now covered the sky. They began to turn about each other, a spinning gyre flashing now bright, now dark, a growing, blinding cavity in the space that lay now ahead, now *around*; the roaring pushed so hard against Jonah's eardrums he thought they would burst and the light would come splashing into his head and bursting out of his eyes, brilliant as sunlight, and then he would be shining like the Helix, shining so bright it would not let him go and he would be forever a part of it, a shining, fractured self ablaze in this forgotten corner of a ravaged world, far from home.

The roaring dissolved. Though it was gone Jonah could still hear it, and would hear it for several hours to come; the awful pressure was gone too, and that was a blessing.

'Grandfather Tree?' he quavered, opening eyes he did not know he had shut.

He was still flat on his back, still staring straight up. The turbulence was gone, the cracks in the blue were gone. There was a sky above him once more, but it was not the sky he knew.

The sky was dark red, the colour of wine. The air was dry as sand.

'Alive we are,' said the lesky. 'This is a good thing.'

A cloudless wine-red sky, speckled with small grey shapes. The shapes circled each other like curious insects. Small and close, or large and distant? Jonah could not tell, so strange was the blank, bland sky against which they floated.

'Your surprise is not reassuring,' said Jonah. He sat up very slowly. His head felt as though it had been scrubbed clean from the inside.

'The Bark – I told you he could do anything now!'

One of the grey specks darted sideways, then receded until it was lost. There was a very soft humming sound, fragmented by the wind, which fell here just as it fell on other parts of Stone.

'Another part of Stone,' said Jonah. 'You took us across the line of the Helix. You flew us straight upwards and we have broken through the spiral. Into the future.'

'That you might call it, ye. The shortcut we found, wouldn't you say? The one we wanted!'

18

'I would like to go back, I think,' Jonah said, unable to take his eyes off those circling specks. He felt shaky. 'I fear Annie might have another of her visits. I do not like to leave her alone for too long. This world . . .' he waggled his hand at the sky, 'it is very . . . strange.'

'Time enough there is to explore,' replied Grandfather Tree. 'Another day.'

'Another day . . . um, will going back down be as singular as coming up?'

Jonah spent the return journey below decks. Inside the Bark, thankfully, the passage through the Helix created little more than a few seconds of turbulence, no worse than that caused by a small boat crossing the wake of a steamer. For that, he was very grateful.

Both man and lesky were subdued; for his part Jonah felt uneasy, as though he had walked out on to a circus tightrope and then stepped hastily back, surprised by the depth of the drop. They did not converse during the descent, nor did they say very much as they parted.

'Now we can go wherever we choose,' said Jonah as he stepped from the catwalk on to Ruane's hand. The Bark, hovering just above the knuckle of the Goddess like a bizarre wooden jewel, cast a long shadow across the sea.

'Then we must choose carefully,' replied the lesky. His face had formed momentarily from the timber framework surrounding the hatchway. As he spoke the hatchway closed, erasing his face like a magnet disrupting a pattern of iron filings.

Ruane was a giant with the torso of a woman and the grey and craggy tail of a whale. Despite the near-human proportions of Her upper body and the angular beauty of Her face, Her sheer scale made Her as alien as any creature Jonah had encountered on Stone.

Closely related to the selkies who had colonized Her life-bearing body, Ruane was gentle and strong. She breathed the air, just like Jonah. She dived behind the waves only when it was absolutely necessary – and only after giving considerable notice to the seal-people who relied on Her for so much. Ruane was vessel and harbour to these simple sea folk, protector and provider. And Goddess.

And She was Jonah's friend.

Equally strange was the ocean through which She swam. The waters, raised up to Stone's near-vertical pitch, were held against the will of gravity by charm alone. Sometimes, especially from the air, it looked less like an ocean and more like a massive waterfall whose movement had been slowed to the merest crawl.

And the Goddess? She was a mermaid immersed in that waterfall, a mountaineer embedded in a liquid cliff, a salmon defying the currents trying always to force it down. She was an awesome and unlikely sight.

Her flank was a shoreline. Jonah paced along it, picking his way between the living flotsam and jetsam. A pair of golden crabs, each with hands instead of claws, scuttled sideways as he trod on the lump of driftwood beneath which they had been hiding; the turquoise eyes of an otherwise unseen beast glistened from within a pile of seaweed; one length of the seaweed itself twitched and hissed, clearly alive.

Today Jonah chose to skirt round the selkie settlement. The seal-people were pleasant enough company but their slow and generally aimless conversation seemed to suck the time right out of the day. He always felt uncharitable when he thought of them this way but they were, essentially, dull.

Gerent and Malya would be working among the selkies, trying in vain to interest them in nets or weapons or some other tool or skill. And no doubt the selkies would

20

show interest for a while and then grow bored, and the Neolithics would grow frustrated and so another day would turn. His thoughts were confirmed when he passed a heap of half-made ropes on the edge of the settlement. Carefully begun, they were woven tightly for only a few yards of their length; thereafter they were loose, their raw ends splayed in surrender. Beside the ropes was a pile of headless arrow shafts.

He had to smile: for all their faults the selkies were at least reliable.

His Neolithic friends were just visible as pale shapes against the soaring ocean. A cluster of selkies, their seal-bodies low to the ground, seemed to be watching them with something approaching interest. Their unusually attentive postures drew his eyes back to Gerent and Malya, who were clearly in the throes of a titanic argument.

They were too far away to be heard but their actions alone betrayed them. Gerent raised his arm as if about to strike the woman he loved. Malya did not flinch and he lowered it a moment later, spinning on his heel to stalk away towards the sea. Malya stood and watched him depart with her arms held rigid at her sides.

Belatedly he heard shouts, the remnants of whatever harsh words had passed between them, old sounds chasing the light of their movements across the belly of a Goddess.

Annie was waiting for him at the shack, restless and impatient.

They had built this rude shelter as soon as Ruane had assured them that, as long as they were living on Her skin, She would not dive fully behind the waves. They had thrown it together from driftwood and clumps of dried weed, but it was all they needed in a climate where the sun was warm and rain almost unheard of. Situated halfway up the terrace of Her ribcage, it gave them an

21

unparalleled view along Her flank and tail, and out to the far-distant vertex of Stone's mighty sea.

'Are you all right, my darling?' he said, taking her in his arms.

The tan of her skin was startling against his rather pink flesh; her hair was dark too, almost black, and flowed over him like the waters of the ocean. Her touch, her *contrast*, enchanted him. She was, in his opinion, quite the most beautiful thing in this or any other world.

'Don't fuss, Jonah! Of course I'm okay. Fed up of waiting around, I can tell you that much.'

'You too?'

'What?'

'Nothing. Has she come to you today?'

'She's coming now, Jonah, in case you couldn't tell!' Her hands were trembling and her eyes were drifting in and out of focus.

'Oh, my dear! We must get you inside.'

'Don't *fuss*! Holy Jesus, how did I get myself landed with an English nanny for a man?'

'But . . .'

'Right here is okay, it doesn't matter. Just tell me one thing – did you get across the Helix? Will the Bark go where we need it to go?'

Jonah nodded. 'We are going up, Annie. All the way to the very roof of Stone.'

'Good. Shit, here she comes! Just make sure I don't fall over.'

Obediently he steadied her, watching her eyelids flutter as her gaze turned inwards, feeling her hands spasm as he gripped them with his own. She muttered something under her breath – then all her muscles relaxed. It was an odd sensation, to feel her both limp yet not really requiring support. It was like holding a puppet with the power to work its own strings.

He released his hold, observing her intently as she took

a single step forward, then a single step back. Her hands, hanging at her side, were now utterly still. When her eyes opened however, they were very far away.

'Annie?'

There was a pause, as if the name had had to travel a very long way before reaching her ears.

'I'm here, Jonah, I'm okay. Just watch what I do, like before. I'll be back soon, I promise.'

And so, not for the first time, Jonah watched in trepidation as Annie went out west.

2

Annie Out West – 1

The jerked beef looked like a line of flags waving in the night breeze. Properly dried, those thin strips of meat would stay edible for months to come; right now, eating was the last thing on Annie's mind.

Going out west like this was a bit like having what her mother used to call a *dreamin' dream*. That was the nonsense phrase Katherine Harker had used to describe the experience not only of waking up within a dream, but also being able to control the dream's events.

Annie could remember only one true dreamin' dream of her own (in which she'd dressed all the male members of her family in scarlet frocks and had them perform the Virginia reel in a hurdy-gurdy house, much to the amusement of her mother and her many cousins, who stood watching and stamping their feet appreciatively on the booze-stained boards).

She often had dreams of the other kind, where she was out of control and at the mercy of events. A lot of these were good but those that were bad usually involved what her mother called the *Snallygaster*, an invisible serpent that would slither in through a window during the night and wreck the house while everybody slept. To defeat the Snallygaster – which was only an invisible old ghost after all, all you had to do was blow

24

it away. Only in the dreams Annie just didn't seem to have any breath.

The Snallygaster dreams were scary. But they weren't dreamin' dreams.

That line of jerked beef was an authentic touch. She'd seen beef hung out like that on many a wagon as it toiled its way out west. She'd liked the taste well enough then, if not the stringy texture, but here and now . . . she was pretty sure these replicas were laced with poison. She would look at them, and enjoy the memory of them, but she wouldn't eat.

And the wagon itself felt real enough, with its hard seats and tattered canvas awning. The ox and cow in the traces weren't the same animals she remembered from her own past, but they smelt strong enough to be real.

Other wagons were strung out before and behind hers, their sounds making the symphony of the trail: the clank of tools in the panniers, the creak of the axles, coughs from the drivers and stifled giggles from behind the uplifted sheets . . .

'Annie?'

Every other detail sank into shadow as she heard the voice.

'Annie, sweetheart. It's time for your story.'

Mama!

Without warning she was *there*, filling the cramped wagon with her sweet mother-scent, embracing the daughter whose eyes were filling with tears, who was choking too much to speak, whose arms gripped her mother's neck with such ferocity that they were pushed gently away.

'My little dear, whatever's come over you? Settle down now, and hear a tale.'

The embrace, in the manner of dreams, transformed into the tight swaddle of her childhood bed. Her mother was still there, beyond the covers, close enough to love but not to touch. Annie tried to free her arms but the bedclothes bound them tight. As in a dreamin' dream she knew none of this was real, but the power to exercise her will was no longer there.

'Lie back, sweetheart. Don't you struggle now. Don't want the Snallygaster to get you.'

Soft Mississippi tones. Oh, Mama!

In the sky the moon was full, filling the floor of the wagon with deep blue pools. Her mother's face was in shadow, invisible in the night.

'Now where did we get to? Oh yes, Rapunzel. Well she stayed in the tower a long time. Many, many years. Her hair grew mighty long in all that time, mighty long. Then, one day, a fine young prince rode through the forest and saw her at the window, plain as day and beautiful as night.

'"Rapunzel," he cried, "let down your hair!"'

And so Annie listened once more to the story that had always been her favourite, crying silent tears in the dream that was not a dream, crying as she listened to the sound of her dead mother's voice.

She didn't remember closing her eyes, but when she opened them her mother was gone. She was alone in the wagon. And now the wagon was alone on the trail.

Darting to the rear she pushed aside the lines of beef and stared out into the blue-black of the night. The moon was high, its shadows short. Far to the north she could see a plume of dust: the rest of the wagon train. Low hills obscured the horizon; rocks jostled the wheels. She'd left the beaten track.

Jumping down from the wagon she trotted forward past the front wheels, easily outpacing the slow beasts.

'Whoa,' she said, tugging at the cow. It didn't respond, merely ambled on. The smell of the oxen was both familiar and pungent. More than anything she could see or hear, it made her believe in the scene.

Unable to stop them she hoisted herself on to the cow's back. A saddle had been made ready for her. Had it been there all the time? She couldn't recall.

But then this is only a dreamin' dream.

The saddle was cinched as tight as it would go but the cow's thick skin was loose on its bones. The swaying motion lulled Annie and she found herself wondering if it were possible to fall asleep inside a dream. And, if it were, whether or not she would dream the dream of a dream . . .

The trail – for it was still a trail, however ill-maintained – began to rise. The moon was falling now, and the shadows of oxen and wagon stretched far ahead, leading them on up the incline.

Beside the trail ran a wide creek, chattering in the darkness. Its voice became a welcome companion to Annie until they parted company at a set of gentle falls. The silence, for a while, was unbearable.

When the moon failed altogether, and with no sign yet of the dawn, the stars became brilliant. Annie looked up at them and cried. They were so beautiful. The night sky of Stone was devoid of stars, a vast and soulless wilderness. In many ways she'd grown to love that weird, tilted world, but when the night came there was really no competition.

She raised her hand and traced a path across the Milky Way, seized the Big Dipper and scooped herself a great draught of heaven.

They continued along the brows of hills, along elevated crests and scarps. Always the trail was the high place on land that was lifting higher and higher. They rounded a bend and saw mountains but the skyline, indistinct in

27

the meagre light, wasn't familiar. The geography was all wrong; suddenly she wasn't in Kansas any more.

The sound of the creek returned the instant they came around the corner, and as the oxen laboured up and over a steep ridge Annie saw it had become a torrent. It wasn't especially wide, but the water was fast-flowing and barred their way completely. They were nearer to the source and it was an angrier, swifter stream than before.

For the first time since she'd found herself on this dream-wagon, the oxen stopped walking. She climbed down from the cow, patted its neck and stepped forward. At the bank of the river she knelt, dipped her hands into the icy water. Something cut through her peripheral vision and she looked up in time to see a shooting star sear the spattered blanket of the sky.

Night dragon, she thought. The slash of light disappeared round the curve of the world. She imagined it bouncing clear of the atmosphere again and flying free, still burning, burning . . .

She raised her cupped hands to her lips, and was about to drink when she heard voices whispering in the water.

. . . light . . . moon . . . name . . . sun . . .

While the water drained between her fingers she stared entranced at the delicate dance of the starlight on the froth of the river. She thought there were two voices, entwined like ivy. Or maybe it was only the water, fooling her ears.

. . . sun . . . name . . . moon . . . light . . .

The more she strained the less she could hear. Soon the words were lost altogether in the river's babble. She stood up again, wiping her hands against her skirt; somehow she knew the water, like the jerked beef, had been poisoned.

Dawn was still some way off but behind her the starry sky was beginning to lose its opulence. To the west the mountains were solidifying out of the darkness, a long, buckled spine of shadow rising like an ancient defence. Cut through the middle of the range was a steep-sided notch, a high valley through which the trail she was on would inevitably lead.

A mountain pass.

The river proved shallow enough to ford. Sure-footed, the oxen drew the wagon safely across, with Annie walking beside them. At one point she slipped and nearly fell; thoughts of Archan's poison flowing over her face helped her keep hold of the saddle. Once across, she climbed back aboard the wagon.

Inside, waiting for her, was her mother.

'Mama!' she said, backing away. It was her mother's face all right, but . . . 'Your eyes!'

'All the better to see you with, my dear,' purred Katherine Harker. She reached a hand towards her daughter's face.

Eyes of steel, thought Annie, staring into two round mirrors.

'Say what you need to say, Archan,' said Annie. 'I see through the disguise, so you may as well spit it out.'

Her mother smiled, revealing gleaming silver teeth.

'Oh, but my dear.' That voice, so familiar! 'Is that any way to talk to me, when I've come so far to see you?'

'It's all you'll get, you bitch!'

For a moment Annie thought she saw her mother's real face behind this cheap replica. She flinched, half-believing that she'd as good as slapped her own mother on the cheek.

She'll lose her temper now, she thought, knowing the dragon of old. But the dragon didn't. Instead she moulded Katherine Harker's features into a dazzling smile. The voice however was ancient and cruel, and impossible to mistake.

'Oh my dear, you have found strength! How amusing!

29

That a faery should think itself capable of fortitude when it is barely even *real*! Even in its prime your species was nothing but a notion adrift on the breeze, an aethereal fancy made solid only once every hundred years. And in recent ages what have your kind – you *men* – done but grub in the soil and build monuments to yourselves? The basilisks soon discovered the folly of architecture – what is Stone but the greatest folly of all? – but you have surpassed even them with your love of *making*. The soil enslaved you long ago, and the soil is where you look ever and always. Fitting it is that the soil is where you all return, at the end of your pitiful days.'

'And you are different, Archan?'

'You need to ask me this? You *dare*? I, the last of the dragons – an *immortal* dragon who looks not merely to the sky but beyond it? Not only will I outlive you, faery – I will out-*be* you! So tell me, knowing all this, do you still feel strong?'

'Strong enough for you.'

The wagon lurched. Katherine hissed like a snake and lunged at Annie, who caught her mother's wrists in her hands. Their faces pressed together; this close, the breath spilling from between those shining teeth was thick and foul-smelling. The skull beneath Katherine's fine skin flashed red. Annie tightened her grip, forcing herself to watch the pain flicker in her mother's brow. The inhuman metal of Katherine's eyes clouded a little. Annie clenched her hands, wincing as her Katherine's wristbones grated together.

'You cannot defeat me,' came the growl from her mother's mouth.

'Maybe not,' replied Annie. Her voice was steady now, still and cold. The pre-dawn sky was bright behind Katherine's head; it looked as though her hair was glowing. 'Not here at least. I might have you in my hands, Archan, but you're still a mighty long way away.'

'Ah,' Katherine said, 'but I'm gettin' closer all the time, girl!'

Annie could actually *see* her breath now, thin red streamers falling from her lips like trails of blood.

'We've met like this before, Archan. Twice. You got anything new to say?'

'I have plenty to say, *faery*! Tell me: do you remember the first time you dreamed of me?'

Annie shuddered, her confidence wavering. Archan stabbed Katherine's fingers towards her captor's throat; Annie drew back, but didn't let go.

She did indeed remember that first dream, only too well. It had risen without warning in the middle of one of Stone's dead black nights, a short and dreadful nightmare in which she had seen Archan's face plunging towards her out of the darkness like a steam locomotive.

At the last moment the apparition had slammed to a halt . . . and transformed into the face of her mother. The likeness was perfect, except for the teeth, which were the evil serpent's silver fangs.

'Hello, my dear,' her mother had said, stabbing at her with a long forked tongue. 'I'm back!'

The dream had spanned only a few seconds, or so it seemed to Annie when she woke up, sweating and clutching at Jonah. Now, looking back, it seemed to her it might have lasted for hours.

'Oh Jonah!' she'd blurted. 'Oh shit, Jonah – it was her!' And at once Jonah had known who she meant.

The second dream had been longer, but although Archan had tried rather harder to frighten Annie again somehow it had the opposite effect. The scares were cheap and ultimately unconvincing. Annie had emerged from this second dream not cowed but invigorated.

She'd been stumbling alone through a field of sharp,

volcanic rocks, tracking something she could not see. Suddenly she'd come upon a gibbet sticking straight up out of the pumice. From a crudely knotted rope swung the body of her mother. The rope creaked, and Annie heard the scuttling of the mice nesting in her mother's clothes. The corpse's eyes clicked open, flashing silver, and the lips peeled back to reveal those same needle-teeth. Katherine croaked, her breath like rust.

'Get a new act, Archan,' Annie had said. The words seemed to buoy her up, tangible things in the damp air. 'This one's gettin' a mite predictable.'

Katherine's face scowled.

'Brought you a message, girl,' said Katherine's voice.

'Spit it out.'

'I will spit you out, when I have eaten you whole and split your bones to powder!'

'This is my dream, bitch, not yours. What's the message?'

The body rotated completely around. The head remained motionless as it did so. Annie tried to ignore the sound of her mother's vertebrae being torn apart.

'You might have locked me out of this world but I have found my way into another. What's more, there is a place – a very special place – where these two worlds meet. A crossing point, if you like, a place to *pass*. And I am going there – in fact, I am already on my way. But what I would *really* like is for you to be there too. And Jonah, of course. In fact, you could bring along all your friends. It could be quite a reunion. A very brief one, of course . . .'

'What is this place? Where is it?'

Katherine's head, the neck to which it was now only loosely attached creaking like a storm-bent tree, tilted up towards the blue-grey sky.

'Up there,' she grated. 'The summit of Stone. The place where . . . where . . .'

With a hideous ripping sound Katherine's body detached from its head and bounced on to the pumice. Sharp volcanic shards slashed a hundred cuts into its skin. Annie watched with cold detachment as her mother's disembodied head waltzed on the end of the rope.

'We'll be there, Archan,' she said as the silver eyes turned first cloudy then black. Dark blood dripped like tears. 'If you want a showdown then you got yourself one, sure as shit falls off a shovel!'

It was this second dream that had really fired Jonah's imagination.

'The very tip of Stone!' he had proclaimed. 'The place where the future comes to an end! What did she call it? A crossing place?'

'It's a trap,' said Annie.

Jonah nodded. 'Of course. But also a final chance.'

Archan jerked in Annie's grip, jolting her mind back to the interior of the wagon and the reality of *this* dream.

'You dreamin', girl?' she cackled. 'That second time we were cut a little short, you might say. There was something I wanted to tell you about that special place up there.'

'Then say it and go. I'm sick of your games, Archan.'

Katherine's face pressed close, its eyes bulging. 'Oh, my dear, I have plenty more games, plenty a' play for a rainy day as dear ol' mama used to say!'

'Say it, if it's important!'

'Oh, it *is* important. The most important thing of all. And the one thing I forgot to tell you – its name.'

'Its name?'

'Yes. I believe you do not know a thing until you know its name. Names have power, Annie – you'd do well to remember that.'

'The top of the world, you said. That's where we're going.'

Behind Katherine's head the dawn came like an explosion, setting her hair ablaze. Far to the west the opposing flanks of the mountain pass flashed like flame.

'There,' Annie said, looking at the slash of sky flanked by indomitable stone. In this dream it might be a mountain pass, but in the waking world it was the very peak of Stone.

'That's right, my dear. Stone-tip and mountain track – the two things are one but they share the same name: *Sunlight Pass*. That's where we're headed, you and me and Jonah makes three. That's where we'll meet for real, at last and at the end.'

'Sunlight Pass,' repeated Annie and her mother melted into the air like the ghost she was.

The ox and cow plodded on, drawing Annie and the wagon out into the west, up the first of the steep gradients leading to the sharp-edged notch in the mountain.

Heading out west towards Sunlight Pass.

3

Climb

The story of Malya's courtship with Gerent was the strangest Jonah had ever known.

He had first encountered these young lovers during his earliest days on Stone, when he had stumbled upon the Denneth, the Neolithic tribe to which they belonged. Darwin might have asserted that Jonah and Annie were their superiors by virtue of approximately five thousand years of evolution; in reality the Neolithics possessed sharper eyes and keener ears than either of their nineteenth century companions. Malya could wield a sword better than any man Jonah had ever seen and, in most situations demanding deductive reasoning, Gerent could out-think them every time.

He sometimes thought the Neolithics were living proof that evolution worked in reverse.

Like Jonah, the Denneth had been transported to Stone from the Earth by a cataclysmic volcanic eruption. As far as he could determine they had originated from the land mass that would come to be known as Scandinavia; he liked to think of them as prototype Vikings. Once Gerent and Malya abandoned the Denneth and their requisitioned castle their forbidden love blossomed. The son of the king and the daughter of the shaman found the happiness which had been denied them all their lives.

But the happiness was short-lived. Malya's wicked father, Frey, flew in on his stolen dragon wings, cornered them on an exposed timber ledge and killed his own daughter in cold blood.

Gerent's grief was profound but even death could not keep the young lovers apart. Fully aware of Jonah's ability to twist Stone's archive of memories, Gerent forced him to change the course of history and bring Malya back into his arms. In doing so, he also forced a fork in the river of time, causing nothing less than the twinning of history and the creation of an entire new world. All in the name of love.

And now, just when they should have been at their happiest, they seemed further apart than ever.

The final split came on the eve of the departure. The journey had been delayed for the best part of three days. Of primary concern was the fear that Stone's charm-filled air – which contained enough nutrition to make both food and drink a luxury rather than a necessity – might very well exhibit different properties as they travelled into the uncharted upper realms.

'Up there,' Jonah explained, 'above the Helix, are completely new worlds. Who knows whether the air will feed us in the same way, or translate our languages as it does here? Will we be able to breathe it at all? We can count on nothing. We must take supplies.'

While Malya transferred the armoury she had created on to the Bark, Gerent tried to rally the indolent selkies into helping him cache food and drinking water. It was hard work, and he ended up catching large quantities of fish himself, using the nets he had become so expert at making and losing his temper with increasing regularity.

Once caught, the fish were strung up in long lines to dry in the heat of the sun.

'Jerked fish,' said Annie as she saw the first batch laid

out on a mat of sea ferns. 'Well, I guess if you can't get beef . . .'

'It is an old Denneth tradition,' said Gerent. 'A safeguard against a lean hunt.'

'There's nothin' new under the sun.'

The stockpile grew. Ruane herself helped bring it aboard the Bark, plucking it from where it was stacked on her own flank and depositing it with infinite care into the hold set aside by Grandfather Tree. Fresh water was easier to arrange: the lesky piloted the Bark out to sea and opened an outer hatch, allowing Stone's ocean to flow into sealed chambers. Basilisk charms filtered and cleansed it, making it more than palatable.

Throughout the proceedings Gerent was everywhere, busy even when there was no need to be busy, pursuing his ever-futile task of marshalling the selkies. He planned and worked and lost his temper until soon he was angry all the time, the permanent frown like a tattoo on his brow.

Jonah was with him when he finally lost control.

They were together at the shore, heaving at the drag lines of one of Gerent's giant keep nets. The wind was brisk and waves were frothing across the mountain of fish inside the net. The two men were heaving with all their might, struggling to stop the net sliding down the shallow incline and back into the water. Malya was watching with her hands on her hips.

'There's no point, Gerent,' she said. 'We've no time to dry them now – they'll only go to waste. Let them go.'

'They're caught now,' snapped Gerent. 'They'll be eaten.'

At that moment Jonah tripped and fell flat on his back, the rope skidding from his grip fast enough to leave a scorch mark on his palm. Left with the full weight of the catch Gerent hauled valiantly for several seconds before yelling to Malya for help. Instead she just shrugged and turned away.

The current snatched the drag line from Gerent's hands and several hundred freshly-caught fish disappeared into the surf.

'Best place for them.' Malya laughed and that was when she found the point of Gerent's sword pressed beneath her chin.

It was the only time Jonah had ever seen Gerent outdraw the warrior-woman. From the ice in her gaze he suspected she would not let it happen again.

'I brought you back!' he said, his upper lip curled back like a dog's.

'Jonah brought me back,' she replied. Her eyes were cold like ice. 'You held a blade to his throat too. Maybe one day you'll learn how to ask nicely.'

There was a silence; it seemed to Jonah that it went on forever. Then Malya spoke again.

'I can't keep thanking you forever, Gerent,' she said.

'I don't want your thanks! I don't need anybody's thanks! I just need . . .'

'What? What do you need, Gerent?'

'Never mind. You wouldn't understand.'

'Probably not. Are you going to put your sword away or do I have to knock it out of your hand?'

And there it ended. Slowly Gerent lowered his blade and slipped it back into its sheath. Then he stalked away down the shore without once looking back.

Later, in the orange glow of the sunset, Jonah and Malya talked together.

'Gerent is like a man possessed,' he said. 'I cannot understand what has come over him.'

'Yes,' said Malya. She shivered and rubbed one hand through her close-cropped blonde hair. She was pretty as Jonah imagined all Scandinavian women were pretty (even those from a time long before the name Scandinavia had even been coined); she also looked immeasurably sad. For a moment he thought she would cry, then she surprised him with a smile. 'I used to think love was strong – now I'm not so sure.'

'Oh Malya, Gerent is angry because he feels power-less. He was born to be a king, yet he has no people. It was he who understood you could be brought back from the dead, but he could not perform the task himself – he had to force me to do it for him. And now that you have returned . . .'

'Yes, Jonah?'

'Love *is* strong, Malya. But so are you – stronger than many men. Stronger, perhaps, than Gerent.'

She scowled. 'So I make him feel powerless too? Is that it? Well that's aurochs-shit – I'm just as I've always been.'

'Yes,' agreed Jonah, 'that you are. But take this obsession of his with the selkies, for example. He tries to order them, to rouse them to action – to *rule* them . . . just think about it, Malya. I am no great judge of men but I can see that Gerent is suffering inside. Just as I can see that he still loves you more than life itself.'

Malya shut her mouth, which was open ready to argue back, with a snap. Then she crossed her arms and lay down on her back.

They were resting together in a special place, side by side on the smooth slope of Ruane's cheek. This was one of the few places it was possible to have a decent con-versation with the Goddess. The ground beneath them was warm, living flesh. Now it rocked with the syllables She spoke.

'I thought you two came here so that we might make our farewells,' said the Goddess.

'Indeed we did,' sighed Jonah, lying back beside Malya on the pliant, organic ground. 'Please accept my apol-ogies, Ruane.'

'None are required.' Far down the slope of Her jaw they could see mountainous lips articulating the words. Her voice was like a kindly storm.

'Ruane, do you think he still loves me or has Jonah completely lost his mind?' asked Malya. It always pleased Jonah to hear Malya talking to the whale-woman. There was something blissfully informal about her manner. He suspected Ruane appreciated it too; surely it was lonely being a Goddess.

The cheek beneath them rose and flexed: a smile.

'Behold,' intoned the Goddess. 'The sun sets.'

Together they watched it slide behind the immense drapery of the ocean. For an instant Jonah saw not a sun but a child's ball thrown against a wall. Except the ball did not bounce off – instead it plunged in, was swallowed.

Annie was toiling up the slope. She reached them just as the last beams of daylight dissolved behind the falling clouds, orange light turning to silver-blue. The leggings she wore were faded so that the brown and black stripes were almost indistinguishable from one another; the sleeveless white shirt was no longer white but a variegated grey. The warm light had turned her tanned skin to gold. She looked to Jonah like a woman who had walked around the world without stopping.

'Did you finish your painting?' Malya asked. 'Can I see?'

'No,' said Annie, hugging her painting box to her chest. 'I mean, I'll show you in a minute.' She sounded tired, uneasy.

'I'd like that.' Malya leaned back again, her hands clasped behind her head.

Annie stood watching the darkening sky, her back to Jonah. While she had been painting she had tied her hair up in a black cloth; it was knotted at the back of her neck, tight enough to make a virtual skull cap. Jonah preferred to see her hair loose and longed to see it flowing free against Stone's fabulous back-drop.

'We're ready to go, aren't we?' she said.

'You know we are, my dear,' yawned Jonah.

'Too exciting for you, darling?'

'A man must sleep.'

By now the sky was thick purple. Beside it the sea was beginning to pulse with yellow nocturnal light, the glow of the charm prowling its depths.

'I will miss you all,' Ruane said. Reduced in volume, her normally massive voice was not so much a sound in the air as a vibration in the ground. 'It is quiet now the Shifters have gone. I always welcomed their company, even when I was a selkie. But they no longer live on the skin of the Goddess; they have taken their changing ways elsewhere.'

Like the selkies the shape-changing Shifters had once lived on Ruane's body. Unlike the selkies, the Shifters were curious about both themselves and their world. After two of their number had helped Jonah fight back Archan, the remainder rediscovered their collective sense of adventure and embarked on a great migration across the face of Stone. They promised to return one day, but would not say when.

'They were a noble race,' agreed Jonah. 'But you have your own people for company.'

'If you mean the selkies, I have outgrown them. I have a duty to them, of course, which I will continue to uphold, but when I grew from Ruane the selkie into Rata Kadul I left behind much of what I was before. It is the way of things here in the ocean: when I die another selkie will be chosen to grow and take my place, but there can only ever be one Goddess at a time. The selkies are simple, strong creatures, but even in their presence I am lonely. And I will be lonelier still when you have departed.'

41

'We will come back again,' said Jonah, glancing at Annie as he did so. She would not meet his eye.

'Do you really believe that is likely, Jonah Lightfoot?'

Jonah struggled to hold back his tears. 'We need not say goodbye until morning, Ruane.'

'But I thought that was why you came here tonight,' whispered the Goddess. 'To say goodbye.'

In silence they watched blackness envelope the world of Stone. Yellow ocean light rolled around Ruane's cheeks, bathing them in faint colour.

'Well,' announced Malya suddenly, 'I think it's about time we saw what Annie's been painting this afternoon!'

They were all glad of the diversion, though Annie hesitated before unveiling her latest works.

'I've done a lot of paintings lately,' she said, stalling for time. 'Still, there's a hundred and forty-four tiles in this box, and I'm still barely halfway through them.'

Her work comprised a series of miniature oil paintings. Her canvases were the small ivory tiles making up the Mah Jongg set she carried in the wooden box.

Before Stone, her travels on Earth had taken her all the way from Kansas to the East Indies. The paintings she had made along the way included such exotic views as sunset over the Galapagos Islands and storm clouds prowling the coast of Java. During the time they had spent on Rata Kadul, she had supplemented this Earthly collection with a number of views of Stone.

Her more recent life-studies were pictures of selkies at work and play, views looking out across the upturned ocean, usually with some part of the Goddess in the foreground – a giant pair of flukes, for example, or an outstretched hand.

Usually she worked on only one tile at a time, and usually she only painted from life. This evening was different in both respects.

Jonah looked at the pair of tiles she had been working

on, grunted, and turned them towards the yellow light in an effort to make them out more clearly.

'There is little to see,' he said.

'They ain't finished,' said Annie.

The first tile was flecked with crimson and yellow, an approximation of flames; the second was all cool blues and whites. Fire and ice. And in the centre of each was a stab of silver that might just have been an eye.

Turning them over he saw the flames had been painted on the back of a tile marked with the sword-shape of the Red Dragon; the ice had been matched with the unmarked blank of the White Dragon.

'Are these eyes?' asked Jonah. 'Are they Archan's eyes?'

'I don't know.' Annie replied. 'I think they might have come to me in a dream. Most likely a dreamin' dream. But, yeah, I reckon Archan sent them. Tryin' to keep me on my toes.'

'You mean she has made you paint them? But what do the pictures mean? Do you plan to finish them?'

She shrugged. All at once he saw that she was as tired as he was, probably more so.

'Who knows?' she sighed. 'I'm pretty sure they're to do with the other Stone, the one you made when you yanked dear Malya out of the past. It's been preying on my mind lately, you know, the notion that there's another world out there somewhere. Another Archan.'

'But my darling, you know very well that it is a logical . . .' began Jonah.

'. . . impossibility that we'll ever meet up with this other world. Temporal paradox or some damn thing. Yeah, you've told me all that but I can still *smell* her, Jonah! There's two Archans out there! Somehow, sooner or later, we'll have to deal with the both of them. *That's* what these pictures are about, if they're about anything at all other than Archan herself trying to scare the bejeezus out of me!'

Malya, who had been looking at the dragon pictures with distaste, shook her head and turned away.

If Archan had intended the pictures to be scary then in Jonah's opinion she had succeeded. Even unfinished the images radiated such a sense of doom he could not bear to look at them for long. They were scary because they were *real*, just as the journey they were about to undertake was real. It was all real: journey, destination, the certainty that Archan would be waiting for them when they got there, the likelihood that this time their luck would run out . . . all real.

Their discussion of the paintings left Annie melancholy and drained of all energy. Her face wan in the shimmering light, she made her apologies and set off towards the hut.

'Do you want me to come too, my dear?' Jonah asked.

She paused, raised her hand and set her hair loose; it descended like a growing shadow. 'No, that's okay. You stay a while. I'd rather be on my own.'

'But if Archan comes to you . . .'

'She won't, not tonight.'

Jonah watched her disappear behind the curve of Ruane's jaw. Beneath his feet the ground moved as the Goddess tilted her head, creating an easier slope for Annie to walk down. He watched the empty space she had left for a long time before he felt Malya's hand on his shoulder.

'She loves you very much, Jonah,' she said. 'Nothing can change that.'

'Everything changes,' whispered Jonah. 'Nothing goes.'

'What's that?'

'Hmm? Oh, nothing Malya. Basilisk lore, old words.'

He turned and found her standing very close, looking

at him with shining eyes. He was struck by her beauty – her cropped hair made her features seem all the more fine. But more than that, he was impressed by what he had reminded her of just now: her *strength*. There was an energy about her, a sense that she was indomitable. This Neolithic woman, whose people had crossed from Earth to Stone five thousand years before Jonah had even been born, was . . . *daunting*.

'Archan has not really come up against you yet.' Jonah smiled. 'I wonder what you will make of each other.'

'My sword arm is strong.' Malya returned his smile; her version was ferocious.

'It will take more than swords to defeat the dragon. But . . . it is a good enough start.'

'I am glad you think so!' Her fierce enthusiasm was welcome after the gloom; it was also infectious. 'I've gathered an armoury to make the king of the Denneth proud! We have two dozen long-swords and a dozen spears. I've made only three bows, but the lesky can always make us more and we have arrows aplenty. I've also discovered a burning oil: I made it by catching those flabby creatures with the tentacles and squeezing out their bellies. It's stored in a special space in the lesky's hull. It can be poured over our enemy and ignited!'

Jonah arched his eyebrows. 'You have been busier than I realized. Well, we've a dragon to conquer and some might suggest fighting fire with fire. Who knows? Perhaps it will work.'

'But we have more than that, Jonah!' Malya's eyes were blazing now. She held his upper arms, almost embracing him. 'We have love!' She looked away, suddenly bashful. 'By that I mean the love of warriors. We are bonded, all of us. We will fight side by side, hand in hand. We will feel each other's pain and avenge each other's deaths without thought for ourselves.'

'I hope I do not have to avenge anyone.'

'When I first knew you I thought you weak, but now I know that is far from the truth. You hauled me out of the river of time, Jonah. You brought me back from the dead. In many ways you are the strongest of us all.'

She dropped to her knees. From nowhere she drew a sword. It was short, Romanesque, with a bronze sphere on its hilt. Jonah smiled: it was the same sword he had seen Malya retrieve shortly after their first meeting on the roof of the Denneth castle . . . oh, it seemed so long ago! The sword he himself had once held, the first he had ever wielded.

She reversed her hold, confident with the blade as she offered the hilt to Jonah. He took it instinctively for it had finally dawned on him what she was doing. He fought to suppress a smile as she bent her head.

'Accept my service, Jonah Lightfoot,' she said. 'I will protect you and serve you until I die.'

'Unless I should die first.'

'With me as your protector, that's not very likely.'

Time and again Jonah had found himself in the company of characters he had once thought existed only in legend: the noble, knightly Esh, who herself had died to save him and his companions; the mighty dragon Torus, asleep in its lair on a mountain of bones; the evil winged wizard Frey, who used magic for power and struck down even his own daughter when she stood in his way. Now a womanly knight had pledged him her service. He wondered if this was what it was like to be Arthur, and chuckled as he remembered that he too had once pulled a sword out of Stone.

'Rise, Malya,' he said. He tapped her shoulders with the blade of the sword. 'I accept your service, but we will fight side by side, if it should come to that. I am nobody's master and, though I am no match for you in swordplay, I will endeavour to protect you as much as you will protect me.'

'The love between us all is a real thing,' Malya said. 'And it is love that wins battles, however strong the arm that wields the sword.'

'Some might dispute the truth of that, but few would deny the sentiment.'

Standing, she drew close to him once more and kissed him once, hard, on the lips. He reeled back, overwhelmed by the passion in the sudden gesture. 'I serve you because I love you, Jonah!'

With that she turned and marched away. Ruane had turned again, and Jonah had a clear view as his Neolithic knight traversed an upraised tendon bridging the hollow between the jaw of the Goddess and her collarbone. Eventually the darkness claimed her, but not before she had turned for a last time and raised her sword in salute. It glinted, reflecting yellow, magical light, and Jonah did not yet know that she was doomed.

Beneath him the ground moved.

'Goodbye, Jonah,' said the Goddess. 'It is quite a mountain you must climb.'

'Farewell, Ruane. Until we meet again.'

'Perhaps.'

As Jonah walked back to his temporary home he could not stop thinking about Annie's paintings, or rather about the tiles on which the paintings were made.

We brought them all this way, he thought, he mind thick with fatigue. *All this way . . .*

Later, when he was drifting into the borderlands of sleep, the tiles tumbled with him into his dreams.

He was airborne, flying through a flock of ivory boulders. Each was as big as a house and each bore an inscrutable Chinese mark. Each occupied its own special place in the surrounding sky. They jostled him as he spread dragon wings, nudging him forwards along an unseen track.

Red light bloomed ahead, spilling across the tiles.

Ancient thoughts surrounded him. The thoughts assembled themselves into words, sentences, a list of instructions. On every side the tiles responded to the instructions, revolving like great, square moons. It was a dance, Jonah realized, an elaborate ritual in which every single piece had its own special role.

The gameboard. With every piece in its place.

A grid of red light, a sense of purpose, of disparate strands weaving into a composite thread. Something falling. A sudden, dense sound, like a fist striking soil, followed by a chain of words he could not make out. All around him, the six voices of the Deathless merged into one, the basilisks intoning the rules of the game.

As he started to waken he felt the dream slipping away from him. He tried to cling to it; as a child he had fought in this same way to keep hold of his dreams about flying. But always they had melted, too fragile to withstand the light of the day, like ice crystals in the sunlight, as this dream too melted.

It was while packing his few possessions into the Bark that he first began to fear for Malya's future.

Unlike the Neolithics (who were habitual scavengers) neither he nor Annie had accumulated much in the way of baggage during their time on Stone. Even those few things they did own – with the exception of Annie's painting box – had ended up tucked in the furthest corner of their hut, buried beneath a disarray of odd items of clothing they had either picked up or made for themselves. Forgotten, they had lain there for all the days they had spent on Rata Kadul and looking through them was like meeting old friends.

The first thing Jonah found was a small knife Gerent had carved for him from the beak of a squid-like creature prevalent in Stone's upturned ocean. Useless for cutting anything, it had a primitive beauty Jonah could not deny.

Smiling, he laid it aside for careful wrapping. Next were Annie's journals. The first of the red-bound books was filled with accounts of their earlier adventures on Stone, the second with her largely unsuccessful attempts at poetry.

'Think I oughta stick to painting?' she had said after a recitation of 'Sky over Yellow Light.' Struggling for compliments Jonah had opted instead for honesty, holding his nose and turning his mouth emphatically down. The corner of the book was still bent where she had struck him with it.

At the very bottom of the pile was a rectangular object wrapped in coarse linen. He knew what it was of course, nor was finding it any great surprise. What did amaze him was how long it was since he had looked at it. None of them bothered to track time here on Stone – without moon cycles or even seasons one day ran seamlessly into the next – but he knew it had to be weeks if not months since he had held it in his hands. This, which had once been his talisman, his one connection with the Earth and with his own, personal history.

Feeling like a man who has betrayed an old friend, Jonah unwrapped the cloth from around his first edition of Charles Darwin's *On the Origin of Species*.

But even before he had raised it into the light, as soon as he lifted it in his hands he knew something was wrong. Desperately wrong.

He closed his eyes, unwilling to look at it. He hefted it, testing its unexpected weight. That was the first clue: its weight. Then he peered at it, rubbed his fingers across it, willed his senses to be wrong. But they were not.

The book had turned to stone.

To look at it was perfect, except that the colours were gone, leaving a blankness the colour of slate. The textures were correct: the nap of the leather, the rippled edge of the well-thumbed pages, the embossed lettering on the spine, but all the colour had been sucked from it. And it was heavy, far too heavy. He did not have to try opening it to know it could no longer be read. If Darwin's words still existed inside this petrified slab then they would never been seen by his eyes again. It was solid as . . . well, as stone.

Then it came to him.

This is not the original book. I left that behind on the shore of Krakatoa when the volcano erupted and threw me here to Stone. This is the book I drew out of the memory rods.

Yes, he had fished this book out of the river of time, quite intact and indistinguishable from the one he had possessed before. At the time – and for some time after – it had seemed perfect. The real thing.

But now it had turned to stone. Just as a fish lives for a while having been landed on the bank, gasping and thrashing in the unforgiving grass, so the book had lived. For a while. But now . . . now it was simply dead.

Jonah felt unutterably sad. The friend he had come to greet had passed away in his absence. Here, weighing heavy in his hands, was clear evidence of the limits of his powers here on Stone.

He was about to put the stone book down when he stopped. A violent trembling fit gripped him; his bowels turned to water.

I brought Malya out of the rods too, just as I brought out the book.

His hands went limp and the book fell to the ground. It struck hard and broke into many pieces, blunt fragments adrift in a sea of fine grey dust.

Jonah had been expecting a great send-off, if not a fireworks display then at least a crowd of selkies waving as the Bark began its ascent. But the innate apathy of the seal-people won out, and only a handful turned up to wish them goodbye.

The adventurers passed between the selkies, touching hands. Malya, who had grown closest to these strange and lazy sea-folk, exchanged embraces with several of the younger ones, but even as they were boarding the Bark the gathering was already breaking up. Happy to show their faces, the selkies were clearly unmoved by the prospect of the launch itself.

So it was in muted fashion that the Bark cast itself loose from Ruane's side. Jonah, Annie and Malya stood together on the perimeter deck, unsure about what to say or do. Grandfather Tree was busy inside the Bark, doing whatever it was he needed to do to set them on their way.

Gerent, standing some distance away round the curl of the deck, ignored them all.

The Bark rotated a little as it glided out into the sky, affording them a glorious view of Ruane's upturned face.

'Good luck!' boomed Ruane. Her face was sad, but the very depth of Her emotion made it radiant. With jade eyes shining like beacons and hair fanned wide in the water She looked every inch a Goddess.

'Goodbye, Rata Kadul!' they called, waving frantically as the Bark slowly spun the other way, eclipsing the view.

The last they saw of the Goddess before She was obscured by the hull was one mighty hand extended from the water. It was truly enormous, yet its pose was as exquisite as that of a porcelain doll.

'Now that,' said Annie, 'is what I call a lady!'

Jonah squeezed her hand, grateful for the contact. Behind them Gerent and Malya stood apart, the love they had once shared blown away as if on the wind.

His gaze lingered on Malya and his stomach turned over in terror.

*   *   *

51

Soon after the launch the Bark was approaching the land mass Jonah had seen during his first ascent. Still wreathed with smoke, it hung above them, an entire continent that was no more than a bloom of algae on Stone's immense ocean. The Bark was rising in leisurely fashion, and they had ample time to inspect this uncharted territory as it sank first towards, and then past them.

It looked almost Earthly, a tilted landscape of fertile vales and bleak highlands. Dull brown rock punched through smooth humps of moor. There were no trees, but an abundance of small, squat bushes bearing fruit that resembled bananas. And everywhere there were craters; it was from these that the smoke was issuing.

'Can we get closer?' Annie shouted across the Bark's deck. 'I'd sure like to get me a taste of that fruit!'

'You think I couldn't grow you fruit?' grumbled the lesky. Nevertheless the Bark pitched forward and moved in towards one of the larger plantations.

'You just pilot the ship,' said Annie, eagerly surveying the approaching terrain.

With its upward velocity slowed to nothing, the Bark hovered beside a clump of bushes, close enough for Annie to be able to reach over the rail and pluck one of the long, greenish-yellow fruits from its stalk. After a moment she managed to penetrate its tough skin and crowed with delight when she tasted the soft, pink flesh inside.

'Tastes like cornbread,' she said, then grabbed several handfuls of the fruits and tossed them to her friends. 'Try it – it's good.'

Jonah snatched up a pair of the fruits as they came slithering down the deck towards him. While they all wrestled with the skins, Grandfather Tree pulled the Bark away again, though not before he had opened a hatch in the side of the vessel and scraped a good quantity of the bushes into a hidden hold.

Tossing the skin overboard, Jonah bit into the flesh.

Nearby, Malya was doing the same thing. Watching her pleasure made his stomach churn again.

How do I tell her she is doomed? Oh dear God, why did I have to know?

Casting his gaze across the near-vertical landscape he spied a particularly large crater nearby. Something about it caught his eye. He circled the deck to get a better view.

'Grandfather Tree?' he said, pointing. 'Would you take us over there please?

'The day moves on,' warned Gerent. He had discarded his fruit half-eaten and was eyeing the remains with suspicion. 'We should be going up.'

'Indulge me, please. After all, there may be something to scavenge.'

A distraction, he told himself. *There will be nothing to see. You are fooling nobody, least of all yourself.*

And, overlaying these and all his thoughts: *How do I tell her?*

Clustered together, eating silently, they all peered over the rail as the lesky steered the Bark towards the crater.

Thin straggles of smoke drifted outwards from its depths; around it the landscape had been blasted clean. Jonah imagined a giant cannonball hitting Stone, and wondered who might have fired it.

The crater was about a hundred yards across. It gaped before them, an unseeing eye. Its interior was hot and sterile.

'There,' said Jonah, 'at the centre. There is something there.'

'Then let's leave it there,' said Annie. 'Come on, Jonah. Gerent's right – we can't waste time at every beauty spot along the way. Not that I'd call this exactly beautiful.'

'No, I know . . . but there is . . .' He rubbed his temple, memories of a dream touching a nerve somewhere inside. 'Please.'

Is this only a distraction? Or is it something more?

As they entered the crater it transformed from an eye to a mouth. Its ragged lip eclipsed the rest of Stone, so that now there was only the crater's curved back wall before them and the smoke-strewn sky behind them. Inch by inch the Bark drew level with a rough outcrop of rock bulging from the very centre of the crater.

Balanced on the outcrop was a small rock. It was black as jet, very different to the brown crater into which it was set like a dark jewel.

Jonah reached for it; as he did so one of Stone's dizzying shifts in perspective made him feel as though he were in a tiny dinghy, stretching out to touch a looming harbour wall. His fingers closed around the rock – it was no bigger than his fist. It was rough and pitted and felt as warm as his hand. His companions watched as he held it before his eyes, turning it over and over.

A fresh jet of smoke belched from a crack in the rock just a few yards above them, and they felt the Bark tilt as Grandfather Tree beat a hasty retreat.

'Not a living place,' observed the lesky, manifesting himself as a flexible wooden face pressed up out of the deck between Jonah's and Annie's feet. His broad mouth, usually lined with brambles, was currently filled with half-eaten pink fruit. 'Root and rock – they do not mix!'

'What is it, Jonah?' said Annie. She too was fascinated by the rock.

Jonah was only half-listening. At first he had thought this might be an egg of some sort, but now he could see it was just a rock. It looked like Stone-stuff – the fundamental building material over which all this land and sea was laid like meat on the bone – but the more he stared at it the more he came to believe it was not of Stone at all.

He believed it had come from an entirely different world.

He shook his head, rubbed his eyes. He grew aware

of his friends' expectant stares. 'No revelations,' he confessed. 'At least, not yet. Come – we have dallied long enough.'

As the Bark left the smoke-shrouded continent beneath it Annie wrapped her arm through his and pecked his cheek. 'Your head's full, Jonah Lightfoot, ain't it?'

'No more than usual,' he replied.

'One thing I've been meaning to ask you. Why d'you leave your book behind?'

'What?'

'It ain't with the rest of the baggage. Seems you left most all your stuff behind, Jonah. What's up? You given up being sentimental?'

'Something like that.'

'Anything you want to tell me about? I know what that damned book meant to you.'

Jonah sighed and placed his hands on her shoulder, looking her square in the eyes. 'It came from another world, Annie my love. Another time, another place. Yes, it did mean a lot to me once but, well, the time came to lay it to rest.'

'Hope it had a good burial.' Her eyes worried at him, seeking what he was not telling her.

'Ashes to ashes,' he said. 'Dust to dust.'

This time Grandfather Tree approached the Helix more cautiously.

'Turbulence up there,' he explained when Jonah asked why he had slowed down so much. The Bark was coasting upwards, slowing progressively as it neared the edge of the Helix.

'There was turbulence before . . .' said Jonah. Then he saw what the lesky had already seen: thick black clouds far more energetic than the cracked blue gyre through which they had passed the first time. They looked more than ominous: they looked deadly.

'Heading upStone.' The lesky halted their ascent altogether and turned instead into the morning sun. 'Calmer it might be, further along.'

UpStone and *downStone*: the two fundamental directions in which free travel was permitted by Stone's strange and unwritten laws. Fly too far out into the open sky and an unwary aviator would be flipped round by folds in the very fabric of the air . . . and end up travelling back in towards Stone again. Up and down were regulated by the Helix. Which left side to side.

Standing on a ledge with one's back to Stone, staring straight out into the sky, one could therefore choose to turn either left – *upStone* – or right – *downStone*.

Straightforward enough, although in making that choice it was worth remembering the memory rods stretching both upStone and downStone as they curled round Stone's immense spiral. Their temporal aspect meant that to travel upStone was to travel – relative to the Earth – into the future. DownStone led into the distant past.

On Stone, even such a simple task as choosing which way to go was a hazardous business.

Anxious moments passed as the Bark sped upStone – a direction the lesky sometimes described as 'along the grain' – dodging the occasional streamer of vapour that shot out of the Helix. Far from improving, to their dismay conditions got steadily worse. The very air around them became dull and thick and the sea lashed at them, growing choppy before the stiffening gale.

'Calmer it is not,' said Jonah, clinging to the deck rail. The others had retreated below decks.

Whichever way he turned his head the wind still burned his face. And it was *hot*, more like the draught from a furnace than Stone's usual warm breeze.

'Let us stop here, Grandfather Tree. I need a moment to think.'

The lesky withdrew into open sky. The clouds remained

hunched overhead; occasionally a jet of steam spat down towards the vessel. The sound of the Helix was a low and steady thunder.

At length Jonah shrugged. 'There is no way to know when the Helix will calm itself. It might be hours, but it might equally well be days. And we do not have days.'

'Risk it?' There was an enthusiasm in the lesky's voice Jonah considered somewhat misplaced.

The Bark's interior confused Jonah. It was a warren of curved passages, tight vestibules and doors, countless doors. Each door was marked with a Mah Jongg symbol, but nobody – not even Grandfather Tree – had yet worked out what they were meant to signify, if anything at all.

'Nothing to do with me,' he said when quizzed 'Bark rebuilt himself. Basilisks designed him – basilisks put the marks there, not lesky. Pretty though.'

Jonah still had no idea how a group of six immortal creatures which had existed for all eternity could be even remotely interested in Mah Jongg.

The others were waiting for him in the drum-shaped room Jonah had christened the bridge. While there were no controls here – at least nothing a human being could operate – there was a sense of it being at the very heart of the ship.

From behind the livid green walls there came a low and constant humming sound, and both floor and ceiling were studded with strange growths. These growths were gnarled and moss-covered; some sweated syrupy resin onto the floor, from which it drained via an array of narrow orifices; others pulsed like arteries. Some were pale-skinned, almost transparent; inside them little wheels whirred round and round, driving complex mechanisms that stretched and flexed like organic clocks. It was fascinating and incomprehensible and utterly entrancing.

Lightning arced between two of the lumpy wooden

outcrops, connecting floor and ceiling with a brief but dazzling tracery of clean blue light. A sharp tang like gunpowder wafted across the room.

'We are going to try to run the gauntlet of the storm,' Jonah announced. 'We are, despite the weather, going up.'

'Thought you might try something dangerous,' said Annie, smiling like a big cat.

'I suggest we all lie flat on the floor,' Jonah went on. 'Grandfather Tree!'

There was a muffled protest, then the lesky's voice burst from the ceiling, though there was no sign of his face. 'Ready?' he shouted.

'As we'll ever be,' said Annie. She lay next to Jonah and seized his hand.

'Do it, lesky!' said Gerent, wrapping one arm around a convenient pillar. Malya took up a similar stance on the opposite side of the bridge, her free hand resting on the hilt of the Roman sword.

Judging by the expressions on their faces, Jonah considered, they all felt nervous. And a little foolish.

Almost imperceptibly they began to gain weight under the Bark's mild acceleration. Then, with an accompanying flurry of electrical sparks from one of the wooden control pillars, the flying ship started to pick up speed more rapidly. The floor vibrated and something rumbled behind one of the walls. Jonah felt Annie's fingers crushing his own. There was no sense of foolishness now, only apprehension sliding into fear.

There was a jerk and the floor tipped sideways. Jonah slithered several yards on his back before fetching up against one of the pillars. A second later Annie cannoned into him. He heard a crack and hoped it was not one of his ribs. A second jerk threw them the other way, except it was not so much a jerk as a spasm, as if the whole interior of the Bark had twitched like a muscle. Throwing a glance to the side Jonah saw Malya clinging to her post with both arms now in an effort to prevent herself from careering down the still-sloping floor and into the wall.

Then, with a tearing groan like a ship striking a reef, the Bark righted itself.

The entire room was vibrating now and with his teeth trying to drill their way out of his jaw Jonah found time to imagine that the cylindrical room was indeed a giant drum. The floor bounced against his back, tossing him as though he were a doll. There was a pause, a blissful silence, then they were heavy again, suddenly and immensely heavy.

Jonah tried to lift his head and found he could not even move it an inch. His arm was dead weight on his chest. With a supreme effort he dragged it off; it struck the floor like a sandbag. His vision greyed, then began to close into a tunnel. The only sound he could hear was the roar of the blood draining from his head. Suddenly unconsciousness seemed a very attractive proposition.

Just as he was about to black out, the force compressing him against the hard wooden floor relaxed. Momentarily he had no weight at all, then his body seemed to crumple back into normality. An aching, bruised normality, but one in which he could at least consider sitting up and looking around.

'That was rougher than the first time we went through,' he groaned, allowing Annie to pull him up. On the opposite side of the circular room Gerent and Malya too were picking themselves up and rubbing their bruises.

'How much more of that before we reach the top?' asked Malya.

Jonah arched his back, hands massaging his spine. 'I confess I do not know how many crossings we have to look forward to exactly. Several hundred, I imagine.'

'Several hundred!' Annie exclaimed. 'Hell's bells, Jonah – they all gonna be like that?'

Like a pale wooden fountain Grandfather Tree erupted from the very centre of the floor.

He seemed to delight in varying the way he manifested himself and this time his body coalesced from a tornado of what looked like wood shavings. Manlike down to his waist, his lower body was an indeterminate swirl of sawdust. His face formed, adorned with a crown and beard of brambles. Liquid green eyes shone from borehole sockets, and he was crowing like a cockerel.

'Takes more than a storm to stop the Bark! By the taiga, that was thorny! But, make it we did, and safe we are. Storm's beneath us now. Across the thread we've come, through the Helix. Into a new world!'

'The same world we saw before?' Jonah said.

'The same. Dark red sky, very dry. On to the deck you should come. Feast your eyes! A whole new world!'

Jonah led the way above deck to the cockpit. Above them was a new sky, vast beyond the scope of any sky they had seen before, on Earth or on Stone. It was dark and clean, a cloudless vista the colour of wine, or blood. Arid wind poured on to them, scented with spice. Pale flecks circled high above them, like spinning grey stars

Dominating one entire half of the vista, of course, was Stone, that world-sized wall which had once seemed so strange to Jonah and Annie but which was now strangely reassuring. A friendly face in an foreign land. Its surface looked scratched and pitted, but whether by natural erosion or artifice they could not tell. They were too far from it to make out individual features, but to Jonah's eyes it looked . . . *brutalized*.

'This is the future,' said Annie. 'Well, I'll be damned.'

'Future indeed,' agreed Grandfather Tree. 'Lesky travelled wide and far, once upon a time. Came to this time once. Many turnings ahead, this time. Many futures away. I remember little of it, but I remember it was . . . strange.'

'Strange it is,' said Jonah. '*Everything* is strange here, except perhaps for the line of Stone and the spices on the wind. But the wind is so *dry*. The sunlight is . . . flattened somehow, and as we talk it seems that our voices lack vitality. And though it is warm the ends of my fingers feel icy cold . . .'

Annie gripped his hands in her own. He felt the same contradictions in her flesh: palms aglow and fingertips like ice.

'Weird place,' she said. 'Let's get out of here.'

'It is but the first step on a very long road,' said Jonah. 'Grandfather Tree, are you ready to take us up? We have many skies to cross.'

'I am,' replied the lesky. 'But others . . . they may not be so keen.'

They followed the direction of his woody finger. While they had been talking several of the airborne specks had grouped together into a larger body. As they watched, the mass of specks separated again, resolving themselves into twelve distinct forms, growing bigger all the time, getting nearer.

'Natives?' suggested Jonah. 'I wonder if they are friendly.'

The wind shifted direction a little, then began to break into gusts and flurries. Fragments of sound fell with it, a series of distant explosions.

'That's what they wondered about the Apaches,' said Annie.

One of the shapes was faster than the others. It darted from side to side as it descended, so it was hard to make out its precise shape. Jonah's over-riding impression was of a stooping hawk dropping towards its prey. It was not a reassuring comparison.

The darting movements intensified as the shape drew

close enough to study. It was wide and sharp, bird-like but not a bird. A pair of wings was swept forward from a smooth central body. They did not flap, but nor were they entirely fixed; instead they flexed and folded, even opening up occasionally like parasols. Near the tip of each wing was a glistening sphere. It was falling in absolute silence.

'Ah ye,' said Grandfather Tree. 'I remember these now.'

Towards the rear of the hawk-thing was an irregular jumble of forms, darker grey than the wings and body. Before they could even begin to wonder what these were the thing was upon them.

It dropped the final hundred yards in less time than it took to blink, growing massive above them, more massive than it had first appeared. Still there was no sound. At the last moment it deployed a large antenna – something fanlike, blurred beyond recognition – and flipped on to its side. At one instant it covered half the sky, an angry eagle, then it was gone.

A second later the sound splashed across them, a guttural screaming followed by a prolonged and rag- ged hiss.

'Faster than sound!' said Jonah, surprising himself with his instant understanding. But there was no time to think, because eleven more of the hawk-things were plummeting towards them.

'Below decks!' bellowed Grandfather Tree, and that was when Jonah felt Annie sag against his arm.

He grabbed for her at the same time as Gerent. The Neolithic seized her round the waist while Jonah took her arm. Her eyelids fluttered; her head rolled from side to side.

'Dreamin' dream . . .' she moaned.

'Damnation!' Jonah thumped the deck with his fist. 'Of all the times to choose! Gerent! Help me lay her down.'

They manhandled her as gently as they could to the bowl-shaped floor of the cockpit. A shadow fell across Jonah. He glanced up, assuming it was the flock of hawk-things blocking out the sun.

But it was Malya, poised above him with her legs spread wide and a sword in each hand, ready to repel all boarders. His perfect lady knight.

'. . . trail's too narrow, Jonah . . .' Annie's voice was a croak. '. . . gonna lose the wagon . . .'

'Hush now, my darling. You are safe now. Go with the dream if you must. I will be here when you wake up, I promise.'

What happened next happened so fast that Jonah only assembled the sequence of events later.

Ten of the eleven hawks flashed past as swiftly as the first, but the last of them slowed, veering first away from the Bark then turning in towards it, flattening its stoop into a shallow dive.

Malya's blades shone silver as she lifted them high, then a blast of air threw her to one side. She landed hard and lost her grip on one of the swords, which went clattering off round the curve of the hull to fetch up against one of the Bark's stabilizers.

The deck jumped. Jonah looked around for Grandfather Tree but he had disappeared back into the hull. Thunderous sounds from beneath his feet informed him the Bark was underway again. Evasive manoeuvres.

Gerent fell backwards as the Bark lurched down and to the side. Jonah reached for him, catching his arm in time to prevent him being thrown up and out of the cockpit bowl altogether. Something grey eclipsed the sky and a tornado was there and then gone, faster than thought.

Just before the hawk's guttural scream came there was a brief, meaty thud, then a dreadful scratching sound like fingernails drawn across a blackboard. Fine, warm liquid sprayed across Jonah's face, then the sky cleared and the hawk was gone. All that remained was a dwindling trail of fire in the sky. The air spun and the screaming lingered, but of all the twelve things there was no visible sign.

The Bark tilted further, and the wind against his face informed Jonah they were travelling sideways at some considerable speed. He looked down and saw blood pouring from Annie's leg.

'Annie!' he screamed.

She was unconscious, or dreaming still, he could not tell which. Something – it must have been the hawk – had tossed her on to her side. Her right leg was splayed out at an uncomfortable angle, the striped leggings ripped open the full length of her thigh. They were soaked almost black with blood.

Jonah seized the torn fabric and ripped it further, exposing a straight slash about a foot long. The blood was not pumping – at least her arteries were intact – but it was flowing at an alarming rate. Panic clamoured in his mind and he fought it back. For a moment he had no idea what to do next. *Shirt!* he thought. He pulled it over his head, rolling it into a wad which he pressed hard against the wound. The white cotton bloomed red but he kept up the pressure, head lowered, hair hanging in his face.

Something whistled like a kettle, then that rough, guttural screaming was back. A hawk was swooping low over his head, a hook trailing from its underbelly. The tip of one of its wings was torn and smouldering. The hook dragged across the Bark's hull, tearing into it and creating that nails-on-blackboard sound Jonah had heard during the first attack. A gash appeared in the hull less than six feet from where he was kneeling, its edges smouldering.

There was another shudder. This one felt like a solid impact, as if something had struck the Bark head-on.

'Grandfather Tree!' Jonah shouted at the deck. 'Get us out of here!'

The lesky's face appeared from a patch of bubbling wood.

'Can't!' said the lesky. 'We're cut off! Heading upStone – the only way.'

The distant terrain of Stone streamed past as they began to head upStone, forgetting the descent for the time being in favour of a simple flat race. Annie lolled, dead weight in Jonah's arms.

Still he could not really judge what the hawk-things were – were they vehicles or creatures? The former seemed most likely, but those two spheres, one on each wingtip, and the barely-glimpsed nests of activity at the rear of the craft had looked wholly organic.

It is as if the pilots, whatever outlandish creatures they are, have melded with their machines!

The pursuit continued far upStone. Then, without warning, the hawk things began to close in. Jonah was about to call to the lesky again when a hand closed on his shoulder. He yelled, then turned and found himself staring into Malya's wide eyes. Gerent was close behind her, teeth bared.

'Duck your head!' he said.

Jonah did so. There was a tremendous bang, then the air was filled with splinters of hard metal. Mixed in with the particles was an oily rain. He spread himself as far across Annie as he could, trying to protect her from the falling debris.

Lifting his head he saw that six of the hawks had disappeared. In the Bark's wake was a massive plume of smoke and whirling fragments.

'How did we . . .' he began, but Malya cut him short.

'We didn't,' she said. Then she pointed up. 'That did.'

Something new was descending, something that dwarfed the hawks. An enormous bat-winged vehicle, sleek and multicoloured and spiralling in towards them at punishing velocity.

'Last chance, Grandfather Tree,' he whispered, not even sure that the lesky could hear him any more.

A silvery line lanced down from the multicoloured bat, striking one of the remaining hawks. The others split up to avoid the killing beam. One was too slow: a spinning wing severed from another hawk sliced it in half before it too exploded into flames.

The Bark juddered almost to a halt, nearly throwing Jonah and the others altogether clear of its deck. Then it dropped like a stone, back towards the Helix.

Clouds lifted around them, howling like wolves, and the wine-red sky began to fade. Thunder replaced the howling. The clouds became dark and momentous, sacks of vapour moving faster than clouds had any right to move. Jonah had a brief sensation of being smothered – beneath a giant's bedclothes, perhaps – then the light failed entirely and they were plummeting through black night. He clung to Annie, no longer knowing whether he was staunching the flow of blood and no longer really caring. They were close together – that was all that mattered in this nightmare.

Dreamin' dream. He wondered if Annie was aware of any of this.

Then the blackness from the outside world fell into his head and he knew nothing at all.

Alien thoughts tumbled, great square shapes in motion. He felt Stone resist the Bark's attempts to subvert its laws, felt the repulsive power of the Helix, felt the Bark press down like a beetle fighting its way through the surface tension of a pond.

In the turmoil he was aware of time flowing round him like liquid.

I pulled Malya out of the river long after I pulled out Darwin. She has a long while to live yet. Time enough to find an answer. Time enough . . .

Sunlight exploded, clean and Earthlike, and the clouds peeled open to reveal a sky of the most dazzling blue striped with zebra clouds.

'Back where we started,' he said, hugging Annie hard.

The fall continued. The Bark plunged through the warm sky of Stone, leaving swathes of vapour trailing above it like white smoke.

We will fall right through and out the other side! thought Jonah.

By and by the Bark slowed. Now it was drifting rather than falling. It had developed a noticeable list to one side, and when it changed direction it did so with clumsy jerking movements. Beside it Stone was a cracked grey wall built from granite blocks at least half a mile on a side. It was huge and daunting.

And it was unaccountably familiar.

Then Jonah realized why.

Of course! We were chased upStone before we dropped back through the Helix. Therefore we have not returned to the ocean we left behind. This place must be very close to where Annie and I first entered Stone!

He drew geometry in his head, tried to sort the tangle of distances and dimensions. Meanwhile the Bark had entered a thickening pall of smoke. Someone had lit an enormous bonfire on the surface of Stone and they had fallen right across its path. Flames heaved into view, licking out from a gash in the very skin of Stone.

Jonah looked on in awe. This too was a familiar sight.

A cavity in the great wall. It is not a bonfire at all: it is a brand new threshold!

When a large volcano erupted on Earth, this was what happened on Stone. The explosive force was somehow channelled, flipped over to cut a tunnel through to a new world. They were first-hand witnesses to the opening of a new threshold, a passage between Earth and Stone.

It was too much to take in, too much coincidence that

67

they should have broken through the Helix precisely in time to witness this catastrophe.

Stone enjoys coincidences – that's its game.

Esh had said that to him once; now more than ever he believed it to be true. One of the mysterious race of the Ypoth, Esh had been a true native of the tilted world and therefore the nearest Jonah had to an authority on Stone. He wished she were here now, to help him make sense of all this.

He was halfway into an impromptu prayer when the Bark teetered sideways, carrying them clear of the reaching fingers of ash.

Already the outpouring of volcanic material had stopped. The sprawling cloud had been severed at its root and was now beginning to disperse, prey to the falling wind. Jonah imagined some mighty door slamming shut in the newly-carved tunnel, plugging the rift like the Dutch boy plugging the dyke with his finger. Somewhere in there the Ypoth would soon begin to emerge, ready to repair the damage.

Fires continued to blaze inside the wound. Pale sticks fell like rain and as the Bark coasted nearer (Grandfather Tree was clearly as curious as the rest of them) Jonah saw they were actually whole trees, stripped of their branches and torn off above the root. Many of them were ablaze. Tucked just inside the tunnel entrance was a huge bonfire, a tangle of tree trunks knitted together like a defensive wall; the volcano on Earth must have been heavily forested. Grandfather Tree's voice floated above the sound of cracks and crackles, tutting at the loss of so much good wood.

'Look there,' whispered Malya, gripping Jonah's shoulder.

She pointed out a large green object wedged into the bonfire. Flames were creeping across its flanks. Jonah to could not work out what the thing was, but it was obvious that the creature clambering across the top of it was a man.

Gerent cried out to Grandfather Tree before Jonah could open his mouth, but the Bark was already moving in towards the hole. Cinders boiled past them like hot, black snow; the air grew hot. They could hear the wind whistling past the hole, fanning the fire and sucking the disintegrating trees out into the sky.

Then, as the Bark dived between clouds of thick black smoke, they heard a new sound. It was unexpected, incongruous, the sound of music and a woman singing. The music was unlike anything Jonah had heard before, played by instruments he could not quite identify. Was that really a guitar? The music was raw and filled with energy, fractured by the wind but vital nonetheless. A hypnotic, repeating rhythm.

Music to die by, he thought as he saw the man stand upright on the teetering green object and wave to them, nearly slipping off in the process. The fire was an orange storm scant yards behind him, spitting as it advanced.

The woman continued to sing, except to Jonah it sounded as though she were screaming.

The man's feet were planted on the front section of a vehicle that was like nothing Jonah had seen before. Its surface was smooth metal that must once have been mirror-bright but was now streaked with filth. Its front was all metal bars and grilles, and round glassy things that had to be lights. These were cracked and, like the rest of the vehicle, heavily grimed. Large windows surrounded a cabin, and the whole vehicle was balanced on four enormous wheels. An embossed metal tag pronounced its name was *Cherokee*.

A horseless carriage! It was so far beyond Jonah's experience that he knew immediately where the man had to have come from.

'We have travelled too far upStone,' he said. 'This man is from my future!'

The side of the Bark nudged the green, mud-slimed

vehicle, almost knocking the man off. At once he leaped aboard the basilisk ship.

His decisive action almost certainly saved his life; no sooner had his feet left the metal than the trees on which the vehicle was resting collapsed. Seconds later the whole bonfire sprawled backwards. Explosions tossed out branches like spears, but the Bark was already speeding away from the mayhem, the rescued man fighting to maintain his hold on the swaying deck.

Malya danced across to the man and helped him crawl to the cockpit bowl. He fell in beside Jonah, a tall bald man with dark skin and bright eyes. He wore brown denim trousers and a battered leather jacket; his clothes and skin were coated in fine grey powder.

A man from the future, Jonah thought in wonder.

Then Annie moaned and lurched forward. Fresh blood oozed from beneath the bunched-up shirt Jonah was holding still against her thigh. She opened her eyes, found the stranger staring into them. She fixed him for a long moment. Then her eyes glazed over and she dropped once more into unconsciousness.

The man fell forward, paralysed by a sudden coughing fit, then looked up and croaked, 'Where the fuck am I?'

4

Annie Out West – 2

The sun rose in a different landscape to the one in which it had set. The track beneath the wagon wheels felt the same – pitted and pebbled – but the mountains no longer resembled the Rockies. In fact, it didn't look like America at all.

'That's dreams for you, girl,' said Annie. The landscape beyond the traces was lush and green. 'Full of surprises.'

The track wound round mountain slopes which had been carved into terraces. Below her (she was already quite high; the air in her lungs was thin and cold) the natural gradient was almost impossibly steep. Enormous steps had been cut into it; on them was laid out a patchwork of flooded fields. Low orange light glistened off the water, making long shadows of the earth banks dividing individual plots. Rude towers rose high, marking boundaries, their own shadows stretching for miles. Tiny figures toiled in the fields; it looked as though they were walking on water. The terraces marched down and down into banks of cloud like the very staircase of the gods and Annie wondered where on Earth she was.

The oxen plodded on up the gradual incline.

Later in the morning they passed near to one of the highest of the terraces. Some men were building a new tower beside the ruins of one that had fallen. Its timbers were blackened. Beneath it lay a heap of crushed green metal. The men waved to Annie as the oxen hauled the wagon past. At the very top of the half-finished tower sat a man with a drum, beating out an urgent rhythm; when Annie went by he stopped drumming and called out to her. She could't make out individual words, but he looked and sounded Oriental.

The sun had risen almost to noon by the time they left the flooded terraces behind. Now the slopes really were steep. The track was little more than a notch hacked into the side of a rocky cliff. To her right the mountain rose towards heaven, while to her left it fell into a cloud-filled abyss worthy of Stone itself.

Fallen rocks made the going slow. Annie frequently had to jump down and guide the oxen through a maze of boulders, or even lever some of the larger rocks aside. The wagon tipped and jostled on the uneven surface and soon she was walking all the time – the oxen were sure-footed enough but she was afraid the wagon would tip over completely and drag them all into the chasm.

As morning turned to afternoon they rounded a pillar of bald black rock and saw high peaks looming ahead. The track threaded its way through them, finally disappearing into the darkness between two opposing walls of rock.

Even there, miles ahead, the only direction was up.

'I hope we don't meet no-one comin' the opposite way,' she said to the oxen. Almost at once she heard a voice.

It echoed off the mountains. She couldn't tell where it was coming from; at first it didn't even sound human. Then as it grew louder and clearer Annie recognized it as the voice of a man. The words were strange; she thought it was probably the same language used by the man with the drum.

The oxen negotiated a difficult bend. Now the voice was

72

very near indeed. Accompanying it was a sound Annie did recognize: the patient clip-clop of hooves on rock.

'Oh shit,' she groaned. Then he came round the corner.

He was a short man; the fact that he was hunched forwards made him seem shorter still. He was huddled in black robes, while around his waist was tied a dark grey blanket patterned at the edge with red and blue squares. On his head was a black and white hat shaped like a bowl, only turned the right way up, as if it were ready to catch the rain. Behind him trailed a pair of mules.

His eyes were hidden beneath heavy Oriental folds and she realized the language she'd heard earlier was Chinese. She called the oxen to a halt and watched uncertainly as the man and his mules drew up. The man looked terribly familiar.

'Hello Annie,' he said, bowing low. His back was hunched and round. 'I fear your oxen must go.'

She blinked. 'Go? What do you . . . who are you? What do you mean, "go"?'

The little Chinese man picked his nose, examined the findings and flicked them over the edge. 'Old Tibetan custom. A traveller must make others aware of his presence. That's why I shout. You didn't shout. The price you pay is to lose your animals to the mountain.'

'Lose my . . . You mean they go over the edge? No way!'

'Old custom,' he repeated with a mischievous smile.

Annie wrapped her arm round the bigger ox, surprised at how fond she had grown of these uncomplaining beasts. Even if this were only a dream she was damned if she was going to see them sacrificed because of some tradition.

Only a dream, she thought. *Hell, Annie, you better not get lazy here.*

'I won't do it!' she said.

73

The man seemed to consider this for a while, then shrugged. 'Okay,' he said. 'It's your dream. But they'll have to stay here. The path's too steep. That's why I brought you a mule.'

'Oh my god,' she exclaimed. All the breath went out of her and she clutched at the ox for support. 'It's you! The last time I saw you was in San Francisco, the day before I got on the ship. You gave me the painting box, the Mah Jongg tiles!' She found there were tears in her eyes. 'You set me on my way.'

'And again I am at your service.' The Chinese man bowed low once more. As he rose again his eyes were sparkling beneath their hoods. 'Now, leave everything here and come with me. Another journey beckons, and for this one you need only yourself.'

Suspicion came late, so late in fact that Annie was already climbing on to the larger of the two mules when she thought, *He's Archan! He's a disguise, like my mother! It's another trick!* She stared at him, eyes bulging, her fingers digging into the mule's sparse mane. He looked back at her, that flicker of amusement on his face again. Then he shook his head.

'Look at me well,' he said. 'It's important we start in the right place. All journeys must start in the right place. Look at me well, and listen to me well. And when you listen to me, also *hear* me well. *I am not the dragon.* Do you understand me?'

She nodded.

'Do you believe me?'

She nodded again. He sighed and shook his head.

'Think again. Do you *see* me?'

Blue eyes that were full of laughter. A stoop like an old man, yet he was not as old as she had first thought. In fact there was no age she could fit to him at all – he might have been twenty or eighty, she just couldn't tell. Small, supple hands.

74

'Yes,' she whispered. 'I see you. I believe you. I know that you are not Archan.'

And she *did* know it, as surely as she knew this was her dreamin' dream. This was the same Chinese man in whose outhouse she had slept on her last night in San Francisco, back home in another world.

That night had marked the end of her journey overland from Kansas. It had been a long journey, sometimes wild, often just dull. She'd told Jonah some of it but suspected the whole of it would remain locked in her heart until the day she died.

After years of love and abuse in more or less equal measure she'd finally chosen to leave Rance, the husband who in the end had loved her more with his fists than with his heart. Her mother had been right – the Snallygaster was real and she'd married the bastard.

And, yes, it had felt like an ending, the end of years in a little sod house on the Kansas prairie, the end of her marriage and all her youthful days. After weeks on the trail she realized it was also a beginning. She didn't miss the abuse, not at all. The love she kept a long time in her heart; most times she thought that too would stay in her heart forever.

She'd been almost a year on the trail. She supposed it had been an adventure, the sort of tale a writer might make into a book, but in her mind it was just a series of more or less unconnected incidents. Sometimes it seemed to her it had happened to somebody else entirely.

A wagon train much like the one in her dreamin' dream carried her to Salt Lake City, where she stayed for a while, selling her drawings and waiting at tables. Later, with the call of the Pacific in her ears, she joined another train over the Rockies. Having survived attacks from both mountain lions and mountain men she ended up in San Francisco. As soon as she smelt the salt from the bay she knew the

75

Pacific was no more an end than her escape from Rance had been. It was just another beginning.

The same day she arrived in San Francisco she met this diminutive Chinaman with his upturned hat and impeccable English. His outhouse (a tiny wooden lean-to adjoining his shabby dwelling on St Louis Alley) was empty and she was welcome to sleep there. The alley was crowded and noisome. The din of surrounding Chinatown was both confining and comforting, like being bandaged from head to foot with noise. Tomorrow, the Chinaman promised, he would help her find passage on a suitable vessel.

She never thought to ask how he knew she wanted to go to sea, to sail on out west as far as she could go.

Next morning he was knocking on her door, beaming and describing the ship on which he had already secured her a place. It was headed for the impossibly exotic Galapagos Islands.

'How much?' she asked. 'I've got some money, but . . .'

But he only shook his head and laughed and said he knew the captain. How likely was that, when to be Chinese in San Francisco was to be roughly on a level with the curs on the streets? Another mystery she hadn't even thought to question.

Before leaving for the dock he had given her an ornate mahogany box with brass hinges and a delicate clasp.

'I made it for you,' he explained.

'But how could you? This must have taken you weeks . . .'

There she trailed off, because she had just opened the box.

Inside were stacked what looked like hundreds of little white tiles. But it was the paints and the brushes and the little pots of liquid that really caught her attention. She started crying almost at once.

'You've kept your drawing up but you haven't painted

since you were a little girl,' said the Chinese man, as if he had known her all his life.

'Rance thought it was dumb.'

'Start again.' He closed the lid; their hands touched. 'And take care on your journeys, wherever they take you.'

The ship took her to Galapagos, barren and beautiful, and still she travelled on. She came to Java and, a few miles off its western coast, Krakatoa. There she found a beach and on the beach she found Jonah. After that there was just Stone.

Here in a dream landscape with her fingers wound into the mane of a mule that stank worse than the oxen she had just decided to abandon, Annie realized the Chinese man's mysterious way, not to mention his intimate knowledge of her, had never struck her as odd until now. He'd given her the box, kissed her forehead like a father and walked her to the dock. He had waved to her as the ship departed, then turned and walked out of her life. She'd hardly thought of him since.

And, until now, she'd never even asked his name.

'My name?' He frowned in response to her question. 'Even I don't know all the names I could go by, but the one that suits me as I am now is Tai Yi Huang Ren.'

'Tie what?'

'A mouthful for you? So. You might simply call me, "Mister Ren".'

'Mister Ren,' she smiled. 'It's good to see you again.'

'So! All is well! Now, let's be on our way. Ha, mule, go!'

The path did indeed get much steeper.

Annie wondered what the oxen would do; she'd unhitched them from the wagon but they showed no inclination to move from where they stood: they were still chewing the cud when she and Mister Ren disappeared around the trail. They were either patient or stupid, probably both. Hunger would drive them back down the mountain, she supposed, assuming dream-cattle actually got hungry.

Paddy fields still clung to the hillsides, the terraces ever more precipitous the higher they went. Then they entered a layer of damp cloud, and for a time there was nothing. The mules plodded on and Annie could think of nothing to say to her new guide; nor did he say anything to her. The silence was oppressive, a watching enemy.

Breaking through the clouds was like surfacing from beneath the sea. The cloud layer stretched into infinity, a dazzling white ocean, smooth as newly-laundered bedsheets. Only where the mountains pierced it did it fold into streamers and tendrils of vapour, breaking against the rocky shores of these apparent islands. All sense of place evaporated, beyond the knowledge that they were somewhere on Earth. West, East, high in the Rockies or lost in the Himalayas . . . they could have been anywhere. What mattered was the not the location, nor even the destination, but the journey itself.

'So how come you're here?' she asked. Maybe talking would help distract her from the ache in her backside.

They were riding single file with Mister Ren in front, so all she could see was the Chinaman's rounded back. His head rocked from side to side as the mule ambled on; he seemed rather more comfortable in her dream than she was herself.

'I like to step in occasionally.' His voice meandered back, quiet yet penetrating. It was like he was speaking into her ear. 'And Archan has been particularly tiresome of late.'

'You know about Archan?'

'Of course, yes. An important time is drawing near. The Deathless have bungled things rather too often for my liking. So. It's time I had my say.'

Annie wished he would stop, turn to her, so she could see his face. Was he smiling? Or frowning? She couldn't gauge his mood, nor the real meaning of his words.

'Who *are* you?' she said.

Then he did stop, and he did turn to face her. The reflected light from the cloud blanket surrounded him in a brilliant aura. Within the halo his eyes shone green. Even his black robes seemed aglow.

'You've met me before, Annie West. Yes, yes, in San Francisco, but think harder. Can you not remember another time? A more recent time?'

He was laughing now, revealing small, perfect teeth. Annie shook her head, perplexed. Mister Ren reached down and took the hem of his robe, then lifted it over his head in with a single sweeping gesture.

At first she thought he was carrying a shield beneath it, but why carry a shield on your back? Surely it was more use held in front, or on the arm. She hustled her mule closer, to get a better look. When she looked again she gasped: it wasn't a shield at all. It was a shell.

Segmented, black as night, like a tortoise-shell carved from ebony. She couldn't see how it was attached to his back – it might very well have been part of Mister Ren's anatomy for all she could see – but it wasn't the fixings she was looking at. Instead her eyes were drawn to the familiar red sigil drawn on the side of the shell.

It was a Mah Jongg mark, the sword-like shape of the Red Dragon.

'Esh!' she exclaimed. 'But . . . you died at the Threshold. Or does this mean . . . *are* you Esh, reborn in my dream?'

Reclosing his robe, Mister Ren grew solemn. 'I was in Esh as I am now in Mister Ren. The Ypoth you knew as Esh was, you might say, one of my earlier lives.'

Annie recoiled. 'Then what in hell are you? Are you another wandering spirit that takes control of people whenever you feel like it? Because that doesn't sound any better than what Archan does.'

'No, no, Annie, you misunderstand me. No taking control, no wandering spirit. No, I was Esh in the completest sense, just as I am Mister Ren in the completest sense. So, Mister Ren is all me, though he is not all that I am. And Esh was all me too. As Esh, I was your friend and companion during your difficult early days on Stone, whose real name is Amara. I taught you and Jonah something of Amara's ways, and I guided you to the Threshold, where Jonah made his first stand against Archan.'

'You gave up your life for us there,' said Annie. 'So what are you now – reincarnated?'

'Not as simple as that, no. But it's a start.'

She couldn't help but laugh. 'You're like Esh in one way – you talk in riddles!'

'So – I do not mean to. Perhaps I've been around the Deathless too long. Now they were the ones for being obtuse! Sometimes I wish I'd never made them.'

All the wind went out of Annie's lungs. She sagged against the mule's scrawny neck.

'*Made* them? Made the *basilisks*? Made the things that made Stone, or Amara, or whatever the hell you want to call it?'

It was too much to take in. Mister Ren's smile widened, but it remained a smile of truth, not tease.

Then she said, 'Oh shit, Mister Ren, you're not God, are you?'

The little Chinaman's smile wrapped right around his face and he doubled up with laughter. Tears squirted from his pale green eyes and he held his sides as he rocked to and fro in the saddle, a broad pantomime of amusement that was all the more absurd for being genuine.

'God!' he spluttered. 'Well, that's a fine one, young Annie!' And he continued to chortle as she looked on in amazement. 'Not God, oh no, no, not God. Don't know anything about God – though I daresay he knows a thing or two about me. No, I like to avoid names – they can get you into a lot of trouble if you're not careful – so for now you call me Mister Ren, just like you used to call me Esh. As for what I *do*, well, I make things. I've made all sorts of things in my time, but the one thing that always bothered me was that they kept on running out. You know – like winding up a spinning top and watching it spin until it drops on its side and scoots away across the floor? So I set to work making something that would last forever. Took me a long time, then I hit on it. You'll have guessed already what it was.'

'The basilisks, the Deathless Ones. They were made immortal.'

'Close, Annie. I made them afterwards, to make use of the thing that lasts forever. Yes, I made the basilisks, but before I made them I made immortality.'

By now the pain from Annie's back and buttocks was almost unbearable. She swung her leg over the mule's back, ready to dismount.

'Look, I'm sorry, Mister Ren, but if we're gonna have a chin-wag could we take a rest to do it?'

He looked up the trail. A deep frown created a mosaic of tiny wrinkles across his forehead and suddenly he looked a thousand years old. *Strike that*, thought Annie, *more like a billion*.

'Well,' he said, 'yes, my fanny hurts too.'

Wincing somewhat with the effort, the little Chinese man who had made the basilisks clambered off his mule and squatted down next to where Annie had seated herself with her back resting against the sheer cliff face that flanked the trail.

'Smoke?' He drew a long ivory pipe from beneath his robes.

Annie declined, watching in fascination as he tamped a large wad of sweet-smelling tobacco into the bowl and lit it simply by blowing on it. It seemed entirely appropriate that the spicy aroma of the smoke was the same as the air of Stone.

'So you made Stone too then?'

Mister Ren brandished his pipe. 'No no no! Keep up, Annie. The *basilisks* made Amara. I made . . .'

'. . . the basilisks. Yeah, okay, I get it. But it's still all yours, in a way.'

'In a way.' He gazed out over the clouds. 'That's why I won't allow Archan to break it apart.'

'Where is she, Mister Ren? How's she found a way back? I thought we'd taken care of her pretty good this time.'

So Mister Ren told her how there were indeed two dragons now, how Archan had made contact with her twin self in the parallel world Jonah had inadvertently created. He told her how Archan had taken control of Areken, forcing her twin to commence the perilous journey up the face of Stone to its tip. There, in the place known as Sunlight Pass, was an opportunity for Archan to cross back into the version of Stone inhabited by Jonah and Annie. An opportunity to wreak revenge on those who had defied her, and to recommence her mission of destruction.

The little brushstrokes were news but the bigger picture was one she'd been able to see for a while now. She'd known Archan was on her trail again – wasn't that how the dreamin' dreams had started? And ever since Jonah had created that other world she'd feared the repercussions.

There are two Archans out there. She shuddered at the sure knowledge.

'If she can get at her twin, this *Areken*, and she can get at me . . . then why doesn't she just come on over into our Stone and be done with it? Why all this chasing up to the roof?'

'Because she *cannot* "just come on over". You and your friends did a good job at the Aqueduct. I was proud of you. You shut her out good and proper! She really is trapped beyond the barrier you made; all she can do now is influence the minds of those creatures with whom she has unusual affinity. Her twin sister, of course, is one, despite the fact that they are literally worlds apart. And you are another, Annie West. She knows you well – after all, did she not live inside you for a time?'

'I've got her measure,' muttered Annie. The reminder was unwelcome.

Mister Ren's eyes sparkled. 'Yes, yes! You've got her measure, Annie, and that gives us hope. She comes to you in your dreams, but she lacks the power to take control as she once did. She's far away and weakened, Annie, never forget that. Far away and weakened.'

'Hmm. But pretty soon we'll meet her up close again, won't we? Is she gonna seem so weak then?'

'So. Up close . . . yes, that will be another matter. But resist her while you can. We may learn something in the meantime to give us the strength we need.'

Annie stretched her arms above her head. The air was thin and she felt short of breath; it was cold too, like winter.

'You keep saying "us". You mean you're not cut out for this either?'

Mister Ren shrugged. 'Why do you think I need your help?'

Mister Ren had almost finished explaining what he needed when Annie felt the cliff shaking against her back. She had time to glance up, then the boulders started raining down on them. One struck her thigh, ripping the thin fabric of her leggings and opening a deep gash in her flesh. The pain was sudden and intense, blindingly *real* considering this was supposed to be a dream, and she screamed.

Mister Ren hunched over, presenting his back to the avalanche. Pressing herself back against the rock face, Annie screamed again as the rocks crashed down on him . . . but not one of them touched him. It was like watching a stream parting round a stone.

The avalanche was frenzied but short-lived. Soon the flow of rocks had slowed to a trickle. No more struck Annie, or even came near her, but the gash on her leg was howling for attention. Blood had pooled beneath her, dark and sticky, and she knew she ought to apply a tourniquet. But she felt weak and faint and the dream was already slipping away from her. Here she was, in the middle of a dream, falling asleep. Her vision blurred, her head slumped to the side. From the corner of her eye she watched Mister Ren shrug off the last of the boulders and glare up at the mountain which had unleashed them.

'A feeble effort!' he shouted. Was that a tremor in his voice? Or were her own senses trembling? Then he rushed to her side.

'Annie! Wake up, Annie! Don't leave, not yet! There's more I must say to you.'

'Gotta go,' she mumbled. Her head was so heavy. Her leg had started to throb now, the pain an immense, excruciating heartbeat. 'Wake me up at the summit.'

'No, no! Not yet! Listen!'

She heard his urgent instructions through the sea-wash of blood in her ears, wishing she could wake from this dreamin' dream and return to a world where her leg didn't look like a side of meat on a butcher's slab.

'Comin' back, Jonah,' she whispered as the Chinaman's words dissolved into nothingness. 'Comin' home . . .'

5

Passenger

The man's name was Tom Coyote. He was thirty-five, just three years older than Jonah, and he had been caught up in one of the major volcanic eruptions of the late twentieth century.

'Mount St Helens,' he said through cracked lips. His eyes were glazed, looking at something other than the Stonescape drifting past the Bark. 'They said she was gonna blow.'

'What year are you from?' asked Jonah. Grandfather Tree had extruded a mug shaped like a giant acorn and filled with a warm, sugary liquid, which the man was cradling in his shaking hands. His hands were large, Jonah noted, and almost swallowed the mug whole.

He was taller than Jonah, who was himself a little over six feet, though Coyote was narrow-shouldered and much thinner; the way he was huddled over made him seem shorter than he really was. Grey ash lay around him where he had begun to brush it from his face and hands; his clothes were still caked with the stuff. Around his neck was slung a strange glass-eyed device with the word *Pentax* embossed on the front.

Coyote's voice cracked as he laughed. 'Year? What *year*?' Big hands still shaking, he lifted the cup to his lips, but brought it down again without drinking anything.

Then he whispered, 'Right. Okay, yeah. 1980. It's May, 1980. Anno domini. The mountain blew up.'

Jonah had already answered the bald man's frantic questions about what had happened to him and where he was. He described Stone and its relationship with their home; the words came easily, and the reality he found himself articulating was clear and logical in his mind. What was harder to deal with was Coyote's reaction.

'Parallel world. Shit, I might have known. You got Elvis here too?'

Jonah recalled his own first hours on Stone, his own sense of dislocation, of outrage even, of pure disbelief. His heart went out to this man who, like him, had been catapulted out of the jaws of a volcano and into a whole new world.

'This is not a dream,' he said. 'I spent my first days here wondering when I was going to wake up. That was time wasted. I can assure you that you are alive and, as far as we can determine, well, and most assuredly awake. Tom Coyote – welcome to Amara.'

He left the newcomer with Malya and went below decks to check on Annie.

Unseen, Grandfather Tree opened the doors ahead of him as he marched through the winding corridors of the Bark. Root-like appendages dangled from the ceilings, twitching and twining around each other, while from behind pipes and panels came muffled scratching sounds. All around him the Bark was repairing itself.

Gerent was sitting with her in a small, quiet room deep in the vessel. The air in here was warm and thick, concentrated in a way that Jonah could only describe as *wholesome*.

With Gerent's help he had managed to clean and bandage Annie's wound, which was deep but not as fearsome as they had first thought. No major blood vessels had been severed and looking at the neat dressing (a soft green cloth supplied, like Coyote's cup and a replacement for Jonah's bloodstained shirt, by their talented lesky host) he was confident the remarkable healing powers of Stone's charm-filled air would soon repair the damage.

Tasting the flavour-filled air, he realized Grandfather Tree had in fact compressed a great deal of the healing charm into this cramped space. *She will soon be walking again*, he reassured himself. *When she awakes, that is.*

He was fairly sure that Annie's continuing unconsciousness was the product of sleep rather than coma, though he did worry that she was still in the grip of one of her dreamin' dreams. If she was, then it was by far the longest one she had experienced so far. He wondered what Archan might be saying to her that could take so long.

'Has there been any change?' he asked. Gerent shook his head, his long blonde hair swishing against the upraised leading edges of his wings.

'No, Lightfoot. But she breathes well, and shows no sign of distress. She will sleep away the pain and wake in her own good time.' Despite his encouraging words his voice was glum.

Jonah sat down next to Gerent, squeezing between the Neolithic and the edge of the low wooden couch on which Annie lay. With the three of them in there the little room was full, but the cosiness was companionable. He took a deep breath, feeling the life-giving air infiltrating his lungs.

'Where is Malya?' Gerent's attempt to sound casual failed miserably.

'Above decks,' said Jonah. 'She has taken over from me in interrogating our new passenger. Poor fellow, I expect it does feel like an interrogation to him. He won't even know what has happened to him for several days, not properly at least. Still, he seems a resilient sort of chap, despite the obvious shock. Oh, Gerent! Just imagine! This man is from the year 1980! I . . . I cannot begin to think what to ask him. That vehicle he was riding in, for example – by what means was it powered? Is it a gasoline-powered horse-less carriage as I suspect? Are such marvels commonplace in his time? And as for that peculiar music he was listening to . . .'

'I liked it,' said Gerent.

'Yes . . . well, it might have suited your primitive Stone Age ears but I can assure you that to a Victorian gentleman it sounded distinctly unsavoury.'

'The charm of Stone works many miracles,' said Gerent, 'but you are still the most pompous man I know.'

Jonah smiled at the dig, and at himself. 'We do not see you flying very much these days, Gerent,' he said, running his hand across the nearer of his red and black wings.

'The mood rarely takes me.'

'Malya used to like seeing you in the air,' Jonah said. 'She thinks you look graceful when you are flying.'

'Why does she tell you these things, and not me?'

'Perhaps you do not want to hear. Gerent, those wings are part of you now. I thought you had come to accept that, but now you seem to despise them.'

'I do despise them!' Gerent pulled the wing away, his sudden anger overwhelming in the confined space. 'They are not mine – I was not born with them but bonded to them by an evil spell! Do you know how it feels to wear wings made by the man who destroyed my people? Sometimes I cannot even bear to look upon myself! Were it not for Frey and his evil deeds I would be king of the Denneth, as is my right. But no – the dragon whose scales he stole has taken his revenge: the castle is incinerated and my people are no more. Now there is only me, and what use is a king without his subjects?' He stopped, his eyes filling with angry tears. 'And were it not for Frey then Malya would never have suffered an awful death, would never have had to see the eyes of her father turn cold as he took her life away.'

'The Malya who is with us now was not killed by Frey. We rescued her from that fate. She does not have that dreadful memory.'

'But I do, Lightfoot! I do!' He hung his head. 'And every day I look on Frey's wings I am reminded of it. Every day I look on them. And on her.'

'On *Malya*? Dear God, Gerent, does it pain you to look upon the woman you *love*?' Now Jonah was angry too. 'What would it take to convince you, Gerent? Must she be taken from you again? Would that be enough to make you understand the love you share? Do you want to see her *die* again?' He looked away, heart pounding, watching the shallow rise and fall of Annie's breast.

A spasm passed through Gerent's wings. He rose, clambering over Jonah to get to the doorway. He left without a word.

A few moments later Annie stirred in her sleep.

'Is she with you now?' Jonah whispered in her ear. 'Stand up to her, Annie, my love. Show her your strength. Resist her with all your might.'

She was smiling, he noticed, and he wondered if she might be dreaming about something other than Archan altogether.

A touch of his hand to her brow confirmed she was not feverish. Not that he feared infection: neither of them had suffered so much as a cold during their time on Stone, and their occasional injuries had healed with uncommon speed. Scarring too was minimal. Nevertheless, it was reassuring to see her at peace.

'Who are you with?' He snuggled as close to her as he could. He closed his eyes, imagining night around them, pretending they were together in an ordinary bed.

Jonah was enough of an English gentleman to find

their relationship just a little uncomfortable. After all Annie was still legally married to Rance and, as far as they knew, he was still alive and well and living in Kansas.

We left our old lives behind, he consoled himself from time to time. *They lie now wherever our clothes lie, on the remains of Krakatoa's beach, or beneath the waves of the Straits of Sunda. We are doing only what we feel to be right. And we love each other* . . .

'Annie West. Annie Lightfoot.' He nuzzled her cheek. 'Well, what's in a name?'

A knot in the wooden wall twitched, then rearranged its shadows to form the old and elfin face of Grandfather Tree.

'Up to the deck you should go,' he said. 'They're arguing. Could turn ugly.'

'But Annie . . .'

'I'll watch her. Go. To you they will listen.'

The lesky emerged further, growing arms and hands with long, mobile fingers. He stroked Annie's arm with these gentle twigs.

'Call me if there is any change,' said Jonah as he levered himself up off the floor.

'You think you can order me about you got another think coming! Jesus Christ, you got any idea what kind of day I've had? Just let me hang out here for a while, just 'til I get my head together, you know? What am I gonna do, steal your fuckin' ship?'

Jonah watched from the shadow of the hatchway as the bald man ranted. He was directing his anger squarely at Malya. Gerent was standing behind her and a little to the side, watching the proceedings with interest. Malya was scowling. In her hand she held the Roman sword. Its keen edge gleamed. Coyote's eyes kept returning to it.

Jonah looked at Coyote, tried to seek out anything he had missed. He was cleaner for one thing; grubby water was pooled in a depression in the deck beside him and Jonah guessed that Grandfather Tree had liberated some of their drinking supply to facilitate a wash.

Revealed was a tall thin man, dressed for the outdoors. Rugged and, it had to be admitted, handsome. Around his neck was the small, dark object labelled *Pentax*; it swung to and fro on a thin strap, its metal corners and glass eye making stars in the sunlight. The man's hands were restless, now pressing into his pockets, now sliding over his head as if combing flat the hair he did not possess, now fiddling with the device about his neck. Jonah had already guessed this was some kind of futuristic photographic equipment; he resolved to quiz Coyote about it later.

Coyote was glaring at Malya, but there was a curious expression on his face, something beneath the anger. At last Jonah recognized it and again felt his heart open to the man's plight – it was simple and honest confusion.

'Is there a problem?' he said as he stepped up out of the hatchway. 'Malya – why have you drawn your sword?'

'I asked this . . . person to leave the Bark,' she said. 'He refused. I decided to encourage him.'

'Why?' Jonah tried to keep his voice light. 'What crime has he committed?'

'No crime. But we have a mission, Jonah, in case you had forgotten. We don't need passengers on our quest.'

Coyote laughed at this. 'Quest! Oh yeah, oh man, that's just too much! What is it, the pot of gold at the end of the rainbow or you just lookin' for Oz?' He leered at Malya. 'Is that hair your natural colour, blondie?'

'He is tired and confused,' Jonah said. He was close enough now that he could lower his voice and pitch his words for Malya's ears alone. 'We cannot simply abandon him – the shock might be too much for him.'

'He does not look like a man who shocks easily,' she said. Jonah had to agree, but continued to press his case.

'Then we should at least find a more appropriate spot to put him ashore, as it were. This place . . .' he waved his hand at the grey wall of Stone past which the Bark was drifting, '. . . is no better than a desert. Let us travel a little way downStone, where we know there is at least water and perhaps some settlements into which our friend might be introduced.'

'He goes,' said Malya. 'And he is no friend.'

Jonah could no longer contain his anger. Why did the Neolithics have to be so petulant?

'For goodness sake! Will you stop behaving like a child? This man deserves rest and a chance to recover his senses. It's all very well for you: you are a denizen of Stone, this place is all you have ever known. But I know only too well the torment of crossing over from our world to this. I wish someone had been there on my arrival to welcome me and explain the circumstances in which I found myself. I'll be damned if I will not do at least that for our friend Coyote!'

'Hear hear!' cried the bald man. He rushed forward to embrace Jonah, applauding as he came. Gerent nodded at him as he went past, a tacit approval. 'Thanks man, I mean, I owe you one.'

'Yes, well, you are very welcome,' said Jonah, trying to extricate himself from Coyote's bear-hug. 'I cannot promise you a berth on our ship, but we will extend our hospitality for as long as we are able, at least until the Bark is ready to tackle the Helix again.' He paused, then added, 'In any case, I should very much like to share a conversation with a man from the year 1980. You must live in a world filled with wonders, sir.'

Coyote released him, leaving him short of breath and with aching ribs. 'Wonders. Yeah, right. What year did you say you came from?'

'From the great and glorious year of Queen Victoria's reign – 1883.'

'Queen Victoria. A limey. An *old* limey. Right. So who

are these guys?' He nodded at Gerent and Malya. His gaze lingered especially on Gerent's wings.

'Oh, please do forgive them. They are Neolithics, that is they come from the Late Stone Age, or rather their ancestors did, since they themselves might more accurately be classified as natives of Stone.'

'Stone? Oh yeah, this place. Right.'

'Um, yes. You see, people from all ages have found their way on to Stone. The resultant population is a melange. A sparse population by most standards however, thanks to the contraceptive effect of the airborne charm.'

'Woah, man – you're losing me now. I'm still catchin' up with Queen Victoria. You're trying to tell me this Stone's a kind of melting pot, right? A place where anyone can turn up any old time, never mind his race, creed or colour? Just like the good old US of A – "Bring me your tired, your poor". Right?'

'A "melting pot". Yes, I suppose so.'

Coyote lowered his voice, his eyes on Gerent. 'So what's with this guy's wings? Cavemen never had wings, not in the history books I read. He gives me the creeps, I gotta tell you . . . hey, what's your name?'

'Jonah. Jonah Lightfoot.'

'Pleased to meet you, Jonah.' Coyote stuck out a gnarled hand. 'I'm . . . oh well hell, you know who I am already.'

'I know your name is Tom Coyote,' replied Jonah. 'Would you care to tell us a little more about yourself, Tom?'

'Don't mind if I do!' Jonah found the sudden enthusiasm disconcerting, but he could not contain his curiosity about this future-man. 'You got any chairs we could draw up, Jonah?'

'The deck is comfortable enough.'

'Then I guess that'll have to do.'

*   *   *

'I'd been on the mountain a week. There were a lot of journalists there, like me, and photographers and all the usual circus. I'm based in Seattle, but there was such a ruckus about St Helens I figured I may as well head on downstate and see what stories I could dig up.

'Well, I toured around, talking to the locals, you know. There's some strange old boys up on that mountain. Or there were, I guess I should say. One guy I interviewed lived in this old shack, way up on the north slope. Jack Coogan his name was, said he'd lived up there all his life and wasn't gonna let some bunch of smart-aleck geologists turn him out of his home. I guess he's dead now. His house'll be nothing but cinders, that's for sure.

'Oh, there were plenty of others – geologists and vulcanologists and god-knows-what-ologists, all swarming over the mountain. I guess some of those guys are dead now too, got just a touch too keen on being the first to break the news. Like me. I lost all my notes – they were in the Jeep. Still got my camera though. Don't imagine there's many places round here I can get the pictures developed.

'I was on my way back to see old man Coogan this morning. Thought I could get some human interest going, you know, a "stubborn old codger" angle. "I know this mountain like my own child and I say she ain't gonna blow, but if she does I'm goin' with her!" That kinda thing.

'It was hard to believe it was gonna blow up. All the geeks were positive, kept showing pictures of how the north face was bulging out, an extra five feet every day, they said. There were the quakes too, up to five on the Richter. But the sun came and went, and the clouds came and went, and people were still walkin' and talkin' on that old mountain. It was busy but . . . kinda sleepy too, I guess.

'So there I was, tooling up the track towards Jack's place again. Deep forest, but it opened out higher up. I could see the mountain dead ahead, framed by the trees and clear against the sky. The north face. It swelled up, then it just . . . blew up. It was like the whole mountain was falling towards me, deadly fast but in slow motion too, both at the same time. Weird. I grabbed the camera and reeled off a few shots but I already knew this was no time to be taking pictures. The ground was shaking and I could hear wind – nothing like an explosion, just the meanest wind you ever heard in your life. And everything was going dark. I flipped the Jeep round and started speeding back down the dirt. She was bouncing all over the place. I knew the track wasn't this rough, it was the mountain doing most of the moving. I looked in the mirror and saw the forest breaking up behind me. The trees were just snapping off like matchsticks. Something exploded not far back and this shape somersaulted past the window. A fir tree, big as you like, spinning end over end like a damned Popsicle stick. I ducked – like it would make any difference – but it had already gone past and was crashing into the rest of the trees at the side of the road.

'I floored the accelerator and looked in the mirror again. I could see this cloud, this grey cloud, bearing down on me. Then I realized the cloud was *all* I could see. No sky, nothing in the side mirrors except this wall of cloud. It was like it had wiped out the whole world, there was just me and this wall. The forest was splintering before it. It was like you'd imagine a tidal wave, just slicing through everything, ripping it all up as it goes along. The cassette deck was cranked up real loud. Blondie. *Atomic*. So there I was, driving for my life down the side of an erupting volcano with Debbie Harry screaming in my ears.

'The cloud was getting closer every second, too fast to believe. I mean I was pushing eighty despite the road and this thing, this wall was just gaining on me all the time. Two hundred miles an hour, easy, maybe more. Just far out. Then all the trees around me were dropping like dominoes and the Jeep wasn't on the road any more, she was lifting up into the air. *This is it*, I thought and then this light appeared. I hadn't realized how dark it'd really got until this light burst in and I could see a patch of blue sky ahead. Out left I could see the ash cloud overtaking me but on the other side was a black wall, like a tunnel wall, racing past. Then I *was* in a tunnel, jouncing along with burning trees flying every which way. I hit something on the road and the Jeep careered sideways, nearly tipped over, then something else scraped the roof, something like a bar spanning the tunnel from side to side. Then I was clear and there was just the trees and the fire and the ash cloud again, only now the cloud was thinner, weaker somehow and the trees were piled up like a dam. The end of the tunnel got close all of a sudden and I jammed on the brakes and skidded to a halt a few yards short. More trees were piled there and I just missed slamming into them. Then the trees coming from behind crashed into the back of the Jeep and knocked it forwards, and the cloud was pouring over everything and everything seemed to be catching fire. Debbie was still screamin' and I stayed inside as long as I dared, until the cloud was mostly gone, then I jumped out and on to the bonnet and started hollerin' . . .'

Tom Coyote pressed both hands on top of his head, bearing down as if to stop the memories erupting through his skull. His eyes were watering; Jonah saw the grey trails the tears left on his cheeks and thought, *this man must be riddled through with volcanic ash*.

His father had once related a memory from his own childhood of the so-called 'year without a summer' when Tambora, with an eruption four times as powerful as that of Krakatoa, had disrupted weather systems across the globe. This tale, like most of the tales from his father's past, had always been ancient history to Jonah. Exploding mountains were the stuff of legend; they did not belong in the here-and-now.

These days he knew different; he saw Coyote did too.

'You are lucky to be alive,' said Jonah. He thought for a moment, then smiled and added, 'My father was a newspaper reporter like you.'

'Yeah? Mine tested A-bombs.'

'Were you assigned to a newspaper in Seattle? I fear I know little enough about the American newspaper industry. Are there indeed still newspapers in the twentieth century? Or is information dispersed by other, more miraculous means?' He was babbling, he knew, but with each question he asked another bubbled up beneath it. A man from the future!

'Newspapers – yeah, we still read newspapers. Most of them are just as full of crap as they always were. UFOs and half-naked women. But I don't work for any paper – I'm kind of freelance, I guess you could say. I go my own way.'

Jonah wondered what A-bombs and yew-foes were and filed away the remark about half-naked women. What kind of libertine society existed in the impossibly distant time of 1980? Instead he asked Coyote about the vehicle he had been driving down the mountain.

'The Jeep, yeah. Well, it's an automobile, you know.' Coyote's tone was growing sullen. He kept putting his left hand to his head, touching smooth scalp with probing fingertips.

'Is it a descendent of Monsieur Bollée's self-propelled carriages? Mind you, I always considered those steam engines unwieldy in the extreme; no more than one would expect from the French of course. How is it propelled? Is it gasoline, as Mister Benz has predicted?'

'Gas, yeah, right. Look . . . what's your name again – Jonah?'

'Yes.'

'Look, Jonah. Thanks for sticking up for me but right now I'm dog-tired and pretty much pissed off. Someone's blowing the last trump in my head and all I want to do is shut it out and sleep it off. No offence, but can we save the lecture on the internal combustion engine 'til the morning?'

Jonah was about to stumble through a flustered apology when a branch thrust its way out of the deck between him and Coyote. The bald man lurched backwards, his eyes widening. The branch sprouted a single human hand, in the middle of which was a mouth.

'Jonah,' said the voice of Grandfather Tree. 'Found something I have. Come and see, right away.'

'Why have you left Annie on her own?' said Jonah. He was angry at having his conversation with Coyote interrupted and positively enraged at the lesky's abandonment of an injured woman.

'I haven't!' The fingers splayed wide around the wide-lipped mouth, expressing surprise and dismay with remarkable facility. 'Hence the unorthodox anatomy. There's too much to be done for me to be rooted to just one spot. I'm with her, the rest of me – safe she is. Stop talking! Come now!'

So saying, the partial lesky cruised off across the hull, the branch-arm carving the wood like the periscope of a submarine. Jonah offered the open-mouthed Coyote a forlorn grin before hurrying after it. Malya joined him, leaving Gerent alone with their visitor.

'What's the lesky found, do you think?' asked Malya as they jogged together across the deck.

'I cannot imagine,' Jonah replied.

'We must be wary of strangers,' said Malya. 'I do not trust this man, Jonah.'

'Trust him? Well, no, I suppose we hardly know him. Gerent seems to like him however. All the same . . .'

He stopped, trying to determine how he really felt about Coyote. The bald man was not exactly charming, in fact, there was something about him that Jonah found intimidating. But while he did not exactly warm to Coyote he most certainly sympathized with him, and for that reason alone he was willing to offer the man any courtesy he could.

And, he had to admit, he was fascinated by the future!

'Don't let him seduce you, Jonah,' Malya said. 'He's dangerous.'

The branch-arm came to an abrupt halt, and signalled them to do the same with an outstretched hand, like a policeman directing traffic.

They were standing on a grooved timber balcony from which jutted the usual array of probes and sensors. Several of these instruments had been sheared off by one of the hawks; those that remained were making languid turns like miniature windmills. Wedged between two of the stumps was a chunk of silvery-grey material. It was hissing quietly. Jonah bent to examine it, heeding Grandfather Tree's entreaty not to touch it, nor even to get too near.

The thing was roughly cylindrical, broken at one end and coming to a rounded cap at the other. He knew at once where it had come from.

'It is a piece of one of those flying machines.' The impulse to reach out and grasp it was strong but he resisted. 'It must have broken off during the attack.'

'Look close,' said the lesky. 'See on this side: a puncture there is.'

Holding on to one of the surviving probes, Jonah leaned out over the edge of the platform and peered at the other side of the cylinder. Sure enough there was a tear in its dull, metallic skin. He shivered; it reminded him too much of the wound in Annie's leg. Inside he could see something pale and pulsing, something that was undeniably organic.

Footsteps echoed behind them. Turning, Jonah saw Coyote and Gerent wandering on to the balcony, deep in conversation.

'Tried asking your buddy about those wings of his,' said Coyote. 'Changed the subject on me – prefers talking about fish, would you believe?'

'There are some things I prefer not to talk about,' said Gerent.

'What the hell's that?' asked Coyote.

Jonah explained briefly about the hawk-things which had attacked them. Having described their appearance he found himself dwelling on his confusion about whether or not they were living beings.

'They seemed simultaneously fabricated and yet alive,' he said.

'Cyborgs,' said Coyote. 'Like the bionic man. Half and half.'

'Really? Do such creations exist in your time? Well, it might be an explanation, I will grant. Grandfather Tree, why did you ask us not to touch this . . . *cyborg*?'

'I'll demonstrate!'

The lesky's temporary mouth melded back into the palm of its branch-bound hand, then the branch glided over to a small reservoir set into the hull and scooped up a handful of water. Returning to the cylindrical object the lesky carefully trickled a few drops on to it.

The result was immediate and catastrophic. Acrid yellow smoke poured from the cylinder, belching across the platform. Eyes watering, Jonah and the other onlookers backed away, rubbing their stinging eyes. Seconds later there was a flash of yellow flame and a further outpouring of smoke. Coyote lapsed into a new fit of coughing.

*   *   *

As soon as the flames had died down they returned. Where the cylinder had lain was a pile of white ash; its organic contents had been reduced to a smouldering black stain on the wood.

'Guess it don't like water,' said Coyote, rubbing his head.

'Exactly!' came Grandfather Tree's triumphant cry. 'At last I remembered! The air up there – it was dry. It is a waterless world. The machines – they're made of a metal that burns in water.'

'Yes,' said Jonah, 'I have heard of such chemical elements. I believe sodium behaves in such a way.'

'Then we have a weapon against them!' said Malya. 'Come – we have wasted enough time. Lesky, can you use your stocks of water to repel the flying demons?'

'Ye, ye, oh ye! Squirt them we will!'

'Then your time is up, stranger.' Malya faced Coyote. 'You must go, now.'

Coyote's eyes narrowed, flicking from Malya first to Gerent, then to Jonah. Neither of the Neolithics betrayed their feelings; all Jonah could manage was a wan smile.

'I am sorry,' Jonah sighed. 'But I do believe Malya is right. We must continue on our journey, and I would not put your life at risk by suggesting you stay aboard. You do at least know a little about your new home, and as for the rest . . .' He trailed off, failing to find the words.

'No.' Coyote shook his head. His face was dark and brooding and for a moment Jonah felt fear. Then the negation was clarified. 'No, you're right. I've outstayed my welcome. Thanks, Jonah, for saving my skin, and for the low-down on this place. I guess the rest is up to me.'

The optimism was false, they all knew that. But they all kept up the pretence as a solemn Coyote shook each of their hands in turn. Gerent, looking a little disappointed now, acknowledged the tall man with a brief nod of his head. Malya would not meet his stare, which intensified as he gripped her hand in his. He held it for what seemed an age, and though she was more than able to match his grip for strength, still she would not look him in the eye.

'Don't mistrust what you don't yet know,' Coyote said as he let go of her hand.

He flashed a quick smile at Gerent and his arm raised and lowered, as if he were about to reach for Gerent's wings but thought better of it. Malya scrubbed at her palm with the heel of her other hand while Grandfather Tree eased the Bark in towards the surface of Stone.

Scoring the steep wall here were innumerable deep grooves and crevices; in places it looked like a dry lake bed turned up on end. The cracks were thick with moss and fungus, crusty with age and eroded by the wind. Although this stretch of Stone corresponded to his own future, Jonah thought he had never seen anything that looked so *ancient*.

There were no large structures adhering to the wall, hence his initial dismissal of the region as a desert. Now he was forced to revise that assumption, for set into the cracks and crevices were thousands of squat dwellings. They were small and round and packed tight together, like cells in a hive. Many of them looked damaged and deserted, but a few displayed the tell-tales of habitation: smoke trickling from chimney holes, squares of fabric strung on lines between neighbouring walls. As they flew nearer, movement was visible: people, humans, clambering through the densely-stacked villages.

There are people here, Jonah thought. *At least he will not be alone.*

The Bark was making for a ledge system several hundred yards above the highest of the crevice-villages. The widest ledge ran horizontally both upStone and downStone; clearly the lesky wished to give Coyote the option of ignoring the settlements and striking out on his own.

Some of the villagers were waving, as if they saw giant wooden chandeliers flying through the sky every day of their lives.

Jonah looked at Stone. He felt like a mayfly coming up against the Himalayas. Dizziness clawed at him, a dizziness he had not felt since his early days here. Did he imagine he had understood this place? He knew its shape, could manipulate the fibres holding it together, was about to explore it to its very summit, but still the sheer size of Stone took his breath away.

The Bark continued to glide in towards the ledge, which turned out to be ten times as massive as it had first appeared. Another of Stone's tricks – the tinkering with scale and perspective. It was not a ledge but a roadway the width of London's Royal Mall, a deck of polished granite attached to Stone's near-vertical face with great iron bolts. Each bolt was as big as a factory chimney, driven at an oblique angle through the granite and into Stone itself.

With the same precision Ruane had used to deposit Jonah on the Bark, Grandfather Tree aligned the flat part of the deck with the edge of the roadway, making it the simplest thing in the world to step from one to the other.

I could get off here, Jonah thought. The idea was as cold and sudden as a rush of ice water. *I could get off and disappear into one of those little round huts and never be heard of again. I could turn my back on Stone, on the memory rods, on Archan and all the rest of them. I could forget my destiny, or fate, or whatever it is that keeps me crawling across the face of this forsaken, miraculous world and simply . . . diminish.*

But even as he thought this, even as he watched Tom Coyote move from floating Bark to solid Stone

103

he was also thinking of Annie, how she would not let him give up now, and how he could not give up on her.

'Watch out for me when I'm dreamin' my dreams!' she had instructed him. 'Be my guardian angel.'

She was dreamin' her dreams this very minute but it felt as though he was the one who needed an angel at his shoulder.

'Annie,' he whispered.

'Jonah!'

It was her voice, carrying through the wind. He whirled round and there she was, standing with the help of a lesky-made crutch but standing all the same. She was bent forward, her body clearly in pain, but her face was alive.

'Annie! Are you all right?'

'Never mind me! Get that man back on board right away!'

Jonah looked in confusion at Coyote, who was regarding this new development with interest, then back at Annie. 'Him? But . . .'

'No "buts", Jonah. He's coming with us. We need him, Mister Ren says so.'

'Mister who?'

'I'll tell you later, but right now we need that man on board this ship and we need to get our asses movin'! We've pussyfooted around long enough and it's time to get goin'.'

While Gerent and Malya gaped, Jonah rushed to Annie's side, grabbing the arm that was not held up by Grandfather Tree. She sank into his arms, glad of the additional support.

'I knew we could trust him,' he said so that only she could hear.

'That's the thing,' she whispered back. 'We can't – he's a rattlesnake. But we ain't got no choice, Jonah, we just got to take him with us or this whole trip'll be for nothing.'

With a broad grin Tom Coyote crossed back over the narrow gap between Stone and Bark.

'Permission to come aboard?' He dipped his body towards Annie in an almost-bow, grazing the flat of one large hand unceasingly across the top of his bald, brown head.

6

Fabricators

Once Grandfather Tree had been able to cruise the
memory rods like Jonah. He had been the first adept
to arrive on Stone, many, many years earlier. The ability
actually to change the rods had been taken from him by
the basilisks – only Jonah and Archan were now capable
of that remarkable feat – but he had spent many years as
a voyeur, a tourist of worlds.

Day after day he had travelled through the rods, visiting
the Stone-bound memories of a thousand realms: desert
world; world of endless mist; a wondrous world where
the soil flowed like the sea and the mountains were made
of water. The acrid metal world that existed before the
world of charm. The savage world of nature that followed
and within it the natural faeries who ruled its smoke-filled
lands. And between them all – the cataclysmic Turnings
wreaking the changes when each world became the next.
The heartbeat of eternal change.

Everything changes . . .

In among all those worlds, a world from Jonah's
future, from all their futures, many Turnings ahead.
A sky the colour of red wine and filled with hawk-like
flying machines. A place where . . .

. . . all life was manufactured.

The machines were alive, and everything that lived in this world was a machine. There were no families, only variants; there were no births, only units rolling from production lines. Yet the machines lived, and were aware. That was the way this world worked.

The machines were at home in the sky. The sky was where their gods could be found. Their gods were the Fabricators, the huge, gliding factories in which the machines were constructed. But they were more than just factories – they were repositories of all the wisdom of the many machine races, of all the archived plans and schematics, the myriad inventions and components and variations. They were fabricators and inventors, dangerous experimenters and deep thinkers. They made, and they ruled, and they were revered.

Closest to the gods were the hawks, the silver-grey fliers who protected their makers and masters. Like most deities, the Fabricators fought dreadfully among themselves, and more often than not it was the hawk squadrons that were called upon to represent their interests in battle. Fiercely loyal to their makers, the hawks could be counted on to fight to destruction. As for the Fabricators themselves, they spent their flying servants with abandon. After all, it was easy enough to make more.

Beneath the hawks were a host of lesser machines, all designed to service their masters. Most lowly of all were the quarrying gangs and their servant mechanisms. Of limited intelligence, these lumbering behemoths were built to consume and process raw materials into useable resources. Big-bellied hawk variants flew the processed materials up to the Fabricators, where the integrated manufacturies set to work to make more and more machines.

Life was hard in this world where life was not a miracle but a product. Machines were loyal to their guardian Fabricators, and the wars between rival clans were prolonged and bitter. Any intruder into this brutal realm was treated with suspicion, if not outright hostility. Even on his first visit, when he had been wide-eyed and keen to explore, Grandfather Tree had not stayed for long . . .

'It is fascinating,' agreed Jonah, cutting the lesky short.

His wooden friend had been about to launch into a more detailed description of some of the complex hierarchies existing in this alien world, but Jonah feared there was no time for such luxuries. There was one point he wanted to clarify however.

'What of the fleshy material we have observed? The eye-like globes on the wings of the hawks, not to mention those strange trailing tentacles.'

'Ah ye, their greatest invention. Bored they came, some of the Fabricators. Other ways they sought for reproduction. Then they hit on it: organic life.'

Suddenly Jonah understood. 'The spread of industry! Just as man has made machines to do his work, so these machines have made . . . well, if not man then his equivalent!'

'A topsy-turvy place,' agreed Grandfather Tree.

Jonah's mind raced: a world inverted from his own, in many ways its opposite. Yet it possessed the same levels of social strata, the same petty squabbles escalating into wars. So much changed, so much the same.

He looked at the ceiling, imagining the heights of Stone they still had to cross.

Future worlds up there, every one. So far advanced from my own . . . yet perhaps they are all really the same. Does history repeat itself – or rather does it circle round and round like a fairground carousel? In the end, does it all simply turn?

So many worlds, each with its own siren-call. They reverberated through the memory rods like songs through a harp, calling to him, harmonious and seductive, inviting him to abandon his physical pursuit and explore these new realms from within. It was thè call of the memory rods and he was resisting it with all his might.

It had occurred to him recently that he would not be sorry if he never navigated the rods again. He had already meddled with history once too often. the ability to alter the past was a lethal weapon, one he never wanted to wield again.

Jonah peeked out through a side portal. The Bark was rising once more towards the Helix, travelling much faster this time. The wind was monstrous. Airborne dust scoured the hull and Stone itself was a featureless blur. He ducked back inside and the portal closed up like an iris.

'Bark's fixed again. Full of water too,' the lesky shouted above the howl of the wind. 'Let's go squirt some hawks!'

Though she could walk only with great difficulty, and was still in considerable pain, Annie had insisted on being at the centre of the action during the second ascent. Jonah in turn had insisted on her not being on the bridge proper, given the battering they had all taken there the first time.

Grandfather Tree had duly created an annex to the bridge, complete with couch and straps to restrain Annie during violent acceleration. She was not entirely happy, but acquiesced without too much argument. Jonah joined her there after his discussion with Grandfather Tree. For what felt like the hundredth time he asked her about her latest dream. She had told him enough about Mister Ren to fire his curiosity; now he wanted more.

'There's no time to tell you about it, Jonah,' she said impatiently. 'Before we do anything else, before we can even think about anything else, we've got to get through this first world. It's one of the hardest worlds to cross; the others won't be so bad, not 'til we get near the top anyway. There's work for us to do on the way – all of us, but especially you, Jonah. Especially you.'

'What about Coyote? Does he have work to do too?'

Her brow furrowed. 'I don't know, Jonah, and that's the honest truth. I wasn't told anything much about him, except we need him with us and he's . . . well, he's dangerous.'

'Dangerous to us?'

She thought for a moment, then said, 'Just dangerous. But that doesn't matter, not yet anyhow. Nothing else matters except beating Archan to the top of Stone. If we get there before her there's a chance we can win. If we don't then we're lost for sure. Everything's lost. All the rest of it – what little I know – I'll explain along the way.'

'If we get past the hawks.'

'If we get past them.'

Jonah kissed her. She felt stiff in his arms. 'This Mister Ren,' he said, 'is he dangerous too?'

The sudden light in her eyes was enough to convince him otherwise.

'Oh no, Jonah. He's like the sun – he shines when everything else is dark. I don't think he's capable of doing anything bad at all.'

'Is that why he needs our help?'

No sooner had they crossed the Helix than they spotted a large flock of hawks rallying upStone, thirty grey wedge-shapes weaving ever closer.

Grandfather Tree had created ten portholes spaced equally around the bridge, round eyes affording a pan-oramic view of the wine-red future world. They were not literally apertures in the walls but artful projections of charm, relaying views from Bark-eyes set into the hull. The effect was convincing though, even down to the red-flecked streams of light pouring in through those portholes facing the sunset.

DownStone, in the direction of the glowering sun, there was a second squadron. It contained at least as many hawks as the upStone phalanx. They were all getting nearer.

The Bark was travelling in a smooth vertical line,

climbing at a speed that left even the sound it made behind. Its purpose was clear: to pass through this hostile world without engaging the enemy for a second time. Measuring its speed against that of the hawks, Jonah saw that was not going to be possible.

A pair of hawks from the downStone group loomed suddenly large in one of the portholes, momentarily eclipsing the sun. They moved in perfect synchrony, turning their noses upwards as they matched trajectories with the Bark.

Despite his apprehension Jonah was fascinated: the nearer hawk was close enough that he could see every detail on its hull, every scratch and pock-mark. The fleshy globes on its wings were flattened by the punishing airflow; streamers of flesh hung like tentacles beneath its aft cockpit.

What weapons do they have? he wondered, recalling the crudity of the first attack, when the hawks had used trailing hooks and even their own wings to slice into the Bark's wooden hull. Did they not carry projectiles, or some means of hurling fire like the giant bat-winged ship that had intervened before?

'Not fire!' he exclaimed, ignoring the puzzled looks of his companions. 'It was a beam of water!'

The nearer of the twin hawks darted up to the window. It must have been only yards from the hull when Grandfather Tree emptied a dump tank full of water across its fuselage.

The effect was instantaneous. The vehicle's thin metal shell collapsed and ignited, erupting in a brilliant yellow fireball. Then, its upward motion abruptly terminated, it was sucked away below them as though some invisible rope had been tugged. Its twin hesitated before a narrow jet of water sliced it in two. It vanished even before the flames could take hold, appearing not so much to fall as fold itself into nothingness.

The two Neolithics cheered simultaneously, raising their fists in identical gestures then glowering at each other, unsettled by the shared moment. Jonah felt elated.

'Bravo, Grandfather Tree!' he shouted. 'They did not even get close!'

'Close they got,' said the lesky. 'But they're weak! Forgive me, I must concentrate.'

His voice cut off as four more of the downStone hawks arrowed towards them. A watery broadside created a lethal, falling cloud that ripped them to shreds before they were within a mile.

The Bark lurched Annie cried out as supple branches clamped across the uninjured parts of her legs, preventing her from rolling off the couch. Jonah was not so lucky, falling hard against a wooden cabinet protecting one of the Bark's inscrutable mechanisms. He cursed and wondered why he had not asked the lesky to make couches for them all.

Water exploded beyond the round vision panels and four more hawks were disposed of.

'Some damage . . . that time.' The lesky's face crossed from one edge of the ceiling to the other in an eye-blink.

There were more detonations outside, and a series of rolling turns that threw Jonah and his companions first one way then the other. Clinging on to a thick stump growing from the top of an instrument-outcrop, Jonah watched with growing excitement as Grandfather Tree picked off the hawks one by one.

Yet still they came. No sooner had the lesky dispatched the last of the downStone flotilla than the upStone hawks were upon them. These latter were more disciplined than their cousins. Larger, paler, they flew in tight formation and were able to dodge the jets of water with comparative ease. Grandfather Tree responded by converting more charm into raw velocity and soon the hawks were struggling to keep pace.

Gradually the hawks lost ground. They surged aloft once more in a vain attempt to match the Bark's remarkable speed, only to fall back even more emphatically. Soon they were just motes of dust, barely visible against the thick burgundy of the sky.

'Halfway,' panted Grandfather Tree. His face careered the opposite way across the ceiling, pausing midway to proffer a brief and bramble-filled smile. 'Not out of the woods yet.' Chuckling to himself he disappeared again.

Beyond the window, Stone itself was heaving back into view.

So far their largely vertical ascent had taken them further and further away from the ten-degree slope of that indomitable wall. Now, with the promise of a little breathing space, their lesky pilot was taking the opportunity to alter their flight path, vectoring them back inwards before they struck Stone's space-twisting boundary, the outer perimeter of the sky beyond which it was impossible for anything to pass.

Stone emerged from the dark red sky, a vast grey sheet scored with countless vertical scratches. As they drew nearer, larger features that had at first looked like simple discolorations were revealed as deep scars and trenches. The scale – as ever on Stone, and especially in this alien atmosphere – was impossible to gauge, but the closer they approached the finer the detail became, and it was soon clear they were flying past a quarry of truly gargantuan proportions. The surface of Stone here had been not so much excavated as devastated.

The Bark eased off its approach one mile short of Stone's ravaged surface (by Grandfather Tree's albeit rude reckoning), though it maintained its punishing rate of ascent. Constructions were visible from this distance; Jonah balked at the sheer size of the things he was seeing.

A giant machine bit into the surface with teeth the

size of icebergs. Fat cables dangled over canyons greater than Colorado's deepest; massive boulders poured down them, strung like dew on a spider's web. A curved trellis spanned the gap between two tortured outcrops of grey Stone-stuff. Scurrying across its intricate branches were what looked like millions of tiny brown insects. Some swift estimates informed Jonah that those insects, swarming over the trellis like termites over a downed tree trunk, were each at least as big as a London town house. They moved in a multitude of individual streams, complicated contraflows in a pulsating artery.

'It's incredible,' said Annie 'What are they doing, d'you think? Are they trying to get to the memory rods? Can you look inside, Jonah?'

Still reluctant to reawaken his affinity with the rods, Jonah closed his eyes and allowed his awareness to reach at least a little way into the fabric of Stone.

I suppose it can do no harm merely to look.

In his mind's eye Stone's hard flesh became flimsy and transparent. Layer by layer it melted away: first the scurrying machines, then the girders across which they moved. It was like peeling an onion to expose its heart.

Behind the elaborate mining constructions lay the open-cast pits themselves, then the Stone-stuff into which they had been carved, immeasurably dense yet quite sheer to Jonah's heightened perceptions. It was within this stratum that he expected to find the memory rods, and he found them indeed, straight black cords that were in no way transparent but into which he could see all the same. Hard ebony, yet imbued with the same flurry of movement he had observed on the termite-covered trellises. The ceaseless flow of the river of time.

'The rods are there,' he said, 'but they are buried much deeper than we are used to. They lie several miles behind the skin of Stone; even these machines would need to dig a long way back even to come close to them.'

'Oh. Good. Was it . . . was it okay, Jonah? Did you feel all right?' Her tone was light but there was an undercurrent of concern.

'I found nothing that surprised me. Why do you ask?'

'No reason . . . well, all right, if you want to know: you ain't been memory-travelling for a while now. D'you think you're still up to it?'

'Why? Do you think I will need to go somewhere?'

'Not just yet . . . but soon, Jonah. Very soon.'

'Is this something to do with your mysterious Mister Ren again?'

'You got it!'

How can I ever travel the rods again, when each time I do so I put so much at risk?

A cry from Malya interrupted his thoughts. She was pointing out of one of the windows to a huge shadow sliding down the wall of Stone. It swallowed the city-sized quarries in terrifying silence. Vastly elongated by the setting sun, it was too distorted to betray the nature of its source.

'Grandfather Tree!' Jonah said. 'We require a better view!'

The light level in the bridge dropped, then, without warning, the entire ceiling disappeared. Or rather, the entire upper half of the Bark disappeared; it was as if a lid had been lifted away, leaving the vessel's occupants vulnerable on the exposed floor of the bridge.

'I wish he'd warn us before pulling a stunt like that!' said Annie.

But Jonah was less concerned by the lesky's trick than by what was revealed in the sky above them. There, slowly revolving in air that was now the colour of dried blood, was the big brother of the bat-winged ship that had intervened during the first ascent.

Unlike its smaller counterpart, this flying machine had not two but four wings. These were equidistant around a central hub so that the machine resembled nothing so much as a set of vast windmill vanes turned on their side. A windmill that had to be at least two miles across. Its smooth undersurface was iridescent, a pearly membrane breaking the dying sunlight into a thousand rainbow beams. It was directly overhead, and the Bark was travelling up towards it at several thousand miles per hour. A collision course.

'Lesky!' said Gerent. 'Divert the craft!' There was an ominous silence. 'Lesky! Do you hear me?!'

No response.

Jonah exchanged a glance with Malya. She opened her mouth, about to speak, when the instrument pedestal beside her bulged. Green light spilled across the Neolithics' faces as Grandfather Tree, his own face hideously distorted, thrust his way up from the floor, shouting, 'Can't . . . turn!'

'What do you mean . . .' Jonah began, but already the lesky's deformed features were flowing back into the pedestal like thick sap. 'Grandfather Tree! What is happening?'

'. . . Help . . .' came the lesky's voice, wavering and impossibly distant. '. . . me . . .'

'Damnation!'

Above their heads the ceiling remained transparent. The lazy blades of the Fabricator already filled the sky.

'Jonah!' Annie's cry made him jump. 'You steered the Bark once!'

Four pairs of eyes were upon him. Annie's were wide, imploring, full of love and fear. The Neolithics regarded him with a trust he found almost overwhelming. But the eyes that bored deepest were those of Tom Coyote.

Their passenger had spent the entire ascent seated on the floor with his back against one of the taller instrument extrusions. He had watched the battle with keen eyes but not a flicker of real interest. But now he was rising to his feet and walking over to Jonah.

'You got some magic ways about you, too?' he said. 'This I've just got to see.'

'There is nothing to see,' snapped Jonah. 'The best advice I can give you is to stay back and hold tight!'

So saying he dropped to his knees and did something else his adept-powers permitted him to do: he plunged his hands through the yielding wooden floor . . .

. . . *and deep into the heartwood of the Bark.*

He had steered the Bark before, when it had been merely an ocean-going vessel and before Grandfather Tree had been woven so completely into its fabric. Since the final bonding of lesky and Bark he had not presumed to explore again its inner workings. Such an act, uninvited, would have been a violation of the worst kind; and Grandfather Tree had never invited him in.

But now it was different. Even as he forced his hands into the sap-meat of the living ship he knew Grandfather Tree was in serious trouble.

Jonah's affinity with the Bark had two distinct aspects.

First was the similarity of the lesky's original root system with the network of memory rods. Indeed, once upon a time the two had been inextricably linked. This was how the lesky, in his days as an adept, had been able to explore the rods and all the histories they contained. Echoes of that old root system remained in the Bark even now, and navigating them was, for Jonah at least, as easy as walking.

Secondly, the Bark was a basilisk device. Jonah had met the basilisks several times and was beginning to get a fair impression of how their minds worked.

Subtle and manipulative, these once-immortal creatures had been just as susceptible to squabbles and wrestling as the average man – or for that matter the massive Fabricators against which they were now pitted. The basilisks had been mighty indeed –

Stone's existence was proof of that – but Jonah could not help but think of them as fundamentally flawed and somehow human. So, in immersing himself in their vehicle, he should have found much that was familiar.

But something was very wrong. There was something else in there with him – an intruder.

The basilisk ghosts wafted past him as he careered through the inner spaces of the Bark, seeking out Grandfather Tree. Baleful and aloof, these insubstantial spirits all but ignored his plea for help; the only acknowledgement he gained was the nudge of a phantom claw from the one named Ocher.

Look down, the basilisk ghost seemed to be saying.

So down he went past buried chambers and conduits, through secret spaces not meant for humans. Runnels of charm percolated through foam-like wood, the life-sap of the ship.

Further down the heartwood was splintered. Liquid pressed on every side; he was twisting his way through the maze of internal walls dividing the water reservoirs near the bottom of the craft. The water sloshed, a spectral presence in this hard realm of timber and magic. The broken wood slashed at his thoughts as he sped past; he paid it no heed. Where was the lesky?

Belatedly he commanded the Bark to slow down. The order chased off through the splinters like a rabbit through a copse, heading for the bridge. He hoped he had not left it too late. Then he prayed it would work at all.

With a jolt he found himself sliding into the Bark's ventral spire. This upside-down finial was the lowest extremity of the entire vessel; Jonah allowed himself a pair of eyes and, lesky-like, the chance to peer out from the hull. He felt the sap around him turn cold as he registered what it was he was seeing.

A large chunk of the Bark's lower quarter had been cut completely away. Beneath the Bark, expanding into the wind, a vast cloud of dust and wood-chips was falling away with the severed piece of hull. Water sprayed haphazardly from *a ruptured tank. All that remained of the hawk that had performed this horrifying surgery was an accompanying cloud of still-glowing embers and fine grey powder.*

From the amputated section of hull came a dwindling, wailing voice, '. . . help . . . me . . .'

Grandfather Tree was inside.

Jonah was paralysed. He could neither move nor cause the Bark to move; he could barely even think. All he could do was stare at the falling scrap of wood. It was Bark sap, he knew, inflaming his reaction to the point where he was virtually incapacitated. Trees, it seemed, were more at the mercy of their emotions than men. He tried to grit his teeth, but of course he had none.

The reminder that he was not reliant on his physical body gave him the courage he needed. Leaving one eye here at the base to track the severed hull section he sent the other speeding around the Bark to the very top, where it could assess the threat of the Fabricator. The two images overlapped; for a brief moment he felt like a chameleon, perceiving the world from two entirely different viewpoints.

The Fabricator was too close. Though his command to decelerate had been heeded it was too little too late. The collision was inevitable. Once he had piloted the Bark through a storm-wracked ocean; now, in this hostile alien sky, he had not the slightest idea what to do. He had to . . .

'. . . get out!'

Jonah yanked his hands free, spraying wood chips across the floor. Annie was on her hands and knees at his side, a fresh blood-bloom on her dressing.

'Something has infiltrated the Bark,' he said. 'I don't know where to go.'

'No place to go, Jonah!' she yelled. He glared up at the Fabricator, scything the air with huge sweeps of its iridescent blades. 'Gotta do something!'

'But it's so . . . it's all *lesky*!' Jonah gasped. 'I had

119

no idea . . . I cannot control the Bark the way I did before.'

Tom Coyote loomed behind Annie, staring down at them from his prodigious height. 'Burst the tanks!' he said. 'Rocket propulsion!'

Jonah gaped at him as multicoloured light poured into the bridge, dappled reflections from the colossal under-belly of the spinning Fabricator. 'Equal and opposite,' he said and thrust his hands back into . . .

. . . *the unfriendly Bark.*

All was confusion. How could it have changed so much in so short a time? Gone were the familiar shades of the basilisk ghosts, gone was the homely resin-scent of the lesky. The Bark's wood was petrifying around him, sap first congealing then solidifying.

I shall be trapped like a fly in amber!

Not solidifying – freezing.

Yet still the Bark yielded to him. Progress was painfully slow, a mere crawl; surely they would strike the Fabricator before Jonah could reach the water tanks.

All the Bark above him was a fossil, its outer surface shredding beneath the scouring action of the wind. Protective shells peeled away, exposing the fragile interior. The bridge was flayed open, exposing his friends to the elements.

No! This is not happening!

Brittle timber flexed again beneath him. Something like a growl quaked from the heartwood. Jonah changed direction, seeking out the source of the sound. There was no time for this but he had to do it all the same. Something about the noise had awakened dark fears that would not be ignored.

Run! Fall away from this place! Escape, Jonah, escape!

Were the thoughts his own? Almost certainly not.

He was no longer crawling but lunging forwards, splitting the softening timber like a woodsman. Grandfather Tree would curse him for the damage he was causing but unless he moved quickly all would be lost. Again there was the groan. Now he could see something moving in the heartwood, something small and foreign embedded in the very core of the Bark. It was smooth and blue like old ice. Red light flickered on and off inside it, partly obscured by tiny flapping shapes, like the wings of a moth as it circles a candle.

The intruder!

It was ice, he could see that now. It should have been melting, so warm was it here in the heartwood, but instead it was expanding, sending out tendrils of frost to latch on to the woody fibres of the Bark, turning them to stone again. Again Jonah tried to resist this process of icy petrifaction, but this time to no avail.

It stank of Archan. She was here!

Then he remembered he was human.

A pair of hands sprang into being before him – his own, hot with human blood. With an animal cry he clamped them around the block of ice.

The red light flared, burning his skin, but the pain just made him hold on even tighter. Steam boiled from between his fingers and the moth-shadow fluttered, ever more frantic. Gradually the heartwood threw off the frost-tendrils, turning green once more and throbbing with the pulse of the sap. Jonah could feel the ice melting in his clutches, shrinking away as it poured itself out in harmless rivulets. As the last drops hissed into nothingness the red light winked out and the flapping wings stopped altogether. When he opened his hands there was nothing left at all.

She will not be defeated so easily when we meet her at Sunlight Pass, *he thought.*

It dawned on him that the Bark was filled with voices: Annie's, calling to him to be quick; his own, screaming, out of control; the sextet of the basilisks urging him to prevail over Archan . . . call her name and watch her fall . . . *they bellowed. And beneath them all, he discovered he could still hear Grandfather Tree.*

'Turn . . .' *implored the lesky.*

Soaring through the rejuvenated Bark-wood as though it were no more substantial than air, Jonah hurried to the outermost shell of the many-layered hull. Behind this protective skin were buried the water reservoirs Grandfather Tree had so diligently filled. Many were only half full as a result of the airborne battle, and some were empty altogether, but overall Jonah guessed they still had at least two thirds of their original stock on board.

Moulding the internal partitions like clay (and rejoicing at the ease of it, at the beautiful familiarity of it!) he dumped all the water into a single spherical tank, which he simultaneously compressed and heated. Then, without further thought – for he was sure the last possible minute had come and gone many times over – he punched a fist-sized hole in the hull.

The effect was instantaneous. As the jet of steam and water squirted from the side of the Bark Jonah was thrown clear of the tank and hurled back into . . .

. . . the arms of Annie, who clasped him to her as the sudden acceleration rolled them together across the floor. Behind them Malya crashed against Coyote. He prevented her from tumbling all the way to the floor by grabbing her wrists; she threw him off, spitting like a cat and recovering herself only by wildly spinning her arms. A dimness filled with dark rainbow hues rolled over the bridge and the sky disappeared. The Bark had been swallowed by the shadow of the Fabricator.

The water continued to jet from the punctured hull for the best part of thirty seconds, during which time the bridge was filled with a constant screaming wail. Then, abruptly, both sound and acceleration ceased and they were gliding in absolute silence beneath a monster.

The underside of the blade was like a city, reticulated by deep channels and blocky structures. Inverted rivers of colour raced through the grooves, connecting the blocks with shimmering strands of fire. Under different circumstances it would have been quite beautiful. As it was, it was a rock against which they were about to be dashed.

It grew darker. The silence was unbearable.

Red light splashed across the bridge, the sudden reappearance of the lesky as welcome as the brightest dawn. The trailing edge of the blade hove into view. It was ragged, set with spikes and sensors reminiscent of those decorating the Bark. Lightning stretched between the largest of these, a lethal web of jagged blue scratches hungry for the Bark. The scratches of electricity became fat volt-filled snakes, a lethal and restless net slung directly in their path.

'Do something, Jonah,' Annie said.

'I have done all I can,' he replied. A sudden movement caught his eye: it was Tom Coyote, raising both fists and pounding at his skull.

They were inside the lightning. It banished all shadow, flickering and dancing so fast that they were consumed by its furious glow. Then, miraculously, the lightning was gone, the turning blade of the Fabricator was gone. All that remained above their heads was the sky's blank and darkening canvas, blood-black in the dying rays of the setting sun.

'We made it!' Annie shrieked.

'Then let's get the hell out of here!' said Coyote.

Jonah leaped to his feet.

'Not yet,' he said.

Emptied of the water that had been its only ammunition against the hawks, the Bark screamed back down through maroon twilight. Charm spilled out in a broad fan above it, fundamental magic driving it down; the air compressed beneath it glowed brilliant orange. Sparks and fragments of burning branch lifted past the bridge in a constant stream, ventral antennae eroded by the blistering wind.

Jonah's hands were engulfed in the floor again, but his consciousness was only partially immersed. It was strange, sharing his own senses with those of the Bark. The seam where his skin melted into the wooden deck was blurred; it tingled, an unpleasant sensation he did his best to ignore.

'I can no longer pilot the Bark as I once did,' he had reiterated to Annie just before forcing his hands back into the vessel. 'It has changed so much – it has been tailored to Grandfather Tree, you might say. Trying to control it is like trying to wear a suit tailored for another animal altogether.'

'So what's the point in going after him?' she said.

'Grandfather Tree is my friend.'

'Mine too, in case you'd forgotten. I meant what can you do?'

'I cannot steer the Bark with any degree of accuracy, but I do believe I can make it fall at some considerable speed.'

'Fall?'

'Yes. The rest is up to the lesky.'

And so the Bark fell, charm pouring from its reservoirs straight out through the top of the hull. It was a desperate manoeuvre, as ultimately uncontrollable as the water jet that had diverted them around the spinning Fabricator blade. And when the Bark ran out of charm, it really would fall, and this time there would be no stopping it at all.

'How much charm is left?' Annie asked when he told her this.

'I have no idea. The Bark will not tell me. Enough, I hope.'

Jonah's theory was simple: Grandfather Tree had been alive when the part of the Bark he was occupying had been sliced off. And he had still been alive as the severed part had fallen away. There was a good chance, Jonah reasoned, that enough charm remained in the wood for the lesky to remould it, at least a little.

He was gambling all their lives on the hunch that Grandfather Tree had sculpted himself a lifeboat.

'Hawks,' said Gerent.

The fierce glow of their magical comet-tail lit up the forms of the marauders, but the Bark's rate of descent was too great and the hawks struggled to keep pace. Away to the left were the slow-spinning sails of another Fabricator, even larger than the one they had so narrowly evaded.

Jonah had managed to open a small Bark-eye on the bottom of the hull, but the air-glow was impenetrable. He had no idea what was down there. *Are we to cross back over the Helix yet again?* he agonized. *Perhaps this journey is impossible after all.* Failure, all at once, seemed inevitable.

'There!' shouted Malya, so loud that he jerked his hands quite free of the floor.

The charm-tail died away, leaving only the twilight gloom. Jonah lunged forwards, trying to make out what she was pointing at.

Far to the side, spinning wildly in the Bark's substantial bow-wave, was a small object. It looked exactly like a sycamore seed.

'That's him!' yelled Jonah.

Ignoring the fact that the swarm of hawks was now closing again, he punched his hands into the nearest console. Bark-wood resisted him – each time he interfered it grew less tolerant of his presence. A comparison came to him: *a dog, restless for its lost master.*

Resistant though the Bark was it did yield to his will and sent a braking plume of precious charm straight downwards. Pressed hard to the deck, they waited until the Bark's motion had been reversed. Now it was rising again, but slowly. Rising towards the fragile spinning form that was the lesky's lifeboat. Rising towards the hawks.

Gasping, Jonah freed his aching hands. They were bleeding from a dozen scratches; brown splinters protruded from beneath his fingernails.

'I hope I do not need to do that again,' he said.

The sycamore seed fell with painful slowness. The actual closing speed was greater, given the upward velocity of the Bark. But would it be quick enough? Jonah did not think so. Gritting his teeth against the pain he pressed his hands to the console once more . . . only to have his efforts resisted completely.

'Damn you, Bark!' he gasped. He was pushing with all his strength. 'It is your skin I am trying to save too.'

Curses proved no more effective than brute force. He drew back, breathing hard.

Gerent came to his side. 'Can you do anything?'

'I don't know . . . I am trying to get us moving a little faster.'

'That is a big thing, yes?' said Gerent. 'Can you do a small thing?'

'A small thing?'

'Open a door?'

The sight of Gerent rising on red and black wings above the Bark drew Tom Coyote close to one of the windows. He stood, towering over the others, watching with his mouth agape at the winged man.

'He flies,' said Coyote.

'What did you expect?' said Annie.

Malya was clinging to Annie, both holding her up and leaning on her for support. Jonah stood poised by the wooden console, his splinter-filled hands splayed wide as though he too were trying to grow wings. The only thing he had managed to coax out of the Bark – other than opening a dorsal hatch for Gerent – was the release of a trio of light-charms from the external cockpit. They bobbed to and fro, tracking Gerent as he sped towards the revolving sycamore seed, their light leading him through the dusk.

Above him, the hawks had assembled themselves into a long arrow formation, and above them a Fabricator was circling ever nearer, electricity coruscating across its entire underbelly.

Gerent shrank to the size of a doll, then he was clutching at the sycamore seed. The seed was twice as long as he was tall but, Jonah guessed, very light. Grasping it to his chest, Gerent flipped on to his back, tucked his wings in close and started a power dive back towards the Bark.

If the lesky is dead, then so are we all, thought Jonah.

Though his wings were reduced to minimal triangles, the broad fan of the seed's single blade was causing too much wind resistance. Gerent bent over; it looked as though he were talking to the seed. Then, with a sudden, shocking gesture, he ripped the blade free of the nugget of wood to which it was attached and cast it free. It flashed out of sight, torn away by a vicious eddy.

Before Jonah could even take a breath Gerent was large again above them, then dropping out of sight around the curve of the ship. Seconds later there was a thud as he crashed against the hull. They all turned to the bridge's main doorway. All except Tom Coyote, who was still staring into the dark sky with a blank expression.

When Gerent burst in Jonah felt momentarily revolted: the nugget he was clasping to his chest looked exactly like a severed human head. Then he saw the face was that of his friend: Grandfather Tree, looking haggard but with an unmistakable green gleam in his eyes. Even as Gerent thrust the disembodied head into Jonah's arms, fresh brambles were beginning to sprout from the lesky's mouth.

'There!' said Grandfather Tree in a voice far bigger than they had expected.

With a roll of his shining eyes he indicated the console beside which Jonah was standing. Jonah dropped the nugget on to the top of the wooden pillar, in which a shallow depression was already forming. Like a bead of mercury the nugget rolled around in the dish, gradually losing its solidity until it was flattened to a disc. Then, with a glutinous sucking sound, it was absorbed down into the pillar.

For a moment nothing happened, then the whole Bark shuddered. Sap sweated from every console and mechanism on the bridge, casting an eerie green light across the floor. The ceiling crashed shut, blocking out all view of the sky except for a small round hole immediately above their heads, a new window in place of the shaft leading to the cockpit.

'Flat!' thundered Grandfather Tree.

They had experienced enough of the lesky's flying to know what he meant.

The acceleration was greater than anything they had yet experienced. It glued them to the floor, making it impossible to raise limbs and difficult even to breathe; Jonah suspected if he tried to turn his head he would probably break his neck.

Through the new window they saw the hawk swarm approach and then scatter, blown clear by the sheer speed of the Bark. Fabricators moved in but the Bark avoided them with easy swoops and turns. The air-glow returned, above them now, but just before Grandfather Tree closed the window on the sky there appeared beyond the glow the familiar cracked whirlpool of the next Helix.

The last thing Jonah saw before the window closed for good was the Helix expanding to absorb them, the gateway to yet another new world.

7

Archan Rising – 1

Archan had always believed in the power of white.

Long ago, when she had been a mortal dragon alive in the great world of charm, she had been one of the Twelve, a member of Halcyon's elite and globe-spanning dragon council, reading minds and making decisions and wielding great charm. In those days it had been rewarding to rule her fellow dragons, but she was not without her fears. A dragon of power she was, respected and feared, but when she died would she be remembered?

She changed the way her body looked, tried to make herself memorable. She made herself white – unblemished, unforgettable white.

The shape-shifting continued until she had exceeded all that was considered normal, even among the exotic ranks of the charmed dragon. She deleted her limbs and bleached her scales. Her wings she retained, engines and symbols of flight, but in reducing herself to a pure serpentine line she removed even her eyes, relying instead on penetrative charmed senses that revealed so much more than mere vision.

White serpent, she eventually cut herself off from dragon society altogether. At last she was free to pursue her greatest ambition.

I shall not be forgotten. I shall live forever.

Along the way she committed murders, mostly for sport. How could a dragon understand the nature of immortal life if she did not appreciate the flimsiness of mortality? Most of her victims she took as lovers beforehand. She was strange, but her very strangeness made her desirable. The more she shunned her fellow dragons the more attention she attracted. Yet in the end even the cycle of loving and killing was not enough and she left dragon society altogether, taking up residence in the abandoned Earthly citadel of the basilisks. Here, for the first time, she started to understand how eternity might become hers to own.

The world turned, shedding the charm from its skin and embracing the ways of nature. Soon after, Archan placed herself at the heart of the gathering of the Deathless, the collective suicide of the oldest creatures in the world. It was there that she inherited all that the basilisks left behind. It was there that she became immortal.

And though she had changed colour many times since then, she was still, in her heart, white.

She remembered a white dragon from her younger days. Her memory of that dragon was vivid, perhaps because of his colour, perhaps also because of what she had done to him. Whichever it was, she believed the day she had killed him was the day she had started to fall in love with the purity of the white.

He had come to her cave at the end of a long summer day. Over the dragon settlement to the west of the mountain the sky was filled with slender winged shapes testing the thermals and riding what breeze they could find. Archan had long ago tired of such things. When she took to the air she preferred to make the sky do her bidding, not the other way around.

He came seeking physical embraces, which she gave

him. After only a year on her own in the secluded ravine she had already become an object of lustful curiosity for most of the young males down the mountain. Bets were made, bluffs were called and a steady flow of initiates climbed the slopes to her hermit's retreat.

Most of them returned, their silent bliss crucial to the life of the myths surrounding the dragon they had gone to visit. Just as crucial were the rumours about what had happened to those who did *not* return.

This one dragon, the white one (whose name Archan, quite naturally, did not remember) had been pleasing enough in his physical appearance but quite feeble in mind. After exploring his body she had begun to explore his mind, touring the empty desert of his stunted imagination, wondering at the spaces about which his meagre thoughts billowed like forgotten leaves.

While she was inside him a thought came to her: was it possible to own a mind that was *entirely* empty? Or rather, could a dragon live without a mind to guide it? Was such a creature possible? If so, what might it be used for?

It was an intriguing notion.

So she scoured his mind. It was like licking out a dragon's egg without breaking the shell, she decided later. This was another hobby of hers.

What remained was a shell of white scales in the shape of a dragon. It breathed and blinked and when she entered its mind it moved its limbs in accordance with her instructions. Yet it had no will of its own and it had neither thought nor memory of thought. It had no past and no future. She brought its body against hers and looked through its eyes into her own (in those days she had still possessed those crude organs) and felt the primal dance through both its loins and hers and the act was hers alone to relish and discard. Its scales were white and that was meant to be, for they were white and pure and bright as the light of the summer sun.

And they belonged to her. They belonged to Archan.

Later, when she had plucked the scales from each other, one by one, and cast them one by one into the mountain stream, there was nothing left of the white dragon at all. Except it seemed to Archan that its whiteness remained and so she claimed it for her own. It had been hers ever since.

Now there was whiteness not just in her but around her too. This was the void into which she had been locked, the emptiness outside the world of Stone. But this whiteness was different: it was not pure, it was not even clean. It had no aspect that could be described; it did not even resemble the abominable wasteland of deep space.

It was the whiteness of *nil*.

Her physical body was trapped here. Here, beyond the ragged edge of Stone, beyond the last bitemark she had made in Stone, she lay. The void, she reassured herself, was not entirely empty. *She* filled it. When she had entered the void she had been red and black, a monstrous distortion of the dragon form. Now she was white again, white like the void, and she was anything but empty.

Archan's will alone was what protected Frey's body inside the Helix. By rights his flesh should have been shredded by the crossing; his mind certainly should have been pulverized.

Regarding the latter, Archan was unconcerned. But since she was now wholly reliant on this pitiful faery body for survival, she had a vested interest in keeping Frey's blood pumping through his veins. His spirit she could do without, but she needed his meat.

It was charm that kept them all intact as the turmoil of the Helix tore at the vulnerable flying faery. From her white prison cell Archan was forced to use charm upon charm upon charm – her own dragon charm as

132

well as that which she had sucked from the basilisks. Not to mention the prodigious well of ancient magic with which she was now replete, having gorged herself on the infinite lower reaches of Stone.

A passenger of a passenger, she thought to herself as the wicked winds ripped gouges into Frey's skin. She sent healing charm across the gap between the worlds, not bothering to dull the pain, only to close the wounds. The pain was good, the pain reminded her what it was to live. Besides, the pain was not really hers.

The bond with Areken was gratifying in its strength. And she could still reach Annie, although only by way of a nebulous dream-world, and the wretched faery had been quick to recognize her dragon adversary's limited powers in that domain.

As for the splinter of lesky-wood she had hoarded in her white prison – it had allowed her to connect with the Bark all right, lasting long enough for her to plant a seed of ice inside the ship as it fought with the Fabricators. But the damned faery Jonah had taken care of that and the splinter was now drained of what little power it had possessed.

Which left Areken her strongest link with this or any other world. Without Areken it was entirely possible she might never have escaped the white at all.

Never? Even eternity is longer than never.

Most galling was the fact that she could not use the memory rods to get at Jonah. She had some creative ideas, such as reshaping the moment of his conception so that he was born with all his nerve endings on fire and his eyes filled with termites.

But the barrier surrounding her white prison prevented all such contact with Stone – *her* Stone. She did not dare tamper with the memory rods in Areken's version of Stone. There was no telling what escalation of paradoxes she might set off were she to tinker with those.

No, until I break through at the summit of Stone I will be patient and use only my charm. Until the dawn comes to Sunlight Pass. Then I will have my revenge!

Besides, if she was honest with herself, it was taking all her energy to keep control over Areken. Her vigilant mirror-self prowled back and forth through Frey's shattered mind, ever prepared for the chance to strike back at her malicious twin.

But Archan would remain alert. She was not about to slip, not this time. This time there would be no mistakes.

With a drawn-out, idiot scream pouring from its mouth, Frey's body was dragged into the world of the flying machines.

Winged shapes surrounded it almost immediately. Through Areken, Archan used Frey's watering eyes to observe the onrushing attackers, remarking to her sister on their passing similarity to airborne dragons. Her sister did not respond; either she did not agree or simply did not care.

The first flying machine dived close but did not make contact. A reconnaissance pass. The second came closer still, peeling away at the last possible moment, its propulsion units making a low keening whine. The third flying machine severed Frey's right leg just below the knee.

Blood sprayed across the machine's silvery wing, which burst immediately into flames. Suppressing the cry of outrage from the half-mad faery still buried deep in the cave of his mind, Archan sent a bolt of undiluted charm to the site of the wound and cauterized it with a flash of green fire. The pain was sharp and immense and, to Archan, quite delicious.

Below Frey, what remained of the flying machine spiralled out of control into the deep red abyss. Following it, spinning like a seed on the breeze, fell Frey's leg.

The wings on the faery's back continued to flap. Archan

was amazed they worked as well as they did: she had never seen a more unwieldy contraption of charm. The scales might have come from a dragon – along with the glowing ball of charm at their roots that kept them working – but the handiwork, the harness, were all faery. Crude, in other words. But work they did, and now she was relying on those wings to carry them all the way to the top of Stone.

Still, given the hostility of the natives in this unwelcoming world, perhaps a helping claw was needed.

She had brought with her into Frey's weak faery mind only a small selection of the millions of senses available to her. The mind was small, and to bestow it with too much power might literally burst it apart. Now she activated a number of additional charms with which she was able to probe both the flying machines and their larger parents.

The data came in immediately: the machines enjoyed a symbiotic relationship with their organic sub-systems; they could be destroyed by water, or water-based compounds; they were fast but had little intelligence. Turning her attention to the larger Fabricators she learned to her surprise that they had no motive power at all – they were gliders, relying entirely on the thermals and currents of this world's blood-coloured sky for their lift and manoeuvrability.

Well, the water was simple enough.

Using charm to apply sudden heat, Archan created a thin layer of sweat all over Frey's naked body, where it mixed with what was left of the decorative mud to form a sticky paste. Further extensions of charm spread the glutinous liquid over the leather harness and the wings it supported. Then she inverted the temperature control and turned the water to ice. With his body and wings frozen in place, Frey's body locked like a statue. Without the wings driving it up, it began to fall.

'Are you insane?' screamed Areken.

'Some might think so,' Archan replied, 'but we know the truth, my sister. However, I do rather need your help.'

'I'd rather die.'

'That, as you well know, is not a likely prospect. However, if you refuse to help me this feeble faery body will eventually strike the Helix. If it survives that encounter it will then be shredded against the side of Stone. You will be cast free, a formless spirit adrift in eternity once more. Powerless, again.'

'As will you be, and you fear that fate every bit as much as I do,' said Areken.

'Fear it, yes. But you forget I still have a body here in the white, in my version of reality. I will become a prisoner again, admittedly, but with plenty more opportunity to devise a means of escape. You however . . .' She let the thought linger unformed.

Areken raged, lashing at the icy sculpture of Archan towering over her in their mutual mind, but she already knew she was beaten. And she also knew she had no time to waste with tantrums.

'What must I do?'

'I have filled the faery's wings with flight charm. You know its workings as well as I. Even though the wings are immobile you can fly the creature. I have other things to concentrate on.'

'So you aren't as all-powerful as you'd have me think!'

'My strength is not at issue, sister! I am distant from you, that is all, distant in every conceivable respect. My influence is therefore . . . diluted. But do not underestimate my will! If anything, its power is amplified. If you defy me you will regret it for all eternity. And eternity is something else you know the meaning of every bit as well as I.'

No more was said, but Archan felt Areken's trapped dragon mind take control of the charm she had pumped into the wings. Giving her sister access to the charm was risky, of course, but there was no choice and Archan believed that fortune was kind to those who were bold.

Except I am more than bold, she considered. *I am . . .* adamant.

The effect of the ice-skin was better than she could have hoped. The flying machines, faced with a creature apparently made entirely of water, simply gave up their attack and fled.

Frey's battered body floated up through the sky under the control of two dragons – one maintaining its protective tomb of ice, the other directing the filaments of charm that kept it aloft. This silent and uneasy truce lasted well enough to bring it within striking distance of the next strand of the Helix.

Three Fabricators circled at the upper limits of this world's dismal atmosphere. Identical twins of the giant machines which had threatened Jonah and his companions, these four-winged gliders cycled around each other in a simple, repetitive dance. They were no more than curious, Archan judged, but that did not mean they were not an obstacle.

She did not want to fall. She was not as casual about this mission as she had claimed. Of course not, how could she be? Inside her heart she held as much anger as Areken, probably more. But unlike her sister she had learned the wisdom of patience, the strength that came not from the fire but from the ice. From the *white*. The delicious anticipation of long waiting and final retribution. She had learned not so much to control her temper as to stockpile it. The stockpile was very large now, and growing still, but it was not yet the time to release it.

'Do you have any ideas, sister?' Archan asked.

'One or two. They are gliders, yes?'

'Our thought processes are closely matched.'

'How could they be otherwise? Do you want to do it, or shall I?'

Archan smiled to herself. 'Oh, I think I should have the honour. I would not want you to get ideas above your station, after all.'

Archan piloted Frey's body through the narrowing gap between the Fabricators. The nearest of them skewed suddenly, scything closer. Turbulence bubbled out from under its wings.

Drawing on the vast reserves of charm at her disposal, Archan amplified the freezing effect by which she had immobilized Frey's wings. Transmitting the magic between worlds was like trying to squeeze a troll into a snail shell. Great swathes of ice-laden charm spilled back into the white, but enough crossed over to fill the blood-red sky with snow.

Immune to the water crystals, the Fabricators continued to close in. But the air temperature was dropping rapidly. While warm currents continued to rise on every side, the funnel of air containing the Fabricators grew cold. Suddenly heavier than the rest of the sky, it simply fell. Unable to gain the rising thermals quickly enough, the spinning gliders fell with it, leaving Archan to navigate her way through the frozen air using the power of charm alone.

The last of the snow fell just as the ice in which Frey was encased began to vaporize. He was surrounded by an expanding cloud of steam. The backs of his legs and arms turned bright red with scald-marks. The dragons allowed some of the pain through to his caged mind. The agonizing sensation was at once welcome and unbearable to him, informing him as it did that he was still alive. As the blisters formed Frey started to scream. Then for the second time he entered the strange nether-realm of the Helix and for him the world turned not white but a wide and welcome black.

8

Placement

Jonah lost count of the days. They crossed world after world; in none of them did they find anything approaching the hostility of the Fabricators.

Many of the worlds seemed altogether barren, though within the desolation the variety of terrains was staggering.

As strange as any was the world they passed into immediately after fleeing the wine-red skies of the Fabricators. Here the air was utterly pure; there were no clouds, nor even any haze to diminish the distance. The vertex marking the distant curve of Stone was a knife-cut across a yellow sky. Jonah could detect no trace of Stone's usual spice, though Malya claimed she could still smell it, very faint on the breeze. Grandfather Tree assured them the air was as crammed with charm as it had ever been, but charm of such an exotic breed that their feeble faery senses could barely register it.

Stone itself looked like a steeply-inclined thatched roof from some homely cottage in Oxfordshire. A close fly-past confirmed that the fibres from which the surface was woven were about the same thickness as Earthly straw, but immeasurably stronger.

'We had better not start a fire,' Jonah said as Gerent, leaning precariously over the side of the Bark with his wings spread wide for balance, snatched one of the pliable strands from the weave. Between them they embarked on an impromptu tug'o'war which left them both sprawled laughing on the deck, with the fibre lying unbroken between them.

Jonah rose first, extending his hand to assist his friend but Gerent became suddenly self-conscious and the laughter died in his mouth. He brushed away Jonah's offer of help and loped below deck to bury himself in his quarters.

Giant pegs were driven at regular intervals into the wall of straw, but at no time during the ascent did they spy whatever beings had put them there; nor, in fact, did they see any sign of life at all. Even Grandfather Tree, the most widely travelled of them all, knew nothing about this place and so, as they dropped below deck in readiness for the next Helix crossing, they added it to the long list of enigmas Stone had offered up.

To begin with they returned to the open deck after every crossing.

Worlds slid past, worlds of lumbering giants and scurrying midgets, worlds populous with unearthly beasts and worlds that were merely upended deserts. They passed a nightmarish world where Stone was smothered with electrical sparks, its surface restless with jittering energy beams. They passed another whose surface was insubstantial, a pillow of goose-down large enough to nestle the Earth.

There was one constant however: in every world the sun looked out from the sky, maintaining its course through the day, though its colour changed frequently and sometimes it shone more or less brightly. They climbed and climbed through world after world, and through them all the sun remained their watchful companion.

The fully restored Grandfather Tree, as exuberant as

ever despite his brush with death, found ways to increase their speed so the crossing times were cut to less than an hour and it became more trouble than it was worth to traipse in and out every time there was something new to see. Despite the wonders outside, the travellers became bored. The lesky maintained a few viewing windows on the bridge and that was enough to satisfy most outbreaks of curiosity.

Jonah knew he was getting tired of it all when, having watched a five-mile-wide eyeball blink at them from a deep and dismal chasm in a limestone-rendered Stone, he simply turned away and yawned. As the Bark continued its ascent the eye shed a single tear that broke apart on the rock and crashed like Niagara into the abyss.

Annie, on the other hand, was in her element. Though her wounds were healing well she was even less inclined than the others to move around and so she sat and painted.

'I told you I was feeling artistic,' she said as she and Jonah sat gazing at a misty veldt. Here Stone was lush and green; in the sky small bat-like animals were racing the Bark, chirruping at each other in high-pitched voices which Grandfather Tree relayed into the bridge.

She showed him the tile she had just completed, a loose array of tiny strokes on the smooth ivory. The endless stream of worlds past the windows had provided her with an endless source of material; to capture it she had developed a sketchier style somewhat freer than her usual painstaking miniaturism.

With a few seemingly random splashes of green and yellow she had captured the grassland to perfection; thin brown slashes described the elegant dips and dives of the bats against the misty air. Looked at too closely it was a meaningless jumble; held at arm's length the illusion was breathtaking.

'It is beautiful,' said Jonah, 'but why bother? Forgive

me, my darling, but I do not see the point in this fanatical work. Of what possible use can these compositions be?'

'Your Mr Darwin was very diligent when it came to recording the facts.'

'My Mr Darwin was on a voyage of discovery; we are heading for Armageddon!'

'Well,' she said, stretching her arms above her head until her shoulders cracked, 'Mister Ren says I gotta do it, so . . .' She stared up at Jonah from the couch, half-smiling, eyelashes lowered. 'You're crotchety because you've got nothing to do, ain't that right? Well don't think you can take it out on me because . . .'

'Annie, I never . . .'

'I know you didn't. Now, d'you want to hear about Mister Ren or not?'

'Do I have any choice in the matter?'

'None at all, my English lover. And that's what's making you so crotchety. Come sit with me and I'll tell you a story.'

She had already told Jonah a little about her last trip out west, but only a little. Now she told him everything.

'I am not clear.' Jonah frowned as she described in detail what she had learned on the mountain trail. 'Are this Mister Ren and Esh one and the same?'

'Well, yes and no. Kind of. I don't think this Chinaman *is* Esh, not the way we'd like him to be. But if the two of them were horses you'd say they were out of the same stable.'

'Hmm. What about these latest paintings of yours? What have they to do with our Chinese friend?'

'That's easy. He told me I had to put a painting on every tile. He said not to miss a single one.'

'But *why*? What is so important about these damned tiles?'

'I don't know for certain, but if we've carried them all this way there'd better be a good reason! And yes, I asked him that same question, before you look at me like that. But he didn't answer me, not properly. What he did say was this: "First the tiles must be painted. And then they must be placed."'

'Placed?'

'Yep! That's where you come in, Jonah Lightfoot! You and me – we got a set of instructions to follow. He said he'd like to have told you himself, but at least I was the prettiest messenger he'd ever seen.'

'How charming. So what are these instructions?'

'Ah, I remember that part word for word. He said, "The tiles, Annie. Tell Jonah the tiles are the key to getting rid of Archan." They're seeds, Jonah – the Mah Jongg tiles are seeds. Mister Ren gave them to me before I left San Francisco and between us we brought them here to Stone and now it's time to sow them.'

'Seeds?' Jonah said. 'Sow them? But sow them where?'

'Just what I asked him!' she crowed. 'And you know what? The answer's in those damned Chinese symbols. They've hounded us every step of the way: the mark of the Red Dragon on Esh's shell, the matching symbol you lifted out of the floor like a sword, the sign of the North Wind on the locks that opened up the Aqueduct ... There's a different one drawn on practically every door in this ship, for God's sake! Since we've been on Stone we've not moved more than ten paces without tripping over one inscrutable squiggle after another!

'Those symbols are markers, Jonah. They mark the places where the seeds have to be sown. They're ... I don't know, crossroads or places where weird power's focused or ... wells dug into the roots of Stone. I don't know what they are, and neither does Mister Ren, not really, but he does know they're powerful. And it's up to us to get them working. Well, up to you really. You gotta set the primer, Jonah. Then we stand back and watch it all blow.'

Jonah said, 'And when it does all blow will it take Archan with it?'

'You bet!'

'So what must I do?'

'Simple – you use the memory rods to travel all over Stone, back to every place we've been where there was a Mah-Jongg mark, and every other place you can find besides. Each trip you make you take a tile with you. Place the tile on the mark, making sure they match. When all the tiles are in the right place . . . that's when the fun begins.'

Use the memory rods . . . Jonah shuddered at her words and saw her eyes narrow at his reaction.

'It sounds too simple,' he said hurriedly. 'Why were we not told to place the tiles as we went along? Why wait until now?'

'Just what I asked him. Great minds, eh?' Annie was quiet for a moment. 'Mister Ren never expected Archan to get this far. He underestimated her too, just like we did. He only ever gave me the tiles as a last resort.'

'The last resort. Is that what we are, Annie?'

'It's all we ever were, my darling. Our Mister Ren – he's been around a long time, and he likes to keep an eye on things. One of the things he's kept a real close eye on over the years is Archan. He always knew she was trouble. But after she snatched immortality from the basilisks she got blown out of her body and ended up locked away at the North Pole for so long he got lazy. There's only so much trouble an outlaw can make from inside a gaol cell, you know. But then, the minute Mister Ren took his eye off the cell door she headed straight for the hills. And so he made himself a posse and set them to round her on up.'

'And we are the posse.'

'That's right, pardner! He knew you could handle the memory rods and reckoned you could handle Archan too.

He thought your traps might be better than his, but they weren't.'

'That does not make me feel particularly clever!'

'Hey, it's a compliment! Mister Ren thinks the world of you, you know. Take it on the chin – you did your best.'

'I did my best twice and still she is coming back for more.'

'Okay, but this time we got our secret weapon.'

'Secret weapon? A box of ivory tiles?'

'Yeah. But there's a hell of a lot of them!'

They stared at each other then burst out laughing. Jonah appraised the tiny, oblong tile he was holding, then held it out in his fist towards Annie and mimed pulling a trigger.

'Bang!' he laughed, wiping tears from his eyes with his free hand. 'I just killed you with a Three Bamboo!'

'Well hey there, you varmint,' drawled Annie. She narrowed her eyes and rummaged in the painting box. 'You shoulda reckoned on my trusty Green Dragon here – can split a raisin at eighty paces!'

They hugged and pummelled, simple physical contact releasing the tension. When Jonah drew back he saw bright anticipation in Annie's face, knowing it matched the excitement in his own.

'You have to put a painting on the back of each tile before I can put it in its place?' he asked.

'Uh-huh.'

'Why?'

'God only knows.'

'How fast can you paint?'

'Fast enough, Englishman! Now it's time for you to tell me something.'

Her sudden change of direction caught him unawares. 'What do you mean?'

'I mean, Jonah, you switch your tail every time I

145

mention the memory rods. Something's changed, hasn't it? What's changed? Why are you so scared?'

He looked away, out of the window, and saw a trickle of slime oozing its way out of a series of pores in Stone's pockmarked skin. It glistened in the sunlight like sticky dew.

'No reason,' he lied.

Telling both himself and Annie he needed a breath of fresh air before embarking on his mission, Jonah made his way out on deck in time to watch the transit of a version of Stone entirely covered with strange and beautiful buildings. It was like a tapestry of cathedrals.

He thought about the memory rods and realized that he was terrified.

I have resurrected Malya only to condemn her to death a second time. What further havoc will I wreak when I go back in there?

Something clicked behind his head, an alien sound he could not place. Spinning round he found himself staring at a small convex reflection of his own face. He thought at once of the fish-eye mirror his father had brought back from Holland and hung on the parlour wall; his face looked bulbous and deformed, much as the parlour had done when, as a child, he had peered up into the mirror, trying to see round the hidden corners it seemed to contain.

The mirror dropped away, revealing the weather-worn features of Tom Coyote. The mirror was the lens of Coyote's miraculous twentieth century camera. Coyote nodded a greeting and wound the film advance lever with his thumb.

'Quite a sight,' he said, nodding at the palatial surface of Stone. 'Thought I'd record it for posterity.'

Coyote had already explained the camera's workings to Jonah. The device was miraculous to him in terms of its size, but he was curiously gratified to learn that the principles of photography had not changed greatly since his own time. A synthetic flexible strip had replaced unwieldy glass, and the chemicals used were capable of responding much more efficiently to the action of light, but it was essentially the same piece of apparatus used by the earliest Victorian practitioners of the art.

'Only problem is there ain't nowhere to process the film in this Godforsaken hell-hole,' Coyote had said. 'Still – might as well snap away, I guess. You never know, I might get paid for it. If I ever get me home, that is.'

Coyote had allowed Jonah to inspect the camera, describing in some detail the film transport mechanism, but had cautioned him not to open the back. 'You'll fog that baby,' he warned, 'and I got a load of pictures of that damn volcano just belchin' its guts up into the air. Don't want to wipe out all that history now, do we?'

Jonah had seen enough of volcanoes to last him a lifetime, but he had no desire to spoil Coyote's work. After a query-laden inspection he handed the camera back, awed by its complexity, pleased that he understood its essential workings.

'Is it important to take photographs in 1980?' he said. 'For a journalist such as yourself, I mean.'

'Picture speaks a thousand words, Jonah, ain't that what they say?'

Jonah took seriously Annie's assertion that this twentieth century man was dangerous – after all the warning had come from none other than Mister Ren – but Coyote possessed a powerful charisma Jonah found hard to ignore. Like the rods, Tom Coyote was both fearful and seductive.

'Look,' said Coyote. 'I know your buddies think I'm Norman Bates or something but I gotta tell you, I'm just a regular freaked-out guy, you know what I mean?'

147

'Um . . .' Jonah began, struggling to wade through Coyote's twentieth century phraseology.

'Look at it my way, I'm still in shock or post-trauma or something, whatever. Okay, I'm not saying I'm not an in-yer-face kind of guy, I'll admit that, but in my business you gotta be pushy. I'll bet it was the same with newspaper hacks in your day, right?'

Jonah was about to answer that nobody had ever called his father 'pushy' but Coyote was in full flow.

'What I'm trying to say is this: a lot of people don't like me because I'm too tall and too rude and maybe sometimes – only sometimes mind – I can come over a little aggressive. I fight my own battles and I fight them to win, but that doesn't make me a bad guy. Determined, yeah, and I won't say I'm not single-minded – I always get something if I set my mind to getting it – but I'm not a bad guy, no way.'

Tom Coyote's eyes were burning with a ferocity that could just as easily have signalled truth as fiction; Jonah found that in his presence he could not easily separate the two. Part of him wanted to like the man, to give him the benefit of the doubt. But . . . was dangerous the same as bad?

Tigers are dangerous. Only men are bad.

'What you thinkin', Englishman?'

'I was thinking about a task I have to perform,' said Jonah. 'A very important task.'

'And you're afraid, I can see that. Saw it right away through the goddam camera! Hey, you know what I'd do in your situation?'

'No, but I suspect you are about to tell me.'

'Close your eyes and think of England!'

Jonah did indeed close his eyes, but England seemed a very, very long way away.

Coyote turned out to be right though – in the end it *was*

thoughts of England, the home he believed he had put behind him forever, that gave Jonah the courage he needed to plunge into the memory rods once more.

Both he and Coyote had returned below decks. After watching the tall, bald man settle down for a nap between two of the larger consoles on the bridge, Jonah kissed Annie, used a lesky-made bowl to gather up the seventy tiles she had already painted and made his way to the travelling-room Grandfather Tree had prepared for him deep inside the Bark.

On the door leading into the hidden chamber was a Mah Jongg symbol: Nine Bamboo. Rummaging through the wooden bowl Jonah found a matching tile. The image on its reverse was one of Annie's more recent sketches: a tense blue study of lightning in a brooding sky. Stone was a thin slash of grey at the very edge of the composition, quite subordinated to the massed clouds.

Acting without thinking, Jonah turned the tile so the grid of bamboo symbols faced its twin on the chamber door. He pressed it against the smooth timber. It travelled the last quarter-inch on its own, as if an ivory-sensitive magnetic field had just been activated. When he took his fingers away the tile stayed clinging to the door, oblivious to gravity.

Eyes narrowed, he watched as the painting came to life. Lightning split the painted sky, blue-white lines like liquid pouring through clouds of thick ultramarine. He even fancied he could hear the crack of electricity finding its earth. The animation was transitory; no sooner had it begun than the tile melted into the door. As the little block of ivory disappeared the colours of the painting were fused into the door pattern. Jonah was in no doubt that he had put the right tile in the right place, and that in doing so he had begun the connection to some new and greater earth.

He also understood the importance of the paintings: to

work properly the tiles had to be alive. Without Annie's work they were as dead as . . . well, as ivory.

A place for every one and every one in its place.

From the door immediately above the Mah Jongg sign a familiar face appeared.

'Well, Jonah, it's a start!'

'Grandfather Tree, I cannot decide. Should I fill the rest of the places on the Bark before I venture into the rods? There are Mah Jongg symbols on so many of the doors in here.'

'Ye, Jonah. And now we know why they're there! Powerful he is, the Bark – much more powerful than even I imagined.'

'Indeed. So what should I do?'

'Don't you know?'

'Are all leskies as exasperating as you?'

'No, no, no! Many much worse!'

'Then are you going to offer me your opinion?'

'Jonah – you're the one. You know. I don't. Help you I can, advise you I might . . . but interfere I cannot. Your journey this is, nobody else's.'

Pursing his lips Jonah grunted his agreement. 'Let me in then, please,' he said. 'The rest of these doors can wait – I have a long way to go and the sooner I set out the sooner I shall return.'

The lesky's face jerked out of sight, the planes of his cheeks and twists of his brambly beard vanishing piece by piece, as though he were being carved in reverse. Then, silently, the door slid into the wall and Jonah stepped into his travelling-room.

The instant he crossed the threshold he knew this was the right place. Memories swelled up inside him, and at first he thought they came from the rods. Then he recognized them for what they were: his own, natural human memories from a particular summer in a particular place, with a particular girl.

'Lily!' he gasped. He could almost see her.

Lily, his first love, who had seduced him on her father's farm in Kent, whose love had guided him through those early summers when his body had not known whether it was man or boy but had been eager to learn the difference. Lily, whose name conjured the scent of her unruly blonde hair, the ever-present flush of her cheeks, the tally of meadows and hay-lofts and secret dells. The simple sense of adventure they had shared together, and the knowledge of the danger were they ever to be discovered.

Thoughts of England!

He forced himself to look around the travelling-room and in doing so saw what had triggered the sudden surge of nostalgia. The walls were pale. In the planked floor was a large square hole through which he could see a second lower level and, through an identical hole, a third. Unidentifiable equipment was piled on all the floors: linked pipes and long trays, wheels and cords and coiled threads of what looked like spider silk. The stack of rooms reeked of barley and seemed terribly familiar.

'The mill!' he said.

'Problem?' Grandfather Tree appeared, poking his nose and eyes out from one of the stout beams supporting the low ceiling.

'N-no,' stammered Jonah. 'No – it is just that . . . this place reminds me very much of somewhere I went when I was younger. What is it?'

'Mill.' The lesky added his briar-lined mouth to the facial ensemble, allowing him to offer an unhelpful grin.

'Yes, that is what it reminds me of. I was asking about its function within the Bark.'

'You ask, I say. Mill it is: charm-mill.'

'And what, pray tell, is a charm-mill?'

'A place that mills charm.'

'Grandfather Tree!'

The lesky laughed aloud. 'All right, all right. The Bark: he travels now through many different worlds. Most have charm, some more, some less. But most have it. Charm, it is a constant, a universal quality throughout history. Your world of nature – unnatural it is. Ha! But charm varies. Bark, he drinks the charm. His power source it is, his life-sap. But many flavours has the charm, many guises. In your world and time it was all but invisible. Much charm is coarse, unrefined. Bark must grind it down before he can use it. This is where he grinds it.'

'I thought I asked you for somewhere quiet and secluded.' Jonah was eyeing the apparatus with new respect. On the next floor down was a huge drum-shaped container; inside, he assumed, were the grinding stones.

A mill for the grinding of charm, he thought. *Now I have seen everything!*

'Oh, worry not, Jonah! Bark is replete. This mill – he will not use it again for a long time. Reserves are good, and good progress we make. Peaceful it will be, Grandfather Tree gives you his word. Now, why has the mill so arrested you.'

'You do not need to know.'

'But I'm curious!'

'Then you must remain curious. I may tell you later. Now, please, leave me here with my thoughts and Annie's tiles.'

'But I should watch over you while you're in the rods.'

'Oh, very well, I suppose you will do that anyway, Grandfather Tree. Really – sometimes I believe you are eavesdropping on everything that occurs on this ship!'

'It is my right. Bark and lesky are one now.'

Jonah pressed his hand against his forehead. A dull ache was developing there.

'Yes, of course you are. But could I have a least a few moments to myself? Could you leave me alone with my own memories, just for a short time?'

'Naturally I will, Jonah,' replied Grandfather Tree, suddenly grave. 'I promised to serve you, and serve you I shall. Call me if you need me, please.'

'I will, I promise.'

When the lesky had gone Jonah opened his heart fully to the memory that had so surprised him.

His quest temporarily put aside (but not really forgotten, for he sensed this was a vital part of it all) he drifted back in time to a morning in the summer of 1865, when he and Lily had first dared to explore the abandoned water mill at the very edge of her father's southernmost pasture. His exploration of the memory was pure and natural, a simple and miraculous restoration by the deeper part of his mind; in reliving the story he did not use the memory rods at all.

Or so he told himself, as he breathed in the musty smell of ancient barley and . . .

. . . *turned to see Lily pulling her cotton smock up over her head. Her body was long and pale, sparsely freckled and quintessentially English (or so Jonah imagined, never having seen any other girls naked, English or otherwise).*

She held the garment out in front of her, enjoying the dance of the morning light on the fabric. She herself was standing directly in the path of a dazzling beam of sunlight that had found its way in through a tear in the wall. Glowing dust encircled her body, floury light offering the curves of her hips, her breasts, through the thin material of the smock.

'We should not,' he said. 'Not here.'

'Oh, Jonah. Why not here? Is it so different to everywhere else we've done it?' The smile on her burning face was sly.

'No . . . but something about this place . . . it makes me uneasy.'

'Why? 'Cos they all say it's haunted?' she teased.

'They do?'

He was fourteen. Six years had passed since he had witnessed the deaths of his father and brother, but although his feelings of guilt about that fateful day were laid largely to rest he was still uneasy with any talk about the dead.

It was while chasing Jonah that Henry and Albert Lightfoot had been crushed beneath a toppling concrete dinosaur, one of the many exhibits in the grounds of the relocated Crystal Palace high on Sydenham Hill. An incredible death and one for which he had for a long time felt responsible.

People who died incredible deaths might very easily become ghosts, which meant that a place such as a haunted water mill was a place where the past might suddenly catch up with Jonah Lightfoot in a bleak and bloody rush. And at fourteen years of age, he had no desire to relive that day outside the Crystal Palace at all.

Little did he know that the miracle of the memory rods of Stone would one day give him the opportunity to do just that . . . and more. Not only to relive the memory but to change it too. By changing the flow of time around that absurd concrete Iguanodon he would be given the chance to raise his father and brother from the dead.

At fourteen years of age he would not have believed that, given such an opportunity, he would refuse it. That he would turn his back on doomed Henry and Albert and leave the dreadful day of death exactly as it had been.

The man he would become, while voyaging in a strange other-world called Stone, would come to realize that his decision not to change the past was a sound one. Tinkering with history was a dangerous business. Had he chosen to save them he would have dropped another great boulder in the river of time and caused its stream to diverge: he would in fact have created a whole new world, just as he did when he rescued Malya. But that world, once made, would have drifted away from him. His reward would have been the knowledge that Henry and Albert lived on, his punishment that he would never share in their restored lives.

So when Lily told him the mill was haunted his ardour was

dampened – not for long of course, since he was a fourteen-year-old boy, but it took at least ten seconds of Lily gyrating behind her upraised smock to bring the smile back to his face. As soon as it was there Lily lifted the smock up and over her head and pressed her freckled, naked body close against his, trapping the falling smock between them as she kissed his lips, his cheeks, his forehead, then pulled back enough to let the smock drop to the floor and slipped her hands inside his clothing, surrounding him first with her fingers and then with her body, urging him down to the floor with her moving hips, singing his name and riding down the ghosts.

Later, with bodies still bare and hair full of barley dust, sawdust, fine white stone dust, they clambered up through the watermill to the bin floor at the very top of the deserted building.

A single square window framed a cramped view of what had once been the mill-pond, but was now a crusty depression overgrown with nettles. Through the window they watched a rabbit pick its way between gorse bushes. Bees danced below the eaves just outside the window, their legs clotted with pollen. The day was hot and close; a September storm was on its way.

Jonah's sense of foreboding increased as the light outside failed. The rabbit paused in its exploration of the dried-up mill-pond, its tail the single bright spot in a mass of vegetation turned dark. Then it bolted. Black clouds piled high, their shadows flooding the land like oil. The buzz of the bees was gone.

There had been a storm the day the dinosaur fell. The same storm, it seemed to him now, had been waiting for him all those six years, waiting for the moment to strike again and claim its third victim. During those years he had been simply serving his time before the sentence was carried out. Now the executioner's axe was about to fall.

Something cold touched his neck and it was as much as he could do not to cry out. The touch became a caress and then Lily's hand was snaking round his shoulders, drawing him away from the window and back into her arms.

He gave himself over to her embrace, turning his back on the storm outside as she pressed him against the sill. Sudden hail lashed in through the open window, pounding his naked back. Summer heat and icy rain, the plump softness of Lily's breasts against his smooth chest, the hardness of her nipples, fear and love.

Lily had somehow lifted him up on to the window sill – her farm brawn was more than a match for his young city muscles. Her hands were roaming through his hair, down his neck and chest to his navel. The hail had turned his back to ice; the sound of it pummelling the exterior wall was like a fusillade of muskets. It was then that the sill gave way.

There was no sense of transition, no memory of actually falling out of the window. He saw Lily's horrified face become small, a frozen portrait of outraged shock set with perfect symmetry inside a dark wooden frame. He fell with the hail, for a second an integral part of the storm, while a flat sheet of lightning simplified the sky. Then he hit the waterwheel and for an instant there was no light at all.

He was still on the wheel when he came to. As with the fall he had no sense of change, no sequence of waking through time: regaining consciousness was like flinging open a door.

The hail was peppering his naked belly and legs and lashing his face. His erection had already subsided. He had fallen square on to the top of the wheel, and found time to be glad it was long rusted into place. Were it not he would almost certainly be lying underneath it by now, probably with his neck and several other essential bones broken into a number of pieces. But his fall had done nothing more than dislodge a scattering of moss and mud from what had once been the most efficient breastshot water-wheel in the county. It had also knocked the wind from him and set a steam-hammer pounding in his lower back, but he did not think he was seriously damaged.

A lightning fork darted from the ground to meet its twin falling from the heavens and he recalled how earlier the storm clouds had appeared not only to descend upon the land but also to rise up from it, like a reflection springing from a mirror to meet its maker.

There is a symmetry to things, *he thought.*

There was a ringing sound in his ears; he shook his head and it went away.

Sky above, earth below, the two mutually reliant. Each a reflection of the other, with no way of knowing which is an echo of which.

Thought clung to him like pollen to the leg of a bee. Lily's voice was screaming at him through the open window. She was very close – he had fallen only a few feet. He started to wonder how on Earth he was going to get down from the waterwheel.

'Holy Jesus, Jonah, are you all right?'

'Yes, Lily. I think so.'

And he was. Though he had fallen he felt elevated. Sprawled here naked on the very top of the immobilized wheel he was acutely aware of his place within the storm-lit scene. A young man alive between sky and soil. The hail had dissolved into a thin spray of icy rain. Grey-green hills underpinned the arch of the sky. The planet turned through space. His body was pinned to it like a butterfly.

I am fourteen years old, *he thought.* And this is a good place to be. Between the soil and the sky. My name is . . .

. . . *Jonah Lightfoot.*

There was more to the memory but it was already floating out of reach. Yet the crucial emotion remained.

The knowledge of one's proper place. The truth of one's name.

Jonah allowed himself a quick peep down through the hole in the floor to the grinding room and beneath that the meal floor where, presumably, the reconfigured charm was stored before dispersal throughout the Bark. All was quiet and still; he could not imagine what it must be like in here when the mill was in operation.

The first tile out of the bowl was all-too familiar: the sword-shape of the Red Dragon. Clenching it tight in his fist he closed his eyes and remembered the places he had encountered it . . .

. . . *a monolithic structure projecting from Stone like a plank from a giant pirate ship. A structure towards which he was falling before his dragon companion Kythe snatched him from certain death in her talons. The Red Dragon clearly marked on the surface of the monolith* . . .

. . . but this tile was not intended for there. Nor was it for the identical shape he had seen cut into the bones of Archan herself when he had last faced her across the Aqueduct. He had no doubt he would have to place a tile into *that* unholy place sooner or later. Right now he trusted it would be much later.

No, he knew without thinking that this Red Dragon tile – one of four in the set – was for the hard black shell of Esh.

With his eyes still shut he concentrated on the feel of the tile in his fist. He had not even looked at the painting on the back but he knew it was of the coast of Java seen from the ocean, the first picture he had ever seen Annie working on.

The memory rods were scratching at his mind like cats. He even fancied they were purring. He was already fearful, but the suspicion that the rods might actually be alive made him shake.

Not cats, he thought. *Tigers!*

The corners of the tile were hard and blunt. The ivory was warm. He curled his fingertip into his palm and touched . . .

. . . *the yielding surface of the Threshold floor. Standing, he felt it give beneath his feet. Opening his fist he saw the little tile lying there, painting side up. The Javanese coast was alive in the darkness; waves of oil and pigment rose and fell while clouds slid across a painted sky.*

He had entered a memory of his own travels across the surface of Stone, and now that he was here a little of his fear left him.

This is the past, *he told himself,* your past. Tread carefully, change nothing but what you must and all will be well.

Early on, with Esh the Ypoth as their guide, Jonah and his friends had made their way to the Threshold. The Threshold was a great oval rift, a permanent breach connecting Stone to Jonah's home world. Connecting it specifically to a point in time known as the Turning of the World, the crucial pivot between the opposed worlds of charm and nature. Here it was that Jonah had first defeated Archan, sending her plunging back through infinite time on a journey without end. Or so he had hoped, but the journey had ended. Archan had wriggled out of that trap as she had wriggled out of so many others. Nevertheless this was a time and place with particular resonance.

Making his way through the shiny black cavern Jonah was amazed at how familiar it all seemed: the wide walls meeting the floor in a seamless curve; the root-like knots into which the memory rods were entwined to form an almost impenetrable jungle at his back; the slab-like Guardians, slow-witted protectors of this vulnerable place, lining the mouth of the cave like standing stones.

No sooner had he found his stride than he faltered. Before him, embedded in a ruptured section of floor, was Esh's corpse. He sank to his knees, unable to quell the tears. With his free hand he touched the smooth black carapace, traced the lines of the Red Dragon engraved there.

Esh had saved them all, sacrificing her own life in her defiance of the Guardians and giving them time to make their escape. In dying she had been assimilated back into the fabric of Stone, the same material from which she had originally been spawned. The hope that she might in some

159

way live on within Annie's Mister Ren was almost too much for Jonah to bear.

Esh had been his friend.

He pressed his face against the carapace, crying like a child.

By and by the tears abated and he was able to raise his head and look at Esh's face. It was a mess, the semi-human features melted like tallow into the floor. The wide tortoise mouth drooped, her eyes were forever closed. Further down her body almost nothing remained of her long insect limbs.

'Oh Esh,' he said softly. 'I am so sorry.'

The grief was sweet and cleared the last traces of fear from his heart. Esh had feared nothing. Now, with her beside him again, he knew he had the courage to go on.

Transferring the tile into his left hand he was about to press it into the symbol on Esh's shell when he heard a faint noise. At first he thought it was a voice; in fact it was the whispering not of lips but of wings.

Gerent had appeared in the distance, his angel-silhouette unmistakable against the brilliant sky. The row of slab-like Guardians twitched as he swooped over them but did not move to follow. Thereafter he flew low, hugging the floor as if unwilling to trust his wings to keep him aloft.

Of course, *thought Jonah,* at this stage he had not had them for long.

Jonah dropped into the shadows behind Esh's body. At the same time his body faded to near transparency, making him quite invisible even to Gerent's keen eyes.

As a seasoned traveller of the rods he was now able to exercise an extraordinary degree of control over how he manifested himself within an individual memory. He could experience events as an active participant, an insubstantial spirit, even from within the mind of another. And, like Archan, he could even take over that mind and bend it to his own will. That, he had already vowed, he would never do.

He was equally determined not to make any changes to the memories. This scene in the Threshold was one from his own past: if he altered the proper flow of events here he was putting in jeopardy his very existence.

Gerent glanced at Esh's body as he sped past. Jonah tried to make himself small, terrified lest he should be seen.

He already knew where the Neolithic prince was going: shortly after they had made their escape from the Threshold Gerent had returned to collect the book Jonah had left there: Darwin's On the Origin of Species. It had been a risky thing for Gerent to do, given that a new battalion of Guardians was already waking.

Jonah clenched his fists and suppressed a moan. Being reminded of the book reminded him of Malya. Poor, doomed Malya . . .

The back of the Threshold resembled a tangle of giant mangrove trees, so twisted were the rods there. Gerent rummaged through them for a moment or two before breaking free again with the book in his right hand. His left hand he held out to his side like a tightrope walker to make up for his lack of control over the wings. Again he flew close to Esh; this time he paused, hovering for a moment before touching down in front of her.

Jonah had by now made himself completely invisible; still he flinched back against Esh's shell, certain he would be discovered.

Gerent walked up to Esh and peered into what was left of her face. The expression on his pale, Nordic face was unreadable. The dragon wings convulsed behind his back as if eager to take off again.

I am not here, Jonah thought.

His phantom heart pounded in his transparent chest. The more he travelled the rods the more sensitive he became to their vulnerability. When first using them he had rushed in like a fool; now he strove to make his tread as light as an angel's.

Gerent bent down and tugged at something beneath the opposite edge of Esh's shell. Jonah suppressed his curiosity, unwilling to move a single ghostly muscle for fear of giving himself away. If he had breath he would have held it.

When Gerent stood up straight again he was holding a short spike of black Stone-stuff. It was one of Esh's claws. He hefted it then tried brandishing it. It looked like a small dagger in his hand. Satisfied, he stowed it in the leather pouch slung about his waist.

As he turned away Jonah had to smile: the Neolithics were scavengers by nature, and neither Gerent nor Malya was likely to pass over a useful tool if it was there for the taking.

He was about to breathe a mental sigh of relief when Gerent's head rotated back in his direction. Blue Stone-Age eyes scanned the shadows in which Jonah was crouched; his lips twitched. Paralysed, Jonah prayed the torrent of thoughts in his head were not making as much sound as they seemed to be.

He will see me! . . . He will see me and history will change! . . . Perhaps he will linger too long and be killed by the Guardians, or perhaps he will simply take fright and return and tell the others (including me!) what he has seen and we will all behave differently and history will change . . . was I not a fool to believe I could even set foot in the past without rewriting it? Am I now doomed to turn to stone, I and all my companions around me?

Blue eyes narrowed, and the brow above them frowned. Jonah froze: the Neolithics had such acute senses!

A slow blink, then Gerent was shaking his head and turning away again. Dragon wings thumping the air, he took off and sped back towards the entrance. The menhir-shapes of the Guardians were definitely restless; another five minutes and it would have been too late.

Jonah flopped back against Esh's shell, his whole body shaking. Had Gerent sensed him? Had he affected events enough to change them, and if he had would he ever know it? He waited for the wrench, for some clue that history had split apart again, but nothing happened. Gradually he allowed himself to believe that everything was all right.

Still invisible, he climbed to his feet and shoved the tile into the centre of the mark on Esh's shell. The mark flashed bright red for a split-second then settled to a dull glow, barely discernible.

'Know your place,' he whispered.

Floating like a lost soul through the thick air of the Threshold, Jonah found the closest knot of memory rods and plunged back into . . .

. . . the mill.

Breathing hard, elated and apprehensive, Jonah found two more Red Dragon tiles. Holding them tight he looked down at the . . .

. . . matching symbol glowing from the surface of the monolith, staring at the sword-shape he had once drawn Excalibur-like from the floor. Without hesitating he knelt and placed the first tile in the centre of the blade. It vanished and the mark on the floor glowed a little brighter.

A minute twist in time and he was inside the monolith, where a second Red Dragon shone from the floor. It too accepted its tile without complaint.

Rising before anyone should come, Jonah spun back into . . .

. . . the Bark, encouraged by the speed at which he had made the placements. Just as quickly he found two matching North Wind tiles, the only others he knew for certain had to be placed into his own Stone memories.

He had encountered the North Wind mark at opposite ends of the Aqueduct, the great bridge spanning an otherwise impassable divide in Stone. Jonah would have to navigate through the rods to a point in time before the Aqueduct had been destroyed. This suited him well, since it meant there was no risk of meeting either himself or any of his friends. Nor Archan, for that matter.

The reminder that memories of Archan too existed within the rods was not a welcome one.

Drawing his thoughts back into the past he made his

way through the sinewy unreality of the memory rods and emerged into . . .

. . . *a broad tunnel, surrounded by fast-flowing water from which a square island stood proud; in its centre was cut the mark of the North Wind. It looked now, as it always had, like a man and a woman dancing together.*

The mark was large; Jonah recalled how one of the Shifters had allowed its amorphous body to flow into the engraving, filling it like cement and activating the locking mechanism set deep into the island. Activation of the sister lock at the other end of the Aqueduct had started the gradual collapse of the bridge.

He placed the first tile.

Across the gap in the fabric of Stone which he still thought of as the fire-break, *lay a strange realm of living metal. It was in this bizarre landscape that the second island resided. Trying to ignore the sluggish coppery ocean, the repetitive movement of the silvery wall and its billion staring faces, Jonah threw down the second North Wind tile and made his escape back into . . .*

. . . his sanctuary on board the Bark.

Now he was not only panting but sweating. He was puzzled: he did not recall expending this much energy when he had used the rods before. And these were such short jaunts by comparison to some he had made.

Then realized: never before had he been so careful not to disrupt the memories he entered. Whatever changes he made in actually placing the tiles were insignificant – they had to be, or Mister Ren would never have suggested he do it. But it was other changes he feared, and he was so cautious now that his trips were undertaken with back hunched and muscles tensed. He tiptoed, he skulked, he crept and crawled. His was the exertion not of the athlete but of the spy.

Propping his back against something that was half-tree,

half-spinning wheel, he took a series of long, slow breaths. The barley-like smell of milled charm was as strong as ever; Jonah floated on it and wondered how he could find the rest of the Mah Jongg symbols that were still hidden away inside the memory rods.

The answer came immediately: the basilisks.

It was a while since he had communed with them, or rather their ghosts. He had felt their presence in the Bark during the battle with the Fabricators, but it had been fleeting; apart from Ocher's nudge . . . *look down* . . . they had kept themselves out of his way. Why was that?

The basilisks built Stone, which they called Amara, as a safety net. When they built it they were immortal, but they feared their immortality might one day be taken from them. So they built a place, a secret world, where all their memories could be stored. If they were ever to die, their memories would survive. And memory is history, and history is story, and story is truth.

And truth will never die.

The basilisks, by their own choice, *had* died. They were not immortal after all, they were merely the vessels in which the immortality had resided for a while.

Immortality is not a condition but a thing!

Why had he not thought of this before? If it were true it meant that Archan was no more immortal than the basilisks! If the thing that was immortality could be wrested from her then she was as vulnerable as a baby. *Could* it be taken from her and, if it could, where would it go?

She can *be defeated!*

Holding on to that thought, Jonah dipped into . . .

. . . *the rods in search of the basilisk ghosts.*

He found them almost immediately, six floating, reptilian shapes immersed in a tangle of glowing red filaments. They bobbed like corks in a fiery ocean then veered away, leading him deeper into the skein of memories.

. . . Wait! *Jonah called. He could feel his thoughts speeding through the rods like vibrations through the silk of a spider's web* . . . I must speak with you! Please wait!

But the ghosts hurried on, whispering to themselves, casting baleful looks back over phantom shoulders. His attention concentrated on their trail as they meandered both through and between the rods, Jonah was unaware whether he was travelling into the past or the future. Knowing the basilisks it was probably both.

Time flowed around him, undisturbed by his presence so gentle was his touch. He would change nothing, treat the rods not as clay but as conduit, merely a road to be travelled. He was skating over black ice and leaving not a scratch.

Just when he thought the ghosts would lead him on this chase back to the very beginning of time, one of them stopped and swivelled to face him. Jonah found himself staring into the featureless metal eyes of Ocher.

It was ugly and squat, the product of an unholy union between lizard and bulldog. Its primitive anatomy afforded it two arms and a long, prehensile tail. Sharp silver teeth sparkled in a wide and brutal mouth. It was also almost wholly transparent; in many ways, it was not even really there.

. . . This is an important moment, *said the basilisk ghost.*

Its words pounded through Jonah's body, making his ribs sing. It was not a voice but a drumbeat.

. . . You must help me defeat Archan, *Jonah replied.*

. . . Help requires knowledge. We know the parts but not the whole. The Maker alone knows the whole. Nevertheless this is an important moment. This moment is one of the parts. Ocher might say the most important of all.

. . . The Maker? Do you mean Mister Ren?

The basilisk waggled its head.

. . . You must experience this moment.

. . . What do you mean, what moment?

Jonah looked around him and realized the ghosts had led him to a specific place within one of the rods. A specific memory. He could smell smoke and ash and fire; he could hear rumbling explosions and falling trees. It all sounded terribly familiar.

. . . Krakatoa? *he asked, but the basilisk ghost shook its head.*

. . . Another mountain, another day. Both you will come to know.

There was another sound intermingled with the noise of the volcano: the steady thump of drums, the screaming voice of a woman. For a moment Jonah could not place it, then he had it.

. . . The song in the automobile! Mount St Helens! Coyote . . . why have you brought me here? I am chasing Mah Jongg marks, not delving into the pasts of my companions! I have already vowed never to do that again – it brings nothing but pain for all concerned.

. . . Enter the memory rod! Do it now! Learn a new truth about Thomas Coyote! You must know why he was fleeing the mountain.

. . . I know very well why he was fleeing the mountain! I should have thought it was obvious! He was fleeing the mountain because the mountain was hurling a billion tons of earth on top of him, and believe me I know what it feels like to have an erupting volcano on your tail!

. . . Memories lie, as you also know. This one does not. This one you must see.

. . . No! I refuse! If I enter the memory of Tom Coyote's last moments on the mountain I run the risk of changing them. No, Coyote is too close to me now, to all my friends, for me to risk the consequences. You of all creatures must understand the fragile reality you have constructed here on Stone. I do not need to go there!

. . . Amara is fragile, but that is its strength.

. . . Damnation! Must you always talk in riddles?!

To his surprise the ghost lowered its head. It exhaled, phantom breath billowing around its jaws.

. . . Ocher would beg forgiveness. What you see does

not represent what the basilisk was: this form is as feeble in mind as it is in body. Thoughts in this form are . . . disordered. This is less a spirit than a reflection. Less a memory than an imprint. Fossil mind. Petrified. Like a fossil it retains the shape but not the essence. Riddles occur but they are not intended.

Jonah sighed. He felt little pity for the ghost, but he did feel regret that he was not able really to appreciate the basilisks. Compared to what they had once been this wraith was little more than a vegetable.

. . . Listen to me, *he said with as much patience as he could muster* . . . You talk of fossils. I have learned the futility of drawing things from the past – books, people, knowledge. In the end they all fossilize, they petrify. They turn to stone. I will not interfere with the memories of Tom Coyote, not without good reason. But I do ask your help – no, I *demand* your help on another matter. The reason I came to find you is this: I must know if there are other places on Stone where you have hidden Mah Jongg symbols than those I have already located. *Are* there any others? Please, you must tell me.

The ghost of Ocher considered this for long moments.

. . . If the information is shared, will you then explore the memory of Coyote?

. . . You do not give up easily, do you? Listen – if you tell me what I need to know, then I will consider – *consider* mind you – the possibility of investigating Tom Coyote's memories. But I will do so only if it is proved to me to be vital to our mission to destroy Archan, and even then only as a last resort. And even *then* I will only observe. I will touch nothing, change nothing, bring back nothing. Do you understand?

. . . Your words are clear. Proof may be forthcoming.

. . . In which case I will keep my word. I am a man of honour.

The ghost of Ocher glanced behind it as if seeking its lost siblings. Then it exercised its long, silvery claws while regarding them with the intense scrutiny of a child performing mental arithmetic.

. . . Seventeen locations remain, including two at Sunlight Pass. All can be accessed using the memory rods, except the two at Sunlight Pass. Those can only be approached in the flesh. Here.

Grasping one of the shorter claws sticking out sideways from its wrist (like an Iguanodon's thumb-spike, Jonah recalled), the ghost snapped it off at the base. Jonah winced at the sharp sound.

As the broken claw was held out to him it solidified; he snatched it up just as it began to sink through the ghost's transparent flesh.

. . . The locations are encoded in the claw. Use the knowledge well. And remember your promise.

. . . An Englishman's word is his bond.

The basilisk ghost withered into the air like cigar smoke. It did not even say goodbye. Jonah turned too, clasping the claw against his chest and . . .

. . . rising back into his body in the charm-mill. He stretched, yawning. The backs of his eyes were aching and his mouth felt dry and tasted awful.

Clutched in his right hand was the basilisk claw, hard and smooth and undeniably real. He had no doubt that, given a month or two, it too would turn to stone.

Embedded into it – and quite open to his charm-heightened awareness – was a multi-dimensional map of the remaining Mah Jongg locations, scattered across the surface of Stone like meteorite strikes. Most were distributed seemingly at random.

— Three struck him as odd however. They appeared to be cut directly into the surface of a badly twisted section of memory rod. Also they were very close together. There was something different about this tight little triangle of marks, he was sure of it.

None of the locations was familiar to him; all of them (except the two of course, at Sunlight Pass) appeared to be quite accessible.

'Well, Jonah Lightfoot,' he said to the room, 'you have plenty of places to visit, so you had better start right now!'

As he lifted the bowl of tiles again he acknowledged that, however pathetic the basilisk ghosts might be, he would never have found the remaining locations without them. And as he dropped back into the netherworld of the memory rods to place the next tile, he found a single thought lodged in his mind like a pebble in a shoe.

If immortality is taken from Archan, who will have to bear it next?

An unerring compass, Ocher's claw took him far and wide, forwards and backwards through time, around and along the dimensions of Stone to hidden corners where inscrutable symbols lay waiting in forgotten corners.

A tiny Two Character lodged behind a lightning-struck tree.

An East Wind scratched into the underbelly of a dormant, many-headed serpent.

A cluster of adobe buildings that, viewed from afar, were arrayed in the shape of the Seven Bamboo.

These scenes and more adhered to the near-vertical skin of Stone, and into each of them Jonah Lightfoot placed a precious tile. As he did so he disturbed nothing. He was himself a ghost, less even than a breath on the breeze. He changed nothing.

One was a flower tile – the Orchid – and it was fitting that the place set aside for it was inside the head of a giant orange bloom, fully twelve feet tall and jutting from a piece of Stone made from highly compacted soil. Tiny landslides broke out periodically, only to be caught by clusters of these enormous flowers. Jonah floated like an invisible bee before its huge stamen, applying his secret pollen. The sun beat against him and it felt like summer.

In this way he filled twelve of the seventeen spaces pin-pointed by Ocher's claw. For the time being he held back the Triad (as he had christened the three rogues clustered on the twisted memory rod). Something kept him from placing these just yet, a sense that they were special.

Which left only the pair of tiles to be used in the endgame at Sunlight Pass itself. The pair of tiles Annie had started painting on their last night on the ocean and which she had not yet finished: Red Dragon and White Dragon, the serpent twins.

There were still the tiles for the doors on the Bark however, over fifty of them. His eyes glazed as the dream washed over him again: a great migration of ivory blocks, tumbling end over end. Too many to count, too many to keep track of. For a moment he lost all sense of what he was doing and why. Then his head cleared and he went on.

A place for each and each in its place. One by one, steady as she goes.

The lesky helped. Jonah would delve into the bowl and bring up a tile, which Grandfather Tree would tut over for a few seconds. Then invariably his green eyes would light up and with a cry of, 'Follow me!' or 'Ah ha!' or frequently both, he would slide away down a series of twisting corridors with Jonah in hot pursuit.

Having arrived at the door, the lesky would watch gravely from whichever wall he was embedded in at the time while Jonah touched the tile against the matching pattern in the wood. Then the lesky would cry, 'Next!' and off they would go again.

As the last of the door tiles slipped into position, Jonah heard the click-rasp of Coyote's camera again. The tall man was standing in a hatchway at the far end of the corridor, dark against the daylight bleeding in from outside. He raised his hand in an informal salute and ducked back out of sight.

'Grandfather Tree,' said Jonah, 'what do you make of our passenger? What I mean to say is, do you observe him when he is out of sight of the rest of us? Does he do anything . . . unusual?'

'Ha! Do I spy on him, you mean!'

'Well . . . oh, for heaven's sake, yes, if you like! Well?'

Grandfather Tree grinned. A broad trail of brambles erupted from one corner of his mouth; he crushed the berries between mobile lips before they could escape and sucked up the juice.

'Ye, watch him I do. Annie's warning I heard. I take it seriously too.'

'Very well then – what have you observed?'

'Nothing.'

'Nothing?'

'Ye, nothing. Coyote – he does nothing but sit. Sometimes he walks. Often he works his camera-box. Boring he is . . . outside at least.'

'Hmm. But what about inside?'

'Lesky cannot say.' Grandfather Tree paused, scrutinizing his human companion. 'Jonah Lightfoot could, had he a mind to.'

'No!' he snapped at once. 'I do not have a mind to! I refuse to invade Tom Coyote's memories! He may be good, he may be bad, but his mind is his own.'

'Forgive a foolish lesky, Jonah! It was a notion, that's all, just a rustle in the leaves.'

'All right. And that is how it will stay.'

The lesky looked so forlorn that Jonah could not stay angry with him for long. Glancing back into the bowl he decided to change the subject.

'There are only these three left now, Grandfather Tree. I have been putting them off but I can do so no longer.'

'So, to the rods again!'

'Yes. And then I think I have earned a nice hot bath!'

Floating in blackness, free of his body but not fully transferred into Stone's realm of memory, Jonah pondered the Triad.

Green Dragon. A complex jumble of strokes in which his Western eyes saw the profile of a man wearing a deerstalker hat. He had not met any green dragons on his travels so far, but no doubt there had been such creatures, once upon a time.

Eight Bamboo. A straightforward suit tile with eight narrow rectangles, each coloured in red, green and blue, representing small bamboo poles. It had no particular significance to him, although he had always found the configuration of the eight poles a little odd: they were positioned in two groups of four, one above the other. The top group resembled the letter 'W'; the bottom, its mirror image, resembled an 'M'.

One Circle. Another fundamental tile, the first of the Circle suit. Concentric circles. It looked like a rosette, or a church window.

They were no more or less mysterious than any of the other tiles in the Mah Jongg set.

Then why do I feel so apprehensive?

The other tiles had been scattered far and wide, but these were different. All three in a triangle, on the skin of a twisted memory rod.

'You gotta set the primer, Jonah,' he heard Annie say. 'Then we stand back and watch it all blow.'

For the first time since starting this peculiar task Jonah had a very real sense that Stone was a powder-keg.

No, not a powder-keg. A firework. A Chinese firework. What are those conical ones that spew out sparks and smoke? Roman candles? Just like miniature volcanoes . . .

The placement of the Green Dragon, the Eight Bamboo and the One Circle would not set off the explosives, oh no. It was not time for that yet. But he had a feeling he had been running out a line of gunpowder for a fuse for some time now and in placing these three tiles ... well, he believed that in placing them he would finally put a match to it. With the fuse lit the clock would be ticking. And nothing would stop it.

Belatedly he decided to look at the paintings on the reverse of the Triad tiles. On the back of the Green Dragon was a storm scene. There was no ground, only a sky filled with lightning. Slashes of rain sparkled like crystals. On the back of the Eight Bamboo was a field of gold and a rough sod house. It was Annie's home in Kansas, a place he recognized from the times he had travelled there, courtesy of the memory rods of Stone. She must have painted it from memory, and quite recently too; he could not remember ever seeing it before.

The third tile, the One Circle, was an enigma. The painting was of a table-top, covered with paraphernalia: pencils, a blotter ... and a book. The book was open, its pages uplifted as though by a breeze. He did not recognize it at all.

Anxious not to waste any more time, Jonah pressed forward into Stone. Black walls peeled apart around him, admitting him into a deep, broad chamber. It was silent. Spanning the chamber were the memory rods; they looked to be lying horizontally, like fat tightropes, though Jonah knew they were slightly inclined, rising imperceptibly as they spiralled their way upStone. Closest to him was a rod with twice the girth of its neighbours. It was knotted, gnarled and ancient. On its slick, black skin were embossed three Mah Jongg symbols. Of course, they matched the tiles in his hand exactly.

Fortune favours the bold, *he thought.*

He stepped across the chamber and held up the Green Dragon. The memory rod chimed like a tuning fork. Jonah pressed the first tile in.

9

Frey

For a long time there was nothing but the pain. Frey
had no idea what was causing the pain, nor how long
he had been suffering. There was barely a consciousness
that qualified for the name 'Frey'; there was only the
pain. Later came change. The pain did not diminish, but
now Frey found himself clutching at the tiniest strand
of self-awareness, like a drowning man waking to find
himself clinging to a floating branch. To cling was to live,
so cling he did. His name became his life-raft.

Frey. I am Frey!

He was well-practised at inflicting pain on others, so
he cast around for some wretched soul with whom to
share it. But there was nobody. Just him, locked inside
his own mind.

I was unconscious. Now I am awake.

Basic thoughts, the most basic of all. But thinking them
was like moving a mountain. Tentatively he explored.
Though he was awake again much of his mind was
closed to him; it was like returning home to find most
of the rooms locked and barred. Those parts he could
touch were filled with pain.

My leg! Something has cut off my leg!

He remembered bird-shapes diving through a thick red
sky. All his skin was scorched. That was by far the worst:

he felt flayed. His eyes were nearby but he could not see out of them. They were open, he could sense that much, but something else was looking through their windows.

The dragons!

Memory burst open, a room he had thought locked but whose door had just given way. He cringed as he fell in through the open doorway, each memory a new agony.

A dragon controls my body! And it in turn is controlled by a second dragon, its master but also . . . its sister?

Much was hidden behind dragon barricades but this fact they had not bothered to conceal.

Sisters!

The dragons had possessed his body, but Frey understood that it was a delicate balance. Too heavy a hand and he would collapse under the strain; too weak and he might regain enough strength to expel the invaders.

But why keep my mind alive at all, if my body is all they need?

There could be only one answer.

If my mind dies my body dies too. They need me!

The knowledge gave him power, which was why they had surrounded him with pain.

Back to the pain, always back to the pain.

Enough pain and he would be incapacitated, unable to process even the simplest thought let alone construct a plan. Frey understood both pain and power well: he had used both throughout his life, and to great effect. But again it was a balance. Too much pain and the most basic, vital functions might begin to shut down. He might, for example, forget how to breathe. Too little . . .

Before they noticed how aware he was he let out a colossal scream. There was no sound of course, not really, but in his tortured mind he heard his cries reverberate around the dark bone cave that had become his prison cell. Having yelled long and hard he whimpered for a while, one imaginary ear cocked to gauge the dragons' response. There was laughter. That was good. As long as he screamed he was clearly in pain. As long as he was in pain he was clearly no threat. He screamed some more and listened some more. He listened to the dragons bickering behind their barricades. Most of all he listened to the silence beyond, for he had begun to formulate a plan.

Frey had never been one to ask for help, but right now he thought he probably needed some. And he had a crazy idea he knew who to ask.

Frey had been the first shaman of his tribe to understand the true nature of magic. His predecessors had made a great show of their powers, communing with the unseen spirit world and working medicine both good and evil, but they had been frauds every one, and they had known it. Theirs was a tradition not of sorcery but sleight-of-hand.

The shamans had been fakes even when the tribe of Late Neolithic human beings known as the Denneth had lived on the Earth, in the icy region that would one day be known to Jonah Lightfoot as Norway. They continued to be fakes when the concept of *tribal master* melted into the concept of *king* and one of the earliest monarchies was formed. They remained fakes even when a dense volcanic cloud suffocated half the tribe and nudged the other half across the gap between worlds. Only when they had been on Stone for several generations did a shaman come along who understood that here, on this great wall of a world, the magic was real. He was Frey.

One of his most spectacular feats in his days as shaman was the capture of the dragon Torus. After drugging and torturing the hapless beast, after extracting scales and spines from every part of the creature's body, Frey constructed for himself a set of charm-powered wings. Even after the beast had escaped the wings remained

Frey's pride and joy, justification for his role as medicine man and spiritual advisor to the king and his people. They were all the proof he needed that he could work the charm.

But one thing continued to puzzle Frey. The magic was real enough – any fool could see that – but what about the spirits?

The legends of the Denneth were as old as the tribe – older, some said. As shaman, Frey was their guardian and, like most of his predecessors, he had always regarded this particular duty as mere storytelling. The relating of fiction to ease a troubled soul. The perpetuation of myth. But if Stone had made the magic real, might it not have done the same to the spirits? Were they here too?

He thought about the spirits through the pain, imagining them not as advisors but as rescuers, avenging angels descending to free him from the dragons' grasp. Almost immediately his innate scepticism rose up.

The spirits are not real! You told the king and his fools they were and like fools they believed you, but you never heard their voices as you said you did!

But this was Stone, where the magic was real, and Frey knew that somewhere on this mighty wall the spirits were real too. All he needed to do was call to them and they would come.

Not that it was an enticing thought for, according to legend (and Frey knew *all* the legends – as a shaman that was his job), the spirits were a pretty unfriendly bunch. Like the Denneth they had evolved over time, changing from aethereal mountain-ghosts and sky-spectres into rather more tangible forms. In recent years the spirits had begun to develop recognizable and quite elaborate characters. They were in fact becoming gods.

There was Ordin, for instance, to whom a warrior might pray before a battle. Once a faceless and formless spirit-of-the-dead he was now the head of a sprawling family of gods and demi-gods. A poet now as well as a warrior, he was much less predictable than his generally sympathetic ancestor. If a tribesman prayed to him before battle Ordin was as likely to cut off a supplicant's head as lend strength to his sword-arm. And as for Loké – he had disposed of any number of his fellow gods and was reputed to have even less affection for mortal men. The gods fought constantly, both with each other and with the various monsters against which fate had pitted them: Ferrir and Ymir and Rok.

As gods went they were wholly unreliable, but Frey believed that if he prayed to them they would come. The magic was real, and so were the gods. The gods might bring him the strength to overthrow the dragons. The gods might be just as happy to kill him, but at least he would still be rid of the dragons. And the pain.

Either way he would be free.

One of the dragons called to him from behind a barricade of ice.

'Faery! Do you wish to see where you are?'

Why were they talking to him? Before he could ponder this his sight was returned to him, a devastating explosion of light. He screamed, not for effect this time but in sheer terror. For a moment he thought the shock would kill him.

He reeled, then recovered. The view was blurred: his eyes were damaged and would never again bring the world into proper focus. Nevertheless he could see light and shade, long splashes of cloud in a deep blue sky, the hulking solidity of Stone.

'W-where am I?' he said. He did not have to pretend to be weak.

'Journey's end,' replied the dragon voice. He had no idea if it was the intruder or the intruder's intruder.

'Almost, at least. After the hawk attack we thought it best to keep you unconscious. It seemed the easiest way to keep you alive. We have come far and now the final strand of the Helix lies directly overhead. Above it lies the very tip of Stone.'

'Why are you telling me this?'

'You tortured one of our kind, faery. That is an unforgivable crime. We want you fully aware as we conclude our journey. We want you fully aware as you suffer your just punishment. The pain you feel is a prelude. Now you will really start to hurt.'

Frey withdrew into the furthest recess of his prison cell. Had he thought himself capable of control? What a fool he had been! This was justice, his reward for a life of evil, for torturing the dragon had been but one of many crimes. He had administered a poisonous drug to his king that allowed him to manipulate the royal mind, making him, Frey, ruler in all but name. He had raised a daughter as his heir and, when she rejected him, murdered her in cold blood. He had killed people, or had them killed, for speaking ill of him behind his back. The blood of many men was on his hands and now he was going to pay.

Why had he done these terrible things? For the first time in his life he faced this question and found he had no answer. Then he realized this was the first time he had ever acknowledged his actions as terrible. The realization made him scream louder than he ever had with the pain.

When he recovered a modicum of control he scolded himself for his self-pity. Given his life to live again he would act in just the same way. And in the meantime he was still in acceptable shape. The dragons wanted him to suffer, therefore the dragons still needed him alive. Therefore he still had time to turn the situation round.

But he needed help.

*   *   *

180

Frey recommenced his prayers in earnest, calling to both new gods and old spirits. He called to Ordin, father of the gods. He prayed Thor would bring Mjollnir the hammer to smash the dragons flat. He named a hundred names, calling them to him, desperate to believe in them but still, somewhere, harbouring grave doubts that they existed at all.

Don't be a fool! he warned himself. *If you are faithless they will not come. The magic is real – so are they!*

But still true faith eluded him. So he resorted to a tactic with which he felt more comfortable: bribery and lies.

If you come to my aid, he called, while at the back of his mind lurked one of the more obscure legends he had related to wide-eyed children back in the castle of the Denneth, *I will give you a prize!*

He listened to his thoughts in panic as the prayer unspooled itself. More occupied with shielding his thoughts from the dragons he had little time to ponder the wisdom of going out so far on such a slender limb.

Gods and monsters, he was thinking.

The gods feared nothing more than they feared the dreadful day of Rarnok, when their sworn enemies would rise up and engage them in a terrible final battle. From the blood of the slaughtered gods a new world would rise. They, in the end, were to be the sacrifices.

Gods and monsters . . .

The name came to him in a rush.

Ormungad! I will tell you the whereabouts of Ormungad the world-serpent, whom you could never find! Ormungad, who is destined to slay Thor with his poison and herald the end of all things at the end of all days. The world-serpent shall be yours! In return you have only to free me.

The children had loved the tales of Ormungad. Sworn enemy of the gods, the giant serpent lay dormant at the bottom of the deepest ocean, hiding from its foes until the final day of reckoning. The gods – Ordin in particular

– spent much of their time searching for this and other monsters. They believed the more they could kill before the day of reckoning the shorter the final battle would be. Ormungad was one of the few who constantly eluded them, which made the giant serpent the best possible bait with which to lure the gods to him.

Of course, in dangling such bait Frey was taking a tremendous risk. If the lord of the gods even sniffed the lie his wrath would be no less than that of the dragons.

But then, maybe Ormungad is real here too.

Frey supposed he had nothing to lose.

The dragons worked the wings attached to his back and together they rode up through the last section of the Helix. Typhoons ripped his tattered flesh and dragon charm was sent in to stem the blood-flow. The storm abated and Frey's body passed into total darkness.

It waited, wings flapping steadily, for the dawn. But the dawn did not come. All remained black, both Stone and sky. After waiting longer than they deemed wise the dragons consulted and agreed that the tip of Stone was a place where the sun simply did not shine. Frey paused in his prayers. The instant he stopped praying his gods replied.

10

Triad

Green . . .

. . . *dragon.*

Storm clouds puffed like ulcerous cheeks, spilling fire and water through their wounds, sky built to flatten the Earth, ground quickened by rain, new streams celebrating new life as electricity embraced the Crystal Palace.

Sydenham Hill, 1859.

A memory conducted by the rod.

So much light.

Metal bones alive with St Elmo's Fire, an epileptic aura, a lightning fork bolting realms together, rabbit-jumping up to meet its falling twin, ball lightning fizzing and forgetful in the epicentre of the Palace, an aimless flame unsure of which way to burn. Volts in motion, massive amps. Every flash of light like a tear in the walls that hold worlds back.

Tiny creatures flee the Palace. Two-legged, splattered with fickle storm-light, they run well, their gait a repetitive fall barely snatched from collapse by each successive step. One large, one smaller. Father and son. A third creature, the second son, watches, but this one is different. It has no body here, it is watching from afar, an uninvolved spectator. It watches as the running creatures pass beneath the shadow of a falling monster. Steel hoops bind the concrete. The monster has not lived for millions of years but it still has the power to kill.

Ghost-Jonah watches as the dinosaur crushes Henry and Albert yet again. No matter how many times he views the scene he is appalled.

He drifts closer, refusing to see the human shards poking from beneath the Iguanodon. Drifts round behind the monster, sees the markings on its exposed base. Buried in the soil since its construction – or perhaps since real Iguanodons walked the Earth – is the Mah Jongg sign he has been seeking. The dinosaur's flanks are streaked with mud; beneath the mud lies bright green moss.

Ghost-Jonah puts the tile in its place and the dinosaur comes to life. It lurches to its feet, contemplates the tiny humans it has demolished, then turns and looks down at ghost-Jonah. But even as it turns it is fading. A face bearing not a trace of humanity manages to look unutterably sad.

Henry and Albert have faded too, and the storm. But the light remains, a bright girder spanning Earth and sky. Between the two is Jonah, standing.

Although he is a ghost, Jonah feels his body thickening around him, enclosing him in its familiar fleshy embrace. Light is everywhere, storm-light. Blood cauldron-hot, eyes stinging at the light, hollow ears, the practised geometry of the joints in his legs, his fingertips. The darkness is gone but the light remains. The light is unbearable in its beauty. Reunited with his body, ghost-Jonah uses it to cry.

Eight . . .

. . . Bamboo.

Ghost-Jonah falls towards the sod house, all Kansas spread around him in the slender blue of moonlight. A new fence surrounds the home that Rance and Annie shared for so many years. Now it is later. Now, ghost-Jonah understands, it is now.

The house looks old but well-tended. The fence holds it, an unlikely jewel, in the centre of a modest crop. The farmstead looks . . . humble.

Ghost-Jonah slithers through the roof. Rance is home, the big man who beat his wife and gambled away his land. He sits in a shaft of moonlight at the worn table laying out cards, playing Patience. This is how he looks to ghost-Jonah now: patient. Ghost-Jonah draws near enough to look into Rance's eyes. He has variously felt pity, jealousy and fury for this man, but now there is nothing within him to reawaken those emotions.

Rance turns over the last card of the deck. It shows not a Deuce nor a King but the mirror-pattern of the Eight Bamboo. Rance does not seem to notice but ghost-Jonah does. Silent and invisible ghost-Jonah drops the matching tile on to the playing card, where it fades and becomes a ghost itself. Rance blinks, presses his fingers to his eyes then seems to see the card for the first time. It is the Queen of Hearts. Lifting it, he places it on the King, opening up a game that had looked certain to be over.

Beyond the window the moon is full.

Before he leaves, ghost-Jonah glances round the one room. Annie's mirror remains by the door though her reflection is long-gone; her quilt is on the bed. There is no shrine, but her presence has been maintained. Everything looks well-kept. Everything is where it should be. Moonlight spills across the floor.

Rance lives. Ghost-Jonah finds that he is pleased.

One . . .

. . . *Circle.*

Creaking sound. The tabletop smells of ink and copper, papers stained with what looks like red wine, miraculous writing instruments strewn. Five chrome balls hang from a steel frame like mirrored suns, clacking in twos and threes, rewriting the logic of momentum. A fist-sized stone with a dark, pitted surface acts as a paperweight. Tied round the stone is a label that reads, 'Meteorite Fragment – Siberia 1910'. His gaze lingers on it. The creaking is the screen door; beyond it, diced by the grille, a volcano has exploded.

Before the noise of the volcano consumes the creaking of the door a third sound intrudes. A wolf-roar, a thrash of gravel. Ghost-Jonah penetrates the door to see an automobile skidding down the mountain track. Bright green, already dulling with dust. Hard music bouncing in its wake. Coyote, going down the mountain.

Open amid the papers is a well-thumbed book of stories by a man called Dylan Thomas. Jonah has never heard of him. Beside the book the five chrome balls have stopped. Outside the window what has come out of the mountain is boiling closer.

The Mah Jongg symbol is hanging on the wall. The rug is round and dense and very beautiful. The mark of the One Circle is large, at least five feet in diameter, a dazzling sunburst, an eye drawing him deep into its centre. But its gaze and its pull are benevolent, and he welcomes them both. Raising his ghost-hand, ghost-Jonah places the third tile into the sun-shape on the Chinese rug. The pattern writhes then hangs quiet. The tile is gone. The circle, like the sun, abides. All is peaceful. The first round of placements is over, and Jonah has not yet wondered whose house this is.

11

Empty

Two days passed. Annie painted without stopping, not even sleeping. She painted tile after tile, recreating the ever-changing view out of the windows during the day and using her memory by night. Jonah urged her to rest but she said she could not.

'Something's driving me, Jonah. I can't stop 'til I stop.'

All he could do was watch the skin around her eyes grow dark and her hair turn lank and dull. The stack of tiles in Jonah's bowl grew and shrank, grew and shrank as he placed them in batches into the corresponding doors on the Bark.

Before being placed, each tile was dropped into an alcove to be dried by a delicate stream of charm. Grandfather Tree also helped by devising substitutes for the turpentine and linseed oil Annie had long since run out of, rich-scented syrups squeezed from his own fingers. She still had plenty of oil paint left, though the tubes themselves were stained and worn. But each completed painting sapped a little more of her energy, and by the time she was down to the last half-dozen tiles she looked grey.

Yet still she painted and still Jonah placed, until just two tiles remained.

The first tile was flecked with crimson and yellow,

an approximation of flames; the second was all cool blues and whites. Fire and ice. And in the centre of each was a stab of silver that might just have been an eye.

The two, the final two. The keystones.

Annie stared at them in their unfinished state for what seemed to Jonah like an age. Then, with a sudden smile, she rolled the tip of her finest sable brush into a puddle of white paint and dabbed a tiny highlight into each silver eye.

'Don't know why I didn't see it before,' she said. She leaned back and put the brush down.

'Is that all that remained for you to do?' said Jonah.

'Yep. That's all: just a little piece of the sun. That's all they needed. Now they're done.' She stretched. 'Now they're all done.'

The Bark continued to plough upwards, crossing world after world. Gerent sulked in his cabin, carving intricate animals from the lesky's apparently endless supply of hardwood; Malya stalked round the Bark's walkways and corridors like a caged animal, checking her armoury over and over again, cleaning blades that already shone like chrome, practising swings and thrusts against her own shadow.

Tom Coyote was prowling the vessel too, snapping away with his futuristic camera. Whenever he crossed paths with Jonah he would pat his pocket and speculate on how much money he would make when he got the pictures home. He had made a den for himself in an unused cabin, and hardly bothered the others at all. His habit of appearing unexpectedly round corners, camera at the ready, put Jonah a little on edge but otherwise he was no trouble at all.

As time went on Jonah observed that Gerent and Malya had started talking to each other again, a development he found encouraging even though the exchanges were mostly hostile.

'Gerent says I'm not to fight at all,' Malya grumbled one day. 'Says he should be the warrior, not me.'

Jonah was pleased that Gerent had said spoken to her at all. 'Gerent is no warrior. We both know that – *he* knows that. He is a thinker, a clever man. He solves problems with his brain, not his brawn.'

'He's brave!' said Malya. Jonah thought it perverse that she should leap so swiftly to his defence.

'Of course he is! I watched him fly out to rescue Grandfather Tree too, and in full view of the hawks. But he yearns for something to control, and in the absence of anything else he has decided it should be you.'

'Pah! He should know better!'

'He does. He just thinks too hard. Remind him that you love him, Malya. And look after him – I think Gerent needs protecting more than any of us. And there is something else . . .' but here he hesitated. Ancient Nordic eyes stared back at him, bright and transparent.

'Yes, Jonah Lightfoot?'

'Nothing, Malya. Except to say . . . none of us know how long we have together. If you still love him – and I believe you do – you should make your peace with him, before . . .'

'Before?'

'Before everything changes.'

Later that same day they all found themselves on the bridge together, all except Tom Coyote, towards whom the conversation turned.

'I have been imagining what it might be like to return home,' Jonah announced. 'It is Coyote who has made me think of it. Every time I see him he talks about what he will do when he gets home, when he sells his damnable photographs to the newspaper. He actually believes this:

that he will return home. Is it the same for any of you, my friends? Do you want to go home too?'

'My home is destroyed,' said Gerent. He no longer sounded angry, just sad. 'The castle I grew up in is no more. It is impossible to go back.'

'I do want to see Kansas again,' said Annie. 'But as for going back for good . . . I don't know. Do we have the choice?'

Jonah rubbed his eyes. 'I do not know. I suppose not. It is just that . . . well, I think about Kythe.'

Like Esh, the young dragon Kythe had been their travelling companion for a time. Having practically cast herself out from Stone's small and insular dragon community, she had come to yearn for the world where her race had its origin. In the end she had actually gone there, flying bravely through a rare form of threshold that allowed travel in that elusive direction – *back*.

'Kythe,' continued Jonah. 'If one dragon can find a way back to our Earth then perhaps we can too. If we choose to.'

'She didn't go back to her own time,' Annie reminded him. 'She ended up in her past, stuck on the Earth years before she was born. Gee, it was years before *any* dragon was born!'

'Yes, that is true . . . but nevertheless there was a way. And . . . oh, I cannot stop thinking about her!'

'You know what I think?'

'What do you think?'

'I think you're even more tired than I am.'

Jonah nodded but his head was filled with the sound of Kythe's dragon wings, measuring time with the beat of his heart. She had been at the back of his mind for so long but just now he could not get her out of his thoughts.

Grandfather Tree was weary too, noticeably slower in his tracking down of the matching door patterns. Resin dripped from his joints and his elfin face was growing more ancient with every hour that passed.

Around him the Bark too was suffering the ravages of repetitive crossings of the Helix. Walls showed signs of flaking, floors had contracted leaving gaping holes along exposed seams. The vessel was filled with cracks and creaks, the sounds of shrinkage and settlement. Many doors were sealed shut, and some of the strange organic machinery scattered through the various chambers had ceased to function.

'What is happening, Grandfather Tree?'

Breathless, the lesky pointed to the door they had just passed by. It was the door to the charm-mill; from behind it Jonah could hear the noise of valves opening and closing, wheels turning, a steady shower like distant hail.

'Is the Bark grinding charm again?'

'Ye, indeed. But the magic – sparse it is. High we are now, nearly at the top of Stone. The charm, it is . . . rarefied. Mountain air, fresh but thin. Bark struggles now. So Lesky, he struggles too.'

'Is that why we are all so exhausted? Because the charm is running out?'

'Partly, ye. Simple tiredness too. Your bodies – adapted to charm they are. To suddenly lose it . . . very shocking.'

'Will there be no charm at all at the summit?' Jonah was devastated. *No magic, no scent of spice!* Tears brimmed in his eyes.

'Can't say. Bark doesn't know, so Lesky doesn't know. Shall we find out?'

'Find out?' Jonah's eyes widened. 'Then we are nearly there?'

Grandfather Tree nodded his wrinkled old face, but he could not muster a smile. 'Ye, ye, nearly there. Passed the last coil of the Helix we have.'

'What?!'

Jonah raced down the corridor towards the nearest window. But though he ran there was no excitement, nor indeed any emotion at all beyond simple surprise. Had Stone's succession of worlds dulled his sense of wonder, destroyed his anticipation? They were here, at the very roof of all the worlds! It was a glorious moment!

So why did he feel cheated? Why was it such an anti-climax?

'You could have warned us we were near,' he said. He had reached a small round aperture in the hull wall. Now he peered into it, only to find the view obscured by a wooden shutter.

'Why?' The lesky seemed genuinely puzzled by Jonah's reaction.

'Oh, never mind. The final world. Well, Grandfather Tree, shall we look out upon it? Can you open this window?'

The shutter juddered to one side. Together they gazed out.

There was nothing outside, nothing at all. If this was Sunlight Pass then it was utterly black.

'Sun soon,' said Grandfather Tree. Then he confounded Jonah further by announcing that the Bark had almost run out of charm. 'Nearly gone it is. Can't fly, so land we must.'

'Can you land in this darkness?'

'Must.'

Once more they gathered on the bridge; once more Coyote was nowhere to be seen. The Neolithics, while not actually conversing, were at least not arguing; Annie was resting in the annex but rose as soon as Jonah came in.

Grandfather Tree spoke to them all from a knot of wood on the ceiling. Flight by charm, he explained, demanded colossal energies. By landing on Stone he could conserve what was left and use it to evolve the shape of the Bark into something that would transport them in a more economical fashion up this dark and final world. Up to the very tip of Stone.

'Spider-legs!' he explained. 'They served Bark once before; now they will again.'

There was a flurry of excitement as windows opened to display branches expanding from the hull's exterior. The sudden array resolved itself into twelve major growths centred on the Stone-side hemisphere of the Bark. Bulbous knots congealed into supple joints; green bark darkened and solidified into a mobile exoskeleton. These new legs jittered and reached, feeling for the surface of Stone. Light-charms flared at their tips, searchlight beams stabbing into the night.

For an age there was nothing to see, then suddenly Stone was approaching at a terrifying speed, visible only as fast-expanding highlights picked out by the moving beams of light. The Bark pitched forwards. The twelve spindly legs stretched, ready for contact.

The light-charms went out at the moment of impact. The Bark slowed like a swaying drunk; through the hull bled the sound of countless cracking knuckles. There was a lurch, then it was over. The Bark, no longer a flying machine, was clinging like an insect to the precipitous face of Stone's blackest realm.

Jonah asked Grandfather Tree to wait a moment before setting off on the long climb up the black wall.

'Do you know this world?' he said. 'You knew the world of the Fabricators – at least, you remembered it once we were under attack. What do you know of this place?'

Grandfather Tree, a cartwheel-sized wooden face hanging from the ceiling, managed to look shrivelled despite his prodigious size.

'No, Jonah. No knowledge of this place. Never been here. Nor has Bark.'

His face was fading. At first Jonah thought the lesky was melting back into the ceiling but then he realized he could no longer see the far side of the room.

A light charm dropped to the floor with a soft thud, like an apple falling from a tree. Another failed behind him. One by one the floating charms died, along with the phosphorescent panels set into the wall. The humans bunched together, united by their primitive fear of the dark.

'What is happening, lesky?' demanded Gerent.

'Don't know,' replied Grandfather Tree. All they could see of him now was the pale green glow of his eyes, but even they were dimming. 'Don't know this place. Wish we never came.'

'Is it Archan?' said Jonah. 'Has she arrived too?'

'No,' answered Annie. 'I'd know it. She's close though, very close.'

A hand found Jonah's – it was Malya's. He gripped it too hard and she yelped. At the same instant the last glimmer of light left them and the Bark was filled with the night.

The darkness inside was as total as that outside. Jonah had never known such blackness. He held his hand up: he could not see it. He brought it towards his face and was still looking for it when his fingers touched his nose.

'Gee,' whispered Annie, a disembodied voice immediately to his left, 'I'm spooked!'

After a brief scrabble Jonah found her hand and squeezed it.

'A world without light?' he said. 'Well, Grandfather Tree, I suppose it would be hard to forget a place like this. Are you ready to go?'

'As I'll ever be,' muttered the lesky. There was a scratching noise, then the floor vibrated and the knuckle-cracking sound resumed outside. They were underway again.

They sat down and talked – there seemed little else

to do. Jonah described the house on the mountain, the room with the table and the Mah Jongg rug on the wall, and asked Annie how she had come to paint it.

'I'm sorry, Jonah,' she said. 'I remember painting it – kind of – but I was damn tired at the time. I don't know where it came from. I never saw the place before in my life.'

'Yes, I had a feeling that might be your answer. I am convinced it is a place from our future, from the year 1980 to be precise. I am sure the volcano erupting outside was Mount St Helens, and I am equally sure the green automobile driving away at speed was a Jeep Cherokee driven by our very own Thomas Coyote.'

'So? What does it mean?'

'That is what I do not know. There was something on the table that caught my eye however – well, several things caught my eye, but the one that particularly attracted me was a stone, a meteorite in fact.'

'A meteorite?' asked Gerent. 'What is that?'

'A rock that drops out of the sky,' explained Annie. 'They come down occasionally on Earth. Some folk call them falling stars.'

'I'd like to see a star,' sighed Malya.

'Come to Kansas and I'll show you a bucketful.'

Jonah smiled: the invisible voices were soothing, more like thoughts than sounds. Thoughts alive in the night. 'Yes,' he put in, 'falling stars. This fallen star looked very familiar too me – it reminded me of something.'

'How could you have seen a rock from 1980?'

'The label said it fell to Earth in 1910, but that is irrelevant. No, it was similar – not identical but similar – to the rock I found in the crater, not long after we had left Ruane. Do you remember? When we stopped to pick the fruit that looked like bananas and tasted like cornbread?'

'So?' groaned Annie. 'What in hell's name does *that* mean?'

'I wish I knew. I feel . . . I feel it has something to do with . . .'

One of the doors to the bridge crashed open, admitting an unexpected stream of light. The corridor outside was brilliant, forcing them to screw up their eyes. A tall man wavered in the fierce glare, one arm raised to his head, feet planted wide apart.

'You gotta see this!' boomed Tom Coyote.

'I was on deck,' he explained, his left hand still pressed against the side of his brown, bald head, 'and it just flew in!'

In his right hand he held the camera, with which he took the occasional snapshot of the thing lying in the corridor.

'It was like this: I was just sat there, looking out into all that darkness, except you can't really look at anything when it's that dark. Then I saw this light burning so bright I thought my eyes'd bust clean out of my head. I had to look away, and when I looked back I could see things floating about round the light, just shadows really but they looked huge, only they were miles away. It was kinda weird. Anyway, I watched with my eyes watering while the Bark moved on past, and then suddenly there was this streak of light coming towards the ship. Well, I ducked right down I can tell you, I didn't know what it was – coulda been a laser beam for all I knew. So this thing shot past like a bullet, and just as it went past there was a kind of buzzin', like an angry hornet, and then a little piece of the light flew right towards me and I jumped back through the hatch but it followed me in. I ran on down the corridor and it was slidin' after me like a great wet fish, spittin' out light and sparks and Christ knows what. Just as I got to here it slithered to a halt and that's when I burst in on you. So what do you think? Weird, ain't it?'

Weird it was, as everyone agreed.

On the floor of the corridor, immediately outside the bridge entrance, was a thin sliver of glowing material. It did look remarkably like a fish, or at least a piece of fish, since the ragged entrails spilling from one side suggested it had been recently gutted.

There were no markings or features such as eyes or gills but along its length were several clearly discernible fins; a flattening at the far end hinted at what might once have been a tail. It buzzed like a dying bee, a noise that soon trailed into silence. Whatever internal light source it possessed was beginning to fade; Jonah guessed that within half an hour the darkness would return.

'Do you have any explanation for what you saw?' he asked Coyote. He could hear a faint grinding noise. The tall man shook his head and took another photograph.

'Nope. The giants – if that's what they were – sounded like they were squabbling though. Maybe they were arguin' over this.'

Gerent knelt down and started to examine the strange thing on the floor. Jonah could not decide whether it was a creature or a plant, or something between. Certainly organic, it was like nothing he had ever seen before.

Annie crouched next to him. Jonah, however, could not keep his eyes off Coyote.

Coyote was agitated. Tiny marbles of sweat had formed on his hairless scalp. His hand was stroking the side of his head, spreading the sweat like a paste. Jonah realized the noise he had heard was coming from Coyote's mouth: it was his teeth grinding together.

'What . . .' he began, but he got no further.

Coyote's eyelids fluttered and he stumbled back against the wall. His left hand beat against his head; his right hand fumbled with the camera, then dropped it. The camera tumbled through the air and crashed to the floor. The door at the back flew open, exposing its workings.

Jonah had never seen the inside of the camera before, but Coyote had explained how it worked so precisely that he knew at once it was empty.

There was no film in it at all.

Coyote recovered himself almost immediately, pulled himself back up to his prodigious height and bent down to pick up the camera. He stopped, registered what had happened and turned to see Jonah staring down at him. Jonah saw the lie first form on his face and then depart. Then Coyote's face changed almost beyond recognition. The expression of unadulterated rage into which it collapsed was so extreme that it hardly looked like the same man at all. For an instant it looked like an animal.

A wolf, thought Jonah in horror.

Grimacing, an extraordinary caricature of his former self, Coyote swept up the broken camera and hurled it at Jonah's head. Malya was already leaping to her feet as Jonah side-stepped the missile, but Gerent was quicker. He shouldered her out of the way, only to have Coyote kick his feet out from under him.

The Neolithic man went sprawling backwards; Coyote followed, moving so fast he caught Gerent before he hit the ground. He punched him three times in the face then yanked Gerent's sword from its scabbard and held it against his captive's belly.

'Follow me and you'll be slippin' in his guts!' he snarled. Spittle sprayed on to the floor.

Malya drew her sword and lunged for him, but he stumbled backwards, turning Gerent into a human shield. Malya narrowly missed disembowelling her former lover herself. Hissing she tracked Coyote's insane eyes with the point of her sword.

'Don't follow me! Coyote grunted. His voice had dropped an octave. 'I mean it!'

With astonishing speed he dragged the semi-conscious Gerent away down the corridor, the Neolithic's head lolling like a drunk's. Malya was about to leap after him when Jonah grabbed her shoulder. She rounded on him, murder in her eyes.

'Wait!' he said. 'We must stop to think about this.'

'Think about what?' she roared. 'Stay if you want but I'm going after them.'

She was halfway down the corridor when Jonah said, 'You promised me!'

Malya stopped, light from the fish-thing dancing on her sword. 'What do you mean?'

'You pledged me your sword. You said you were my servant.'

Slowly, very slowly, she turned to face him. Her whole body was shaking. 'Don't do this to me, Jonah Lightfoot. Please, don't do this to me.'

'Come back, I beg you. If you want to help Gerent you must come back now. If you rush after them Coyote will kill him.'

'You *beg* me?'

'I . . . I command you.'

Malya's shoulders slumped, though her eyes remained fierce. 'You bastard!'

'Grandfather Tree!' said Jonah. 'Can you see where they have gone?'

For a moment there was no response, then the lesky dipped a sheepish head out of the ceiling.

'Gone, ye. They have gone below.'

'Where, exactly?'

'Exactly, um . . . well, when you say exactly . . .'

'Lesky!' growled Malya.

'So little charm,' said the lesky. 'Try to explain I did. Many things lesky could do before but can't do now. Not enough charm to fly – hardly enough to climb now. Much of Bark is . . . in winter. Hibernating, you might say.'

'In winter? What do you mean?' said Jonah.

'Saving energy. Bark – his lower half is blind and deaf,

cold and powerless. Dead weight it is, though dead it isn't. Go there I cannot. That is where Coyote has taken Gerent.'

Malya gripped Jonah's shoulder and turned him away from the morose tree spirit. 'The lesky cannot help us. We are wasting time. We must go after them ourselves.'

'And risk facing a madman in the dark?' Jonah was about to say more when he noticed the camera lying broken on the floor, light from the abandoned fish-form shining off its steel case.

It was empty all the time!

'Malya, give me just a few moments more. Then we will go after them, I promise you. But we have to know exactly what we are up against. There is more to this Tom Coyote than meets the eye and it is high time I found out what it was.'

'How are you . . . ?'

'Just a few moments. I am going to do something I should have done before, when the basilisks first showed me the way. I want to find out exactly what Tom Coyote was doing on the side of an erupting volcano. I want to find out who he really is.'

Malya cast a desperate look at Annie.

'Lightfoot!' She was both impatient and exasperated. 'There isn't time for you to be . . .'

. . . arrowing towards the white shingle house nestled among the pines. The Cherokee was parked in the drive, green paintwork caked with dust. In the back of the vehicle were piled sheaves of paper. Two cameras lay on the passenger seat.

Jonah skirted round the vehicle, confirming it was the same one they had seen Coyote standing on when he had broken through to Stone. Then he turned to the house.

A man was standing before the screen door. He was lowering his hand, having just knocked on the timber post supporting the side of the porch. Round his neck was slung a third camera, a

Pentax. His hair was long and blond, down to his shoulders. Another man answered the door. Bald and weather-beaten.

Tom Coyote, inside the house.

The blond man introduced himself to Coyote. Jonah drifted closer so he did not mistake the words.

'Howdy, Tom. Hope you don't mind me droppin' in on you again like this. I just wondered if you'd reconsidered my offer. Like I said, the Tribune'll pay handsomely for your story. Hell, you might even be a celebrity, get on the talk shows.'

Coyote furrowed his brow and touched his hand to his head in a gesture with which Jonah was all too familiar.

'If the question's the same then the answer's the same. Just go away and leave me alone.'

'Just a few pictures then, Tom?'

The blond man raised the camera and Jonah heard the click-whirr of the shutter.

But something else happened too: there was a dazzling flash from a small box fixed to the top of the camera. It splashed Coyote's face with hard white light and for an instant Jonah imagined he could see his skull leering through from beneath the flesh.

The skull of a wolf!

Coyote's face changed, just as it had changed in the corridor on the Bark. He lunged forward and tore the camera from the blond man's grip. The strap tangled round its owner's neck, drawing a livid red friction burn across the skin. Coyote pulled hard on the strap and hauled the photographer through the door and into his house.

His house! *Jonah realized.* This is Coyote's house. The blond man is the journalist, not Coyote.

But if that was true, who was Coyote? Ghostlike, Jonah slipped through the wall.

The two men were grappling before the Chinese rug; the journalist's eyes bulged as Coyote wound the camera strap twice around his throat and tugged. A guttural croak fell from his lips and his arms thrashed. Coyote's face was screwed into the same wild expression he had worn while dragging Gerent away into the depths of the Bark. A web of saliva had clotted his lower jaw.

Coyote yanked on the strap for one last time and the journalist fell, first bouncing off the side of the desk and then hitting the floor. His head smacked an iron doorstop shaped like a toad but Jonah knew he was already dead.

Coyote stared down at the body. His expression switched from one of fury to one of . . . resignation? The speed of the change was astonishing and Jonah felt the first glimmer of understanding. He also felt exposed: he was floating barely three feet from his Coyote. He felt just as he had during the encounter with Gerent beside the corpse of Esh. His silent heart seemed loud in his ears and he had to fight the urge to flee.

He must not see me! He must not know I am here!

He need not have worried. Coyote not only looked straight through Jonah, he walked straight through him too, marching over to slam shut the door. Then, eyes downcast, he hauled the body of the journalist through a small, immaculate kitchen and out into the back yard.

The yard was small, but it gave on to dense woodland. Coyote dragged the body on up the slope, disappearing into the trees. Jonah suspected the body, once buried, would never be found. Then he remembered this was the side of an active volcano. Coyote could have left the body propped in the chair at the desk and still escaped a murder conviction.

Murder! The man is a murderer!

While Coyote was busy in the woods, Jonah surveyed the front room. There was the Chinese rug hanging on the wall, there the desk with its clutter, all just as he remembered them from his previous visit. The only difference was this time he had arrived earlier. Any minute now Coyote would return and drive off in the journalist's Cherokee, the same vehicle he would later claim as his own, just as he would claim the journalist's identity as his own. When he came back from the woods he would no doubt have the camera hanging around his neck.

Jonah lingered by the desk. Outside the house, Mount St Helens was bracing itself. Jonah looked at the book. It was open at a story called 'The Peaches'. Something about Indians.

Beside the book the cat's cradle of steel balls was clacking out its symmetrical rhythm, set in motion by the impact of the journalist's body with the desk. Then there were the meteorite samples.

Jonah looked at it all, sensing a connection, a fundamental truth about Coyote. He could not tear his eyes away from the nearest meteorite. Making his hand partway solid he reached out and touched its pitted surface. It was cold and rough.

It found its place on Earth, *Jonah thought.*

Outside, the volcano erupted.

12

In Coyote – 1

Everything was dark and that suited Tom Coyote just fine. The latest fugue was over, and he was pretty certain the White Wolf hadn't killed anybody this time. For now he was content just to sit here in the dark and try and find his place again.

Something was weighing on his legs, which were stretched straight out in front of him. Something hard was supporting his back, probably a wall. The object on his legs was man-heavy and breathing, so he guessed it had to be a man.

There was something draped over them both. A cape? A blanket? *Wings!* Yes, it was Gerent, the Neolithic bird-warrior who didn't really look like a warrior at all.

The girl though, she's a real Amazon. Blonde hair cropped short, beautiful hair. Beautiful body too. What I wouldn't give to . . .

He stopped the thought. It was the kind of thought that could bring on another fugue. Holding back the White Wolf was second nature but having to do so frustrated him, made him angry. It was a fine line between anger and fugue, and this was the line along which Tom Coyote walked every day of his life.

He'd been seventeen years old when he'd been told he had multiple personality disorder. Well, that was something he didn't need any fancy trick cyclist to tell him. His mind might be cross-wired but it was very clear to him how it functioned: there was him and then there was the White Wolf, who didn't come out very often.

'No, that's not quite right,' they'd said to him. 'The real Thomas Coyote is buried behind both these personalities. Won't you help us rescue him?'

'No, I won't,' he'd answered. Then he'd run away, a long way away, taking the White Wolf with him.

The White Wolf wasn't very nice at all. The White Wolf (and only Tom himself knew *this* truth) killed people, although he'd killed only one girl before the psychiatrist had gotten a hold of him. Barely two months had passed after his flight from the Las Vegas hostel before he killed two more.

It's having to control myself all the time, he told himself. *Makes me edgy, snappy. Makes me angry!*

He was angry now, mostly because the alternate personality was still close by. The White Wolf was growlin' and prowlin', hidden in the undergrowth but as ready as ever to bite. He'd been told it was unusual for an MPD to have such a clear understanding of his condition, that he was lucky to have an alter that was so self-aware. He didn't think he was lucky at all. He thought the whole situation was shitty. And that made him pretty angry too.

It's not even like I get to be Mild-Mannered Guy and Bad Guy. More like Bad Guy and Even Worse Guy.

And as for all that bullshit about there being another Thomas Coyote underneath it all – the *real* Thomas Coyote, hallelujah! – that was all such a crock.

Such self-pity was common after his fugues. He brooded on the killings: although he remembered nothing of the actual murders he recalled the aftermaths well enough. The White Wolf had a nasty habit of performing the wet work and then ducking into the trees again, leaving poor old Tom to clear up the mess. Admittedly the most recent victim, the blond journalist, hadn't left much of a mess, but some of the others . . .

There had been nine altogether, including the journalist. He hadn't been like the others but he was just as dead. It was testament to Tom's clear-headedness that he had never even been accused of murder, let alone convicted. The other eight had been women, all blonde. If they had short hair that was fine; if they had long hair he killed them first then shaved their heads. A pattern, of course, but there was nothing particularly weird about it. His psychiatrist would've had a field day if he'd known about it, but it was simple enough to Tom Coyote: the White Wolf just liked blonde girls with short hair. It wasn't like it made him a serial killer or anything.

He'd travelled a lot, that had saved him most times, and the girls he'd picked had come from the roughest parts of the various towns through which he'd toured. Not that they wouldn't have been missed by someone, he supposed. Eight years on the road, travelling from the west coast to the east and most of the way back again; eight years and eight girls.

Then he'd settled for a while in a little shack high up on the eastern slope of Mount St Helens and suddenly three years had passed without the White Wolf rearing its head at all. It was there that Tom started to believe there might be an answer to all this.

This place, he thought. *It's this place.*

It was a good place. A Feng Shui sort of place as the Chinks might put it. He earned money cutting wood and building fences and bought himself a Chink carpet and hung it on the wall. He bought himself executive toys and soothing incense burners, all designed to relax him, decrease his stress, calm his anger. Keep the wolf from the door.

He bought books and read them. He bought a second-hand telescope and became fascinated with meteorites. Over the years he built quite a collection of meteorites. They were stones from space that had come to Earth. They knew where they belonged. They'd found their place. Gradually he'd started to believe he might be able to live a normal life.

Then the journalists started sniffing around. Not interested in him, luckily, but in the mountain. But a nuisance all the same. Change was in the air, and worse than that: the rest of the world was watching. The mountain was going to blow, and the world was watching. Tom Coyote was in danger of losing his home and all the world was ready to watch him do it. Ready to watch him fall back down from grace.

They knocked on his door, day after day. All the journals, from the local rags to the Seattle dailies to *National Geographic*. Most of them wanted to cast him as the grumpy hermit who wasn't moving off the mountain for all the tea in China.

Grumpy's right, he thought. *Hell, you want to see me when I'm really mad!*

He tried to calm himself, staring for hours on end at the endless tap-tap-tap of the Newton's Cradle, reading his poetry and his favourite short stories (he'd never gotten on with novels, too long-winded). For a while he thought he'd managed to keep the White Wolf at bay. Then the blond guy from the *Seattle Times* called.

By the third visit Coyote was sick of the sight of him. What's more, he'd just had a call from the *National Geographic* photographer holed up a little way down the mountain saying today was the big day and he'd better get the hell out of there. Everything was coming to a head; the whole day seemed somehow . . . *pinched*.

The knock at the door – just a simple knock on wood! – sent his heart hammering through the wall of his chest.

But it was the flash of the camera, the first picture the Seattle guy had actually managed to take of him, that finally brought the White Wolf back out of the woods.

And as soon as the White Wolf opened his jaws . . . well, he just did the thing he does best of all.

Everything after that had happened on a kind of Tom Coyote autopilot, from the hiding of the body to the stealing of the journalist's Cherokee when the mountain exploded. Everything moved in a kind of homogenized flow, everything melting together, a delicious run of chance and coincidence that included Tom's favourite band – Blondie – being lodged in the Cherokee's cassette machine. After all that, a trip to another world was just like another day at the office. The years of peace were over, the fugues were back in town and everything was up for grabs. So what if he'd fallen through a wormhole and ended up in Oz? The White Wolf had returned and it was time to be angry again.

13

Prisoners

'. . . crawling through that man's past! We've got to get after them – now!' Malya was saying.

Bursting clear of Coyote's memory, Jonah shouldered past her and knelt down by the glowing fish-form on the floor. As far as he could tell this was still the only source of light in the entire ship.

Clenching his teeth and telling himself not to be squeamish, he grasped one of the fin-like appendages and tore it away. Fin and body parted company with a meaty ripping sound, leaving Jonah holding what looked like a fat, glowing tongue. Damp, it nearly slipped from his fingers; when he tightened his grip the flesh yielded like sponge. He looked away, stilling the gorge in his throat.

'I have already done it,' he told Malya. 'I have already looked into Coyote's past, to the very moments before he crossed over on to Stone.'

'So fast?' said Annie. 'Can't've been much worth lookin' at.'

'Oh, there was plenty to look at, I can assure you. Time can be encouraged to travel at different speeds; I simply observed a lot in a short space of time. As for our Mr. Coyote . . . he is a killer, I know that much. But I think we suspected that anyway.'

Annie shivered. 'Knew he was dangerous.'

'He is disturbed, I think. He has two personalities, two minds in the same head. To begin with he was just Tom Coyote – an objectionable man in many ways but no more than others I have met. But now he has become someone else entirely.'

The wolf!

Malya drew her sword. 'Englishman, I have suffered here long enough! Will you give me leave to go or shall I break my oath?'

'You need break no oath. Come on, let us go and get your man back.'

The search was facilitated by the fact that all the doors in these lower reaches of the Bark had been sealed shut. Coyote must therefore have stuck to the main corridor which, with the exception of an occasional dead-end tributary, spiralled down unbroken all the way to the ventral spire, the very bottom of the ship. By checking all the tributaries as they met them they were able to rule out each possible hiding place as they went.

Like Jonah, both Annie and Malya carried a makeshift torch ripped from the fish-form. Like their parent organism they dimmed over time; Jonah prayed they would last long enough for them to find Gerent.

They had gone no more than fifty yards, and the torches were already down to half-strength, when Malya stopped. 'What's that,' she hissed. She clutched Jonah's arm so tightly he was convinced she had drawn blood.

Something was moving down the corridor behind them. It sounded like a medicine ball rolling over a planked floor, a hard and heavy rumble. Jonah turned and brandished his torch at the sound.

A disc of wood, rich as cherry, rolled into the wavering pool of light and stopped. It stood about waist-high, a fat timber gong keeping station with little tics and twitches like a unicyclist at the fair. Carved into one side, like a portrait on a coin, was the familiar face of Grandfather Tree. But it looked ill-formed, modelled not by the master but the apprentice.

'Partly here,' the face said. 'Best he could do.'

'Best who could do?' enquired Annie.

'Lesky, of course. Root he is. Bud I am. Make way.'

Weaving a little from side to side the disc rolled between Annie and Malya and continued into the darkness ahead.

'Wait!' said Jonah, '*are* you the lesky? Or are you simply part of him?'

'Ye, ye, ye. Just call me Bud. That way you go, this way me.'

And with no indication as to which direction he was talking about, Bud vanished into the gloom.

'Not quite the US Cavalry,' said Annie.

'A novel effort though,' said Jonah. 'Come on, we need to keep moving, before these torches give out on us.'

The spiral began to tighten. By now the torches were emitting a fraction of the light they had to begin with. Of the rolling, rumbling disc of wood – Bud – there had been no further sign, nor was there any indication that Grandfather Tree was maintaining any presence down here at all. *Hibernating*, he had said. To Jonah it felt as if, down here, the Bark was well and truly dead. Tension grew.

'Should we ditch the torches?' Annie tapped his shoulder and waggled the light in his face. 'Don't want to let him know we're coming.'

'Then we should have abandoned them before,' said Malya. 'We carry on as we are.'

Jonah looked at Annie and shrugged. Malya was the warrior after all; she knew more about these things than they did.

They moved on, now with Malya in the lead. Her

sword was drawn. In the pale light it looked more like ivory than steel. They had gone a further twenty paces when Jonah's torch, which had been threatening to give out for some time, failed. The two remaining torches were little comfort, seeming not to emit light so much as create shadows.

The pace slowed. Eventually Malya called a halt. The curve of the corridor was so tight they could see no more than five yards ahead.

'He's close,' she whispered. Her voice was as thin as the beams of light spilling from her torch.

'Are you sure?' said Jonah.

'He's close,' Malya repeated.

She bent to one knee and drew her arm back. Then she tossed the fleshy torch into the darkness. It struck the outer curved wall with a slap and rebounded. There was a second fainter impact as it landed out of sight. At the same moment they heard a man's voice – Coyote's voice – say very clearly, 'What the . . . ?'

'Was that such a great idea?' whispered Annie.

'If Gerent is still alive, Coyote is waiting for us. If he's dead, our arrival will make no difference.'

Jonah felt coldness grip his spine. Malya sounded so matter-of-fact. He did not imagine she felt so calm on the inside and prayed, if only for Tom Coyote's sake, that Gerent was alive.

Coyote's voice came again. And it *was* Coyote's voice, not the deeper growl that had come from his mouth when he attacked Gerent.

'That you, blondie? Stay where you are now. Wouldn't want lover boy gettin' all cut up now, would you?'

'Let him go,' said Malya. Her voice was low and level and Jonah amazed himself by wondering what part she would sing in a choir – contralto probably.

'Let him go? Let him go? Can't do that, girl. Not while you're standin' there with your sword all naked 'n' ready

212

to cut me. Can't see you but I know you're there. I can . . . mm, imagine you.'

Was the lascivious tone creeping into his voice genuine or just a taunt? Jonah could not decide. He watched Malya for signs of wavering but saw only the iron grip she had on her sword, the tightness in her jaw. Her legs were half bent, wide-set, thigh muscles hard. Slowly they carried her forward. No weakness there, none whatsoever. Watching her was like watching a perfect machine doing exactly the job for which it was built.

'Let him go,' she repeated. Without any other sound she had advanced so far into the blackness Jonah could hardly see her.

'He won't do it,' murmured Annie. Her mouth was so close to his ear that he jumped in surprise. 'He wants something.'

'Stop right there, bitch!'

Malya froze on the spot. She seemed to float there, a phantom warrior poised before the gates of Valhalla.

'I know you're comin' for me but if you take another step I swear I'll slit him open from brain to belly, d'you hear me?'

'I hear you.' *So controlled!* 'What do you want, maggot?'

'Maggot? Oh, I like that, blondie. I like that a lot! I think the question is what do *you* want? You want lover boy's guts spilling over your ankles? Or you want to take a step or two backwards? I know which I'd choose in your position.'

The words were fierce but did not quite seem to fit the voice. Coyote sounded like a man trying to be ferocious but not quite making it.

Or a boy trying to sound like a man, thought Jonah, suddenly excited. He filed the thought away: he would come back to that one later.

Malya remained motionless, head half-turned so that

Jonah and Annie saw her profile, grey and dim in the dying light of the one remaining torch. She did't even blink. After a pause she said, 'All right, maggot, I've taken three steps back. Now let him go.'

'Englishman?' called Coyote. 'I got a proposition for you.'

Jonah raised his eyebrows at Annie. As long as Malya had been in control he had felt relatively secure. Now he was not so sure he wanted to be here at all.

'A . . . proposition?' he said.

'Yeah.' Coyote sounded relaxed again. Jonah could see Malya's muscles tensing. 'But first tell your blonde bitch friend to BACK OFF!'

Malya did not so much as move.

'She has done as you asked,' Jonah called. He had to clench his hands together to stop them shaking. 'Now, please, tell me what it is you want from us.'

Silence, then a slow escape of breath.

'You're going to find me a way home.'

'Home?' Jonah tried to stall for time. 'I do not understand.'

'Oh, I think you do. You're going to use your fancy time tricks to get me back on my mountain. You're going to find me a little corner where I ain't gonna get disturbed or blown up or have any dirt-raking reporters come knockin' on my door. You can keep this Stone-place of yours and take me right back where I started.'

'But I cannot . . .'

'You ain't listening! You can and you will. Just 'cos you ain't found yourself a way out of this godforsaken shit-hole doesn't mean it don't exist. It just means you ain't been lookin' hard enough. I'm goin' home, and you're gonna take me there.'

'And if I cannot?'

'Then I'll just have to unzip your friend.'

'How do we know he's still alive?' shouted Annie.

Malya was still standing between them and the invisible Coyote, listening to every word. Her mouth opened, just slightly, and she ran her tongue across her upper lip. Jonah watched a bead of perspiration drop from the tip of her nose.

From around the corner there was a sound like a punch bag being thumped, followed by a groan.

'He's a little dopey,' explained Coyote, 'on account of how I keep knocking him on the head. Don't know how much more he can take, truth be told. Maybe you should hurry it up.'

'If he dies you are no longer in a position to bargain,' Jonah said.

'I am certain that will bring him a great deal of satisfaction,' said Coyote in what Jonah considered an inferior imitation of his English accent.

Jonah suddenly realized he could hardly see Malya. She had been inching forwards again without any of them noticing, including Coyote. Surely she would not be so foolish as to attempt a rescue in the dark?

Even as he thought this she tossed her head back to look at him and Annie. She raised the hand that was not holding the sword, all five fingers splayed. One by one she folded her fingers away, starting with the thumb. A countdown.

When she reached two there was a deafening crash from around the corner. On the heels of the crash was a short scream and a metallic scraping. Malya's eyes flew wide open then she was rushing into the darkness, sword upraised, a Valkyrie shriek ululating from her mouth. Heedless of the danger, Jonah and Annie raced after her, only to be bowled over by someone running in the opposite direction. The three of them were scattered to the floor like nine-pins, and only when he raised the glowing scrap of fin did Jonah recognize Gerent.

The Neolithic clutched at him, barking out sounds that

were halfway between sobs and howls; it was a dreadful, keening noise and the echoes it made were terrible in the confined space.

'Shut up, Gerent,' suggested Annie.

Leaving Annie to check him for injuries, Jonah crawled forward, casting aside the torch when it guttered and went out. Light bloomed again as he came round the last corner and into the meagre glow of the torch Malya had thrown.

Malya was there in her usual legendary stance, but it took Jonah a moment to decipher what she was looking at.

Coyote was caged against the end wall of the corridor, legs pumping as he struggled to free himself from a tangle of barbs and branches. His wrists were clamped by thick lianas; he was pinioned as if in a set of mediaeval stocks. Gerent's sword lay abandoned several yards from Coyote's hammering feet. His face was lost in the shadows, though his eyes were just visible as twin points of angry light.

Then Jonah noticed the heavy wooden disc weighing on the bald man's chest like an oversized medal. He also heard a voice that sounded almost like Grandfather Tree's, but not quite.

'No sap down here. Slow me. Did good?'

Jonah barked something that was halfway between a laugh and a cough.

'Good? Yes, my little wooden friend – you did very good!'

Malya had extended her sword arm until the tip of her weapon was almost touching Coyote's right cheek. At the sight of the blade he stopped struggling; his eyes continued to burn, tiny flames in the night.

'Your hair is beautiful,' he said.

'Tell me why I shouldn't slit his throat,' she growled at Jonah.

'Because I ask you not to.'

'You ask? What about command?'

'I ask it, Malya. Please. I would not see him killed in cold blood.'

She yanked the sword away. Coyote's head snapped to the side, and for a moment Jonah thought she had cut him. But no blood flowed and Coyote's eyes continued to burn.

Malya marched back up the corridor in search of Gerent, leaving Jonah alone with Coyote. And Bud.

'Not want him dead?' enquired the partial lesky.

'Yes,' answered Jonah. 'I mean no, I do not want him dead. I . . . we need him alive. Do not ask me why. Can you hold him here?'

'Gaoler me?'

Jonah appraised the blackness. 'It looks enough like a dungeon, I suppose. Are you strong enough to deal with him?'

'Talkin' 'bout me as if I ain't here,' said Coyote. He tugged at the wooden shackles but his movements were listless. 'Just need to go home. Want to be where I belong.'

'Strong me,' said Bud. 'Oh ye.'

Keeping both eyes pinned on Coyote, Jonah tested the nearest of the branches. It creaked but did not move more than a quarter of an inch. It felt strong enough to hold down a bear or two.

Why am I doing this? Why am I letting this murderer live?

But he was no executioner, nor even a judge. If this man was evil he would be judged before his Maker. In the meantime he needed only to be made safe and Bud's prison cell seemed adequate for the task. Besides, Jonah was not sure Coyote *was* evil. Disturbed and dangerous, certainly, probably even deserving a place in a lunatic asylum. But evil . . . ?

I said that we need him alive. Can that really be true?

217

All he could think of were Annie's words when they had first invited Coyote on to the Bark. 'We ain't got no choice, Jonah,' she had said, 'we just got to take him with us or this whole trip'll be for nothing.'

Coyote glared at him and said, 'Put me where I belong, Jonah Lightfoot.'

Annie was waiting for him in the blackness around the corner.

'Malya and Gerent have gone back to the bridge,' she said. 'Thought I'd wait for you. What about Coyote?'

'Grandfather Tree's little assistant has tied him up. I believe he is as safe as if he were inside Wormwood Scrubs.'

'Wormwood what?'

'Never mind. I had not anticipated turning the Bark into a prison, but now that Coyote is restrained I must confess to feeling more comfortable. I believe he is contained, for the time being at least.'

Jonah had left Coyote the torch, for what it was worth, so it was in pitch darkness that they felt their way back towards the bridge. They held hands like children lost in the forest.

'*Could* you have done it?' Annie asked. 'Taken him home, I mean?'

'I do not know. I brought Malya out of the past and into our present, so I suppose there is no reason I should not put Tom Coyote back into the past. Except . . .'

'Yes?'

'Except it would not really be *his* past, would it? I could not place him into a memory where he would be in danger of meeting himself – the consequences of such an encounter do not bear thinking about! In any event, I suspect the rules of Stone would prevent that from happening. No, history would diverge, I think, just as it diverged when I retrieved Malya. A new world would be created to accommodate Coyote, one in which he had not previously existed. It would be only a version of his world into which I placed him. It would not truly be his home.'

'Might be enough,' said Annie.

'However,' continued Jonah, 'I would not do such a thing on principle. It is terrifying enough that I have already created one new world – and a new Archan at the same time. I refuse to do it again. I will not risk bringing a third Archan into existence!'

'Oh. I see.'

'Hmm? What was that, my darling?'

'Nothing. Hold me.'

They stopped, embraced in the darkness. It occurred to Jonah it was a long time since they had held each other like this. The ascent of Stone . . . her injury . . . Coyote . . . he and Annie had been walking parallel paths, passing close but never quite touching.

'I've missed you, Jonah,' she whispered. Then she kissed him.

'And I you, my dear. Why, you are trembling.'

'What about us, Jonah? Will we ever go home? Kythe found a way, dear old dragon. And Coyote wants it more than anything. He thinks you can take him there. But what about us? Can you take us there too?'

'I thought you were content here.'

'I was. But that was before Archan rode on in again. When I thought we might just have found ourselves a paradise here on Stone. We've beaten her back twice before, Jonah, by the skin of our teeth each time. Surely our luck's gotta run out sooner or later. And then there's Coyote, he's . . . oh I don't know, he's just gotten me thinking, I guess.'

'About home?'

'Yeah, about home.'

Jonah thought for a moment, then said, 'About Rance?'

He felt Annie shake her head against his chest.

'No,' she said, and her voice was open and honest. 'No, you told me what you saw, how he's doin' okay. I know you can never go back, Jonah, not like Coyote thinks you can. It's just . . . I'd like to see my home again, even if it's only to say goodbye. I'd like to feel, you know, like I'm not a prisoner here. Like I've got a choice.'

An unexpected vision burst in on him of the world he had left behind. London, his home: a sentimental image of St Paul's Cathedral, its dome sculpted by low winter sun, worshippers crowding the great steps. And the Thames shining in the sunset, as broad and mighty as the river of time itself. Had he really faced up to the prospect of never seeing it again?

He felt a breed of homesickness stirring inside him. London's bustle, the downs and woodlands of Kent, sky above and earth below . . . *home*.

'I know what you mean,' he said. They held each other for a while, lost in the dark.

Jonah was about to suggest they keep moving when Annie pulled away.

'Haven't had a dreamin' dream for a while,' she said. Her voice was edgy now.

Jonah held out his fingers towards her words, still fascinated by the totality of the darkness, the fact that, though they were so close, he could not even see her face.

'Perhaps Archan has stopped sending them.'

There was a faint swishing sound and he knew she was shaking her head, and with some vehemence too.

'Huh-uh, no chance of that. No, she's building herself up, Jonah. I can feel her there most of the time now. She's like a prowler sneaking round your windows and you know you're locked up as safe as you can get but you're just waiting for her to find a way in. Down the chimney, maybe, or up through the floor like a prairie dog. Or maybe she'll just blow down the door.'

'All the more reason to get out of this darkness. This is not the place to have you falling unconscious.'

'Yeah, let's go. Oh, and Jonah?'

'Yes?'

'What I said about goin' home – I meant it. Only, it's not so much goin' home as . . . finding your place.'

Jonah laughed. 'Just like all those little tiles.'

'Exactly. Just like the tiles.'

When they set off again it felt to Jonah as though Archan were stalking them both, a palpable presence in the gloom. He was also aware of the sound of the Bark's arachnid legs creaking and clattering against the wall outside, carrying them ever upwards through the endless night.

14

Archan Rising – 2

Archan was enjoying the ascent through the pitch black world.

Mind in the black, body in the white.

The contrast pleased her.

She was less enthralled by the crowd of half-conceived entities clamouring around her. They had swooped in from nowhere, and they all believed themselves to be gods.

It was Frey who had called them into existence, these would-be deities, little knowing the risk he was taking. Or perhaps he was aware of the risk but considered it worth taking given his predicament. Had she a mind to, Archan might have probed deeper into his thoughts to establish his intentions, but the idea of reaching so far into such a primitive consciousness was abhorrent, like burrowing her snout into a heap of dung.

Frey's gods possessed little in the way of real strength but by Stone they were a distraction! They shouted and bickered, swore at each other and even fought amongst themselves. It was like being surrounded by a swarm of buzzing insects, impossible to disperse, impossible to ignore.

Ghostly forms – the bodies of the gods not yet made real – swam in and out of existence. Here was one who called himself Thor, brandishing an enormous hammer at any of his companions who came too close. Two others were wrestling, the contest made all the more difficult by the tendency of each of them to vanish as soon as their opponent got a grip. One of the wrestlers – when he was visible – kept changing his shape, adding further confusion to the proceedings. His adversary, whose occasional body glowed with its own internal light – kept calling his name over and over again: *Loké, Loké, Loké . . .*

One other name could be heard, shouted by all, rising above the cacophony again and again.

Ormungad, where is Ormungad? Bring us the serpent!

For the first time since embarking on this precarious voyage Archan felt the temper she had long suppressed beginning to rise again. Finally the ice was beginning to melt.

In order to focus her attention she concentrated on the final destination. Somewhere up there, at the top of this black realm, was the top of Stone. The point of the upturned claw, the apex of the conical shell. The place where history wound round so tight that it brought itself neatly to an end.

Did it end? Was that really what happened up here? Did the memory rods, after their eternal journey round and up, round and up, simply wind themselves to a dimensionless point and stop?

She had no idea, nor did she really care, not yet anyway. What she was really clinging to was the idea that there at the tip, there where the memory rods crashed together, *everything* crashed together. Stone, sky, sea and all the worlds that fed them.

And, most important of all, the tip was where *this* Stone made contact with the *other* Stone. The other Stone where Jonah would be waiting for her. Sunlight Pass, the gap through the mountains. The way through to the other side.

*　　*　　*

The gods remained bothersome. She tried various ways to get rid of them: repelling fields of charm, bolts of paralysing energy, even a terrible smell. But nothing worked. Frey's gods were so malformed, so insubstantial that she could gain no purchase on them.

Reasoning that Areken was more fully *here* than she was, and might therefore be able to deploy weapons more effectively, Archan invited her to help. When her sister failed to respond she tried to compel her with taunts and threats. But Areken had curled up in a corner of Frey's ravaged mind like a snail retreating into its shell. Waves of anger radiated from her hiding place, betraying her position but also shielding her from Archan's attempts at excavation. She had neatly and effectively cut herself off.

Though she could have done so, Archan was reluctant to penetrate the defences. They were near to the end of the game now, or the beginning of the end at least. The stakes were high and she had no desire to enter into a full-scale battle with her twin self so close to her goal. The bond between the dragons was strong and so far Areken had bent readily enough to her sister's will. But Archan had no desire to test that bond to destruction. Despite her undeniable power here it was really Areken who was controlling Frey, though under her sister's direction. If she decided to mutiny there might be nothing Archan could do about it.

She is me. Is it any wonder I do not trust her?

The gods flocked after them as Frey's wings took them higher and higher.

She was beginning to suspect that even she and her sister working together, using all the charm at their disposal, would not be able to get rid of them. Which could mean only one thing: there was a power here she had not anticipated, and which she did not fully understand.

Where did they come from?

The answer came back at once: *Frey called them.* But of course that was not an adequate explanation. This was not Frey's world, nor had the gods ever been real to him until now (this much she knew from her earlier, limited exploration of the faery's mind). How could a half-believed prayer in an alien world call into existence a family of gods that had never before been real?

Archan scolded herself. Such an irrelevancy should not distract her from the matter at hand! What did she care if a pack of half-made entities scurried at her heels all the way to the top of Stone? They had no hold over her, they could do her no harm. And yet . . .

Not for the first time, she opened her mind to the memory rods of this, her sister's version of Stone. The rods held memories almost identical to those of her own world but not exactly the same, not exactly. *These* rods she could never touch, for fear of the catastrophe that might ensue.

When Jonah divided the worlds he made two of me. To touch one's own memories is to risk all. To risk a change where one becomes not two but none. If I alter the rods of this Stone, I might wipe myself out of existence altogether!

Was that true? She felt muddled, her thoughts sluggish. Surely she should be feeling stronger now, here where the worlds were close enough to touch? It was as if a barrier had been lowered between her body in the white and her mind in the black, a screen between the Stones.

Fledgling anger breaking free of a slow-melting iceberg. She *would* use the rods, but not before she had crossed back into her own version of reality. Then nothing would stop her. And the first pieces of history she would erase?

Why, all those containing Jonah Lightfoot and his pitiful companions, of course.

The basilisks, she grudgingly admitted, had shown her the way. But they had been half-hearted in their ambitions for Stone. For them it had only ever been a recording device, a means by which their own spirits might be preserved were they ever to become extinct. The preservation of all the rest of history had been a by-product, a mere side-effect.

She, by way of contrast, would become the sculptor of time.

The new Stone, Archan's Stone, would be not the recorder but the transmitter. It would not store reality but define it. Wiped clean of all else, the great wall of Stone would become the ground over which she, Archan alone, would move forever. Its sky would be her sky, its sea hers alone. She alone would be its sun, the light of a solitary world, immortal, eternal, self-defining and ruled only by the state of existence.

Lonely? She had once imagined she might be lonely in eternity, and had worked to find herself an immortal companion. But that had been long ago, a million years or more, when she had been confined to a single world. When she been just a dragon. Before she had become so much more.

Besides, once she was truly alone she would not have to concern herself with the actions of others. She would not feel – as she did now – that things were happening that were beyond her ken. And just possibly beyond her control.

And what of this mysterious place?

A world without a sun, indeed the only place on Stone where there is no sun.

A world where a dull-witted faery broken almost to the point of disintegration can call into existence a pantheon of gods.

A world where I can cross back into the stream of reality from which I was thrown.

A world where everything touches everything else.
A world where . . . anything is possible?

Archan glanced back across the worlds at herself, at where her abandoned body lay in the prison of the white.

A solid dragon skeleton, convoluted and enormous, bones bloated with the history they had absorbed. A monstrous thing really, the antithesis of the pure serpentine form her body had once been.

All at once it repulsed her.

Is this what I have become?

She looked away, looked back inside the faery's cave of a skull, that other prison in which her projected mind now rode.

It seemed she had a place in neither world now. She was wholly *between*. Yet both prisons, equally repulsive, held their attractions. The dragon skeleton was a sanctuary, but also a place of impotence. A dead-end.

And the mind of the faery? That was the stepping stone to either ultimate freedom or ultimate doom, the travelling cage from which she would either be cast down forever, or break free to spread her wings wider than any dragon had ever spread them before.

Risk all, win all.

The doubts would serve to hone her judgement, and make the taste of victory that much more sweeter when she closed her jaws around it. When she closed her jaws around it all.

Looking back like that reeked of self-indulgence. Archan was about to berate herself when she realized how easy it had been to see her body, how much easier than before. The gaps between the worlds *were* narrower here, much narrower. And at the very top? Narrowest of all!

Very well! Let us devise a little test to measure just how much more easily I can reach across one of those gaps.

It was some time since she had met with Annie West in one of her dreamin' dreams. Rather too long, in Archan's opinion. Perhaps now was a good time to re-establish the connection.

Perhaps it was time for them both to go out west again.

15

Shade

Annie could feel her coming.

At first it seemed she was far away. Then the analogy she had drawn earlier – about Archan circling the house like a hungry wolf – bloomed bright in her head and all at once it seemed there was nothing but glass between herself and the dragon.

Archan pressed her scaly dragon face against the window, allowed her steaming breath first to cloud it then to dissipate, cloud and fade, cloud and fade, now eclipsing, now revealing her shining teeth, her blank chrome eyes. Then she stalked round to the next window and repeated the performance. Cloud and fade.

At the third window she extended a claw and drew a groove down the glass. The sound was dreadful, like a child's scream.

I can get in any time I like, it seemed to say. *The choice – and therefore the power – is mine.*

'That's what you think,' said Annie. She turned her back on the scored window pane. 'That window's only real in my head, and if I don't look at it then it ain't there!'

Something pricked at the back of her neck; she thought at first it was the glass flying inwards, smashed by the dragon at last. Then she realized it was not glass flying past her but words, angry words.

'You cannot resist me for long, faery! Turn and face me! Turn now!'

But turn she did not. Unlike Lot's wife she resisted temptation and when the shadow of the dragon appeared at the opposite window she turned away from that too, until finally she closed her eyes altogether to the cracked and sagging frames, refusing to acknowledge at all their existence in the outer walls of her mind.

'I will not let you in again, Archan,' she said.

There was a lingering laugh that grew fainter the more she strained to hear it, then the dragon was quiet. Not gone, just quiet. Archan was thinking now, thinking hard, and Annie knew it would not be long before she tried again, this time with a wilier plan, or perhaps simply with more brute force.

'There! Can you see them?'

Blind, they had to guess from the sound of Gerent's voice where he meant them to look. They were crowded together on one of the flat exterior decks near the top of the Bark. Around them the scented air was thick and hot and black. They could see nothing at all.

'Curse you, Gerent!' came Malya's voice, away to the right. 'Just tell us what you see!'

'If I knew what I was looking at, retorted Gerent. 'I would tell you. If you're so perfect, you tell us what's out there!'

Jonah groaned. The encounter with Coyote, far from bringing the Neolithics together, seemed to have pushed them even further apart.

Wind fell, spreading the spice across their faces.

It had become claustrophobic inside the Bark. So much of the vessel had retreated into hibernation now that the flow of air through the interior was sporadic and inefficient. Moreover the darkness, though equal within and without, seemed less oppressive on the outside.

'Worry not!' Grandfather Tree had said. 'Bark still moves. Redirected the charm is, not lost. Not much left, I'll admit. But enough, oh ye, enough.'

On deck, and breathing the raw air, Jonah remarked, 'The atmosphere seems the very essence of Stone, Grandfather Tree. Surely it is more filled with charm than ever it was. Can you not use even a little of what is around us?'

The lesky hesitated. There was a series of creaks nearby, like somebody fidgeting in a rocking chair.

'Replete with charm this place is. But all of it . . . how to describe? . . . all of it is *spoken for*. Much magic here, but much *need* for magic too. Strange potential here, great potential. Magic here for a reason, not for us.'

While the Neolithics bickered, Jonah strained his eyes into the endless night. Something was changing: somehow it was not quite as dark as it had been. He thought he was beginning to see dim shapes again – no actual source of light but something resembling shadows. At first he thought his eyes were playing tricks (total darkness has a way of conjuring phantom images in even the least imaginative observer) but soon he saw the phenomenon was real.

Speckles of blackness moved within the black, a granular darkness within the dark. Distant giants cut from the blackest paper flitting with sure speed through the night. Degrees of shade, no light. Jonah wondered if it were the charm itself they were seeing. Magic given form and substance, distilled to its very essence and given life.

Something bumped into Jonah, something man-sized. A scaly wing brushed across his face; it was Gerent.

'Sorry,' muttered the Neolithic. 'I stumbled.'

Jonah grabbed Gerent's arm, sensing he was about to retreat. 'Stay,' he said quietly. 'Speak with me, Gerent.'

'What would you have me say?' Gerent's voice was a monotone, as dark as the sky.

Jonah held his breath. Suddenly he wanted to tell Gerent about Darwin's book, about the awful fate to which Malya was condemned. Instead he said, 'Tell me what you make of this world.'

'I make nothing of it. As I make nothing of all that I touch.'

'What do you mean?'

Jonah felt Gerent turn towards him. His voice came close and low, a bitter, invisible whisper.

'Just this, my friend. Once I set out to kill a dragon and free my people; instead I saw the dragon victorious and my people burned to ashes. I loved a woman and she died. I had you bring her back from the dead and now she will not even look upon my face. I should have been a king. Now I am nothing.'

'Had your people lived,' said Jonah, 'you would have been a great king. They perished, but you are still here. We are all still here, Gerent – Annie, Malya and I. We need you, we all need you . . . and Malya needs you more than most. More than ever.'

'Malya can look after herself.'

'Malya's sword-arm is strong, Gerent, stronger even than yours. But that does not make you any less a man. Nor does it make Malya invincible. She is human too, mortal . . .'

Jonah stopped, the breath catching in his throat. He had thought the darkness might make it possible to tell his awful secret, to tell of the executioner's axe poised over Malya's neck, but he could not find the words. Why was it so hard to talk to somebody when you could not see their face?

'What I mean to say,' he said, 'is that *I* need your help. I need your knack of working things out. And I need it *now*, this very minute, if we are to help each other survive, if we are to understand something of this world before Archan arrives and blows it all to the four winds.'

232

'What is the point, if she will come anyway?'

Gerent still sounded disconsolate but Jonah fancied he heard genuine curiosity lurking beneath the surface. Had he fired the man's imagination? If only he could see his face!

'By God, man! This is not the first time I've wished to grab you by the shoulders and shake you until your teeth rattled!'

'Try it, Lightfoot, and you will regret it!'

'Better, Gerent!'

'I know what you are trying to do, Lightfoot!'

'Then help me to do it, Gerent! Look into the darkness with me! What do you see? Giants in the distance, as Coyote described to us. But how can they move so fast when they are so large? They dart like insects!'

'I care not!'

'But I do! What do you make of it?'

'Leave me alone!'

'I will not!'

'Darkness confuses distance!' shouted Gerent. 'Coyote was confused too. Perhaps they are not large and distant but small and close! That much should be obvious even to a moron such as yourself!'

Jonah grinned. Gerent's answer had been spat out with such vehemence, yet it was so obvious that he himself had missed it.

'Very well,' he said. 'Then how is it that we can see them at all, when there is clearly no source of light?'

'Clearly there *is* a source of light.' Gerent was no longer shouting. 'Otherwise we would see nothing. You argue well: it is just that you begin in the wrong place.'

'It is all a question of perspective,' agreed Jonah. There was a pause during which he listened to his friend's breathing – slow and steady, slow and steady. 'Are we any further forward, Gerent?'

He heard a sharp intake of breath, followed by a slow, controlled exhalation.

'Perhaps a little, my friend. Perhaps just a little.'

The rocking motion of the Bark was soothing, like a tree blowing in the breeze. The twelve legs carrying it up the dark face of Stone's peak creaked and snapped, the sound heightening the illusion.

The higher they climbed the more they saw. The blackness filled up with fleeting shadows. There was even an occasional burst of real light, always far distant and never lasting long enough to betray its source. When these bursts did occur however there was always a sense that they were moving downwards, as if whatever had caused the sudden flare was falling, falling . . .

Gerent and Jonah continued to discuss the surroundings but although they came up with many theories they made no real progress; it was hard to reach conclusions with so little evidence.

'Perhaps there is no mystery at all,' Gerent said when they agreed to let the subject rest for a while. 'Perhaps we are simply in the middle of a very long night.'

Jonah nodded then, remembering his friend could not see him, said, 'Yes, perhaps you are right.'

He stopped short. He *could* see Gerent's face, or its profile at least. He moved his head a little and Gerent disappeared; moved it back and he was there again. He could see no form, could see nothing of his features, and so guessed there was no light actually falling upon the Bark. But there was something in the sky behind Gerent, something sufficiently bright to throw his face into silhouette. Widening his eyes, as if that might admit more of what scant light there was, Jonah peered into the gloom, trying to make out what was floating behind his Neolithic friend.

It was hard to make out its shape. He had a vague

impression of wings, or possibly fins. The thing – whatever it was – was drifting and rippling so that its edge was always indistinct. It looked a little like an insect's wing, and a little like a balled-up cobweb; a ghost, a will-o'-the-wisp, a captured flame. A soul adrift in the heavens. An angel.

Then it lit up.

Jonah gasped. By now Gerent was turning to see, and out of the corner of his eye Jonah saw Malya and Annie (actually *saw* them!) jump to their feet and stand together, holding one another. As Gerent twisted round his head slipped sideways, revealing the visitor.

It was a tiny child; at least, there was something of the child about it. *Something small, close by*, thought Jonah. At the core of a dazzling spray of light was a human form, slender and naked, a small boy with shining eyes and hair like gold. The light enfolded him, erupted from him, vibrated like the wings of a humming bird, broke apart like fireworks only to reform and flow back into him like liquid flame. Then the child-form broke apart too, reshaping itself into an old man, a voluptuous woman, an adolescent male, then back to the child.

In all its incarnations it was no bigger than his hand.

Between the changes Jonah thought he saw other shapes: something winged and elfin, a looming, muscle-bound behemoth, a many-tailed beast. But for the most part the being maintained its predominantly human aspect, though he suspected it was presenting itself to them in that way in order to cause them least anxiety.

'Hello,' it said. Its voice was high and clear. Stone's miraculous air translated its speech as well as it did any other. 'You are welcome. We receive few visitors here, so the welcome is doubled. As for the turmoil you bring with you . . . that is not welcome. But it is, we accept, inevitable.'

The Bark had stopped. Grandfather Tree's face was

peering over a control vane some distance away round the circumference of the hull. To Jonah he looked like a naughty schoolboy peeping nervously out from behind a bush and he had to stifle a laugh.

'Th-thank you,' Jonah said. All his companions, the lesky included, seemed to have lost their voices. 'We are not pleased to bring turmoil with us, as you put it. However, whether we came or not I fear that same turmoil would find its way here, sooner or later.'

'This much we know,' came the reply. The creature was still in its child-form, its voice soft and well-modulated. Were this miniature child truly human Jonah might have put its age at five or six; to hear such sophisticated language coming from the mouth of an infant was unnerving. 'We understand our world has been chosen as the final battleground in a manner beyond your control and so we bear you no ill will. The rules of the game are now beyond the control even of those who wrote them. We will not hinder you, indeed we may assist you if circumstances allow. We despise the serpents and all they stand for; we too would see them cast down. If that is what you are here to do, then we are your allies.'

Jonah let out a long, slow breath. Allies? Well, they certainly had no need of any more enemies and this tiny angel positively radiated benevolence.

Gerent, as if reading his thoughts, whispered, 'It seems trustworthy, but do not forget the other forms we saw within it – the ogre and the beast with many tails. Tread carefully, Jonah.'

Reluctantly Jonah had to agree. They had encountered so many mysteries on their journeys across Stone; liberating though it would be to take at least one of their discoveries at face value, especially when the face was so fair, it might also be foolish.

'What can you tell us of this place?' he said. 'And of

your people, of course. Did you, like us, come through to Stone from your own world? Or are you natives of this pinnacle realm? And can you really help us defeat Archan?'

'So many questions!' laughed the floating, shining child. It smiled and nodded at Annie and Malya, who had gathered beside their men. 'I will try to answer them all, if you have time to listen.'

'There is little enough time for us all.'

'Then I will be brief. I think my answers may interest you.'

'Will you begin by telling us what you are? What I mean to say is, are you a man?'

'A good enough start. There is man in me, as there are other things. My kind is complex, though the name of my kind is simple enough. We are *Shades*.'

The world has existed forever, though that has not always been the case.

A strange thing to say, you might think. A paradox, you might say. But listen.

When Tai Yi Huang Ren (as he has called himself in recent times) created immortality he found he needed something to keep it in. Inert vessels would not do so he created six living things – the basilisks – into which he poured that essence of eternity.

Yes, you know this much. I know. But listen, please, bear me out.

Next, Tai Yi Huang Ren created a world for the basilisks to explore. Just as he had poured the immortality into the basilisks so he poured the basilisks into the world.

But he saw that his creation was not symmetrical. The basilisks would indeed live forever, but they had not already lived forever. They had been born, and so their lives were immortal in one direction only.

So Tai Yi Huang Ren created a past in which the basilisks had always existed. In doing this he found he had to create a past for the world too, so that they might always have had a realm in which to live out their immortal lives.

Afterwards Tai Yi Huang Ren looked down on a world whose history stretched into the infinite past and which was assured of an infinite future, thanks to the endless flow of the river of time, which was not his creation.

Looking down, he was satisfied. He had worked hard and so he stood back to let the world turn and the basilisks find their way forward.

History moved ahead in an endless series of jumps – or Turnings. Each period of stability was followed by a brief flurry of sudden change, when all the laws of the old world gave way to new laws. A Turning: a moment where everything changed, everything except the basilisks.

Everything changes, *noted the basilisks.* Nothing goes.

The basilisks built citadels, the greatest of which was Stone. But in building Stone they discovered a strange truth, one which had eluded even their creator.

Though they tried to build Stone straight and true, it did not conform.

They had conceived a wall, simply, but however hard they tried to make it sheer, still it sloped. Though they tried to make it straight, still it curved. No infinite plane this but a twisting spiral. No matter how hard they tried they could not prevent their most fundamental building blocks – the memory rods – from binding together at a particular moment in history.

The basilisks made Stone, but they did not choose its shape. Stone chose that for itself.

I will tell you the reason why.

Every realm of Stone corresponds to a Turning point back in what even we call the home-world. The world of the Shades (which occurs some two thousand Turnings after your world, Jonah Lightfoot) is the crucial one. It is the one world that gives Stone its conical shape, the one world that pulls the rods together to a point.

It is the world of the Shades that made you believe, Jonah

238

Lightfoot, that here is where history comes to an end, because here the memory rods come to an end.

You could not be more wrong. The rods do not end here at all, and I can assure you that history is far from over.

But both history and the memory rods are in peril, very grave peril. We know that you are here to sweep that peril away. That is why we give you our support.

Jonah felt frustrated. Some of the Shade's story he knew and a little he had guessed; yet more was wholly new. But he was still no nearer to understanding what the Shades actually were, and why their world was so important to Stone.

'Please tell us,' he said, 'what this history has to do with you?'

The floating Shade underwent one of its transformations again, this time halting when it had moulded itself into a well-muscled young man. His naked body was approximately the length of Jonah's thumb.

'The world of the Shades is a world without a sun. We are the only denizens of that world. There is no diversity, no evolution. There is the world and there are the Shades, and that is all.

'But there is something even more special about our world. Whereas all the other worlds – yours included – are connected to Stone infrequently, the world of the Shades is connected to Stone *all the time*. All the Shades know of Stone and can pass over to it whenever they choose.'

The little naked man gave a mischievous grin and vanished as though a magician had just passed a hand in front of him. They all gasped. Two seconds later the Shade reappeared.

'I have just been home,' he said.

Jonah felt Annie tremble beside him.

'So,' the Shade went on, 'consider what this means.

239

Though we cannot explore the memory rods as you can, Jonah, we can read a little of what they contain. We know much of what there is to know about Stone, its purpose and shape, when and by whom it was made. Indeed, we are as much of Stone as we are of the world we call our own, the world we sometimes call *home*. We are multi-faceted, our physical forms fed by Stone's endless store of memories. We have within us the form of man, of faery, of blind fish and stone-minded leviathan, of beasts your myths could not even conceive and heavenly creatures you would weep to behold. And yes, we even have the dragons within us too.'

'Then you are like the Shifters?' said Jonah. 'Forever changing your shapes and uncertain which is truly your own?'

'Shape-shifters, yes. But we are content with our bodies. We have no doubt as to who we are because we are all that we are. I am this ... and this ... and this!'

With each phrase the Shade underwent a radical transformation, becoming first a knotted mass of liquid, crawling over itself like a nest of snakes, then an indiscriminate bundle of fur with short limbs and wide eyes. It became a dragon, but it was neither fearsome like Archan nor young like Kythe. This dragon was old and black, its hide tough like charcoal. And it was tiny, of course, a mere toy. Yet its face was kindly and, despite their obvious antiquity, its eyes twinkled. Finally it became human again, a bare-breasted female now, as if to satisfy the male onlookers.

'I am all these and more, as are my kin. We Shades are the living product of the union between Stone and the home-world, the manifestation of the histories contained with the memory rods. Meet with a Shade and you can meet with anyone you care to choose: a hero from your

240

most ancient legend, or your own father. Even your unborn child.'

Jonah shivered, uneasy in the presence of this extraordinary being. The woman the Shade had become, naked and coated with beads of light like perspiration, sought to reassure him. 'I talk of our bodily forms, good visitors. Our minds are our own. Whatever we might look like we are ourselves within. I might change myself thus . . .'

. . . and for a heart-stopping second the little Shade was Jonah's father! Henry Lightfoot's eyes bored into those of his son, while around him wings of light fanned like the wings of Gabriel himself . . .

'. . . but it is a mask, a conceit.' The Shade became the child again. 'I am all these things, but I am really only me. My name is Tangent.'

Tangent went on to explain a little of what life was like for him and the other Shades, flitting as they did between their world and the upper reaches of Stone. The two worlds were equally dark, but Tangent stated that Stone was ultimately more attractive to them because of the lightfish.

'Lightfish?' said Jonah. 'I believe we have encountered one of those, or its remains at least. Can you tell us what they are?'

'Yes, I will tell you of the lightfish, Lightfoot!' Tangent chuckled. Jonah did not believe the Shade's sense of humour was terribly well developed. 'They fall from the Verge, up on high. When we can catch them they are good eating, very good indeed. A Shade will shine for many thousands of breaths after eating a healthy lightfish!'

'The Verge?'

'Yes – we can fly so high, then we are held back by a barrier jutting out from Stone. It is like a ceiling

preventing us from reaching the very topmost peak.
The lightfish swarm there, dark while they cling to the
underside of the Verge and lighting up only when they
fall. We chase them and vie for possession of the largest.
It is a sport, you might say.'

*This talk of the Verge sounds more like the sort of information
we really need to know*, Jonah thought.

'Do you know what lies above the Verge?' he asked.
Tangent shook his head, spraying light like a dog shaking
water from its coat.

'No indeed. Only its name and the fact that it is the
place where the memory rods come to a point.'

'And what is its name?' asked Jonah, though of course
he already knew.

'Sunlight Pass.'

'The place from which all Stone hangs . . . But you said
that although the rods come to a point, they do not come
to an end. What then happens to them? Do they diverge
again? Is there another Stone, an inverted Stone, poised
above this one? Is the shape of the whole not a cone but
an hourglass?'

'I cannot say,' answered the Shade with an infuriating
shrug. 'I have never been there. Perhaps you – with this
remarkable vessel – will be the first.'

'How do we know any of this is true?' asked Annie.

The smile melted from Tangent's infant face and he
became grave.

'Because it *is* true. Just as if you step out from where
you stand you will fall, it is true. Just as the sun rises
in all worlds but this, it is true. Do your people not
believe in their gods without proof of sight? It is the
same with the Shades and their knowledge, except we are
so fundamentally *of* Stone that we feel these truths in our
very bones. Go to the Verge and you may discover how
memory and history can converge and become one . . .
and then how both can go on. Forever.

'Then, when you have discovered how this can be so, return and tell us all how our world really works. We have been waiting for you, Jonah Lightfoot. All of us, all along the way. Can you not see that now?'

Faery-like, Tangent flew beside the Bark as the ascent continued. Everybody remained above deck – except Coyote of course. Jonah expressed some concern as to the security of their prisoner's shackles but, after a brief sortie into the drying, cracked wood of the hull, Grandfather Tree emerged with a confident air.

'Safe he is!' he proclaimed. 'Bud – a good job he does. A chip, I might say, off the old block!'

Jonah groaned at the pun, but was relieved to hear the news.

'So what is Bud anyhow?' asked Annie.

She was lying flat on the deck, arms spread wide, dark hair pooled around her head. Archan was circling her, she had told Jonah; it would not be long before she struck again. She had prepared her mind as well as she could and seemed glad of any distraction.

Grandfather Tree was discomfited by the question.

'Bud . . . er, yes. Well, you could say he is . . . a protégé? Ye, good enough that is. A protégé.'

'But is he you? I mean, has he got a mind of his own? Hey, is he your *son*?'

Brambles twitched at the lesky's lips. His face rotated completely round in the deck, making Jonah feel quite dizzy.

'Son . . .' he mused. 'Well, me he was, at first. A simple me, you might say. But now, detached he is. Going his own way he is. Hadn't given it much thought but . . .' he smiled, then his smile brightened, '. . . but ye, ye, I think Grandfather Tree might be a dad!'

They laughed at his simple pleasure, laughed long in the rippling light cast by their diminutive guide, while the Bark clambered with slow, measured gait up the last few miles of Stone.

Other Shades investigated the motley crew of the Bark as it continued its painstaking ascent, flitting down like fireflies, curious and dainty. Though their wing auras were largely the same their inner forms varied wildly; evidently Tangent's peers were not so sensitive to the preferences of the explorers.

Jonah was reminded of a time long before, when they had discovered a kind of encyclopaedia of life, long abandoned by the basilisks. By running his fingers over the surface of the encyclopaedia he had been able to call up visions of all manner of bird and beast both historical and mythical (indeed, that had been one of his earliest lessons that history and myth were inseparable . . . and equally real). Now, as then, he saw the familiar and the strange, and weird agglomerations of the two, all in miniature form.

These wings carried a shining woman with the head of a dog, these a centaur. Here was a faery, so like the poor doomed queen who had been his friend that he felt tears welling as it swooped past. Then there were things more peculiar, that might not even have been creatures at all: a twisting vine that hissed malevolently; a loosely-woven basket of gossamer threads centred round three gaping eyes; a crystal dome, filled with purple sparks and threads of smoke.

However monstrous these inner forms, they all were contained and somehow justified by the butterfly wings. Even the most evil masks were just that: masks. And that was the way of the Shades, to wear these masks through the course of their curious lives.

Once a great cry went up, and what had become a veritable swarm of Shades spun away towards a falling, buzzing cascade of light.

'Lightfish,' said Tangent. Jonah fancied there was a touch of jealousy in his voice. 'A big one too. There will be feasting soon.'

As they accelerated in pursuit, the lights of the hunting Shades went out. Tangent explained the balance of energy and light his kind was forced to maintain.

'Like your Bark,' he said. 'He chooses between charm to fly and charm to live. Naturally he chooses to live, therefore he cannot fly.'

'You mean when you speed up you gotta put the lights out?' said Annie.

'Indeed.'

A cloak of darkness surrounded the plummeting lightfish, then the feeding Shades were illuminated again in a cascade of colour. Gorged with charm they flew and shone, turning cartwheels in the night, filled with the joy of living.

'Your people seem very . . . content,' said Jonah. 'At least, from what little we have seen that appears to be the case. Is it so? Do you have conflicts, quarrels among yourselves? Wars?'

'No,' replied Tangent. 'We love each other too much. We eat and breed and learn, we enjoy the worlds between which we move. We have all the space we need and yearn for nothing more than we have already. No, life is a good thing and we have neither the desire nor the means to make it otherwise.'

Jonah sucked in his breath, suddenly overwhelmed. That this . . . this being could talk so complacently about a dream which had eluded mankind since the dawn of time! Here was a true utopia, a world without conflict! Eden!

And we have entered into it, dragging ruin behind us! Yet still they wish to help us, when we might destroy all for which they stand.

*   *   *

Two of Tangent's fellow Shades visited them more frequently than the others. One of them had adopted a semi-human form – slender and female with smooth green skin and eyes like a cat's. From what part of history or myth she might have borrowed this template she did not reveal, nor could they tell. The other was a squat beast, all tooth and matted hair, like a little shaggy boar. Yet it spoke with a gentle, generous voice and flew, like all its kin, on glistening wings of pure light. They were introduced as Carpalla and Dun and along with Tangent they formed a kind of honour guard during the Bark's final ascent.

Darkness persisted. The Bark began to slow noticeably, the creaking sounds from its spider-legs growing laboured and arthritic. At one point it paused long enough for a tattered hatch cover to open in the hull. A cascade of battered orange shapes poured out, tumbling into the darkness of the abyss.

'Apologies, Gerent,' Grandfather Tree's voice wafted up from somewhere beneath the deck. He sounded old and immeasurably weary. 'But there was no need for the food. And heavy they weighed. Need lightness now, more than ever. Such a fine catch though. Such a waste.'

Jonah watched them fall. On Stone, it was raining fish.

'Look there! Above us!'

Malya's cry brought them all to attention. Above their heads was a ceiling. Its black edge was clearly defined, set as it was against a field of thick yellow light. Warm light. Sunlight. Eyes adjusting to the sudden change, the travellers gazed around at this strange new part of Stone.

If Jonah had needed any confirmation of the shape of Stone then he had it right here. The Bark was clinging to the side of a narrow cone. The wall of Stone – which they had once perceived as flat just as the first men had perceived the Earth as flat – curved severely to both sides. It felt to Jonah like being pinned to the side of a gigantic church steeple.

Barely half a mile above their heads was a horizontal black disc.

A steeple with a witch's hat planted on its peak! We are looking up at the brim of that hat. We have only to climb over it to see what we have long waited to see: the very tip of Stone itself!

The light spilling from above the brim was dense, filled with smoke. Jonah felt it plunging past him on the constant wind of Stone and wondered if here was the source of both the wind and all the falling charm. The thought humbled him; his hands started to shake. Annie took his hand and he felt her shaking too. He assumed it was for the same reason and did not think to glance across at her face.

'Dear God,' he breathed. 'Are we here at last?'

Annie said nothing. Still he did not look at her, so captivated was he by the vision of the sunlight spilling around the brim of the hat.

'The Verge,' announced Tangent. 'I fear we Shades can go no further. We will wait for you here.'

A lightfish crawled round the perimeter of the hat-brim, its clumsy movements more like those of an inch-worm than a fish, then disappeared up into the light.

So it is *possible to cross over*, thought Jonah.

There was a sudden sound, like distant thunder. The wind? Could it even be the light? The light seemed to have real substance and weight here; he could almost imagine it making a noise too.

The sound became a voice. Air rushed past their faces, cutting in crazy directions, a sudden and unfettered hurricane. Someone screamed, not in fear but in fury. It was Malya, Jonah saw, already climbing up the hull with a sword in her hand and a dagger between her teeth.

Gerent was chasing after her, struggling to pull his own sword from its scabbard.

A face was boiling out of the air, bearded, human, ferocious, clad with a horned metal helm. Gigantic, as large as ever the face of Grandfather Tree had been. Dragging behind it was a fur-clad body, thonged with leather straps. As if seen through running water it wavered, broke apart then coalesced into a whole that was never quite solid, but which displaced the air enough to assure him it was real. In his right hand the bearded giant carried an enormous hammer.

Wild-eyed, he fixed his gaze on the Neolithic warriors who had by now gained the high ground of the Bark's upper hull to face him. Growling, he drew back the hammer for his first swing. Given his colossal size it looked likely he would smash the Bark like an egg with a single stroke.

The Shades had scattered. Annie was still shaking. Jonah turned to her and saw to his horror that her eyes had turned up so that only the whites were showing. A line of spittle ran from the corner of her mouth to her chin. Her whole body was quaking as if it had been galvanized.

'Dreamin' . . . dream . . .' she stuttered. 'Don't leave me . . . Jonah . . . don't you let me go . . . comin' . . . comin' for you . . . Archan . . . comin' for you both . . .'

And with that all the tension fled her body and she slumped to the deck. Jonah barely managed to catch her head and shoulder before they thudded on to the hard wood. There she lay, face open and vacant as an empty house as she headed out west to meet a dragon.

Something ripped through the air above him – the giant's hammer. Jonah watched its shadow swallow his Neolithic friends.

Ancient human warriors . . . the vengeful god . . .

'It is Thor!' he whispered in astonishment. Then, before he could even begin to wonder how they came to be battling against a Norse god, the hammer struck the Bark.

16

Annie Out West – 3

'So. Here we are again. You've done well, Annie West. And Jonah too, both of you have done so well. So far, so far. All the tiles placed correctly – except those last two, of course, but those must wait, Red Dragon and White Dragon, they must wait. Now I believe it might get just a little bit harder.'

Her eyelids felt heavy and her head was thumping. Entering the dream wasn't like falling asleep at all – in fact it felt more like waking up after a night spent drinking cheap liquor. There was a draught across her face, a steady breeze that fanned to and fro, to and fro. And a sound like thunder, a distant storm.

Here we go again.

A hand brushed her forehead and she managed to open her eyes. Smiling down at her was the kind, wrinkled face of the old Chinese man, Mister Ren. The upturned bowl of his hat was teetering on his head as if about to fall off and she reached up to adjust it for him.

'My thanks, many thanks,' he gushed. 'Now – can you stand?'

With his help she climbed to her feet, fighting off the wave of dizziness that came over her as she stood erect. Her thigh ached where the hawk (rock?) had pierced it – funny, she had thought that wound completely healed.

'Last time I was here there was an avalanche,' she said. She looked round with trepidation. 'I was expecting Archan.'

'Avalanche finished now,' came Mister Ren's cheerful reply. 'Look, see.'

She did look. What she saw was a narrow path winding its way between two canyon walls. The walls were unnaturally high, their tops converging in a bright grey band; the path was barely wide enough for two people to walk abreast and ascended at a steep angle into yellow light.

She and Mister Ren were alone on the path. It was warm and bright, despite the oppressive aspect of the towering canyon walls, though far off she could hear the intermittent growl of the thunderstorm. As she listened it grew louder.

'This is it, ain't it?' she said. 'Sunlight Pass. The Bark's at the top of our Stone, Archan and Areken are at the top of *their* Stone and we're here too – same place, different dream.'

'Same place indeed.' Mister Ren was examining something he had just excavated from his left nostril. He flicked it down the path and beamed at Annie. 'Your dream is planted square between the two versions of Amara, Annie West, right between the Stones. If Archan wants to cross over she'll have to come through here.'

'You think we can stop her?'

A shrug. 'Don't know that.' A grin. 'We'll see, eh?'

'Yeah, right. We'll see.' Annie nodded up the path. 'So, what's the view like from the top?'

'Would you care to look?'

'Why not?'

Had she thought the path steep? She hadn't known the half of it! They'd gone barely twenty paces before her calf muscles were screaming. She was about to complain

251

to Mister Ren when she saw how sprightly he still was, and felt ashamed she couldn't keep up with a little old Chinaman.

If you think he's really a little old Chinaman you're sore mistaken, girl, she told herself. *It's just a mask he wears, like the Shades. Why, if you saw what he really was it'd probably burn your mind away!*

Steep though it was the path was mercifully short. After an intense but brief slog up the formidable gradient suddenly it began to level off. Peering ahead through the sweat-soaked strands of hair falling across her face, Annie saw the brow of the hill just ahead.

No, not the brow of the hill – the brow of the mountain. *Hell, for all I know it's the brow of the world!*

Mister Ren was there already, arms spread wide against a vivid blue sky. The canyon walls had fallen away, leaving the summit wide and exposed. Gasping for breath, Annie tackled the last few degrees of the slope and climbed on to the top of the world.

What had she expected? A broad mountain range falling to the sea? A wide plateau peopled with strange lost tribes? Or maybe a smooth stairway rising to heaven?

She saw none of these things. What she saw was a wood . . . except the trees were too regularly spaced for it to be a wood. *An orchard.*

The orchard covered a gentle hill, a soft quilt of treetops moving loosely in the breeze. The path ran down the slope and into the orchard where it became a road, wide and sure and paved with ivory. Though the trees were each of the same unidentifiable species they all bore an astonishing range of fruit: apples and oranges, peaches and plums and pears and pomegranates. Many of the varieties Annie had never seen before. In the pure blue sky above there was not a single cloud to disrupt the sunlight while beyond the furthermost edge of the orchard lay the smooth expanse of an ocean. It was a dream landscape, perfect and true, and yet Annie knew it was also wholly real.

'Does the road go down to the sea?' she said. Then a monumental clap of thunder shut her mouth.

Flinching from the dreadful noise she cast her eyes around. Where could the storm be? The sky was as clear the finest Kansas summer – where were the clouds?

'Not a sky-storm,' said Mister Ren. 'More's the pity.'

Something was disturbing the trees far in the distance, spinning them like a twister though there was no twister to be seen. The spiralling motion drew nearer, smashing through the orchard with breathtaking speed. Before Annie could speak the invisible whirlwind was upon them, the thunder was all around them, the air was filled with thumping and shrieking and flying fruit and she was falling, falling . . .

'Hold tight!' yelled Mister Ren. He grabbed her arm with one hand and his hat with the other. 'It's not her yet!'

Something was taking shape in the rotating air. Just as the Norse god of thunder had distilled from the air of Stone so something was materializing from the core of the whirlwind, something man-shaped but immense. At first Annie thought Thor had found his way here too; like Thor, this latest god was carrying a hammer.

But as the giant solidified she saw that its skin was blue and its head was that not of a man but an owl. Bird-claws adorned its feet and its upper limbs were more like wings than arms. With the hammer it held in one feathered claw it was beating on the drum it held in the other. A beak the size of a small boat snapped open, revealing a pallid blue tongue that flicked and searched. Smoke coursed from its throat and with it came the sound of thunder.

Spinning its head almost completely around the monstrous creature bent its waist and snapped at Annie. Mister Ren fell protectively across her and the giant's beak cracked against the shell-shield he still carried on his back. Membranes darting sideways across its hungry eyes, the owl-god reared up in frustration and pecked again, only to have its blows repelled again and again. After the third attempt it spun its head and beat on its drum. Sparks of lightning flew from the end of the hammer as it pounded and thunder boomed from its throat.

'What the hell is it?' screamed Annie. Now she wished she was back under the rockfall.

'Lei-gong!' shouted Mister Ren. 'Or a version of him at least. A Chinese thunder god. He isn't usually as cross as this.'

'Well what's he doing here?'

'Archan has raised him. She is using the gods as path-finders before she bridges the gap between the worlds herself. No route is sure here in Sunlight Pass. Steps can seem easy but lead to treacherous ends. She is taking no chances.'

The owl-god was changing before their eyes, becoming even more bird-like. Feathers sprouted down the whole length of its body; it discarded both hammer and drum and became a huge crested eagle with lightning crowding its beak and thunder exploding with every beat of its massive wings.

'So. Not surprising.' Mister Ren's calmness was incredible to Annie; she herself was utterly terrified. 'This must be the Thunder Bird. You might know this one, Annie – it's a Native American spirit.'

'Can't say he looks familiar.'

The giant eagle, lightning forming a crown of white about its head, was screeching into the blue sky, beating its wings with increasing frenzy. The thunder was constant now, a steady and mindless series of detonations that made it almost impossible to think. The bird was about as big as the Statue of Liberty.

For now though it seemed more concerned with posturing than finishing off its prey. As long as it was making all this noise there might still be a chance to escape.

'It's your dream, Annie,' said Mister Ren. Somehow his quiet words penetrated the riotous thunder. 'You know that. You've defeated her here before. You can do it again. You can always do it.'

'But this ain't Archan.'

'No. This is one of her servants. So it's even easier to put down.'

'But how?'

'This is your dream.'

And with that aggravating affirmation Mister Ren tucked his head away again, leaving Annie to stare up at the Thunder Bird.

The Thunder Bird found her gaze and stared back, its eye gigantic beady and malevolent.

An ordinary eye, she reminded herself. *Not Archan's eye. She is not here yet. This is my dream!*

Shaking from her head to the tips of her toes, Annie stood up and walked across the flat summit of Sunlight Pass. One of the Thunder Bird's feet was locked in the ground here, claws nailed with sufficient force to split the rock. She passed into its shadow, conscious of its glaring eye, aware of the heat of its breath on her back. She didn't have to turn to know its head had descended to track her progress; she knew the tip of its beak was just inches from the back of her neck.

Now she was heading downslope, over the crest of the pass, down towards the swaying trees. Now she was clear of the eagle's shadow, now the dusty rock surface was clearer. Ten yards ahead lay the first of the ivory slabs from which the road through the orchard was made.

Something brushed her hair, something that crackled and jolted, a finger of lightning testing her defences. She walked on, stronger now, shaking no longer. Behind her the thunder still boomed but it was fainter and somehow less *whole*. Five yards to the road, three yards.

One yard.

She set her foot on the ivory road and the Thunder Bird screamed defeat. There was a tearing sound, followed by the long buzz of electrical discharge, then came a sudden peace. Dancing leaf-shadows cooled her face.

All was quiet.

With both feet on the first of the ivory slabs Annie turned to see the mountain top bare. Bare except for the shell from beneath which Mister Ren was just emerging, a broad smile across his wizened Chinese face.

'Bravo, Annie West!' he cried as he trotted down to meet her on the road. 'I knew you could do it!'

'My dream, huh?'

'Didn't I say so?'

'Care to tell me what happens next?'

'It's your dream!'

'Right, yeah, you said.'

17

Verge

Big as a church, shards of blue lightning following his every move, the great Norse god swung his hammer through the side of the Bark. Jonah cringed against Annie, ready to be hurled into the sky. But no impact came. The hammer met no resistance as it slipped clean through the Bark's hull and out the other side. There was a momentary judder but that was all. The hammer returned to plain view, leaving the basilisk ship unscathed.

Thor's brow lowered in almost comical confusion. Recovering from the follow-through he hefted the hammer, raised it to his eye and tapped its pitted iron head.

One of the Shades – Carpalla – flitted behind Thor's shoulder. Her firefly light remained clearly visible where it should have been obscured.

I can see through him – he is not really here! Jonah realized with excitement. *Perhaps he cannot hurt us!*

Further up the curve of the hull stood Malya and Gerent, weapons outstretched, lips curled back in twin expressions of rage. They taunted the god, urged him to do his worst; instead Thor removed his helmet and scratched his mighty head in puzzlement. Again he brought the hammer down; again it slithered ineffectually through the fabric of the Bark.

Not quite ineffectually, thought Jonah, for again there was the merest jolt as, somewhere deep inside the vessel, some tiny part of the hammer made contact with something else.

Malya was standing before Gerent, holding something out towards him. It took Jonah a moment to realize it was the leather harness Gerent had once used to carry Annie and later Malya herself.

The winged man was solemn for a moment then, with a single fluid movement, he snatched and donned the harness. Malya climbed into it, pressing her back hard against Gerent's midriff; as he took to the air her legs dangled freely between his. Tightly strapped in she had both hands free to hold a sword; in her left she held her own, in her right Gerent's.

Jonah could not imagine what they hoped to achieve. Surely Thor's ghostly flesh would accept their blades without suffering injury? Yet still they flew on, Gerent weaving a course between Thor's slow, reaching hands until they were close enough for Malya to jab at his bulging eye. The sword went smoothly in – and came out clean, leaving no trace of a wound, no gout of blood or humour.

She jabbed again, and again, striking eight or nine times before the god's hand's came up and Gerent was forced to dart away, just in case those phantom fingers managed to gain purchase on them. The god groaned and clawed the eye at which Malya had struck.

The Neolithics continued to buzz Thor, Gerent diving and side-slipping constantly to avoid both thrusting hand and lashing hammer. Malya took every opportunity to deal out blows, all the time trying to strike at least three or four times in the same place, understanding intuitively what Jonah had only just worked out: that only by the cumulative effect of many blows could they hope to injure the god. Soon Thor began to tire, as much from his own futile exertions as from the injuries he had sustained. He looked like a man plagued by a wasp, thrashing hopelessly at a target both too small and too swift for his clumsy reflexes. Jonah even began to feel sorry for him, so dejected did he seem. He looked dull, slow-witted even, and Jonah tried to recall how Thor had originally been portrayed in Earthly legend. He remembered little, only that he had been a champion, if not exactly a hero then certainly not a villain.

Now the god was fading. For the first time his eyes – the left red and swollen – managed to fix on his winged attackers. Was there sympathy there? Jonah could not be sure, but it seemed to him that Thor recognized something in the Neolithics, some trace of kinship.

Head bowed, hammer limp in his hand, the Norse god of thunder melted into the darkness and was gone.

Jonah waited. Would others come? Had Archan somehow recruited an army of gods to wage her war for her? It was not her style – up to now she had preferred confrontation face to face, but then perhaps she had no option; perhaps she could not step so easily between the worlds as she had hoped.

Annie groaned. He lay down beside her, crooking his arm around her head and stroking her cheek with his free hand.

'My dream,' she mumbled. 'Mine . . . biggest damn bird I ever saw.'

'Ssh, Annie,' Jonah said. 'Everything is all right.'

There was a splintering sound nearby and Grandfather Tree's face shot out of the deck, his ancient elf features spread across a wide arrowhead of wood. He looked panicked.

'No,' he said, 'not all right. Not at all. That hammer!'

'What?' *The jolts inside the Bark!* 'What damage has been done?'

'Can't find Bud!' wailed the lesky. 'Bud's not there!'

Jonah's spine turned cold. 'What about Coyote?'

'Gone too! Both gone! Can't find anything. Bark – the hibernation, too hard, too cold!'

Jonah felt sorry for the lesky. But his concern was as nothing compared to his fear of Tom Coyote.

Perhaps the hammer-blow killed him! Killed them both!

Somehow he knew that was not so. There was a killer loose on the ship.

The sky was quiet following the defeat of the god. Gerent and Malya remained airborne for the final approach to the Verge; together with firefly Shades they preceded the slow-moving Bark like pilots leading a galleon to harbour. The closer they drew to that smooth, dark ceiling the brighter the atmosphere became. A lightfish tumbled, an unexpected comet in the haze. None of them, not even the Shades, paid it any attention.

No more gods came.

Malya had twisted round in the leather sling, tilting her face up to Gerent's so that they could kiss. Jonah watched Gerent move his hands across the front of her body while she caressed his face with the backs of her fingers, his neck with her cupped hands, watched without embarrassment as the two of them slipped into darker, more intimate air. Gerent's wings pumped with slow and steady power and their clothes were hanging loose and they were warm human shapes beating out the first and finest rhythm in a bleak and alien space, spreading light and heat and simple joy into all that surrounded them. Jonah watched them and they knew his eyes were upon them, but he knew in turn that they did not mind. He watched them reunited and thought of his book of stone and felt his heart break.

All too soon a shadow descended on Jonah. With the Neolithics absorbed in each other and Annie unconscious, he began to feel lonely; nor, without any idea of Coyote's whereabouts, did he feel at all safe.

Grandfather Tree had retreated into the Bark in search of both Coyote and Bud. Jonah pleaded with him to be cautious, but it was with a ferocious expression on his face that the lesky drilled his way back into the wood. The only proof Jonah had that Grandfather Tree was all right was the continuing progress of the Bark up the final stretch of Stone's curving wall. The boundary between lesky and Bark had blurred to such an extent that it was impossible to mark the point where one left off and the other began – if one suffered then surely the other would falter.

Which made him fear all the more that if the lesky were to be harmed then the Bark might simply fold up its many legs and begin the longest fall this or any other world had ever seen.

With a frantic buzzing sound another lightfish dropped from the Verge, then another. Jonah could see scores of them adhering to the underside of the witch's hat-brim, worming this way and that. Three more fell before he realized something was wrong.

The Shades were conferring, their darting auras positively aethereal next to Gerent's solid and somehow unimaginative wings. Tangent peeled away from his fellows and dived to where Jonah was seated.

'Something has disturbed the lightfish,' he announced, 'as you have no doubt observed. We fear another attack.'

'We repelled Archan's advance party,' said Jonah, 'but she certainly will not have finished with us yet.'

'We believe she used the phantom-god to test the junction between the two versions of Stone. The junction does exist here, so close to the summit, but I do not believe it is wholly reliable until one climbs above the Verge. I suspect she will not risk crossing herself until she has gained the very highest ground. She would not want the gate to snap shut when she is halfway across.'

'So she just sent Thor to soften us up a little.'

'Of course.' Tangent smiled the radiant smile of a cherub. 'She did not succeed!'

Jonah thought of Coyote prowling the pitch-black corridors of the Bark.

'I wonder what made her choose a Viking god,' he said. 'How can we defeat her, Tangent? Brave we may be but will we prevail? Can we prevail? We have a veritable arsenal of weapons aboard this vessel: swords and clubs and barrels of oil that can be set alight and ejected . . . but to what avail?'

Talking more to himself now than to Tangent, Jonah let his eyes return to Stone. There were the weapons he really needed, there behind the wall. Archan must surely have mastered their use by now – could he contemplate facing her with anything less in his grasp?

'Archan has never yet manipulated the memory rods as I have done,' he muttered. 'At least, not to my knowledge. Surely now she has had every opportunity to train herself in their use. She is as much an adept as I am – how can she resist them?'

It was suddenly hot, hot as a summer's day in Kent. Thinking about the memory rods enlivened them in his mind. They coiled like snakes behind Stone's wall, tugging at him, pulling him off balance and he was falling, he was back at the watermill again. No mere remembrance this though: he was *drowning* in the memory! Heat and passion, storm-fall and the hot buzz of the hive. Lily's face, white as a mask, framed by the rotten window. And he felt helpless, as helpless as when he had fallen backwards from the broken sill.

Is that what I have been doing all this time? Falling?

He looked at Stone and saw it flayed open, all its inner structures bare to his secret sight. He saw with perfect clarity the tight spiral of the memory rods where the *now* and *then* dwelt side by side. Except all the gaps between the *now* and *then* had been razed almost clean away; he could perceive that day at the mill just as easily as he could this moment in his present, on the Bark with Annie in his arms, on the wheel with Lily in his eyes.

There was more to the memory rods than there had ever been before. It was *all* here, *all* of it: past, present, future and all points between and beyond. Memories spun across each other like pictures in a zoetrope, infinite lives compressed behind a single window on the world. Jonah looked into the river of time and instead of a flowing stream he saw each individual drop of water contained within the next, so there was no separating them. The river condensed, its mouth turned to its source. Drops within drops within drops, memories stacked upon memories like angels in a showstone. The concentric spheres of creation. The memory rods, here entwined so intimately that every last thought, every last breath within them was shared with and exposed to his seeing mind.

And they beckoned, oh how they beckoned!

I must enter the memory rods again! They are the only weapons I have!

At the last moment he stopped himself.

All that the rods contained he had seen before – at a distance. As long as the billions of rods were held separate – as they were across most of Stone – the memories were diluted. Here though, where all the rods reduced towards a single unimaginable point, to enter them would be to taste liquor more intoxicating than any man could bear, to endure both the worst agonies and the highest ecstasies history had to offer. It would be like skating barefoot across the surface of the sun.

But I am an adept, the only man able to enter at all. If I do not make the attempt who is left to try?

Archan was left, of course.

A storm-hot sky and the voice of the hive.

Looking into the face of the cosmos he could not drive out the smaller, human obsessions. His own humble memories clung to him like pollen: the mill, the storm, his clumsy fall to the waterwheel . . . gazing up at the vast sky as hail collided with his naked body, lying where he . . .

. . . *had fallen, but though he had fallen he felt elevated. Sprawled here on the very top of the immobilized wheel he was acutely aware of his place within the storm-lit scene. A young man alive between air and soil. The hail dissolved into a thin spray of icy rain. Grey-green hills underpinned the arch of the sky.*

His body was pinned to the world like a butterfly.

This is a good place to be, *he thought.* Between Stone and sky. My name is Jonah Lightfoot.

The knowledge of one's proper place, the truth of one's name.

Their names . . . Archan . . . Areken . . . their lying names . . .

Falling to earth to find one's place, falling to Earth like a rock from the sky, like a rock from the stars, the sun, the moon . . . the moon . . . the . . .

. . . moon!

Jonah fumbled in his pocket and brought out the round, black rock. When had he put it there? *Had* he put it there? He could not remember but it was of no importance. It was here now, in his hand.

Moon-rock. A little piece of the moon, fallen to Earth, fallen to Stone.

'Kythe,' he whispered, turning the rock over and over in his hands, 'what are you trying to tell me?'

Skating over the surface of the sun.

It was not so far from the truth. The instant Jonah entered the memory rods he was almost crushed by the pressure of these uppermost twists of Stone.

264

A scientist friend had once enthused about the wondrous effects of pressure on various chemical elements, assuring him that under the right conditions a gas like hydrogen could be compressed to become a metal. 'Alchemy by proxy,' he had laughed.

So too with the memory rods. Squeezed beyond endurance, they were crammed so tight they were starting to become something else entirely.

It was something Jonah had no desire to see, any more than he wanted to open his eyes to the heart of the sun. There were some things a man was not meant to know. What he was searching for was a memory like all the memories he had visited. It was here somewhere, elusive but real.

Trying to ignore the blistering heat he skated through the fire.

He was looking for Kythe, his friend. She had left Stone by way of a charm-drenched whirlpool, a threshold in disguise. Returning to Earth, she arrived at a point in time long before her race had appeared. In fact, she arrived on the very first day of the world of charm.

She was the only dragon in the world. Therefore she was the first dragon in the world.

This burgeoning world of charm was not a safe place for any dragon to stay. The trolls were emerging and they would rule the tortured volcanic lands for many aeons before dragons ever took to the skies. No, Kythe considered it wise to retreat to a place of safety, a place from which she might watch over the slowly evolving world. There she would prepare herself for the future golden age of dragons.

After much deliberation she found a place closely bound to the turning world yet far enough away to ensure her safety. It became her sanctuary.

Cold and grey, devoid of air but replete with charm, the

moon flew free of the Earth's shadow. Jonah soared above her dusty skin, marvelling at a million craters. Grey plains, soft mountains, white powder-stars painted over dark, dry seas. She was the same moon he had gazed up at from the downlands of Kent . . . but for the first time he recognized her as a world in her own right too.

Small and true, *he thought.* Unsung in so many ways.

He flew closer. He was ghost-Jonah, of course, Jonah the time-traveller, regular passenger on the Reminiscence Railway. But usually in his travels he had visited his own world. This was altogether different. The horizon was unEarthly: it was smaller, smoother, rounder, nearer.

This really is a small world.

Stone was the familiar turned on end. The moon was the familiar made soft and then recast. Like the daughter of the Earth one could see her father's features ghostlike behind her own, although she had a personality all to herself. Earth and Stone were no more than kissing cousins; Earth and moon were true blood.

Jonah was close enough now to make out dark motes at the centre of some of the craters. A rough count suggested a little less than half were marked in this curious way; having completed this assessment Jonah descended into the nearest crater to find these dark specks were actually round, black rocks identical to the one he had found in the upright crater on Stone. He was crouching to examine the nearest one when a voice stopped him.

'Hi, Jonah! I can't tell you how great it is to see you again!'

And there was Kythe, an orange dragon made grey by the dust of her chosen world. He smiled and she smiled, the expression spanning both time and type. She threw her translucent wings wide but faltered when she saw his solemn expression.

'I am but a ghost here, Kythe, you do realize that?'

Her dragon face, long and horse-like, dipped to the same level as his own (she was larger than he remembered and now

266

she had to bend to greet him) and her smile grew warmer and sadder. 'You could make yourself real to me, Jonah. We could touch, just for a breath or two.'

It was an agonizing moment. Here she was, his good dragon friend Kythe, suddenly untouchable. Had he not ridden astride her back, had she not always nuzzled him like an affectionate dog? It would take little enough effort to make himself solid in this world for long enough that they might share an embrace, a simple touch of hand and wing . . . and yet he knew it could not be so.

'I cannot,' he said. Now her smile did fade a little. 'That I have come at all is perilous enough. I would not tamper with time any more than is absolutely necessary, and to make myself more real than I am would be to disturb too much of the dust of this world. Dust is real, you know, Kythe – it is as solid as you or I and it makes a difference to things. It is the smallest touches that mean the most, it seems to me now.'

'The smallest touches,' echoed Kythe. She brushed a sad wingtip through the empty space where Jonah's fingers appeared to be.

Jonah expected her to brighten with the childish resilience he had come to love, but she remained melancholy. It came to him that she was not just bigger but older – much older. Kythe, the dragon-child, had grown up at last.

'How many years, Kythe?' he asked.

'Nearly two thousand.' Still that sad smile. 'I have work to do but . . . it gets lonely.'

'Two thousand years alone? Oh, my dear Kythe, how can you bear it?'

To his surprise her smile strengthened a little then and he saw the resilience was still there, an aspect not of infancy but of her nature. Time had slowed it but not removed it, not at all.

'I bear it because by the time another two thousand years have gone by my work will be done. Then I can go back to my world – our world, Jonah – and bring dragons back to where they belong.'

Jonah gazed out across space at the Earth, a dazzling blue jewel. 'What are you doing here, Kythe? And why did you want me to come?'

Kythe spoke, her voice carried not by air but by threads of charm:

'Do you remember a time on Stone – you told me about it once – when you looked into the memory rods and saw a moment from the beginning of the age of charm? You stood beside a herd of unicorns and watched an orange dragon flying down from the moon, leading a great cloud of followers down to the world from the moon in the sky. Surely you know by now that was me, bringing the first dragons into the world.

'Well, that day is yet to come, but come it will and it's my task to prepare for it. When I came through to this world from Stone, the world of charm was so new even the trolls hadn't raised their heads yet. So I knew I had to wait. I knew I had come for a purpose, even though I didn't know what it was yet, and the moon seemed to . . . well, it called to me I suppose. And the moment I got here I knew I'd come to the right place.

'Rocks fall here, Jonah. They fall on the world as well but the air makes them burn away to nothing. Here on the moon they survive, hundreds every day, little black rocks that hit the dust and make their marks. The first one I saw I picked it up, just out of curiosity. I was so shocked I dropped it straight away, just stared at it as it fell back into the dust in that slow, moon-dreamy way.

'It spoke to me, you see. Actually spoke to me.

'You remember how the faery queen sent you messages from the world to Stone? How she spoke into little seashells and cast them into the whirlpool, and how the words stayed rattling round inside the shells all the way between the worlds? I spoke to you that way too, just once, told you I was all right. Well, these little black rocks carry messages too. I don't know who sends them but they come to me through the endless night and I listen to what they have to say and put them in their places.

268

'See this little rock here? This fell today. See, I pick it up and hold it close to my ear and listen . . . oh, so beautiful! . . . and I take it to its place which is . . . just over here, and I place it at the heart of where it needs to be. Sometimes I don't have to take them far, other times I have to fly halfway round this small world before I find the spot.

'So now you're wondering what the rocks are saying to me. They look a little like eggs, don't they? Well, they're not eggs, but dragons will grow from them one day, though not in the way you imagine.

'They're names, Jonah. In these little black rocks are held all the names of all the dragons who will ever live. They come to the moon from some endless place and I listen to them all and put them where they belong. I stopped questioning it long ago, stopped wondering how I knew what to do, where to put them. This is what I came here to do, that's all there is to it, and until it's done and the last name's in its right place then I won't stop. There's no air here but I've got all the charm I need to breathe; it's cold but the names keep me warm. And I know that when I'm done the first of my kin will join me.

'I don't understand how the names can actually become the dragons – I don't think it's my place to know that. I think that when I'm done I'll take a long rest, a long sleep, and wait for them to come to me, wake me up and say, "Hello Kythe, here we are. Will you take us home, please?" And home we'll all go. And they'll be the first ones, the special ones, the ones made purely from their names. The other rocks will stay here and each time a new dragon hatches down there on the skin of the world it'll draw a name to it from the mother moon. The parents will think they chose the name but it won't be their choice, not really. The choice is mine, in a way. They're mine to choose, all the names, all of them, a place for each and each in its place.'

She stopped, breathless, almost glaring at Jonah in her intensity. Her tremendous age poured from her yet she was still in essence young. A virgin queen alone with her toil, content in her

269

solitude, quite ready for the future she herself was dragging into the light.

'What of the black rock I found in the crater on Stone?' he said. 'Did you send it to me?'

'Of course I did!' she laughed. 'Who else? You see, some of the rocks don't have any names inside them. Whenever I find one of these I throw it down towards the world. Most of them burn up, of course; some of them glance off the air and fly back into orbit, still burning. They're trapped by the pull of the world but they're free of the ground at least. These rocks will become dragons too, given time – they'll become the night dragons, which you call shooting stars, and in our lore the night dragons are creatures with no names. A few of the rocks I keep for myself. Whenever I see a volcano flare up down on the skin of the world I breathe your name into one of them and throw it into the fire, hoping it might just find its way through to Stone.' Kythe grinned, exposing satin-smooth teeth. 'It looks as if my aim is better than I thought.'

Jonah recalled the upturned continent with its countless smoking craters. 'I should say you hit the bull's-eye on more occasions than one,' he said.

'I knew you'd need my help sooner or later,' she shrugged, 'so I thought I'd send you an invitation.'

Someone flicked across Jonah's peripheral vision. He looked round just in time to see a puff of grey dust mushroom upwards. It continued to rise, confounding his expectations of gravity. Another of Kythe's dragon names, come to find its place.

'Tell me something, Kythe. Does the name Thomas Coyote mean anything to you?'

The dragon shook her head, puzzled. 'Is it a faery name? They're strange. Why should I know this one?'

'Oh, no reason, I suppose. He is a man who . . . he has caused us some trouble and, well, I know enough about him to know that he too collects little black rocks. I just wondered . . .'

'Nothing to do with me, I'm afraid. But you have reminded me of one more thing I wanted to tell you.'

270

'Go on.'

'I dream a lot – sometimes there isn't much else to do here. Well, not long ago something strange happened. I woke up inside my dream. Have you ever heard of anything so strange?'

'I have to agree it is strange,' said Jonah.

'Yes. Anyway, I woke up in this dream and found myself back on Earth, watching this old dragon legend play itself out. I won't bore you with the details but there was this evil force called the Flame and this little group of dragons had to get rid of it. It was about that time that two dragons – Brace and Ledra – found their way across to Stone and established our little clawhold there. They were my ancestors, you see.'

'Stone can show us much about our past,' agreed Jonah.

'Well, it was all very confusing, fire everywhere, but through the smoke I could see this circle in the air. It looked like dragons . . . connected together somehow. And there was a name too, sort of blowing on the wind. It sounded like . . . Orbos, or something. I forgot most of the dream – except what I've just told you of course – but the name especially stuck with me, along with the crazy idea you might know what it meant.'

She paused, breathless and expectant. Jonah shrugged. 'I am sorry to disappoint you, Kythe. It seems to me I may have heard a similar name before but . . . no, I cannot place it. Perhaps it was just a dream after all.'

'Just a dream . . .' she mused. Then her mood became abruptly brisk. 'Now, what can I do for you?'

'Down to business, Kythe?'

'Oh, dear Jonah! I wish we could chat away like we used to but you know you can't stay here for long. You said yourself it's dangerous for you even to come here like this.'

'I know, Kythe, I know. But . . . oh, I miss you.'

'Miss you too, Jonah.'

They halted, each unable to meet the other's gaze. Then Jonah went on, 'But you asked what you could do for me. I was rather hoping you could tell me. I have responded to your call and

271

every instinct I possess is screaming that this is the right place to be, and the right moment to be here. I know you can help me defeat Archan – I know it is only you who can help me do this. But . . . how? That I do not know.'

Another silence came between them, yet it was a silence not of uncertainty but of anticipation. Shreds of quartz sparkled deep in the grey dust and a shooting star seared the air of the Earth.

Not a shooting star, *Jonah reminded himself in wonder.* A night dragon.

From its dying light he looked back into the stale dust of the moon, saw a little black rock that bore the name of a dragon not yet born. In the moon's black sky hung a greater star, the sun around which all things revolved and from which all illumination came.

. . . light . . . moon . . . name . . . sun . . .

'What did you say?' demanded Kythe.

'Forgive me,' said Jonah, 'I did not realize I was speaking aloud.'

'I . . . I'm not sure that you were. Tell me though: what did you say? It's important, Jonah.'

'It is something that came to me just then, some words that came to Annie during one of her dreams – and you will have to wait a while longer if you want me to explain about those. Anyway, she heard these words in her mind, but every time she heard them they were in a different order. It was as if they were spinning round each other, orbiting with no beginning and no end. "Like a dog chasing its tail," she told me.' He laughed. 'I have no idea why I thought of them now.'

Kythe rose up, wings trembling like those of a fledgling on its maiden flight.

'Come with me,' she said.

She led him across a grey and waterless sea, moving like a creature underwater, wings spread but useless in a world without air, claws extended to kick off the dusty ground whenever gravity's meagre pull overwhelmed the gentle flight charm holding her aloft. She led and he followed, noticing the way her claws lifted little whorls of dust from the ground, noticing the way his own feet left no mark at all. He was truly a ghost in this place and time, a visitor skating recklessly over the surface of the past as if it were a blazing star, fearful of the slightest touch.

They passed crater after crater and every other one held a little black rock at its heart. Jonah looked out to the unfamiliar horizon and saw millions of craters, millions of rocks. For a moment the numbers made him dizzy and he saw wings lifting from each of the craters, grey wings turning to gold in the unhindered sunshine. But when he shook his head the wings were gone, though the numbers remained.

'Here.' Kythe's voice was soft, almost reverent. Jonah looked down to where she was pointing with one outstretched wing and saw a pattern of craters. There were three of identical size ringed equally around a fourth, this one a little smaller. Each of the outer three harboured a little black rock; the crater in the middle was empty.

'Three of the first,' Kythe said. 'These three were among the very first rocks I placed. They'll be among the dragons born on the moon, the vanguard of our race. This one,' she pointed to the nearest of the three, 'is called Sun.'

She paused and Jonah felt his heart pause too. The hesitation tracked through the rest of his body, a bloodless pulse in the space of which he felt a lifetime pass. 'And the others?' he asked without needing to.

She pointed again. 'This one – her name is Moon. And this one is Light.'

'What of the empty place in the middle, Kythe? Will that crater take a rock too?'

'I didn't think so but . . . now I'm not so sure.'

Another night dragon crossed the sky; both ghost-man and dragon-queen ignored it. An idea had spilt between them.

. . . sun . . . moon . . . light . . .

'Name . . . have you placed Archan's name yet?' asked Jonah. Kythe shook her head.

'No rock has come to the moon with her name on it yet,' she replied.

'And when one does . . . might this be the place where it is meant to lie?'

Kythe looked long and hard at the empty grey crater. 'It . . . might be. Until the rock comes I don't know for certain. But, Jonah, I am bound to place it here, if this is where it belongs. I am the mother dragon, I cannot defy my fate.'

'I understand that; I have no desire to unravel the past any more than I have to but . . . could *this* be the place where Archan begins?' This last part he said under his breath, a question not to Kythe but to himself. Understanding, she did not answer. Nor did any answer come, but as Jonah walked away he took some small hope with him.

Seeds, *he was thinking.* Ivory tiles and little black rocks, all pieces with their places to hold and their parts to play.

Holding up his hand he saw that it had faded almost to nothing.

'I cannot stay any longer, Kythe,' he called. When he looked for her he saw a great gulf had opened between them: he was flying high over the dust of the moon, gazing down at craters which glared back at him like a million eyes. 'You have to puzzle it out for yourself.'

'I don't understand, Jonah.' Her words struggled to him on filaments of charm. He had almost left the memory now; its edges were charring like newsprint on a stove.

'It is Archan's place,' he cried, knowing that she knew it too. 'That is what we have found. All you need now is to find her name.'

'But we know her name, Jonah . . .' and that was all he heard before the black edges of the memory rod closed over the moon and extinguished the stars and he fell like a rock back . . .

. . . to Stone.

It was raining fish again, thousands of the hapless creatures plummeting from the Verge to be soaked up by a twinkling cloud of Shades many miles below.

Gerent and Malya had returned to the Bark. They stood facing each other on the upper curve of the spherical hull, hands roaming unselfconsciously, voices quiet in constant exchange. Beside Jonah, Annie was lost in silent sleep, while somewhere unseen Tom Coyote prowled still. Of Grandfather Tree there was no sign.

Lightfish struck the Bark, impaling themselves on the rods and vanes or else bouncing and slithering off around the hull to continue their fall. The sky was alive with shining, spinning bodies. Laughing like children in a storm the Neolithic lovers fled beneath a wooden cowl, waving to Jonah as they ducked beneath its shelter.

Looking up he saw they were much closer to the Verge than before; indeed, the brim of the witch's hat looked close enough to touch. As he watched, six of the Bark's twelve insect legs relocated themselves around the vessel's upper hemisphere. They reached upwards, brilliant blue charm gathering at their tips, and as they made contact with the underside of the Verge a series of jolts fed back through the legs and into the ship, knocking Jonah on to his back. The charm clung like spider silk and, one leg at a time, the Bark released its hold on the wall. Now it was suspended beneath the Verge's almighty overhang, suspended over the abyss that had haunted Jonah since the very first day he set foot on the precarious world of Stone. One by one the other six legs felt their way round and added their strength to the bond. Only when all twelve legs were glued to the Verge's underside did the Bark begin to inch its way towards the outside edge.

He scanned the busy sky for Tangent and the other Shades, finding them at last in a relatively clear patch of air to the side of the Bark and a little below. Lightfish continued to rain past but the rain was more sporadic now; it seemed the storm was beginning to abate.

I have been to the moon! he thought, expecting to be awed. Yet he felt nothing. How real were his experiences in the memory rods? Were they any more than dreams?

He had only to look at Malya, whom he had dragged straight out of one of those experiences to know they were all too real. Yet dreamlike was how they felt to him now. And was not entering the rods in the first place a little like embarking on one of Annie's dreamin' dreams?

. . . light . . . moon . . . sun . . . name . . .

Archan's place, Archan's name. Kythe was bound to place Archan's name-rock when it came. To refuse would only create another time paradox, only split the world and make yet another Archan, nameless perhaps but no less powerful for that. Try as he might he could not see a way through. All he knew was that it mattered.

For now there was nothing to do but watch as the Bark traversed the underside of the Verge, charm-sticky legs trembling as they took it nearer and nearer to the edge. The Bark shuddered with every step, ghastly grinding sounds reverberating through its timbers. It was slowing perceptibly; Jonah wondered how long it could last.

There were no lightfish out here at all. They had either all fallen or else gone into hiding, fearing the fate of their neighbours. What was apparent was a thickening of the air, a syrupy glow which brightened as the Bark pressed its way through. Jonah could feel it damping the movements of his body, squeezing his chest, and for a moment he feared they would be suffocated or even crushed. But there came a point after which the air grew no denser and, although it was uncomfortable, there was no real threat.

Like a spider traversing a ceiling the Bark jerked its

way through the thickened air to the very edge of the overhang. Jonah held his breath as the leading leg tapped its way round the corner and up out of sight, then let it expire as the others followed suit. With an awkward rolling manoeuvre the Bark relocated the sprouting points of its legs again, allowing it to clamber up and over the edge of the witch's brim without tipping the hull on to its side – and spilling its passengers into the abyss.

Just before they left the shadow of the brim Jonah glanced down and saw Tangent hovering beneath the zone of thicker air. The Shade darted close. He placed both hands against each other; in this pose he looked all the more angelic, a winged cherub at prayer. Then he dropped away, a falling star.

Light was everywhere, painful light, and Jonah had to narrow his eyes to slits before he could bear to look. When his vision adjusted he felt giddy, to the point where he put his arms out to steady himself even though the Bark had come to a halt. He blinked, drank in the view, and blinked again. At his side Annie was stirring and mumbling half-words to herself, beginning to come out of the dreamin' dream.

He had expected to see a circular deck of black Stonestuff with a small cone – the apex of all Stone – erupting from the centre. What he saw was rather different; what he saw was unexpectedly *Earthly*.

On top of the witch's brim was an orchard.

The trees were uniformly strange, neither apple nor oak nor elm but some agglomeration of them all. Dark red bark, bright green leaves. The fruits adorning the branches were of all shapes and sizes and less than half he recognized. The sunlight dripping through the canopy seemed changed by the time it struck the leaf-litter, enriched in some way. Abstractly Jonah wondered how thick the apparently solid ground was; if he dug down into the coarse soil how soon would it be before his fingers broke through to the underside of the Verge, opening a trapdoor to Stone's undeniable abyss?

The Bark's deck was lofted to the same level as the tree-tops, permitting a clear line of sight to the very centre of the circular orchard, where there stood not a cone but a statue.

Glossy, black, it was at least as tall as New York's Statue of Liberty, surging clear of the orchard like a breaching whale. Like its Earthly counterpart it had one arm upraised. The other cradled what looked like a large cup against its breast.

But this was not a sculpture of a human being at all.

It was a sculpture of Esh.

The statue was tall and slender, a stretched humanoid form with insect-legs and a reptilian face that was an unlikely combination of woman and tortoise. On its back was hunched a sleek black carapace; Jonah had no doubt that were he to view it from behind he would see – perhaps etched in equally black relief – the Mah Jongg symbol for the Red Dragon. It was Esh, whom he had seen die so that he might live.

He could not take his eyes from her. The sculpture was exquisite, from the twists in the triple-jointed legs to the tug of the carapace against the stringy muscles of the back and shoulders. He began to doubt this was a statue at all, began to believe it must be Esh herself, reincarnated and made immense. His armoured lady knight returned to vanquish the dragon who would devour them all.

Do not be a fool, he scolded himself. *Esh is dead. This is a thing, no more. As manufactured a thing as Stone itself. Do not be deceived by what your heart would see.*

Still, she was beautiful.

The hand not holding the cup was raised high. From the obvious tension in the muscle, as well as the overall posture of the figure, it was clear she was not standing but hanging from this one arm. The hand was a fist clutching a hairline of thread to which was connected, like a child's balloon, the sun.

No Earthly sun this though. It was a tiny ball of light, pure white and quite uncompromising in its regularity, its minuscule perfection. Instantly Jonah knew that this was not just a star but *the* star, the one true sun of which all the suns they had seen on their ascent were merely a reflection. At the same moment he perceived the place of things here at the top of the world.

There was no higher place than the sun. This sun was truly the apex of this and possibly all worlds. Clutching the sun, hanging from it with more determination than even the gods could conceive, was Esh. And hanging from the feet of Esh was Stone.

'What is this place?' said Jonah.

It was not the statue that spoke but Annie.

'Jonah?' she said in a voice from a far land.

He helped her to stand. Still groggy, she looked at the orchard and the sun and the statue of Esh with little obvious reaction. That done, she looked into Jonah's eyes.

He touched her with a tentative hand, fearful that she too might become a statue, touched with one fingertip her cheek, her waist, her breast, her neck. It was a moment so charged with desire that her body jerked with each scant contact. Then she took his finger and stroked it across her lips, kissing the salt from it.

'We're here,' she breathed. 'We made it this far.'

'This far.' He kissed her on the forehead. She was hot; he was too.

'Esh,' she said. Her eyes were dreamy, half-lidded.

'Yes, Esh.'

'It's all so simple, Jonah. All of it. Just tip it over and look at it . . . look at it fresh. That's all you gotta do, all any of us gotta do. Look at it fresh . . .'

'Annie?'

'Where's the river go? That's what you gotta ask your-self, Jonah. Where's the river go? Rest of it's . . . easy. Why, a child could . . .'

Somebody spoke. The voice came from directly behind them.

'Jonah Lightfoot? Annie West? Are you ready to face Archan again?'

Still holding Annie tightly against his body, Jonah swivelled and looked for the first time into the face of Mister Ren.

'As ready as we will ever be, I suppose. But first, I think a little explanation is in order. And please – no riddles.'

'Riddles?' the little Chinese man replied. He was partly transparent, ghost-like. 'What do you take me for?'

18

Sun

Mister Ren said:

'You know a little about me, I think. You know me
as a guide and also as a maker of things – the maker of
immortality above all else, for that is certainly my finest
achievement. So. You probably think of me as a meddler
too, and perhaps a deceiver. Believe me when I say I have
never deliberately misled you – I simply behave as I am
bound to behave. There are rules for us all, even for me.
If I did deceive you, forgive me. But if you do forgive me,
do it later, because there's no time for such things now.

'Jonah, you know most of what you need to know
already. In certain respects you know more than me. But
what I can tell you is how things work up here, above
the Verge. Listen well.

'The Verge, as you will have deduced, marks the last
threshold before the memory rods converge. Here, in the
centre of this orchard, the memory rods come together.
Imagine: all history crushed together into a single thread!
And a thread *is* what it is, Jonah. The rods do *not* disappear
into nothingness, nor do they compress into what in a
later age than yours would be called a *singularity*. Instead
they form a single unified filament, finer than the finest
gossamer, an umbilical cord to the future, the line of
spider-silk from which all Stone is suspended.

'Directly beneath this statue – which, as you have noticed, resembles your friend Esh greatly – the memory rods converge. From the foundation of the statue rises the spider-silk thread. Up through the statue it rises, up through its spine and upraised arm, out through the vein on its wrist and into its hand, where it is gripped. The spider-silk thread continues up out of the statue's hand and straight into the heart of the sun you see blazing above the statue. There it meets with the light of the sun and there is the last Threshold of all. In the heart of the sun lies the one place where Stone and all the worlds are connected fully together. There in the heart of the sun exist no barriers between any of the worlds. There is marked the future of all the worlds where all beings of heart and mind may travel freely across all borders, travel freely into all realms, travel freely into all pasts and all futures and make thoughts and changes without fear of the consequences. In that place, Jonah, everyone is an adept, more powerful even than you and Archan, and more wise. In that place, the first true Golden Age of all the histories of all the known worlds can be said to have begun.

'In that place, which begins inside the sun of Stone and ends far beyond my knowledge, they know of our little worlds and our little Stone. The sun soars above us and we hang from it and they look down on us. Did I say they could cross all borders, these denizens of the sun? It's true, but they choose not to descend to Stone, nor to the worlds it serves. They cannot bring themselves to stoop so low. We are their underworld, Jonah; in their marvellous presence we are not worthy, yet we must hang from them if we are to avoid the endless fall into the abyss.

'It is enough that they support us in this way. Stone is a parasite but without Stone the sun would never have come to be, so its inhabitants tolerate the burden.

The sun is the ultimate evolution of the memory rods, Jonah, the ultimate expression of their form. For Stone is a living thing too, just like man and basilisk and all the crawling, speaking, climbing, falling spawn of all the worlds. And like all living things it seeks nothing more than to survive.

'As soon as the rods were drawn into being they started to twist and climb, surprising even their makers with their tenacity. Like inquisitive ivy they explored, turned, lifted themselves up towards the light. The individual rods touched each other, recognized kin, massed together for strength, became unified and could not be resisted. When they were almost one they created and then crossed the Verge and then their unification became complete and there were no longer individual memory rods but a single line of spider-silk climbing to a new and perfect sun which they themselves had made.

'And in all those future worlds above the Verge came a new dawn and a Golden Age. Future and past became united like the rods and throughout the worlds the barriers came down. A new kind of eternity came, one unbound by the threat of time.

'There, in the heart of a new and perfect sun, the great river of time flowed finally to the sea.'

He tilted his head a little to one side, eyes flashing bright in the dazzling sunshine. 'Come with me now, Jonah. Come, Annie. We have a little time, just a little. I want to show you something.'

A hard deck beneath their feet and the unmistakable song of ship's timbers. Jonah looked up in wonder at the bulging sails, the straining yards. He turned a full circle, head upraised like a man drinking the rain, leading Annie with him as he took in the view. A sturdy ship, this, well-travelled and reliable. The rise and fall of the water's breast beneath her hull. The energetic voice of the breeze.

283

'*You know her, I think?*'

'*Yes,*' sighed Jonah. '*Oh yes, I know her.*'

She was a ten-gun brig called Beagle. Under the command of Captain Fitz Roy, R. N., she had carried Charles Darwin to Tierra del Fuego and beyond, another world away, another age. Now Jonah Lightfoot stood on her deck holding the hand of his woman, Annie West, while the maker of many things stood beside them and watched their simple pleasure.

'*Oh Jonah,*' said Annie, recognizing his joy and taking some of it for herself.

They looked around for the crew – for Darwin himself perhaps – but the ship was deserted apart from the three of them. The sails were trimmed, the rigging set but not by the hand of man. Out of sight the ship's wheel was turning untouched.

'*How do we come to be here?*' asked Jonah. '*Why have you brought us here, of all places?*'

'*Forgive me this conceit,*' replied Mister Ren. '*I have manufactured this vessel for your benefit. Call it . . . a gift. But I have not brought you to see the* Beagle, *rather the* Beagle *is the means I have chosen to show you something far greater. Look out, both of you, and behold the river.*'

Together they walked to the rail and looked out across the water. The river down which the Beagle was sailing was like no other Jonah had ever seen: its waters were black and oily, its waves rope-like and undulating. Yet it was also beautiful, a dark, serpentine stream as wide as the Mississippi and, he suspected, deeper than the Atlantic Ocean.

Dark though the waters were he could just make out shapes moving beneath the surface. Annie grabbed his arm, pointing to a sudden dart of movement near the hull. Another flurry disturbed the Beagle's wake, followed by another more distant. They watched these sporadic signs of life but saw nothing actually break the surface, nor could they discern what creatures they were that swam through these inky depths. Whatever things lurked here kept their identities concealed.

'This is, of course, a metaphor,' Mister Ren announced. 'No river of water this but a river of time. The river of time. You have dipped your toes in it many times, Jonah Lightfoot, and even swum in it for a while. Now you perceive it in all its glory.'

'The river of time,' Jonah said. 'What is this supposed to demonstrate?'

'What do you see?' said Mister Ren.

'Well, like a river, time flows in a single direction. Within its flow lives are lived; I presume that is what we see swimming beneath the surface – the secret lives of unseen beings, perhaps even the lives of men. It is dark . . . like the memory rods.'

'Very good. River and rod, rod and river. The two are one. As the river of time flows so the memory rods climb. So, all very fine. Different to the rivers of your home-world though. Look now at the banks – what do you see?'

'It's getting narrower!' exclaimed Annie. 'The banks are closing in.'

And indeed they were. Distant foothills had become canyon walls. The current, not exactly sluggish to begin with, was now racing, dragging the ship with it; the sails hung slack as it outpaced the wind. Ahead the canyon was high and tight as a mountain pass, slate grey cliffs split by a single blade of sunlight.

'Time flows like water,' explained Mister Ren, 'but where Earthly rivers grow wider as they progress downstream this river gets narrower. Just like the memory rods, it converges.'

A dark slot appeared in one of the side-walls, a lesser canyon into which some of the waters poured.

'The river forks,' said Jonah.

'You know that too,' said Mister Ren. 'You made this junction, Jonah Lightfoot. This is one of the places where you changed the past and split the river into two distinct streams.'

'Dear God!' Jonah clutched Annie's hand as the Beagle approached the jagged wound in the grey rock wall. He had thought himself more or less at peace with what he had done;

now, looking at this crude divergence, he saw he had not so much altered the past as hacked it open.

As the Beagle accelerated past the fork they saw the secondary gorge was crumbling. Even as they watched a slide of boulders crashed into the water, throwing up a viscous spray and clouds of thick vapour.

But there was no time to dwell on it. Now the main river was a slender ribbon of oil compressed by towering canyon walls. Jagged rock reached for the hull; one of the yardarms snagged and splintered like a match. Their speed was impossible to gauge, but the wind it made spread Annie's hair back from her head like a pennant. The band of sunlight raced towards them.

'How many vessels on the river?' asked Mister Ren. When they looked at him without comprehension he repeated the question.

'I didn't see any other ships,' replied Annie. 'Just us, I guess.'

'Exactly!' the little Chinese man crowed. 'Now behold! The river meets the sea!'

The Beagle exploded from the canyon as if propelled from the muzzle of a cannon. The sunlight unpeeled around them, falling across their faces like a cloth of purest, brightest silk. The land fell away, fell behind them as they surged out into the open ocean. There was nothing but sky and sea, and the sea was made from sunlight. And everywhere there were ships.

The ocean was alive with vessels of every conceivable type: brigs and barquentines, ketches and cutters and clippers, junks and jolly boats. Coloured sails like flames on the masts of pirate galleons, submarines breaching like slender whales, a whole flotilla of multi-hulled dugouts, too distant for their occupants to be visible as anything other than dark specks. And for every vessel of Earthly design a thousand more of stranger shape: inflated bladders strapped with twine, glistening iron shells, a ship that seemed all mast and no hull, a tiny square boat made entirely of gold. One far-off leviathan might have served as the Ark, for it looked large enough to carry two of every kind.

Jonah and Annie feasted on the sight. It was a regatta on a scale that defied comprehension. It was at once beautiful and sobering, for it was ultimately too much for them to take in. The ocean shone like a sun; the ocean was the sun. They sat together on the Beagle's *gently swaying deck, allowing the rail to obscure their view of the incandescent sea.*

'Do you see now?' asked Mister Ren. Jonah nodded but it was Annie who spoke for them both.

'Yeah,' she said and her voice was hoarse. 'Yeah, I get it. Us ordinary folk just get swept along by the current, back in the river there. We get born and we live and we die. We live our lives in a straight line, start to finish, ashes to ashes. But these guys . . . these future people who live on the other side of Sunlight Pass or out in the Big Shining Ocean or whatever this damned place is . . . tell me, Mister Ren – does time exist for them at all?'

'Yes, time exists. And it flows still, for there are always currents, even in the ocean. Currents and tides and all manner of marvels and monsters. But here time can flow in any direction – forwards and backwards and even to the side. Up and down and all around! This is what it is like above the Verge, in the heart of the sun from which Stone hangs. And the mariners you see are just a few of those who live here.'

Jonah was shaking his head. 'I cannot comprehend what it means to have time flow in any direction but forwards, but this is surely heaven by any other name. In which case, where do the rest of us eke out our mortal lives but in hell?'

Mister Ren was quick to respond. 'No, Jonah! Oh no, this is not heaven! Nor is your world hell, nor any of the worlds, nor even Stone itself. Although Stone is a place of the dead, in many ways, nor is it without its ghosts.'

'Are they men?'

'Men and more.'

'But what must we be to these . . . well, if this is not heaven then I suppose they cannot be angels? No better than beggars on the street!'

'Jonah Lightfoot!' Annie was indignant. 'You're even more of a snob than I thought! They're no better than you or me, angels or not. And I'll thank you to remember I'm just a farm girl who's done her share of begging in her time, so help me. And as for you, Mister Ren, I thought you said no riddles. This all seems like one big riddle to me.'

'No riddles,' argued Mister Ren, 'just words. But sometimes there are not the words to say what needs to be said. So pictures must be used instead.' He encompassed the ocean with a wave of his arm. 'This is one such picture.'

Jonah felt tired. He lay out flat on the deck and stared up at the sails, taut and pulling hard again now they were on the open sea.

'What will happen to all this if Archan manages to destroy Stone?' he asked at length. 'You said that this place would never have come to be were it not for Stone and the memory rods. Yet Stone depends upon it – quite literally, if it does indeed hang suspended as you say. Might these mariners on a sea of sunlight not welcome the removal of that burden? Might they not be glad were Archan to rid them of the excess baggage?'

'Glad? No, oh no,' answered Mister Ren at once. 'Stone contains their memories too. Your own world, back in the river of time, is part of their past. You yourselves are their ancestors! They would not see all that go to waste.'

'Why bother to show us all this?' Annie flopped down beside Jonah and began absently to stroke his chest. 'It's amazing right enough, but why?'

For the first time Mister Ren seemed ill at ease. He shuffled his feet and examined his fingernails. 'I think Jonah has guessed.'

'Don't play games,' said Annie.

'Jonah?' Mister Ren persisted.

Sitting up slowly, Jonah rubbed his eyes with his knuckles. His eyes were burning; he wanted to sleep for a week.

'Yes,' he sighed, 'I think I might know. It comes back to Archan, of course.' He took Annie's hand. 'Consider this:

288

Archan has two great weapons we are powerless to repel. First of all she can change the course of history. She has not dared to do so yet but the time is fast approaching when she will perform her first experiments. Secondly, she is immortal. But consider this also: if she were to come to this ocean then neither of those weapons would matter! *Here,* everyone can travel through time. By our definition, everyone *is an adept. And here time does not flow in the conventional sense so the concept of immortality is effectively meaningless. If we could bring Archan here – and somehow keep her here – she would be among equals and hence no longer the deadly threat she has been up to now.'*

Annie frowned. *'But she's a monster, Jonah. She's evil. You can't stop her being evil just by clipping her wings.'*

Jonah and Mister Ren exchanged a glance; the Chinese man nodded like a teacher who is pleased with his student.

'No,' Jonah agreed. *'No, Annie, you are right – we cannot stop her being evil. If we brought her here she would continue to do evil things. But she would be just a little fish again, and there might just be some bigger fish here to do more than merely clip her wings.'*

'This is horseshit!' shouted Annie. *'You're talkin' about makin' her somebody else's problem. She ain't a hot potato, Jonah! And how you gonna stop her comin' back down to Stone whenever she pleases, huh? You gonna . . .'* Her eyes widened. *'Oh my God, you're gonna cut the cord! That's it ain't it, that's what you're both thinkin'? You're gonna tempt her up here then skedaddle back down to Stone and cut it loose! Stone falls and Archan's left to do her worst in Paradise! Well let me tell you this stinks! You got any idea? Any idea at all how much it stinks?'*

She beat her hands against Jonah's chest where moments before she had been stroking him. Grabbing her wrists he compelled her to stop.

'I do not like it any more than you, Annie, but it is at least a plan.'

'Stinks!' she cried.

'It may not be perilous for Stone to fall,' said Mister Ren. 'I do believe it will fall forever and so never actually hit anything. Which is as good as not falling at all.'

'Falling's bad in my book,' said Annie.

'Think of it as banishment,' said Jonah. 'Like deporting a convict to Botany Bay.'

'That stank too,' retorted Annie, her anger turning to tears. 'I won't have no part of it.'

'Come here, my darling.'

Jonah reached for her, tried to hug her to him but she battered him away. 'Don't you charm your way 'round me, Jonah Lightfoot! You promise me you won't do this! You promise me!'

He looked for support from Mister Ren. The Chinese man was regarding him with a curious expression he could not quite interpret at first. Then he had it: Mister Ren looked eager, like a hopeful puppy awaiting adoption.

You do not know, *he thought with a sudden burst of insight.* You really have no idea how to deal with Archan at all. You brought us here with no purpose other than to see what we might come up with. You do not need us to help you – you need us to dig you out of the almighty hole you dug for yourself when you first came up with idea of immortality. You do not need us to help you at all – you need us to *save* you, Mister Ren. Don't you?

'Do you deserve to be saved, Mister Ren?' Jonah asked.

'No,' answered the little man at once, and Jonah gave him credit for his immediate candour. 'No, I do not. But I think Stone does, don't you?'

Jonah called a meeting in the shadow of one of the Bark's immense spider-legs. They sat in a circle – if just four people could be said to make a circle – he and Annie, Malya and Gerent. The ground was littered with fruit jostled free by the Bark as it had settled itself at the very edge of the orchard. Over the tops of the trees the upper half of the statue of Esh was clearly visible.

They seemed small, the four of them, small compared to the massive Bark and tinier still compared to the worlds hanging both above and below them. Yet here, at the junction between the past and the future, everything was pinched so tight that perhaps only small people could do the work.

'He hasn't turned up yet,' said Annie. 'I'm gettin' worried.'

She was referring to Grandfather Tree, to whom they had called over and over again, roaming the Bark's decks and venturing a little way into the few corridors still accessible. Gerent had explored deepest of all, fighting his way through a briar-filled tunnel into a cold, black chamber he did not recognize at all.

'It's like winter in there,' he had reported on his return. 'There is no light, no sound. The Bark is dead, I am certain of it. The journey has exhausted it. And if the Bark is dead then the lesky must be dead too.'

'Let us not give up hope,' said Jonah. 'Grandfather Tree is resourceful, we all know that. Besides, there is another reason why we should not abandon the Bark altogether.'

'Coyote,' said Malya.

'Indeed, Coyote. Whatever may have happened to Grandfather Tree we must assume that Tom Coyote is still alive.'

'There is nothing but death in there, Jonah,' said Gerent.

'Nevertheless we cannot take any chances. One of us at least must stay behind to make sure he does not follow.'

'Why do we have to go to the statue?' demanded Annie. 'Ain't that what she'll expect us to do?' She scowled hard at Jonah, prompting Malya and Gerent to exchange puzzled looks.

'Archan is not here yet,' answered Jonah, 'and as long as we have the advantage of time I think we should use it. I believe the place where she will cross over into this world is there, at the very top of the statue's outstretched hand. That place, the tip of that uppermost finger, is where the thread is at its narrowest. It is the weakest point, where the barriers are all but down; it is the gateway through which she will come. If we can meet her there, perhaps deflect her before she has fully come through, then we may yet stand a chance against her.'

'*Deflect* her?' said Annie. 'You got any idea what you're talkin' about, Englishman?'

'Not very much, I fear.' He offered her a lame smile and kissed her on the cheek; she flinched but did not reject the contact.

'What Jonah says makes sense,' said Malya. She was tapping repeatedly at the ground between her feet with the tip of her short Roman sword. 'You don't wait for the enemy to come to you. If there's a chance we can head her off we have to try.' The others nodded at this; even Annie grudgingly admitted that anything was better than just waiting around.

'I will stay,' said Gerent. Malya's mouth dropped open but it was Jonah who responded first.

'I was wondering if it was wise for only one to stay behind,' he said.

Gerent shrugged. 'You'll need a fast sword up there – none is faster than Malya's. She must come with you. Annie's mind is joined to Archan's so she herself may be a weapon you cannot afford to leave behind. And you, Jonah Lightfoot . . . it is your task to face Archan, here at the end of the journey. As for me: I have fast wings and sharp eyes. I am best equipped to patrol the land around the Bark. If Coyote emerges I will spot him and deal with him.'

'He is more dangerous than he seems,' said Jonah.

'He bested me once,' agreed Gerent. 'He will not get the opportunity to do so again.'

His face and mind were set, not that there was any convincing argument against his decision. Gerent had *calmed*; in the dazzling light of the sun he looked every inch a king. Malya looked anguished but held her tongue; much as she was reluctant to leave her lover behind she was even less happy about the possibility of having a killer stalk her through the orchard.

'You take care,' was all she said, slicing with her sword through a fallen apple.

They made rapid progress through the orchard, which was not so different from the orchards in which Jonah had roamed with Lily all those summers ago. Instead of being arranged in a rectangular grid the trees radiated out from the central statue, and the fruits themselves were undeniably strange, but the feel of the place was the same. Dappled light painted domino-shapes on a carpet of fallen leaves; the never-resting voice of the wind chattered high in the canopy.

A twig snapped behind them. Malya whirled, brandishing her sword. The trees were disguised with light, betraying nothing. They waited but no beast came rushing for them.

There was another movement, this time to the side. Several ranks of trees were shivering as if something massive had just passed among them. A scattering of leaves was still moving towards the ground. Something touched Jonah's shoulder and he had to bite back the scream.

'Calm you down!' rumbled the voice of the lesky in his ear.

Heart thundering, Jonah turned to see the old elfin face jutting out from one of the orchard trees. Always wizened, it now looked positively haggard. Nevertheless there was still a sparkle in each green eye and a smile behind the brambles.

'Grandfather Tree!' Jonah pressed his hand to his chest in an effort to still his racing heart.

'The same.'

'What are you doing here? We had all but given you up for lost.'

'Lost – ah ye, not lost. Bark though, he is not a happy place. Too much dead wood. Had to get out, me. Lesky needs sap. This place: a sanctuary it is.'

They gathered round the lesky's tree, listening to him tell of the devastation he had found inside the Bark.

'Poor Bud – beyond finding he was. Dead he may be but . . . maybe not. No way to tell.'

'I'm sorry about Bud,' said Annie. 'What about . . . what about Coyote?'

The lesky shrugged, the gesture rustling the upper branches of the fruit-laden tree. 'Same. No way to track him down. Me – I had to leave.' He explained how he had found his way from the Bark into the root system of the orchard, spreading himself through the entire plantation. 'Part of lesky in every tree now, just like the taiga. Just like home.'

'Can you go back to the Bark?'

'Oh ye, worry not! Get you home I will, at the end of it all. Think of this as . . . a holiday!'

The lesky's eyes watched them as they continued on their way, vanishing from one trunk only to reappear on the next. He hummed as they walked, his ancient woodland song a welcome counterpoint to the rhythm of their feet among the leaves.

Near the centre of the orchard the trees thinned out. The statue's feet – each one the size of a Thames barge

– were planted deep in a mound of moist humus, their smooth blackness contrasting with the orchard's coarse greens and reds and browns. Malya, who had been leading the way all through the trees, marched briskly up to the statue and began an inspection of the enormous feet, seeking a way either up or in. Grandfather Tree followed her as far as he was able, coming to rest in a fallen bough a few yards beyond the last tree.

Jonah held back, seizing a moment alone in this curious place. When Annie saw his hesitation she doubled back and stood with him. Together they watched the Neolithic warrior woman circle round behind the statue.

'Having doubts about your mighty plan?' When he shook his head her voice softened. 'What is it, Jonah? You can't look at Malya these days without your face hardening up. Ain't it about time you told me what's wrong?'

With Malya out of sight there was nothing to see but the tremendous figure of stone.

'That is what is wrong,' he replied, nodding at the statue. He told her then, told her how he had found Darwin's book, how he had broken it into tiny pieces and washed it into the sea. She made the connection fast, clasping her hand across her mouth to stifle the scream even before Jonah had begun to tell her the rest.

'How long?' she gasped, her hand still held to her face. Jonah shook his head.

'I cannot say for certain. I rescued Malya long after I rescued the book, but I fear the book was petrified for quite some time before I found it. She may have many days yet . . . or it could happen at any moment.'

'Will it be quick?' Annie's eyes were startled, awash with tears.

'I do not know that either. I hope so, for her sake. For all our sakes.'

'Can't you do anything?' Now she was crying, big

rolling tears that lumbered down her cheeks, across her splayed hand. 'You can't, can you? There's no way to s-s-save her.'

'I have racked my brains, my darling. You cannot imagine how I have worked to find an answer. But, alas, I fear I have reached the end of my domain. To do any more I would have to be a god.'

'Oh dear God, poor Malya! But, Jonah . . . does this mean everything else you created is gonna turn to stone too? Archan's twin sister . . . by God does this mean that whole other *world* will just shrivel up and die?' She grabbed him with wet hands, her face intense. 'Jonah, it does, doesn't it? All those things you made – they're doomed too! The world that Archan's in right now is gonna harden up just like your damned book! Is this the answer? Is this how we're meant to get rid of Archan, by keeping her trapped in that other world while it turns to stone around her?'

Jonah gaped, overwhelmed by her intensity, shocked that he had not seen it himself. Of course she was right! Of course the same rules applied to *everything* he had duplicated, from books and people to dragons and worlds! Moreover, he had resurrected Malya at the same time as creating that other world, that other Archan, so when she died . . . they would die too.

'How long?' he muttered. 'How long?'

'Does this mean you're givin' up on the other plan?' said Annie. 'The one where the sun-people get lumbered with an immortal dragon?'

'It was never much of a plan in the first place.' Jonah surprised himself by managing a wan smile.

But their excitement died when they saw Malya reappear from behind the statue. She waved enthusiastically and called to them both. 'Come on, there's no time for that! See what I've found!'

'What do we say to her?' whispered Annie, wiping the

tears from her face and rubbing her hands dry against her leggings.

'Just what I have said up to now,' said Jonah. 'Nothing. Perhaps that way she will never know.'

Between the statue's pressed-together heels was a low door. Jonah praised Malya on her detective work, for the door was betrayed only by the thinnest of cracks in the otherwise unblemished black stone. He suspected he could have circled the statue a hundred times and not spotted it once. Her Neolithic eyes had spied it on the first pass.

On the four-foot-high door was etched the sword-shape of the Red Dragon.

In a daze Jonah reached into his pocket. He had no idea where the last two Mah Jongg tiles were. Had he left them on the Bark? Had he lost them overboard? He fumbled – empty, nothing there! Then he had them. Fist clenched tight around the little ivory blocks he withdrew his hand, trembling.

'Steady, Jonah,' said Annie. 'It's just a door.'

Forcing himself to stay calm, Jonah opened his hand and picked the Red Dragon from the pair. Glancing at the painting on the reverse (fiery dragon's head, metal eye, sun-glint) he touched the tile against the symbol on the door.

Nothing happened. Brow furrowed, he took it away and reapplied it. Still nothing.

'Push?' called Grandfather Tree from the fallen bough, but even that did no good.

They tried everything they could think of: turning the tile in every conceivable direction, varying the pressure from feather-light graze to hammer-blow, all to no avail. The door remained shut.

'Damnation!' shouted Jonah. He banged on the door again, this time with his fist. 'This *must* be the place! Why else would the symbol be here? Mister Ren! Esh! Help us! What must we do?'

But Mister Ren was nowhere to be seen, nor did the statue deign to speak. They were, for the time being at least, entirely on their own.

'Maybe we could . . .' Annie began, only to be interrupted by Malya.

'The mark is not in the middle of the door!' she exclaimed, bending her knees and dipping her head from one side to the other. The others crouched with her; after a moment or two of bobbing heads, and with some degree of bemusement, they agreed the symbol was positioned about two inches to the left of centre.

'What does it prove?' sighed Jonah. He stood up again, stretching.

'Where is the other tile?' Malya demanded. He held it out to her: White Dragon, the blank of the Mah Jongg set. On one side was Annie's painting of the ice-dragon, on the other – nothing at all. 'There!' she cried in triumph. 'Red Dragon on the left, White Dragon on the right. So simple we missed it!'

'But there is no mark to the right of the centre line,' said Jonah.

'Exactly!'

A smile growing on his face, Jonah once more pressed the first tile against the Red Dragon symbol. But this time, still holding the Red Dragon in place, he pressed its blank partner into the empty space to the right. There was the faintest of clicks and the door vanished; it did not swing nor slide, it simply vanished, leaving Jonah still holding the tiles and feeling just a little foolish.

'Looks like you ain't finished with them yet,' said Annie. She stepped past him, bending low as she passed into the doorway. 'Better put them in your pocket again before you lose them. Good work, Malya. Don't know why he didn't think of it himself.'

'I wish Gerent were here,' said Malya. 'I prefer sword-play to mind games any day!'

'Do not fret,' said Jonah. 'There may be plenty of that before the end.'

There was light beyond the doorway, dim yellow light. And a narrow staircase leading, quite naturally, up.

19

In Coyote – 2

The goddamn wood-sprite or whatever the hell it was
had gotten to be really annoying. Jawing on and on
like some moron child, filling up the darkness with
inane jokes and disconnected ramblings. He had been
more than pleased when something like a thunderclap
had penetrated the miserable dungeon and silenced the
little brute once and for all.

Hot on the tail of the thunderclap had come something
immense, swishing through the stale air like the ghost of
a hammer. He felt it pass through him, felt it tug at his guts
as it did so, felt it pass soundlessly into the Bark-wood at
his back, leaving him unharmed but taking the lesky's
idiot offspring with it. Bud gave a single yelp as he was
torn from his guard duty, then he was gone. Some small
chinks of light had begun to creep in by then, or else his
eyes had finally adapted to the gloom. Not that he needed
light to tell him he was free: he knew by the sudden
release of pressure on his chest and around his arms that
the chattering wooden disc and its twiggy shackles had
disappeared.

Coyote tottered to his feet. Staggering a little and
grinning a lot, legs numb, blood throbbing into arms
that had been upraised for far too long, he began to

make his way back up the corridor towards a welcome spill of orange light.

The ship wasn't looking great. The enticing orange glow turned out to be a small fire crackling right in the middle of the corridor. Debris lay all around it. He watched the fire for what felt like an eternity, hypnotized by the flames. Gradually it burned itself out, spitting out foul smoke as it was smothered by its own ashes.

Further along the passage was blocked altogether. The floor was buckled, lifted up as if all the demons of hell had tried to hump their way through it. No way out there. Back-tracking, he found only one other corridor; that too was blocked, this time by a plug of resin set hard like a great ball of dung.

Trapped, then.

Tom Coyote grinned. Something would come along.

He slept. There was little else to do and the near-darkness made it easy. The tunnel was getting steadily brighter though: every so often a bulkhead would groan and a new shaft of light would appear. He watched jostling beams of airborne dust and thought about how there were no shadows in the dark.

He slept, as he always did, without dreaming. Sign of a clear conscience. Then, some time after his release from Bud's shackles – it might have been days, it might have been weeks – he fell into a much deeper sleep than usual. He fell and, this time, he dreamed.

It was a lucid dream. He'd heard all about dreams like this from the shrink but had never actually had one. Lucid dreams: the kind where the dreamer wakes up but he's still in the dream. Sometimes he's even able to control it.

Well, he woke up in this dream all right but he sure as hell wasn't the one in control.

It was evening. Surrounded by trees, Tom Coyote was cracking sticks beneath his boots and watching his breath make clouds from the twilight. He recognized California's west coast wilderness at once – the redwoods were unmistakable. Audubon Canyon was a few miles to the north-west of here; in the opposite direction lay San Francisco Bay. This place lay slap between the two, the forest of giants he knew so well from . . .

He whirled round, his boots setting off a storm of tiny explosions in the dry tinder. Echoes bounced back from the trees . . . except they weren't echoes. What he heard were *responses*. There was someone in the woods, watching him, mimicking his every move like a shadow, a reflection. Someone? Some*thing*? A bear perhaps, or a wolf . . .

Movement behind him. He spun again. More cracks, more responses. Nothing to see but dense shadow and the dismal remains of a glowering sky, thick purple behind the towering redwoods.

Got to get outa here!

Thoroughly spooked, Tom Coyote started to run, crashing through undergrowth and weaving between sequoia trunks tall enough to reach the moon. Something ran beside him, breaking all before it. It matched his pace precisely but remained out of sight behind the gloom. Glancing to the left he thought he saw its wake, a blackness in the black, streaks of emptiness trailing long behind a hole in the night. It struck a tree, folded round it and continued, leaving three hundred feet of timber quivering like a landed arrow.

Without warning the land dropped away and he was slip-sliding down a muddy scarp, kicking up a froth of leaves and needles and rich ground-muck until he fetched up against a huge fallen bough. Twice as thick as he was tall, it was a branch not from California but from legend.

Beyond the bough was a clearing and in the clearing

flickered a camp-fire. Seated beside the fire, head bowed, was a small figure who was at once unrecognizable and horribly familiar.

But there was no time to puzzle out the figure's identity because something had crept up behind him. It was there now, hunched over him, spilling icy breath across the back of his neck.

The thing in the woods, he thought in barely-restrained panic, but a glance to the side told him it was not so: the shadow was still loitering there, well out of reach. But if the thing behind him was not the monster . . .

Tom Coyote turned and stared into eyes of chromium steel.

The owner of the eyes told him her name.

'I'm glad I've found you, faery Tom, very glad indeed. I was beginning to think my sister was the only one capable of stealing people's dreams. No, don't move. If you move I shall be forced to make your life very unpleasant.

'That's better. Yes, sit back for a moment, compose yourself. Listen to me – you might hear something worthwhile.

'You know this forest: it's a place from your past. A very important place, as I've come to learn in the short time I've spent here. Here . . . well, we're in your mind, faery Tom. This forest might be a memory of yours but right now it's also the way you've chosen to represent the inside of your head. So unimaginative, you faeries. Still, I suppose it makes a change from a cave. As for me, well, I've come in from the outside, you might say. Or you might say the *other* side. Oh, what does it matter? I'm here now . . .

'I'm going to take a ride with you, faery Tom. I do hope you don't mind – not that you'd have a lot of choice in the matter if you did. I need a claw-hold in this version of Stone if I'm to . . . well, I won't bore you with the details.

You'll find out soon enough what I've got planned.

'I will repeat one thing though, just to make it clear. *Areken*. My name is *Areken*. That's very important to me, faery Tom. Just recently it's seemed my name is the only thing I've got left to call my own. That's changed now, of course: now I've got you!

'But before I can start I have to make a few changes in here. You've got a curious mind, for a faery. A simple mind, on the whole, but not without its twists and turns. Twists and turns are not what I require however – in fact they could be a distinct disadvantage. So I intend to straighten them out.'

Tom Coyote listened without moving. Not that he had any choice, since he appeared to have been paralysed from the neck down. The chrome eyes and the grating voice belonged to a dragon, slender and white, its smooth scales rimed with frost. Winter pulsed from it in waves. Where it touched the trees icicles formed; where it scuffed the ground ice towers sprang like stalagmites, forming a fragile and glassy forest.

When the dragon had finished talking it allowed him to swivel his head. There was the shadow again, marking time behind the trees. It had grown, absorbing part of the darkened sky and at the same time becoming more distinct: a thick neck, a ragged muzzle, sharp ears.

A wolf, no doubt about it! A giant one – a monster!

It was waiting for him in the forest, waiting for him to stray. But the dragon did not want him to look at the wolf, it was turning his head further, turning his body so that he was looking at the camp-fire and the person crouched beside it.

It was a boy, maybe ten, maybe twelve, hugging himself in the night. Unruly hair hung loose, hiding his face.

'Who the hell is that?' asked Tom Coyote, looking back into . . .

. . . the year known to men as 1957. Summer, with the war already faded. A confident, chrome-filled year, bright with new fears and the certainty those fears would be crushed. The year in which Thomas Coyote entered the redwood forest and turned the magical age of twelve, and was told by his father he was no longer a boy but half a man.

Half a man. The sober words matched the grim look on his father's face; the words, like the year, were both fearful and filled with power.

'America's growin' up too, son,' his father said. The pint bottle of rye hovered more or less at the level of his chin; most of its contents Tom could see in his father's eyes. 'The day she dropped the Bomb she came of age. But just like you she's only part-way there. She can't go drinkin' and screwin' just yet, not 'til she's learned how to handle herself. Because she's strong, son, just like you, never forget that. And there's those out there'd like to get the better of her, maybe take her off into the snow and have their wicked way with her. I ain't sayin' it's the Russians and I ain't sayin' it's the Chinks but we gotta be ready for them when they come, you hear what I'm sayin'? Winter's comin', son. You gotta be ready for it, that's all I'm sayin'. Now take a swig. Sooner you start, sooner you'll get to where you're goin'.'

Wondering just where it was his father expected him to be going, twelve year-old Thomas Coyote took the proffered bottle and touched it to his mouth. The smell nearly made him gag but he was supposed to be a man, wasn't he? Or half a man at least.

He tipped the bottle back far enough to let the tiniest slug into his mouth. His father watched, rapt, as he swallowed, eyes streaming, forcing himself not to vomit the foul liquor back into the bottle. He would not be whipped if he did such a thing – his father had never hit him, not once – but the sneers cut deeper than any belt.

'Good enough,' said his father. 'Now, Eleanor. You gonna try some?'

Eleanor Joan Coyote, five years younger than her brother, giggled and turned away.

'Oh daddy! You shouldn't tease me so!'

Thomas watched his father's eyes soften as they looked upon Eleanor. Her contradictory grace – she was both fat and dainty – shone from her even in repose. Everybody loved her, even, grudgingly, Thomas. For the ten thousandth time he forgave his father the obvious favouritism and learned to hate himself just a little more.

That was the end of the camp-fire wisdom. The bottle of liquor accompanied their father into his tent, leaving the two children to whisper ghosts out of the warm night air. Soon Eleanor was dozing. Thomas, who was now half a man, read from his Dylan Thomas for a while. Some time later he was sleeping too.

The fire was low when he was kicked awake. A hand stifled his scream; his father's wild eyes both reassured and terrified him.

'D'you unnerstan' what's goin' to happen to you?' The words stumbled and the liquor in the half-empty bottle sloshed; somewhere in the tent, Thomas knew, the first bottle of liquor was long since empty. Not for the first time he wondered why his mother continued to allow her ex-husband these regular wilderness trips with the kids. She'd left him because he'd gone a little crazy, hadn't she? Why did she still trust him like this?

Because she's like me and Eleanor, *he told himself.* She still loves him.

'I know what they'll do!' His father was ranting on, his voice quiet so as not to wake Eleanor, his lips hard against his son's ear to press the words home, 'I know what they'll do. They'll fly over in the night. Could be any night, could be tonight, son. Could be tonight. You won't know a thing, not at Ground Zero. Sudden white heat then nothin'. A-bomb'll get you every time. Farther out you'll die just as quick, only you'll get to see the mushroom cloud. You know

what we did on the Project? We dressed up pigs. I ever tell you that, son? Don't spread the word now – National Security. Where was I? Oh yeah, pigs. Dressed 'em in fatigues and noosed 'em up so we could find the bacon. Cheaper'n blowin' up real GI's, hah! Project Sunburst. I saw it, son, saw the blast with my own eyes. Like a slice of the sun on Earth. Godawful scary but . . . real gorgeous too. You're gonna see it someday, when they come. They're comin', don't you doubt it. And when they do you gotta be ready with the Bomb. You gotta put yourself in the right place, son. Take th' Bomb and put it where it b'longs. 'S the only . . . th'only way . . .'

His speech slurring badly now, his father slumped forwards. He was not supposed to talk about the A-bomb tests out in the Nevada desert but he did. Thomas wondered if the government would find out and take him away. He had no conception of how important his father had been to Project Sunburst, or any of the other test firings he had been involved with. He knew his father was a mechanic and so guessed he had looked after the vehicles, maybe even the trucks that carried the Bombs themselves, but he could just as easily have been hired to feed the animals.

Pigs in army fatigues! Jesus Christ!

His father came to in time to stop himself crashing into the fire, lurched backwards and immediately fell into unconsciousness again. He was about to fall on top of Eleanor when Thomas, seeing a very real danger to his sleeping sister, jumped up and rolled her out of the way. His father landed heavily with the bottle clutched against his chest. The sound of the glass breaking was muffled but unmistakable; Thomas stared in shock as dark blood began to ooze from between his father's fingers.

Then Eleanor was screaming.

Tearing his eyes from the sight of his bleeding father, Thomas turned to see he had rolled his sister into the fire. She was standing, screaming, with her long blonde hair in flames. Hot *white light crowned her head while smoke mushroomed around the clearing. She looked like a creature from myth, a terrible, beautiful siren shrieking her deadly song. Shreds of scalp had unpeeled and knotted themselves across her forehead; through the smoke her eyes were bright and begging.*

For ten seconds all Thomas Coyote could do was watch while his sister burned.

Reason returned like a blast of winter wind. Screaming himself now, Thomas snatched up the pail of water beside the tent and threw it over Eleanor's head. The flames died instantly; not so the smoke, which continued to pour with dreadful vigour from what was left of his sister's scalp. Her face, he saw with horrified fascination, was quite unharmed. Apart from a few wisps around her ears and the nape of her neck, her hair was gone; in its place was a battlefield.

Behind him his father was groaning. 'Help,' was all Thomas managed to blurt before his father's eyes cleared enough to see what had happened to his precious daughter. Thomas almost heard the crash as sobriety descended, could almost see the alcohol fleeing his father's pores. Ignoring the shards of glass sticking from his palm, his father clawed his way to his feet, knocking Thomas aside in his desperation. He embraced Eleanor then, as she screamed anew, swept her up like a doll and raced away through the trees.

'You little bastard!' he yelled over his shoulder. 'Look what you did to my princess! Look what you did to my little girl! Look where all your readin' gets you! You stay there, you little shit! Don't you move or I'll break every bone in your body!'

Kneeling beside the dying fire, Thomas Coyote bowed his head, letting his mop of unruly hair fall across his face. He would stay here in his place, just like his father had told him to.

'I wanted to help her,' he said. 'I tried to help.'

Later, in the thick of the night, the feel of his own hair became unbearable. Rummaging in his father's tent he found

*the hunting knife and began, slowly and methodically, to cut
it away. When he could cut it no more he turned the blade
on its side and started to shave what was left. Though he was
careful, he cut himself in many places; most of the blood was
dry by morning.*

*When the shock had subsided he found only anger remained.
What had happened to his concern for his sister he could not imagine. No matter, the anger felt good. It felt like the sort of thing a man
should feel. The sort of thing that might one day win a war.*

*'Pigs in fatigues!' Tom laughed as the first trace of dawn
dared the night sky.*

Somewhere behind the distant trees a wolf howled . . .

. . . long and low, a primitive voice for a primitive place.
Thomas looked around, scared and hurt. The redwoods
loomed while at his feet the embers of the camp-fire still
glowed white hot, like the surface of a star.

He brushed back his hair with a twelve-year-old hand
and stood erect. Every muscle in his young body pro-
tested; it felt as if he'd been crouched there for thirty
years.

Beyond the fire lay the body of a tall, bald man,
badly burned. Towering over it was a white serpent.
Fire dripped from its jaws like lava, sizzling as it struck
the ground, the man's ruined flesh. Crouched beside
the dragon was a white wolf. Like the dragon, it had
shining metal eyes; like the dragon, it was as big as
a house.

'I have kept this one,' said Areken. 'It appealed to me
greatly. Now, forgive us, but we must leave you here.
You may roam the forest as you please but remember:
your mind is my domain now. Know your place. Come,
White Wolf.'

The two monsters turned as one and passed between
the trees.

Thomas touched his arms, his legs, his fingers, felt the

raw scrape of breath in his throat, the stroke of sound in the canals of his ears, the thrust of the forest floor against his folded legs, sensed the surety of his name and the truth of his body around him.

There before the flames, trapped between the cold night soil and the first light of the sun's warm sky, Thomas Coyote began to weep.

20

Sunlight Pass

The stairs were steep, the going arduous and even before the second turn of the spiral Jonah's calf muscles were howling in protest. Malya was already ten steps ahead and stretching her lead with every pace; Annie laboured at his side, lips pressed white in silent protest.

Floating beads of charm scattered light like dew, making the statue's curved interior glisten as if wet. Veins of dense colour marbled the black walls – Prussian blues and burgundies and thick bottle greens. A dark mist climbed with them, exploring the way ahead with tendrils of vapour that seemed almost alive. It was, above all, *cloying*.

'Can you hear her, Jonah?' said Annie. Her words had to fight their way through the mist. 'She's close. She's so damned close!'

He nodded, doubting he had the breath to force back a reply.

'No!' Annie stopped, grabbing his arm to hold him back. 'No, Jonah! *Listen* to her! She's nearly here – she really is! Listen hard!'

Jonah realized he had been scared when he had started up the stairway; now he was terrified. But he listened all the same, he could not help himself.

It was faint, but it penetrated the mist with an ease their

merely human voices had quite failed to achieve. It was Archan's voice falling from above, cruel and grating and tinged with fire. She was speaking in many tongues at once, screaming and hissing taunts and abuse in a Babel flood which even Stone's charmed air was incapable of translating. As the seconds rolled by it grew louder, not because she was getting nearer but because the barriers holding her back were crumbling away, one by one.

'Come on,' grunted Jonah. 'We have a long way to climb.'

Malya had already climbed out of sight and they were forced to increase their pace in an effort to catch her up. By the time her heels flickered back into view Jonah's legs were burning up. He shouted for her to stop but she carried on climbing.

'Stopping just makes it harder to start again,' she said.

So on they climbed, up and round, up and round. There was no change in the walls, nor in the twinkling light or the dank mist. The tower spiralled with them and gave no clue as to where they were within the statue. And all the time Archan's voice was above them, raining down upon them, growing louder and sharper with every step they took towards it.

Jonah's thoughts drifted. He thought of Grandfather Tree, whom they had left guarding the orchard, a living moat past which no assailant could conceivably sneak.

Except he is not merely guarding the orchard – he is the orchard.

Then, just when it seemed the staircase would go on forever, all the way up to the gates of heaven and beyond, they reached a door.

Fighting for breath, he fumbled in his pocket for the tiles. Malya flashed a tight grin and waved him away. Then she pushed the door open with her foot. She looked uncharacteristically tired; her face was bright with sweat and her hand, when she lifted it to wipe her brow, was trembling.

'Stiff climb,' Jonah said, returning her smile. She nodded, saying nothing.

Beyond the door was a bright space. Sunlight poured in through a series of square windows set in one wall of a long, narrow gallery. Staggering up to the nearest window, Jonah looked out across the giant cup the statue was holding against its breast.

'Good news,' he announced. 'We are over halfway up.'

Slowly, his hand shaking like Malya's, he withdrew the White Dragon from his pocket.

'Unwritten,' he said. 'Unmarked.'

There was a message here after all, another of Stone's irritating, disingenuous clues. Something else he could not quite grasp. He turned away, disgust rising in him like bile.

'Esh!' he shouted. 'And you, Mister Ren, whoever you are! And the basilisks too, damn them all! I am sick of your games, do you hear me? Do you deserve to be saved, any of you? Why should it fall to me to protect your precious Stone? Why do you toy with me in this way? I should turn my back on you all, here and now! Turn my back and go . . .'

. . . home?

'Jonah!' It was Annie's voice, trembling as his hand was trembling, as Malya's hand had been trembling. He looked her way in time to see her fall to her knees, hands clenched against her breasts, tendons like ropes in her neck. 'She wants me in the dream . . . I gotta go but not . . . not all of me, not this time . . . go on, Jonah! I can keep her at bay . . . so long as I don't go all the way in . . . hurry, Jonah, there ain't much time!'

But he did not go. Kneeling, he cradled her cheeks

313

with his hands, tilting her face up so he could see her eyes. They were wide and clear. Human.

'Dreamin' dream, Jonah,' she said, rewarding his attention with a half-smile, 'but it's my dream . . . she's spread thin, don't you forget it . . . you go on . . . I'll hold her here while you . . .' and here her smile became a dazzling grin, '. . . while you head her off at the pass.'

He found her gaze and held it, demanded it. 'No, my love. I will not leave you here.'

'Hard . . .' mumbled Annie. Her eyes rolled back white for a moment.

'Yes, Annie! It is hard, but you must keep her at bay, just for a little longer. Can you do that?'

Malya was watching from the foot of a second, narrower stairway leading up from the far end of the gallery. Catching his eye she unsheathed her sword and pointed up the stairs. Her hand, he noted, was steady as a rock.

'I will not leave you, my love.'

'Git goin' you stupid bastard!'

She kissed him fiercely, her fingers digging hard into the back of his neck as she pulled him close. She released him but he would not let her go. Instead he scooped his hands beneath her and plucked her from the floor. She was light, lighter than she should have been, as if she were only half-there. By the time he came to the stairs she had recovered sufficiently to walk again, though she leaned on him at frequent intervals. Dazed, partway into a dream himself, Jonah followed Malya up, towards the strident sound of the dragon.

Joining them on this second, steeper staircase was the plaited rope of the memory rods. Hidden during the first part of its ascent through the statue's lower sections, now it burst from one sleek wall to climb like a flower seeking the sun. Malya kept her distance but Jonah could not help but reach for it.

The rope was no thicker than Jonah's arm, yet it was woven from millions of individual strands. All the memories of all the worlds. Touching it both frightened and reassured him, like taking a dose of an addictive yet life-saving drug. Memories chased into his fingers but he brushed them away; he wanted only to let the rods know he was here and that he would look after them. For a while he even climbed it, beanstalk-like.

He found it easier to track their progress now, judging that here they were crossing the statue's collarbone, here striking sideways towards the bulge of its shoulder, here passing into the tower of the upper arm. When the stairs became a black metal ladder Jonah paused, fearing for Annie's safety. She seemed more or less awake now; all the same he made her precede him, hoping he would be able to catch her if she fell.

Halfway up the ladder a single, tiny window revealed a cramped view of the statue's smooth cranium. Dangling off one of the rungs Jonah was able to poke his head part-way through the aperture. Scalding air pounded his cheeks and he pulled back, hissing with pain – he had forgotten the sun would be so close. But that brief glimpse had been enough: he knew they had reached the elbow joint. All that remained now was the forearm, the wrist, the hand with its clenched fingers . . .

He studied Annie as she climbed the ladder. Her movements were smooth but mechanical, like those of a well-oiled automaton. He remembered how light she had felt when he picked her up.

The ladder ended at a flat flagged landing. Jonah fell exhausted to the floor while the two women stood – Malya impassive, Annie rigid. Hard white light flooded down from above, dripping beads of charm which gathered on the flags and chased themselves in circles like frantic mercury.

From a crack between two of the flags, like a fakir's

trick, rose the rope of memories, narrowed now to a thread barely the thickness of Jonah's thumb.

'Jonah?' Annie was calling from far away, her voice as thin as if she were on the other side of a mountain. He ran to her, held her close against him and listened to her distant cries. 'Jonah . . . don't go no further . . . thunder . . .'

Was this the end of the journey? Surely this place did not literally exist at the top of the statue's arm – it had to be an illusion. All at once he was terrified. Though her face was inches from his own Annie's voice came from another world. Reflected in her eyes he saw a black wing-shadow, not a dragon but something huge all the same. A giant eagle perhaps, or a condor; for all he knew it might have been the legendary roc.

'Stay with me, Annie,' he shouted while she screwed up her face, straining to hear him.

Monstrous above them, Archan's voice was a winter wind of incantations and curses. Her words transformed into visible crystal which fell first like feathers then like rocks from space. Jonah watched dumbfounded as the crystal words turned to dragon scales, spinning like sycamore seeds as they flamed in the burning air. Charm encased them, all these falling splinters, fizzing and spitting as it fought in vain to knit them back together.

Slowly the flags succumbed to the onslaught: while the three humans remained untouched the solid ground beneath their feet was pulverized by the raining debris, smashed into an undulating, salt-white beach, whereupon the rain stopped, Archan's voice stopped, everything, for a heartbeat or two, simply stopped . . .

Jonah bent, ran his fingers through the new sand. It poured from his hand, each grain marking time as it fell.

He looked around. It was a dream-world, he was sure of it now. Beneath the glare of the sun the beach might have run forever in every direction. Light above, sand below, both brilliant white, and Jonah in place between the two. But whose dream?

Beside him, prone on the white sand, arms flung back over her head, Annie was in two worlds at the same time, able to . . .

. . . see Jonah, ghost-like, looking down on her as she lay here in the sand. He was wavering in and out of focus – no, to hell with that, he was wavering in and out of *existence*. The two worlds, the two Stones, were overlaid like some trick with mirrors at a travelling fair, each a reflection of the other and in the half-silvered light no way to tell which was the original.

She closed her eyes and when she opened them Jonah was gone. Yet when she stretched out her foot she could feel him standing there, solid beside her. A blink and ghost-Jonah reached towards her; another and he disappeared again.

'Annie West! Do you plan to play conjurers all day long?'

The reprimand was good-natured but urgent all the same. She squinted up into the sun's baking light to see Mister Ren offering her his hand. Accepting it, she allowed him to pull her to her feet.

The dream-world was a simple place, a *fundamental* place. Beneath her was pure white sand, fine as salt. Above her was a sky of light, cloudless and colourless, the underbelly of a star. Beside the beach was an ocean.

She must have walked through the orchard and down to the sea. She did not remember doing so but here she was. Behind her the trees had shrunk, or else grown very distant, she could not tell which. Perhaps they had withered in the glare of the sun. Far out to sea she thought she could see sails punctuating the horizon, but she could not be sure.

317

A black shape dirtied the sky: a bird-shape, an eagle perhaps. Thunder boomed in its wake but it did not descend to challenge her. Perhaps it was eyeing the beach for prey, or else just enjoying the thermals.

'Why does she want me here?' she said. There was no sign of Archan, nor any sound of her. She was somewhere close by though: Annie could smell her.

'Think of yourself as a conduit,' replied Mister Ren.

'I'd rather not.'

'You are one of the few bridges between the worlds. At least, your mind is, by virtue of the fact that it was once possessed by Archan. The act of possession served to . . . how can I put it . . . it served to *redefine* you. Or to rehearse you, if you prefer.'

'I don't prefer either. Look – I'm closin' the door on the dragon. She tries to get into my head again she's gonna get a nasty surprise.'

'That's the spirit! Unfortunately you are not the only bridge.'

'I kinda suspected that. The other one wouldn't be Tom Coyote by any chance?'

'Exactly so. However, our friend Coyote is developing in . . . well, in an interesting direction. He's still dangerous, perhaps the greatest danger, but . . . well, we shall see.'

'You're a smug bastard, ain't you?'

'It is not my intention. I am, in fact, a hairsbreadth from panic.'

The confession shut Annie's mouth for her. Aggravated though she was by Mister Ren's sheer cussedness, his unwelcome honesty brought her up short. 'Tell me,' she said, 'if the worlds are really so close together up here, how come Archan needs a bridge at all? Why can't she just jump across?'

Mister Ren rummaged studiously in his left nostril before replying. 'Perhaps "bridge" is the wrong word.

"Springboard" might be better. No, no, still not quite right . . . but what is more relevant is what would happen were she to attempt a crossing *without* a mind such as yours to act as a conduit.'

'And what *would* happen?'

'Her raw spirit would be naked to the teeth of the cosmos. Such a state cannot be contemplated.'

Annie gulped, quite unable to comprehend what Mister Ren meant but assured of his utter revulsion at the concept.

Naked to the teeth of the cosmos. What the hell lay between the worlds that even Archan would flinch at exposing herself to it? A dull ache crept into her head from the nape of her neck, coursing through her jaw and drilling at her teeth. Sick with fatigue, she dropped to her knees and watched the winged shape circle in the blinding sky.

It was lower now and she could see it was not the thunder-bird she had originally figured it to be. The wings were ragged not with feathers but strips of scale and reptile-skin. The body hanging beneath them was familiar, disturbingly so. A man's body, hanging awkwardly, as if . . .

Her hand flew to her mouth. The man's left leg had been severed just below the knee. Blistered blue paint clung here and there to his ulcerated chest and his head lolled like the town drunk's. Even before his facial features resolved themselves she recognized him: it was the shaman, Frey, Malya's father.

'Can't be,' she murmured. Her skull was vibrating with the pain of the headache. 'He died.'

'Yes,' agreed Mister Ren, 'in another world. Histories change. Everything changes, Annie. You should know that by now.'

As Frey flew beneath the sun she saw his intact leg was grey and heavy. It was in fact made entirely of stone.

Then the sand was bucking beneath her and without warning Mister Ren was thrown ten yards across the beach.

Krakatoa, she thought in horror, *this is where I came in*.

But this was no volcano. It was not the land that ripped open but the body of the flying shaman. Dragon claws erupted from deep within his flesh. She screamed Jonah's name . . .

. . . but there was nobody to hear. He pulled harder, tearing the flimsy wooden partition free of its moorings with a hearty crack and lunging through into the corridor beyond. Inside his head the dragon and the wolf howled in unison, pleased with his work.

He looked around. He had reached the corridor running up to the bridge. There, sprawled on the floor exactly where it had come to rest, was the dimmed carcass of the lightfish. Beside it, also where it had fallen, was the camera he had taken from the journalist's Cherokee.

Marvelling at both the age and the size of the hands which still did his bidding, twelve-year-old Thomas Coyote reached down and picked up the camera. It was dented, and the back no longer closed properly, but it felt hard and good. It felt *Earthly*. He clutched it to the chest of the man he had unknowingly become and listened to the voices fighting in his mind.

It had been an awakening, a return to a new level of reality. Though he remembered all that had happened in his life (including, God forgive him, the ghastly murders . . . Jesus, those poor women!) it was as if it had happened in a single prolonged dream, a lucid dream in fact. A dreamin' dream, as Annie West might have called it. And though he had watched himself grow to manhood, watched the dual personalities first develop and then battle for supremacy inside his own damaged mind, he himself – the essential *he* – had not changed one iota from the twelve-year-old boy who had shaved his head clean beside the embers of a dying camp-fire. For half a lifetime he had knelt beside that fire, unaltered, watching time's river take his body and its two rogue minds on their long, long journey towards the ocean.

And now he stood again, a boy in the body of a man. Tom Coyote was dead, redundant now that the boy he had once been walked again. His body lay in the woods.

But the other, the White Wolf . . . that one was not so easily cowed. It had joined forces with the intruder, the dragon, and now between them they were working Thomas like a marionette.

Free at last, he was as much a prisoner as he had ever been.

I picked up the camera, he told himself, trying to shield from the puppeteers his pleasure at the minor victory. *I chose to do it.*

Still holding the camera to his chest he allowed the beasts to direct him along the desolate corridor and out through a tear in the hull of the Bark. Holding his free hand aloft as a shield against the glare of the sun, Thomas Coyote clambered on to the crooked deck and found himself looking straight into the furious eyes of a man flying on red and black dragon . . .

. . . wings that broke through the sand. They rose on either side of Jonah like the standards of Hell, translucent membranes flapping against a loose fretwork of bones and struts of cartilage. Higher they rose and higher still, spilling sand across his shoulders, into his face, his eyes. Their colossal shadow arched over him, swallowing Malya, who stood dumbstruck at his side, then the nearest of the dunes.

Dream-world, he told himself, but it was all too real.

Muscular coils pursued the wings, humping free of the sand. They shuddered, coughing sand from their backs with a rattlesnake hiss. At first they looked like a nest of smaller serpents, then a complex writhing movement transformed the tangled chain into a single, smooth line: a tail caressing the fractured ground. It, like the wings, was partly transparent, only partly here . . .

A deep trembling had begun, far below their feet: Archan, rising.

Malya was tugging at his sleeve. The instant he turned to her he found the hilt of a dagger pressed into his hand. He seized it, the coarse grip secure against his fingers.

'Shark-skin!' she said, indicating the hilt's silvery covering. 'It won't slip from your hand, even when greased with blood!'

But the fact barely registered with Jonah. He was staring at another blade: the sword she was holding in her hand, the Roman sword he could not imagine her being without.

Malya's sword was grey. Its blade, once gleaming, was now dull and pitted; its bronze hilt, the shining sphere behind the pommel . . . grey too. All grey, like dust.

It had turned to stone.

So had the hand holding it.

Her gaze tracked his. Behind her a dragon's wing billowed like a galleon's mainsail. He looked deep into her eyes and saw that she *knew*.

'Malya,' he stammered, 'I am so . . .'

'How long?' she asked, reiterating the question that had haunted him ever since he had discovered the fossilized book.

'I cannot say,' he said. 'That is to say, I don't know, Malya. I am so sorry.'

'The dragon? She will change too?'

Jonah shivered – in the space of a second or two she had made the connection it had taken him days, if not weeks, to make. They were so smart, these ancestral people, so very smart! 'Everything I have made will turn to stone, including Archan's twin and the world she comes from. But these wings around us . . . if this is the real Archan, the *original* Archan, then she will not be affected. In any event we are too late to hope. She is here already!'

'If she is here then we must face her.'

'But how can you . . . ?' Jonah indicated her ruined hand.

'Where there is life,' the warrior-woman answered, 'there is hope!'

So saying she whirled in the sand and drove her sword of stone straight through the sheer canvas of Archan's wing. Then, a terrible cry ululating from her lips, she carved a huge arc through which glassy blood and sunlight burst like wine and water, a sweet cocktail which Jonah drank in great . . .

. . . gulps of air beneath the pumping dragon wings. Gerent's hesitation gave Thomas just enough time to leap clear of his blade. He crashed on to the sloping perimeter deck, his desperate scrabble for purchase driving splinters of Bark-wood beneath his fingernails. Gerent struck again, this time burying his sword in the timbers six inches from Thomas's nose. Their eyes met and for a moment the Neolithic man looked nonplussed, as if he had seen something unexpected in the face of his enemy. Then, prising his blade free, he drew his arm back for the killing blow.

The whole deck gave way. Unravelling like the spiral-cut peel of an orange it snatched Thomas clear of Gerent's weapon and hurled him on a switchback ride down its disintegrating coils. Inside his head the dragon and the wolf shrieked curses but left Thomas alone to experience the pain of repeated impacts with the Bark's hard hull, the whiplash of the detached handrails against his flailing legs, the constant friction-burn of the deck at his back.

Thomas flew from the deck's severed end and fell the

last few yards to the ground. He landed in a bed of fallen leaves and windfalls, a grown man crying like the child he was inside.

You ain't a child no more, he heard his father scold him with proud anger. *You're damn near half a man!*

The truth was he had no idea *what* he was. He knew he was hurting though, inside and out, and right now he wanted everything, especially the monsters in his head, to just go away.

Lumps of wood rained down, the remains of the deck, forcing him to run for cover beneath the orchard's protective canopy. Swooping close behind came Gerent, his sword scything a path through whatever falling debris his charm-laden wings failed to deflect. Thomas gained the relative safety of the orchard seconds before Gerent came up against the barrier of trees; the Neolithic man folded his wings and dropped lightly to the soil, hefting his sap-stained sword and marching towards the shadows where Thomas was hiding.

Now that Thomas was clear of the Bark the puppeteers reclaimed their prize. The trees of the orchard merged with the redwoods in his head and suddenly his body was no longer his to control. He watched in horrified fascination as his hands were brought up to his chest to lift the camera from around his neck. He assumed they would throw it aside – just a piece of junk the little faery had dared to pick up of his own accord – but instead they deftly unscrewed the lens from the body. Discarding the latter, his hands proceeded to smash the lens against a chunk of rock sticking from the ground. Three blows and the plastic bezels were shattered, exposing one intact saucer of glass and dozens of sharp fragments, several of which stuck into the soft pads of his fingertips.

Snatching up the one unbroken lens, the dragon (for it was she who was really in charge – the wolf she had kept on more as a bodyguard than an accomplice) hauled

Thomas across a nearby clearing and into a patch of sunlight. Hope left him as Gerent, crashing through a deadfall of brush and leaves, fixed on his quarry and rushed forwards. The sunlight was brilliant; Thomas might just as well have been standing beneath a spotlight on a wide open stage.

Areken made him kneel. He felt like a sacrificial offering.

'Raise the glass, faery!' she said. Her thoughts were glutinous, an oil slick spilling ever deeper into his mind. His instinct was to resist but his hands obeyed despite his efforts. He flicked his gaze between the lens and the onrushing bird-man. Gerent was shrieking a battle cry; his sword was a blur above his head.

Plunging through the lens, the sunlight converged to a startling point. With a turn of Thomas's wrist Areken diverted the beam on to a heap of dry twigs. They caught fire at once. Then, turning his hand still further, she guided the deadly beam up the trunk of the nearest tree. Laser-like, the amplified light of a sun that was already powerful beyond Earthly reason sliced the tree in two then ignited the sagging remains. The tree exploded with a hollow ripping sound, sending a mushroom cloud of boiling orange fire and bitter smoke into the sky.

Atomic, thought Thomas.

Then she was moving his legs, compelling him to rise and run through the smoke, all the while turning the lens into the next patch of sunlight, setting fires wherever she could, gradually turning the orchard into an inferno.

He glanced over his shoulder, an involuntary movement that slipped through Areken's supervisory net. The White Wolf growled and cuffed him back, but not before he had seen Gerent give up the chase, falling back behind the gathering flames and throwing his sword to the ground in frustration.

Safe behind the growing wall of fire, Thomas ran on

towards the centre of the circle, towards the great black statue looming . . .

. . . over Annie and Mister Ren. The shadow cast by the shaman's disintegrating body bulged and gaped. Claws were spilling from inside his torso, too many claws to be counted, moving too fast to be much more than blurs. Like needles on some insane sewing machine they whickered out through his flesh from within, spraying blood and lacerated skin down on to the hot sand.

Through it all the shaman's eyes shone like silver in the light of the sun.

Annie watched in horror and revulsion as Archan carved her way out of Frey's mangled interior. It was like some unimaginable conjurer's trick: her massive dragon body – much too big ever to have been contained inside a human form – clawed and gnawed and tore its way out. As it emerged it grew, and it seemed to Annie that to begin with it had been very tiny. It was like watching a locomotive leap from a tunnel, a steady swelling of sound and motion that ended with a raw and breathless rush as it barrelled into view.

'Not Frey!' she said and now Archan was fully *here*, shaking off the last few shreds of human skin like a dog fresh out of a lake, thudding her huge white wings against the air and scanning her surroundings with a slick chrome gaze. 'Not the Frey we knew. It was the other Frey, from the world Jonah made . . .'

'Indeed!' Mister Ren had to shout over the growl of the wind made by Archan's wings. 'She has ridden him into your mind, into your dream. Now she has no need for him, so . . . poof!' With one hand he mimicked an explosion; with the other he held his fruit-bowl hat on against the blast of the wind.

'So what next? How does she get from here to Stone? *My* Stone.'

'As I said, you are a conduit.'

A conduit. A bridge between the worlds. Annie looked around her, looked at the sand, the sun, the sea . . . For the first time she realized – *really* realized – that this entire landscape existed nowhere but in her mind. This place was no more real than the dreamin' dreams of a Kansas trail or the mountain pass through Tibet or China or whatever damn place *that* had been.

All that was one thing, but there was something else too, something even more important.

'This is *my* dream,' she said. Then louder, 'This is *my* dream!'

Beside her Mister Ren was nodding but she was not paying him any attention. Instead she was stalking across the sand, shrugging off Archan's enormous shadow like a spring shower.

'There's no way out of here, Archan!' she shouted. 'You're on my ground now, d'you hear? This is *my* dream and I'll do what I like with it!'

Archan's wings stopped moving. The stillness was so sudden and so total it shocked Annie into matching immobility. For several seconds the massive dragon hung there motionless, a crisp white statue cut like crystal from the very light of the sun. Then, with a slippery gliding motion that was in some way obscene, she curled her neck first round upon itself and then down to the level of Annie's head. They faced each other like this for what felt to Annie like hours, although during the whole time she took not a single breath.

Smoke trickled from between Archan's closed lips. Her head, which was roughly the size of the Conestoga wagon in which she had ridden the trail, swayed from side to side; in her eyes dwelt perfect twinned reflections of Annie and her dream-world.

'Hello, dear,' Archan said and by the time she said 'dear' her voice had become that of Annie's mother. The dragon opened her jaws and there, lying on a bright red tongue in a black funeral shroud with her hands crossed on her chest, was Katherine Harker. The corpse lifted its head and opened its mouth. Fire belched out, furious yellow; it scorched Katherine's lips, her cheeks, turning her face black with soot.

'My dream,' Annie said. Then she closed her eyes and counted to three. When she opened them again her mother had gone. Archan was still there, however: the dream was real but so was the dragon. 'You can't hurt me, Archan. Mister Ren says I'm your bridge across the canyon but that ain't really so, is it? In fact, I'm more like a border guard, Archan, ain't that right? And you know what? You're papers ain't in order – lady, they ain't in order at all!'

Archan's answer was to open her mouth again. Fire flooded not only from her throat but from her teeth, her gums, her snake-like tongue, exploding towards Annie in a lethal river. Annie raised a hand, cringing from the flames, understanding that though she was burning she was not dying, remembering all over again that the dream was hers to command.

With her uplifted hand she deflected the flames back across Archan, who lurched back, spitting curses and scattering blue sparks of charm. Discarding her charred clothes Annie took a step forwards, at the same time permitting new unblemished flesh to form on her blistered body. Rebuilding herself, leaving no trail in the sand, she pushed Archan back to the edge of the ocean.

'Mine,' she intoned as she marched. 'All mine, Archan. You're all mine.'

Spreading glossy wings wide Archan retreated to a position some sixty feet above where Annie stood with her arms outstretched. 'You are strong,' she said, 'for a faery. I cannot, however, imagine fainter praise.' The words transformed into burning rocks that splashed into

the sand all around Annie, a blistering meteorite rain. She
held her ground, telling herself over and over she would
not be hurt. It was not entirely true, of course, and she
would be a fool to believe it was, but it sure helped.

One rock fell nearby, almost crushing her foot in fact.
She bent towards it, curiously drawn to its misshapen
bulk, its steaming, pitted surface. Then a voice spoke her
name – not Archan's voice but another, close beside her
ear. Mister Ren . . . ?

She whirled, raising her fists then lowering them in
relief as she saw that it *was* Mister Ren . . . except . . .

Except he had removed his hat. Her mind raced and as
it raced the little Chinaman smiled, revealing teeth filed
to needle points. From the black shell on his back sprang
wings, red beetle-wings. In place of his cloak he wore a
shroud of bones and skulls, some human, many more
quite unrecognizable; they rattled against each other like
dice, or ivory tiles.

And he had taken his hat off. That was the worst. Of
all the horrifying changes that was somehow the worst.
He's taken his hat off!

She backtracked, desperate to gain time. Her mind continued to race. *Needle teeth and skulls . . .* was it possible?
Or was she going mad?

'Frey?' she gasped as the shape that had once been
Mister Ren opened its eyes and looked upon her. *Here*
was madness, here before her eyes, not inside her own
thoughts. Here was Frey the shaman, Malya's dead father,
turned insane, a ghost within a ghost . . .

Annie held her hands to her head as she backed
away, trying to figure what was going on. This beach – a
visualization of the interior of her own mind. Archan –
an alien intruder, using the imaginary beach as a stepping
stone from one world to another. And now this . . . this
Frey, the steed on which Archan had ridden onto the
beach in the first place and who was now discarded,

only to invade the mind of Mister Ren, who was himself a ghost here, merely eavesdropping on events he could not truly control . . .

She screamed, unable to reconcile this crazy Russian doll arrangement of minds within minds, each mind a puppet of its own invading presence. *Which of us is really here?* she started to wonder before stopping herself. *Are any of us real?* But thinking like that was as dangerous as assuming she could not be harmed because it was her dream. They were all as real as each other: Archan, Frey, herself, even Mister Ren, wherever he had gone.

She screamed again. She could not think of anything else to do.

As if to prove his reality Frey lifted his new Chinese hands and made a grab for Annie's throat. She jumped sideways, found her legs tangling together and fell heavily onto the sand. Frey plodded nearer and bent over her. Tiny skulls jangled in her face; she thrashed her hands through a jostling curtain of bones and teeth, rolling at the same time to avoid the stabbing, claw-like fingers. Frey clutched sand and a knot of Annie's hair, which tore from her scalp. They both shrieked, one in frustration, one in pain.

Annie fetched up against a rogue sand dune. Frey lumbered after her but he was slow, slow enough to give her time to scramble to her feet. Her hip throbbed where she had fallen on it. She backed away from this Neolithic-driven Chinaman and again her sense of reality wavered. Except she was no longer concerned with who was really here but rather where 'here' really was. She had, she discovered, lost all sense of *place*. If everything was twinned – beaches, suns, worlds, even people – then where in Hell's name was reality? Where was the centre of it all? Where did all these things come together? To what, in this crazy dance of dreams, could she cling?

She knew the answer, of course: the memory rods, or

rather the single thread into which all the memory rods had·spun themselves. That was what she could cling to, what they could all cling, to what in fact Stone itself was clinging to lest it drop forever into the pit.

Her head bursting, she looked up at Archan leering down from her vantage point near the underbelly of the sun. *Everything twinned*, she thought. Then it seemed to her that Archan was not riding the air but clinging to it, clinging lest she too should fall. And when Annie thought that the pain in her head went away and she knew where Archan was weakest.

'Where is she?' Annie yelled, resisting the impulse to run from Frey, who was nearly upon her again. 'What's happened to the other Archan, the one Jonah made? You used her to get here, didn't you? Where is she now, Archan? Where's your twin sister? I don't see her but something tells me she's still around, ain't that right? What happened, did she slip her leash or something? I'll bet that made you mad!'

Archan *roared*. It was noise beyond any noise Annie had ever heard, an avalanche of sound that took form just as her speech had taken form, except now it was not rocks raining from the sky but boulders. They thundered down, great growling chunks of rock burying themselves deep in the sand wherever they dropped. One fell directly between Annie and Frey, throwing the shaman back behind a sudden rising plume of sand. Another grazed her upper arm – any closer and it would have knocked her head clean off her shoulders – and the pressure wave formed when it struck the beach hurled her into the sky.

Enough, she thought in desperation, *this is* my *dream!*

She held out her arms and started to fly.

'All right, Archan,' she growled as she climbed towards the sun. Time was melting; gravity had melted too. Below her the beach was coming apart in thick clots. 'All right,

I'll let you through. Let's see if you're really as mean as you think you are. Are you ready? 'Cause I sure as Hell am! I'm goin', you cold-hearted bitch! Are you comin' with me?'

Archan's chrome eyes slipped past, orbiting her like twin moons. It seemed to Annie, as all the light in the sky shrank to a lethal point, that those eyes were registering surprise.

Then, as she tore her dream apart, everything was sucked into that point of light – the vast winged monster that was Archan, the ragged Chinaman that had once been Mister Ren, the shattered beach, the ocean and the trees and Annie herself. They dwindled, and then they passed through into . . .

. . . Sunlight Pass, the place that *really* existed at the top of the statue's arm.

Jonah looked around in astonishment as the beach came apart. The sand rose up in undulating sheets and faded out of sight; likewise the ocean, which hissed into nothingness like a splash of water on a griddle. He was back on Stone, free of the dream.

Beneath his feet was an uneven platform of Stone-stuff: the statue's clenched fist. From the junction of its thumb and forefinger rose the razor thread of the compressed memory rods, a clean vertical slash rising up into the third essential element of the scene: the blazing underbelly of the sun, barely one hundred yards from his head.

Sun above, Stone below, he thought. *Here I stand, between. My name is . . .*

'Jonah Lightfoot!'

The voice was huge and unmistakable. It was Archan's. He turned and there she was.

Jonah blinked, a little off-balance. She was just a dragon. That was what struck him most: she was just a dragon. *It is really her*, he thought in wonder. *She is really here, she has found her way back to me at last. And this is what she looks like, what she really looks like.*

In his previous encounters with Archan she had persistently taken other forms – often other dragon forms to be sure, but false identities all the same. Now she was naked before him, all the glamours cast aside.

She was smaller than he had imagined, not much bigger than Kythe had been when she had travelled with them. Her creamy-white, sinuous body was at least three times as long as he was tall but slender, so much so that the extremity of her tail was little more than a whip. Her head too was slim, featureless but for the cruel slash of mouth. The chrome eyes which had haunted him for so long were quite absent. Her wings were large, admittedly, but no more bulky than the sails of a yacht. There was something unexpectedly delicate about her, something undeniably *beautiful*.

Archan had no legs. She rested on her coils like a cobra, her sharp snout tracing a repetitive figure-of-eight path through the air as she used exotic senses to build a picture of her surroundings. For a brief moment Jonah thought she seemed bemused. Then she spoke again.

'Jonah Lightfoot! Faery! What an adversary you must be that I have remembered your name. Remembrance is the greatest compliment the immortal can offer, do you not know that? When all eternity is to be sifted, mere names become no more significant than the dust between the stars.'

'Some might say that dust is what makes the stars,' countered Jonah, 'and someone with more wisdom than you once told me that names are more important than they seem.'

Archan glowered. Even though she was all but faceless Jonah could see she was irritated.

'I see your friends are still foolish enough to cling to your heels,' she snapped. Jonah looked in the direction she had tossed her head and saw Malya poised beneath the dragon's right wing, sword upraised, head inclined towards Jonah as if awaiting orders. He took a step towards her, convinced she had turned entirely to stone, that she was frozen in that pose forever. Then, to his huge relief, she raised her free hand, warning him to stay where he was with an impatient shooing gesture.

Annie was behind him.

'My darling!' He turned his back on the dragon as he rushed to embrace her. Her face crumpled as he held he tight to his breast.

'I . . . I'm sorry , Jonah,' she wailed, hitching her breaths in short bursts. 'I tried to hold her back but I couldn't . . . I had to let her through, I just had to . . .'

'Hush now, everything will be all right. You did the best you could.'

'I thought maybe I'd gain us some time at least but now . . . now I ain't so sure.' She was gazing at Archan over Jonah's shoulder, her eyes damp with tears and dark with fatigue. He held her at arms' length and looked her over: her clothes were torn and blackened, as though she had been climbing through a burning building.

'I took them off altogether in the dream,' she said, fingering a strand of tattered fabric torn from her blouse. 'Guess it wasn't as real as I thought after all.'

'Oh, it is all real, my darling. All of it.'

Her eyes widened; reflected in them Jonah saw white coils straightening. He turned to see Archan oozing towards them, twisting her body across the dark surface of the statue's fist like a sidewinder carving its way through the desert. All the time her body was twisting and writhing her head remained absolutely level, her eyeless yet perceptible gaze fixed on him and Annie. She encircled them, head raised so that her mouth gaped just inches from Jonah's upturned face. Her body and tail formed a perfect ring around them both; her sail-like wings were furled into narrow bands, like Oriental fans folded for the night.

Malya had followed her and was now waiting just beyond what she presumably judged as striking distance. Archan would strike if provoked, Jonah guessed, as fast as the cobra she so closely resembled. Malya was wise to be cautious.

'What will you do now, Archan?' he found himself saying, the words formulating themselves even before he could think about them. 'Will you bite through the thread? Stone will fall then. Would that be a fitting end for this world? Would that leave room for you in the eternity you have always craved? Or will you simply destroy as you have always destroyed? That makes you a monster, you know, nothing more. Is that all that defines you, your hunger?'

'One might make a distinction between *hunger* and *appetite*,' said Archan, 'but such an argument would be beyond your feeble faery brain. As for destruction . . . well, I prefer the term *conquest*. I have conquered much of Stone already, as you know. It resides even now within me.'

Archan was cold, Jonah realized. Freezing air emanated from her, as chilling as a graveyard breeze. 'Then will you eat what is left of Stone? You have eaten so much of it already. What then? Where is the pleasure in immortality if your *appetite* can never be satisfied?'

'Your attempts to provoke me are pitiful!' Archan laughed, but Jonah thought she was, if not angered, then at least nettled. 'And what I plan to do now that I have made good my escape is no concern of yours. I have wasted enough time with you and your pathetic hangers-on. Now it is time for you to be gone.'

She grinned, that broad slash of a mouth widening to hideous proportions to reveal opposed clusters of silver fangs that seemed actually to be *breathing* within her jaws.

Jonah felt Annie shrink against him, or perhaps it was he who had shrunk against her.

'Wait!' called a man's voice.

Archan hesitated, cocking her head at the interruption. Her deliberation was palpable, a crucial weighing of priorities. Jonah prayed curiosity would overrule vengeance. They had faced each other before and then her hesitation had been her downfall. She would not want to make the same mistake again. Yet here, now, the stakes were so much higher than they had ever been before. Here, now, it was not just mortal lives that were in the balance.

Archan was superficially calm, but in that moment of hesitation, as she decided whether to strike or not, Jonah understood that all her anger, all her bitterness was still there, boiling beneath the icy exterior. And for a man in search of any weapon he could find, that knowledge fell as surely into his hand as a sword with a shark-skin hilt.

Before attending to the interruption Archan wrapped her tail around Jonah's and Annie's waists, cinching them together in a painful embrace. Then she swivelled her eyeless head in the direction from which the voice had come.

It was a man. Jonah could just see the top of his head over Archan's pale coils. A tanned, hairless head that could only belong to . . .

. . . Thomas Coyote's body collapsed on to the rounded knuckle of the statue's upraised fist, close to exhaustion following the ascent. Blood was crusted beneath every one of the body's fingernails and its forearms and shins were blue with bruises. The statue had provided more handholds than its smooth appearance had suggested but it had still been an arduous climb, made all the more arduous by Areken's clumsiness with this crude body. Several times she had been forced to give over partial control to the faery, so unwieldy did its limbs feel to her. Besides, she could feel her anger boiling over, clouding her judgement even as it strengthened her resolve. Determination was everything now, survival was paramount. Eternity was big enough for only one dragon and that dragon was her.

Areken! She repeated the mantra. *My name is Areken!*

She lifted the faery's head, trying to coil a neck that did not want to coil. Dull faery eyes made basic observations: sun above, Stone below. The crucial thread of memory connecting the two domains. Also between the two: a white dragon (Archan!) ready to crush the two faeries trapped within her tail. The primitive (but were they not all primitive?) female stabbing with its futile sword. Beyond this tableau, unseen by the other protagonists, crawled the shaman. He was concealed inside the body of the Oriental, the body used for a time by the maker of immortality himself . . .

Just as Annie had been, Areken was puzzled, confused by the nesting of realities. For an instant she lost track of who she was and from which world she had come, then her anger overwhelmed her.

Sun above, she thought. *Stone below,* she thought. *Dragon between,* she thought. Areken *between*.

She had to destroy them all. There was no other way. Then, at long last, she would be alone, alone and immortal between the twin realms of Stone and sun, with nothing but the thin thread of memory for company.

That, it seemed to her now, was the best possible place for eternity to begin.

Dragging the faery body of Thomas Coyote to its feet, she lurched across the black and sunlit swell of the statue's enormous clenched fist.

'Wait!' she cried in the voice of the faery. She was determined to prevent her sister from crushing the faeries to death. That pleasure should be hers alone to enjoy; she would not be robbed of it.

For a moment she thought she had left it too late, that Archan would despatch Jonah and Annie before these borrowed eyes. Then the white head swivelled towards her and she felt the pressure of a thousand charmed senses against her host's tender flesh. Beside her in the faery mind the wolf-creature was straining at the leash she had wound about its neck. Now she let go that leash, setting the monster free then running with it, flying free . . .

She raced the White Wolf as it stampeded through the imaginary forest inside the faery's mind. She clung to the fur on its back as it toppled trees and sparked fires in the undergrowth with its claws. Then they broke free together, leaping . . .

. . . into existence between the balanced worlds of Stone and sun. Those who watched saw ribbons of light streaming from Thomas's eyes and nose and mouth, vivid streamers that knotted themselves into a solidifying pulp of meat and muscle. From the light, from the pulp, Areken and the White Wolf grew before their astonished eyes.

Thomas screamed as they grew. This frozen boy in the body of a man felt the stolen years fall back inside himself even as the monsters broke free from their prison. With the wolf went all the anger, all the guilt and nightmare knowledge of the murders he had committed. As the beast was unravelled from his heart so his heart fell in upon itself and became whole. Like a cloud the wolf left him, a vast expanding cloud filled with killing light. The outpouring was long and cruel and more painful than anything he had ever known but at the end of it he was left whole and alone. He fell to his knees, trails of light shining like lingering tears on his cheeks.

'Atomic,' he whispered, hiding his face in his hands.

Panting and drooling, their newly-gelled bodies steaming with creation, Areken and the White Wolf glowered at their audience. Areken was an exact copy of her sister, a sleek white serpent-shape; the wolf-thing was something else altogether.

The physical manifestation of Thomas's damaged alter ego was huge and broken. As big as a bear, its fur was coarse and clogged with filth; long yellow canines jutted from its upper jaw like the teeth of a sabre-tooth tiger; its red eyes were both sly and stupid, the eyes of a suspicious moron. It remained crouched at Areken's side, swaying a little and jerking its misshapen head in random tics and spasms.

'Where the hell did they come from?' said Annie, pressing her hands against Archan's scales in an effort to loosen the grip of her tail. 'I thought dragons' bodies were like gold dust round here.'

Jonah had to agree: the only reason Archan – and Areken, in her version of Stone – had resorted to riding around in faery bodies was because they had long ago been ejected from their own dragon forms and left as disembodied spirits. Archan had eventually managed to steal the body of another dragon called Torus, remoulding it to her own design; Areken, her counterpart in a parallel world, had not yet performed that feat.

So where had this new body come from?

'The memory rods,' he murmured. And it was true – he had seen it for himself. While Thomas had been vomiting up those streamers of light Jonah had seen matching streamers pulsing outwards from the memory thread. 'Archan's twin has used the rods to reform her own body – as well as some half-conceived monstrosity to house the wolf-creature – out of Stone's store of memories. She has used the same techniques that I used to bring Darwin's book out of the past, to bring Malya back from the dead, except she has dared to summon her own flesh out of the vault of history. The good news is that none of this new life can be stable – all of it must turn to stone just like Darwin, just like poor Malya.'

Annie rubbed her head with her hand. 'Shit, Jonah. How do you keep track of all this stuff?'

'The important thing,' he went on, 'is that much of what surrounds us is petrifying before our eyes. It is real enough, but none of it is built to last. If we can only stand firm then most of our enemies will simply fall apart where they stand.'

'Not Archan.'

'Not her, no.'

But it was true, at least in part. Whether because of the haste with which they had been formed, or because Areken herself was a creation of Jonah's and therefore fundamentally flawed, no sooner did they spring into life than Areken's body and the grotesque wolf-thing began to decay.

It started with the White Wolf. It had turned around, apparently preparing to attack Thomas – who was still bent double with his face lost in his hands – when a shudder passed down its spine and into its hind legs, which turned grey and lifeless. It turned and sniffed at them; if its face had not been so deformed the look of surprise on it would have been almost comical. Then the same thing happened to its front legs and shoulders. Raising its head into the overhead glare it howled, an oily screech that made both Jonah and Annie raise their hands to their ears. Unable to move its limbs it simply stood there, lank fur bristling with rage, howling at the sun.

Areken was changing too. The body she had made was much less durable than the body Jonah had made for Malya. Grey colour across her wings. The end of her tail darkened too, although the rest of her body, including her expressionless face, remained an unsullied white, for now at least.

'Do we stand a chance now, Jonah?' Annie asked, watching for more signs of petrifaction in both dragon and wolf.

'I cannot say,' he replied with proper English reserve. 'The implications of what Areken has done trouble me more than with the actuality of it.'

'Jesus Christ, Jonah. Don't you ever say what you mean?'

He gave her a quizzical look before continuing, 'By which, my darling, I mean that for the first time our dragon adversary has manipulated the memory rods. This is what I have feared for some time now, that Archan – or in this case Archan's twin sister – would start to tamper with the proper flow of time. And now that one dragon has started neither will be able to stop. The battle, I fear, is just beginning.'

Archan's coils tightened, making it impossible to speak further. Jonah fixed his gaze on the almost invisible thread of the compressed memory rod, but not before he had looked again at the wolf-creature, lurching on legs turned to clumsy stone, bearing down on Thomas with slavering jaws . . .

. . . gaping wide and hungry. Thomas looked away from the face of the White Wolf and into the redwood forest.

'Away,' he whispered to the trees and the trees were gone. Gone too was the smell of charcoal, of burning hair. He was here at last, really here in this strange world of Stone and sun, Thomas Coyote, alone and afraid, although the fear was good, the fear was *real*.

'Away,' he said to the White Wolf. It tottered nearer, its legs inflexible grey stumps; blind grey eyes spun in grizzled sockets. Its fur was sloughing away like broken shale. 'Away,' he said again, watching the tide of stone wash across its body.

Now the monster was inches from his face. Even its

breath was stone now, moisture beading in heavy pellets which gathered like tiny marbles between granite teeth. It stopped, no longer able to breathe. He could see its chest trying to heave against the weight of the rock but to no avail. It was suffocating from the inside out.

Thomas reached into its jaws and broke off a tooth. It snapped easily, spraying dust across a stony tongue. Somewhere in its ruined throat the wolf tried to howl. Thomas broke off another tooth, then another. Soon the wolf's teeth lay scattered like pebbles around its unmoving paws.

Thomas extended his reach and pulled the wolf's entire lower jaw from its skull. It sheared away with a thick ripping sound, like a door sliding open deep inside a pyramid. He dismantled the rest of the wolf, taking it apart piece by piece and tossing the component parts in an ever-widening circle of debris. When he had finished he rocked back on his heels and surveyed his handiwork.

The remains of the White Wolf were colourless on the black ground, colourless in the uncompromising light of the nearby sun. He looked on them and they were nothing to him. Thomas Coyote was alone. The past was nothing to him now, history was dead and gone. He exulted; he was reborn.

He stood and walked across the fist-floor, kicking through the stones and bones as if they were fallen leaves. The two dragons watched him as he walked.

He marched straight up to the coils of the dragon holding Jonah and Annie prisoner and, recalling all he had learned about Jonah's powers during his time on the Bark, said this:

'Jonah. The power's in the past. You know that, don't you? We'll hold the fort here – it's time for you to get to work. Get goin', time-traveller.'

21

Everything Changes . . .

The sunset behind the water mill was magnificent. He had forgotten that, how the sun had boiled and swelled and then flattened before sinking behind the elms in the old West Wood. He watched it now as he cruised through the memory of that day, watched the sky change to violet as the planet fell backwards away from the light. For a time it was neither day nor night but that almost-time between the two, when the stars are still forbidden and the air pauses to catch its breath.

Jonah weighed time and found he had plenty with which to play. Entering the memory stream had been easy (here at the top of Stone there was only one rod to choose from). Now he was inside he could force time to flow at whatever speed he desired. He could remain here for years while only a fraction of a second passed in the world of Stone, where his body was even now in danger of being crushed by Archan. The dragons would follow him in, of course, and bring their own powers to bear, but for the moment at least he could afford to take things steadily.

Could afford, in fact, to take his time.

What he could not afford to do was relax. The dragon twins were as powerful as he was in this memory realm and he would do well to remember that. Though they were not as practised as Jonah at changing the past, they would be much less careful about what they disturbed.

Have I endangered Stone in entering the rod at all? *he*

asked himself. But it was academic. Whatever he did the dragons would find their way in sooner or later; at least here he stood the best chance of facing them on his own terms and with weapons that might actually do them harm.

Weapons? Just what might those weapons be, Jonah Lightfoot? Are you not deluding yourself into thinking you are more powerful than you actually are?

Sliding through one of the mill's lime-washed walls Jonah settled his ghost-form in a dark corner of the grinding room.

They will try to change my past, *he thought.*

Perhaps they would even try to erase him from history altogether. In doing so they would end up splitting the river of time just as he himself had done. They too would become creators of worlds.

Did they understand the consequences of such actions? Jonah had to assume they did. But he doubted that would hold them back.

Does a dragon have a conscience?

Kythe had, but Archan was not Kythe. Nor was her sister.

His thoughts lingered on Kythe. He thought about how she had travelled back in time to the dawn of her race, how she had in a way become the mother of her race. Jonah found this breathtaking – it was like Annie journeying back to Eden to become Eve. This in turn made him think of Krakatoa, which he had likened to Paradise shortly before the fateful eruption.

Annie and I naked on the beach, Eve and Adam. Annie's eyes turning to chrome. Archan in the iceberg . . .

And so he came back to the dragon again, a circular chain of thought. Did the river of time flow in a circle too? From the great ocean of the future was there a small outflow which meandered up into the hills, eventually to turn and grow and become a river and flow back down into the great ocean again?

Did everything simply turn*?*

A noise jerked him free from his musings. It came from the floor above: the bin floor, from the window of which he had fallen on to the waterwheel. At first he thought it was squeaking.

Mice of course, or rats. There were plenty of both in the mill and it took more than a courting couple to send them into hiding. Then he realized it was a human sound, a woman crying quiet tears in the growing gloom.

'Lily?' he said. His voice went nowhere; he was, after all, a ghost.

The air outside was still fresh after the storm but here in the mill the smell of ancient barley was thicker than ever. When he rose through the trapdoor and into the bin room the smell ripened; he could even see it, an aromatic dust clustered in pockets of deep, deep shadow. Still there was no moon outside and here at the top of the mill the darkness was profound.

The sobbing was coming from the north-east corner of the bin floor. It was Lily, Jonah was sure of it now, but why was she crying? As far as he could remember, after she had helped him down from the waterwheel they had gone back inside the mill to sit out the rest of the storm. Jonah had licked his wounds and they had made love again, slowly, to the sound of the awakening bees. By the time the sun went down they were heading back towards the farmhouse.

Night had fallen so why was Lily still here? And why was she crying?

Jonah allowed himself to drift closer to the sound, mindful not to disturb anything in the room. This was a memory from his own past; his presence here could be devastating.

I am not here. I am not a presence but an absence. I touch nothing, I do nothing. I simply observe. Nothing changes. It will be as it always has been. It will be as if I were never here.

The moon had risen, dripping thin light past the broken window sill. His ghost-eyes drank up this meagre glow and traced the line of Lily's curved back, a dark stroke on a shadowy canvas.

Lily?

Something had changed here. Something had happened, something bad.

Willing his phantom heart to be silent, resisting the urge to reach out and caress the nape of Lily's neck, ghost-Jonah backed away, glancing now into the other corners of the room. Rats' eyes opened like bright wounds.

Are they here already? What have they done to this memory? How have they altered my past?

He could hear a new sound now. A tearing sound, interrupted by the occasional 'snap', like breaking branches in a forest. Like the starlight it was coming in through the window.

Lily heard it too. 'Leave him alone,' she said, lifting her head. Her fiery hair was grey in the moonlight, old and wasted. And long, much longer than Jonah remembered. Then she stood and shuffled to the window and Jonah saw that she was old. Very old.

The bare feet kicking up the barley dust were crooked and lumped with corns; her smock draped limp over sagging breasts and age-stretched hips. Grey hair followed her like a bride's train. She was still beautiful though, his English Lily grown wizened and fair. Behind the creased mask of her face shone the eyes he had once loved and which now, he believed, he would always love.

A voice called from below the window but she was blocking his view so he could not see who it belonged to. He walked out through the wall and held himself suspended over the waterwheel.

It is a pity I could not do this the first time around, *he thought.* I would have saved myself a nasty fall.

He recognized the voice and its owner at once. 'Rapunzel,' it cackled, 'let down your hair!'

It was Archan. She was here with him, inside his a memory of a day from his own past. She was here already.

The dragon was squatting on the waterwheel, the tip of her white tail draped out of sight in the overgrown trough which had once been the mill-race. Underneath her soft belly, half-hidden by a swell of muscle Jonah could not help but think of as sensuous, was the body of a young man.

346

Not quite a man, *Jonah thought*. A fourteen year-old boy. Me. Jonah Lightfoot. That is my body beneath her coils. She has killed me already!

He was lying naked exactly where he had fallen. His eyes were as blank and white as the scales on Archan's back, dull despite the moonlight and quite, quite dead.

'Give him back to me,' wept Lily from the window. She was wringing her long, grey hair, twisting it round and round in ever-tightening knots. 'Please, I'll do anything you ask, I promise. Just give him back to me.'

Archan arched her back. Ignoring Lily, she tilted her head towards ghost-Jonah.

'Well, faery,' she said, 'do you think I should give you back? She says she will do anything I ask but I fear she has little idea what a dangerous promise she makes. Should she sacrifice herself for you? And even if she does should I act honourably or should I consume you both? Such a difficult choice to make, as I am sure you agree.'

'What have you done here, Archan?'

'What have I done? Oh . . . call it an overture, faery. Or you might prefer to think of it as an opening salvo.'

'I can change it back. Whatever changes you make to my past I can change it back, Archan. I have travelled further and faster than you through the lands of memory and trust me when I say this: you cannot beat me here. This is my arena. Give up now, while you can, for I will defeat you in the end.'

He was not surprised when Archan laughed, indeed he was ready for it.

'Someone is missing from the party,' he went on. 'Your sister – she is notable by her absence once again. You really must keep her on a tighter rein, Archan. You would not want to have her creeping up on you from behind.'

Archan recoiled from this. Jonah could see the skin around her throat glowing orange as she stoked her inner fires.

She is a tiger, *he thought*, and if you dare to take her by the tail be sure not to let go.

'You don't see eye to eye, do you?' he said. 'In fact, I believe there is considerable rivalry between the two of you. Tell me, Archan. Who will win that battle? Which of you is the stronger? You or her?'

The dragon's throat turned brilliant yellow before she managed to rein in her temper. As the glow subsided she burrowed her needle snout into Jonah's face. There was a faint 'pop', then she withdrew with one of Jonah's eyes hanging from her teeth. Quick as a striking snake her chrome tongue licked the dreadful titbit away.

'A valiant effort, faery,' she said. 'Now, let us see if you are as good as you think you are.'

A gale blasted through Jonah from behind, almost breaking his insubstantial form apart. When he had recovered himself he saw the wind had gathered into a tornado centred directly above the mill. Even from there he could feel its pull; it felt as if something huge and hungry was trying to breathe him in.

Slates began to fly from the roof like playing cards, one at a time at first but with increasing abandon as the tornado took hold. Mangled rafters and the ornate pots from the tall east chimney followed. As the roof disintegrated the suction began to draw things up from the attic. Yards and yards of hessian, uncoiling ropes and battered crates all flung themselves free of gravity's clutches and rode into the storm. A cloud of bats burst free like an explosion of feathers and was swallowed whole. A rusted iron bedstead followed, along with countless sacks and sheets and, most unlikely of all, a stuffed deer.

The tornado ate steadily into the mill. When the roof was nearly gone it started on the walls, plucking up three-hundred-year-old stones like . . .

. . . like little ivory tiles . . .

. . . and tossing them into the night sky. Up went the rain of debris and when the wind reached the line of the windows Jonah noticed something odd: none of it was coming back down again.

Gone, *he thought*. She is not taking my world apart — she is making it gone.

Lily was screaming. Jonah shouted at her to stand back, to get away from the window but her hair had grown impossibly long and Archan was holding the end of it in her jaws. Lily pulled and pulled but her hair was held fast and Archan did not move so much as an inch.

'Rapunzel!' Lily was screaming. 'Rapunzel! Rapunzel!'

The tornado was beginning to lose its coherence. Dark clouds limned with moonlight boiled in from the horizon, erasing the stars. The remains of the tornado hung over the mill like a tumour, casting out lines of vapour and reeling in the fresh clouds even as they raced towards it.

Beneath the advancing storm the land too was on the move. The skin of the world was peeling like the rind from an orange. Up into the roiling blackness went the patchwork of meadows adjoining the downs, up went the line of elms behind the mill, up went the silver line of the river and the great clots of gorse marking the place where the pond had once been sunk. There was no thunder, there was no lightning, but it was a storm just the same. It was a storm of oblivion; it was a storm to make things gone.

Jonah saw all this and he felt it all too, felt it inside his mind. Because this was his memory, all these meadows and trees and touches were moments from his life. And Archan was taking them from him. Archan was making them all gone.

And when they were all gone there would be nothing left of him at all.

Nor would there have been anything of him in the first place.

Jonah Lightfoot would be gone.

He felt dizzy. The storm inside his head was expanding to greet its twin outside; as it expanded it left behind an echoing emptiness, a house devoid of fixtures and fittings, all the furniture, all the memories sucked out through the roof. Even though he was floating he staggered, was tossed by the turbulent air, fell back and lowered his face to his hands.

If she destroys me here then I will never go to Krakatoa. I will never meet Annie, never cross over to Stone, never draw Archan to Stone. Archan will never race me here to the top of Stone and Archan will never battle with me here and so she will never destroy me, so then I *will* go to Krakatoa and she *will* come to this place and . . .

His head was ready to split open. Though it felt as heavy as a cannonball he somehow managed to raise it up. He looked straight at Archan.

The dragon was swallowing something. He thought at first it was a length of cloth, then he saw it was Lily's hair. He watched in horror as Archan gulped it down like a string of noodles; the final delicacy was the limp pancake of scalp hanging from the end. He looked away, wondering if ghosts could vomit.

From the wrecked shell of the watermill rose the two enormous grinding stones. Like coins flipped by a gambling god they cartwheeled into the blackness and were gone. But Jonah was not concerned with mill-stones: the clouds had started to close in on the moon and soon there would be no more light. This frightened Jonah more than the sight of the millstones, more even than Archan swallowing poor Lily's wretched hair. Without the light there would be nothing, nothing at all.

The moon, *he thought.* The moon!

He caught sight of something white moving against the black of the storm. It tumbled erratically, a newspaper snatched by a gale. Then it resolved itself into the shape of a dragon.

'Areken!' *he shouted.*

She flew in fast, banshee ribbons of vapour shrieking from her wingtips. She flew in low, low enough to be hidden from her sister's view by the remains of the mill. At the last moment she arrowed between the still-standing chimney and the collapsed east wall, turned into the wind and passed over Archan's head in a blur.

There was a heavy, hollow thud. Jonah blinked stupidly, unable to believe what he had seen.

Areken had not passed over *her sister's* head at all. She had passed *through* it. Her right wing, its leading edge sharpened to a razor edge, had sliced Archan's head clean in two. The top half – comprising the upper jaw and most of the brain case – dropped past the dead Jonah's body and lodged between two of the waterwheel's paddles. A fountain of blood erupted from her exposed neck as if from a high pressure hose, spraying thick dark fluid into the warm night air.

In the distance Areken stalled and turned, returning for a second pass. Jonah wondered why she was bothering.

The fountain of blood stopped as quickly as it had begun and, for the first time, Jonah saw Mister Ren's immortality at work.

Archan rebuilt herself. A crackling aura surrounded the severed part of her head. It looked like electrical lace. A second later a similar aura surrounded the stump of her neck. Miniature lightning bolts darted between them, growing in both brightness and frequency until there was a veritable spider's web of energy connecting the two.

Then the first aura, the one around the fallen head, started to diminish. Soon there was nothing left but a few rogue sparks fizzing on the damp paddles and when the second aura died away Archan was whole again.

She inclined her head – *her* intact *head* – towards Jonah then, with a final defiant toss, turned to face her sister.

There is no magic here, *Jonah thought with something approaching excitement.* There is no . . . no *charm* to this immortality of hers! All this time I have imagined immortality as a Holy Grail, a state of grace, a perfect and untouchable thing. And yet here it is before me, here is what it means: she can be injured but she can rebuild herself. She ages but she can make herself young again.

That is what it is, but that is *all* it is. It is just so, so . . . so *simple!*

It was magic that powered the immortality, of course it was, but the very concept of it was just so damned crude! Nor had it been any different for the basilisks, he was sure of that. Archan was carrying the flag now but the pattern on its cloth had been the same even in their long days.

To be immortal is to see your body ravaged and renewed, ravaged and renewed, over and over again. To be immortal is to die many times over and never be given the opportunity to rest in peace. To be immortal is to suffer for no purpose. To be immortal is to wait, always to wait, for the next time.

No wonder Archan wanted rid of everything around her. It was not the pleasure of destruction that drove her at all: it was the promise of peace.

'Is that what you want, Archan?' he said in his soft ghost-voice. 'Peace? Is that really all you have ever wanted, all along?'

Another voice, equally soft, spoke in his ear.

'Don't tell me you're feeling sorry for that old bitch, Jonah Lightfoot. Because if you are I'll paddle your ass 'til it shines red as the setting sun!'

Annie!

'What in God's name . . . ?' he said before he was covering her in kisses, ghost-kisses of course but that was just fine because she was a ghost here too. A beautiful, familiar phantom, her touch as real to him as if they were both made of flesh and blood. 'What are you doing here? How in God's name did you get here? Archan – has she . . . ?'

'Hold your horses, Jonah, let me get a word in edgewise.' *Incredibly, she was laughing. Jonah found himself laughing too. The storm in his head had burst like a bubble and now he felt light and free, almost ready to cast himself adrift from this world altogether and just . . . float away.*

'All right,' he said. *The laughter went as quickly as it*

had come but that floating sensation remained. He clung to it, wanting it never to go. It made him feel like a child again. 'All right, Annie, tell me what is going on, please. But make it fast.'

He nodded at the distant clouds, where even now Areken was swooping in, ready for a second attack on her sister. Archan had her back to them, more intent on facing her flying adversary than her human opponents; that at least was a mercy.

'Okay. I'm dreamin', Jonah. That's all it is, really. I didn't realize it before but my dreamin' dreams are my way into the memory rods. Dreams of Kansas, dreams of Chinese mountains I ain't never seen but someone has, Mister Ren himself most likely. All those things were real. All those things were here, here in Sunlight Pass. Here in the memory rod. Jonah, I'm an adept too, at least up here I am.'

'Oh, Annie!'

'And I've come to help you out because it looks like you're sunk in some pretty deep shit here!'

Floating, he was floating. Archan had taken off and she was floating too. The two dragons were grappling in the air like wrestling men at the County Fair but Jonah had no time for them. He was flying past them, rising up into the belly of the storm.

'Annie!' he shouted. 'Come back! Bring me back!'

'It's all right, Jonah,' she cried. 'I'll take care of things down here for a while. You just do what you have to do. Oh, and Jonah?'

'Yes?'

'Tell Kythe I sent my love. All of it.'

The moon . . .

It blossomed like a rose through the muddy clouds, a full bright disc. Jonah passed through the clouds and into a froth of moonlight, watched over by the naked stars. Air and heat fell away until all that remained was a ghost between worlds.

Jonah sped towards the small world. Urgency was with him

353

now; Archan was playing with his mind and time seemed more precious than ever before.

A plume of light caught his eye. Something had hit the surface of the moon, there in the shadow of one of the seas that was not a sea. It had a name, that sea, but Jonah could not recall what it was. He changed course, blinked himself nearer until the moon filled his vision and he was scouring the grey plains like a circling hawk making ready to stoop.

There! A splash of white in the fine grey sea. Finger-trails of dust pointed like sunbeams from the star-shaped crater. Like an eye it looked back at Jonah. He fell towards it, eager to see what had landed there to make such a perfect mark.

The rock was still smoking when he reached it. It was black and pitted and sat like an idol in the centre of its crater. Fresh to this world, it looked both horribly out of place and utterly at home.

By concentrating hard he managed to make his hand real enough so that he could pick up the meteorite. It was large, much larger than any of the others he had seen here. Was it special therefore? Could it be that this was . . .

'Archan's rock.'

He jumped at the sound of Kythe's voice. Turning, he was about to greet her when the smile froze on his face.

She had crept up on him from behind and now she loomed over him, her vast wings translucent in the unshielded glare of the sun. Opaque veins crazed the wing membranes like elaborate window lead; Jonah felt as though he were in church.

'Yes,' Kythe went on. There was something odd in her voice, something Jonah could not identify. 'This rock is Archan's rock. It holds her name. The question is, Jonah, what has that got to do with you?'

'Kythe?' Her face was hard to read, hard to see even. The sun was pinned to the black sky directly behind her head, tipping her eyes deep into shadow.

'I can't believe,' she said, 'that you've dared to come back, Jonah. I can't believe it.' She growled and smoke spurted from her mouth. Jonah took a step back.

'Dared?' he said. 'I . . . what do you mean, Kythe? Why should I not have come back? You knew I would come back. What is wrong? Please tell me.'

She glared at him from beneath the shadows of her brow for a long moment, then grunted, 'Follow me!'

She flew without flapping her wings, an elegant yet conceited mode of flight. The way the decadent charmed dragons had flown before the world had turned its back on them. Charm sprayed from her wingtips like diamonds, its beauty squandered. Jonah followed in silence, the rock in his hand, dread like acid in his stomach.

Kythe stopped at a crater he knew. He saw at once what had changed and thought he knew why his dragon friend was so angry.

'What has happened to the other three rocks?' he said. 'You told me their names: "Sun" and "Moon" and "Light". This fourth rock, Archan's rock, was to be "Name", the last rock of the sequence. That was important . . . somehow. But where are the other three? What has happened to them?'

'I was hoping you could tell me that, Jonah.' Her voice tightened, clipping the words into tiny pellets of sound.

'I do not understand what you mean, Kythe.'

'Oh, I think you do, faery!' The sun was at her side now and he could see the madness in her eyes as they fixed him with their accusing gaze so that he was frozed to the spot, though he wanted to flee. 'Empty your pockets!'

'What?'

'You heard me! Empty your pockets!'

He was feeling dizzy again. Could any of this be real? Could he really be standing up to his ghostly ankles in moon dust while a giant orange dragon spoke to him like an angry headmistress?

'I said empty your pockets!'

He obeyed, he could not help himself. He knew the only things in his pockets were the two Mah Jongg tiles which he still had to place – somewhere – in Sunlight Pass. Yet the objects he found were not smooth and square but round and coarse, and there were not two but three. He brought the rocks out and offered them up to Kythe but she only sneered and spat blue licks of fire into the ground before his feet.

'Traitor!' she shouted. 'How dare you betray the future of my kind!'

'Kythe – believe me, I did not take these rocks from you. I am your friend, you know that.'

'Friend? Ten thousand years have passed since we last met on this forsaken little world. Do you have any idea what it's like to be alone all that time? Alone and immortal might be one thing but I'm not immortal. I'm old, Jonah! I can keep myself going for another thousand years maybe, long enough to lead my dragons down to the bigger world below, but that's all I can manage. I'm tired, Jonah, tired and old. I have no time for games.'

'I have never played games with you, Kythe.'

'You stole from me, Jonah! Don't bother to deny it.'

'It is Archan.' He felt immeasurably weary. The words came out but he did not expect her to believe them.

'You stole from me.'

'Archan is playing with your mind. She is twisting events around, making it seem that I have done things which in truth I would never do. Never.'

'You stole from me!'

'Believe me when I say I would never do such a thing.'

'You stole from me, Jonah. And now you must be punished!'

The madness in her eyes was real, he saw that now – indeed, he could hear it in her voice. But it was not solitude that had made her insane, not anger at his alleged crime. It was Archan. Archan was here, stirring the broth of memory until all the distinct flavours had become a melange. She was here doing more than making mischief: she was beginning the process of destruction from the inside out.

And she was starting with the destruction of Jonah Lightfoot himself.

Kythe was advancing on him, an orange wraith vivid against the grey. Teeth had grown along the leading edges of both her wings so that each looked like a jawbone detached from its skull and grafted into a new location. He backed away, suddenly aware of the weight of the rocks in his hands.

As she lunged at him he hurled the rocks, one by one, at her face.

I cannot believe I am doing this! he howled as one struck her left eye. The others bounced harmlessly off her horns and he was out of ammunition.

Kythe winked her injured eye; the resulting expression was a ghastly blend of coyness and fury.

'How dare you!' she bellowed.

Then Jonah saw the reflections of the sun, two of them, paired stars adrift in this dragon's eyes. He stopped retreating and stood his ground, fingers curled, head cocked. Kythe saw the change in him and stopped too. Then she began to laugh in long, fire-ridden snorts.

'Very good, faery,' she laughed. 'Oh, very good indeed!'

'How much of it is you, Archan?' said Jonah.

'Oh, all of it, faery. All of it!'

The moon swelled. Kythe's body melted away. Colours changed from grey and black to green and blue, stone and sky, sea and sun, and dust became grass and empty clouds rolled in from a horizon that was rolling away. The fallen mill rose and the laughter was Annie's, only Annie was a ghost and her eyes were made of chrome. On the wheel of the mill squatted Archan and beneath her claws was Jonah with white wings and fangs of steel, and there in the sky flew Archan, who was not Areken at all but the same as herself and all she had constructed here, and it was all Archan, all of it.

357

Except Jonah, who was himself and alone in a world where he no longer belonged.

'What have you done to me?' he whispered.

And he was not alone, for Archan, who was everything here, said, 'You are gone, Jonah.'

22

Annie Out West – 4

Annie watched Jonah leave both her and his body behind, watched his eyes turn over white and his chin fall to his chest. Watched him go travelling into the realm of memory.

Just like me, she thought. *Just like me goin' out west.*

Archan too had noticed his departure, though her attention was partly taken by the approach of Areken, who was limping towards her with stone wings raised high and fury in the set of her jaw. Archan hesitated, gauging the level of threat offered by her sister, then Annie felt the coils of muscle relax against her legs. The slackening was not enough to permit escape but demonstrated clearly enough that Archan was gone too.

She's after you, Jonah. She's headin' on in. Hope you're saddled up and ready 'cos she's gonna be kickin' up some dust.

A kind of peace fell over the arena. With Jonah and Archan temporarily absent – in spirit at least – much of the tension had evaporated. Malya was looking warily at Thomas Coyote, who was kicking through the scattered bones of the White Wolf. Even Areken, her body trembling as she fought against the ongoing petrifaction, seemed unsure of what to do next.

Then from behind Archan's coils appeared the head and shoulders of Mister Ren, except Annie knew at once it was really the shaman inside the Chinaman's bones. *Shit – how did he make it back here?*

They all watched Frey's painful progress across the undulating ground. His borrowed legs were splints of stone; also affected were his left arm and the left side of his face, which was frozen in a rictus of agony. It was like the White Wolf all over again – each step saw the borderland of grey migrate a little further across his body. Soon it would reach his heart, his brain, and then it would all be over.

He was heading for Malya. Annie watched Malya's eyes react first with pity and then with recognition, true recognition not of the man's outer shell but his inner soul. Behind the stolen Chinese features she recognized the face of her father, who had once murdered her.

Malya took a step backwards that was every bit as clumsy as those her father was taking towards her. Her mouth dropped open and Annie thought the sword would have fallen from her hand if the two had not been fused together.

Frey was trying to open Mister Ren's mouth but already his lower jaw had locked solid. Through the tiny gap that remained came the faintest moan. Malya moaned too, then took another step back.

He was draped with skulls, most of which had melded together to form a lumpy bone waistcoat. However one of the skulls he had managed to prise free and this one he held forwards in his living right hand, held it as far from the rest of his body as he could manage, as if that would stop it becoming infected. The skull was human in shape but no bigger than an orange. Constantly on the verge of overbalancing, each step a half-caught stumble, he continued to lurch towards his daughter.

'Go away,' said Malya, the words thin and unconvincing.

Unable to speak, Frey swivelled Mister Ren's head

from side to side. Stone vertebrae screeched against each other.

'Go away,' Malya said again. Her voice was a little stronger but now she had stopped retreating and just stood there, watching her father dying before her eyes.

Ten yards was as close as he got. After that he simply shook on the spot, unable to take another step. The colour had gone from all his body except his right hand, in which he still held the single skull. Malya looked at her own hand, the one already turned to stone, and at the stone sword with which it was joined. She put her living hand to her face and pressed it there for a moment before advancing to where her father stood.

'Malya!' shouted Annie. 'Be careful!'

But the warrior-woman did not hear, or did not listen. She *was* careful as she approached Frey but she was also sure. When she was close enough she reached for the skull. As her hand moved under it Frey opened his fingers and let it fall. She caught it and stepped away, watching his fingers turn grey even as she did so.

She stood there for long seconds, seeking something in the blank sculpted orbs of her father's eyes but finding nothing. Then she shook herself, looked round as if she had woken from a dark dream and raised her sword arm again. Her other arm she pulled against her breasts to shield the skull from both gaze and harm.

With the encounter ended Annie found her thoughts returning to Jonah. She watched Areken struggle for certainty and wondered if this dragon too would follow the memory trail. Or would she try to destroy Archan's body in the meantime? Burn down the house while the resident was on vacation, so to speak.

She remembered what Jonah had told her about the passage of time within the memory rods and the corresponding flow of time in the real worlds. The two rarely matched, he asserted, and the traveller of the rods might cross a billion years and leap a billion miles before the body he left behind could take even a single blink.

Goin' out west. Just like me.

It was a moment of revelation like, well, like a rising sun. Could it be true? Was she, Annie West, an adept too?

All those dreams. All that time spent in my head. But is that really where I was all that time? Wasn't that trail just a little too familiar? Weren't those mountains just a little too real? Could I really have imagined those things if they didn't already exist somewhere, somewhere in a real world? Somewhere in the past? Somewhere in the memory rods?

It was a rejuvenating idea. It was also terrifying. If it were true it meant she was no more trapped here than Jonah had been – she had choices, she could fight back.

It also meant she could put herself in the most terrible danger. She could pit herself against a creature whose motives she could not begin to understand on a battleground that was as strange to her as . . .

. . . as the terraced mountain slopes of Tibet.

'But it ain't strange, woman,' she said to herself. Her voice carried though and both Malya and Thomas looked up at her curiously. 'Is it now? It ain't no more strange than that old trail out west. Because you've been there before, been there in your dreamin' dreams. That's where you were all those times, only you never knew it 'til now. Way out west, in the mountain-land of memory.'

Yes, she could put herself in danger but that was all right, because Jonah would be at her side.

She twisted her waist (her hips were still clamped tight by the hard snake-belly in which she was wrapped) until she was looking straight at the memory rod. It was hardly there at all, she saw, little more than a knife-cut through the air. A slender cotton thread holding up a world. Staring at it was like trying to see a star: look right at it and it vanishes, but cheat your eyes a little to the side and there it is, blazing away. This she did, using her peripheral vision to fix the thread in her mind. She imagined the thread splitting open, making a wound through which she might enter.

The wound was real. Darkness was bleeding from it like a gush of light, casting shadows like light and illuminating all upon which it fell with an all-consuming blackness. The thread became the sky and Annie was a gnat. The thought at the front of her mind as she crossed over the threshold between the present and the storehouse of all history was this:

How will I find them when before me is . . .

. . . all the time in the world?

She blinked, sat up. Had it been a fall? She couldn't tell. Nothing felt broken, nor even bruised, though her head ached as if she had drunk just a drop too much liquor last night. She stood up and somebody let off a string of firecrackers behind her eyes. Make that several drops.

Things were rumbling past, very loud.

Slowly the ache subsided and the fireworks died away. Left was a hunger quite unlike any normal craving. It was as if her stomach wanted to smell, or her fingertips wanted to eat or some damn thing. She pushed the sensation away and took a good look around.

It was not what she had expected, not at all.

Jonah had often tried to describe his experiences in the memory rods but despite his best efforts Annie had always found his descriptions wanting. What had stuck in his mind were the memories themselves, not the abstract interior landscapes of the rods themselves. But these ended up being simply descriptions of faces and fields and familiar things and so Annie had imagined exploring the rods would be like exploring her own memories, like leafing through a giant book in which the pictures came to life, grew colour and movement and breathed with the pulse of life, tripping from one tableau to the next with no spaces between, still frames from the zoetrope, endlessly turning.

Maybe it was like that for Jonah. It sure as hell wasn't like that for her.

It was like a gigantic prairie, but one that had never existed on Earth. Wagons were thundering past, many thousands of them – high-topped Conestogas, strange flatbeds hauled by metal animals that looked more like locomotives than horses, drays and Surreys, spiked siege engines and caterpillar-crawlers along with countless more vehicles she could not even begin to describe.

The ocean again, *she thought.* All the boats you could ever want.

On the verge of fainting she pinched herself. She did not wake up – this was no dream.

Shit, Annie! Look around! Work it out!

The wagons hammered past, an endless parade, each wheel with its own direction across the dust of the prairie. Some were pulled by beasts, others by men, still more moved under their own power, belching steam or slipping silently on runners greased smooth of friction. Many carried freight, mostly unrecognisable, tanks and metal shapes and long organic twists of stuff that breathed as they moved.

Dear God! *Each fragment of thought rose painfully, like a bubble in the blood.* What the hell is all this?

And still the wagons moved on.

It began to dawn on Annie that this was what these vehicles did and this was all they did, that this was what happened here. The movement would never stop. These were the memories: not frozen moments at all but movements through time and space, each memory a journey in itself, each memory a way of travelling between way-stations, a means by which all the stuff of the worlds might be transported into the next and constant future.

She sat down abruptly, her backside raising the tiniest puff of dust within the clouds of the wagon-storm. There was something else too, something equally tiny yet independent inside the din. A sound, an absurd sound. Squeak-squeak, *it went.* Squeak-squeak.

On her hands and knees Annie squinted through the racing wagons. A team of twenty horses galloped by trailing a cannon and limber large enough to bring down Jericho. Dust crowded her face but still the sound penetrated. She attached a movement to it, an approaching blur that rocked in time. Squeak-squeak, rock-rock.

A gap in the flood of vehicles and the newcomer was through, larger than she had first thought but still smaller than most of the traffic speeding past. She stood to meet it, for it was slowing as it drew up beside her.

It was a pony and trap. The pony was a grey mare and the trap was made of polished cherrywood. The trap was clean, quite free of the dust clogging the rest of the wagons on the memory trail. Prairie sunlight gleamed off brass fittings; the fine leather upholstery shone nearly as brightly. The driver wore a hat like a bowl turned up and ready to catch the rain.

'Hello, Mister Ren,' said Annie. Now it was her mouth that had been dealt the liquor. Her lips moved but she could not feel them at all. She wiped her chin, convinced she was dribbling.

'Annie! Delightful to see you again! Hop in, please. We ought to get going!'

'You don't say.'

She hesitated, deluding herself for a moment that she actually had a choice in the matter before swinging her leg over the guard rail and squeezing herself into the passenger seat. He doffed his hat, smiled and clucked at the pony, which took them away at a canter.

'Do you mind,' said Annie, 'telling me what the hell you're doing here? Oh, and you could throw in where we're headed too? And don't take all day about it – I've got a dragon to catch up with here.'

'You'll catch up with her soon enough,' said Mister Ren.

A snake-line of circus caravans overtook the trap, gaudy

music splashing from the nearest. They vanished into the rising dust.

'This prairie, it's just a picture, ain't it? Like the beach was a picture, and the mountains and everything else in my dreams? Just a way of seeing things a woman ain't supposed to see.'

'You wouldn't want to see the rods as they really are,' agreed Mister Ren. He gave her a serene smile which might have been meant to soothe but managed only to irritate. Didn't this guy have any sense of urgency?

'Why not?'

'I have already told you the memory rods are alive. Well, like many living things they have teeth. You do not want to stand naked before the teeth of Amara, Annie West. Believe me, you don't.'

He was smiling all the while he was saying this but it was not his smile that held Annie's attention now, it was his words.

Naked before the teeth of Amara . . .

She had heard something similar, and recently too. But where?

Mr Ren said, 'I can find my way around in here but I can't make changes. But you can, Annie. You can! Like Jonah! So! I can take you there but it's up to you to do the work.'

'Work? Take me where?'

By way of reply Mister Ren yanked the reins hard to the left. The grey pony screamed like a young girl and careered sideways, just missing the tail-end of a huge, grimy sled with runners like longboats. Laughing now, he threaded a perilous course through the onrushing traffic, dodging between carts and carriages and strange juggernauts as he took them steadily towards the outer edge of the throng.

'Yee-hah!' he cried. His small white teeth caught the hard light of the sun and turned it to diamonds.

Annie could hardly bear to look. She thought the end had come when the pony galloped beneath the shadow of a tall, big-wheeled trailer pulled by a team of what looked like about two hundred huskies. Between the two pairs of wheels was a high arch of chassis. Mister Ren drove the trap directly beneath it, swerving in behind the front axle before peeling out into the light on the opposite side. A second after they reached safety the rear wheels crushed their tracks into the dirt. Annie screamed but already they were clear.

Beyond the husky-hauled trailer there was nothing but open prairie, a vast glow of green beneath a boiling sun. A single horse, striped red and black like a rebellious zebra, bolted past dragging nothing but broken traces and a tattered rope; Annie guessed that somewhere up the trail a furious driver was throwing his whip to the ground and shaking his fist at his vanishing nag.

The pony slowed to a canter, then trotted for a time, steam lifting from its flanks, until the grass got so deep it could no longer pull the trap. Then it stopped and began to graze, tearing up long clumps of grass and chewing on them patiently, watching Annie with its soft brown eyes as if to say, 'I done my part. Now it's your turn, girl.'

'Well,' said Mister Ren, 'that was a lot of fun!'

'If you say so.'

They walked for a while. The swish of the knee-high grass was comforting but the going was hard. The land which had looked so flat was actually rising steadily towards a distant ridge. As they approached the top of the ridge Annie noticed something odd: all the grass blades were leaning back down the slope. The nearer they got to the top the more exaggerated the effect became. She began to wonder what they would find on the other side.

'Rest here a moment.' Mister Ren's voice was no more than a whisper as he motioned her down with a wave of his arm. 'I need to take a look.'

Annie waited, watching the little Chinaman's ass waggle from side to side as he scurried on hands and knees to the top of the rise. Once there he lay motionless, the black carapace on his back looking more than ever like the shell of some exotic species of tortoise. At last she could stand the suspense no longer.

Keeping low, she followed the line of squashed grass stems to where Mister Ren lay. Then, raising her head up inch by careful inch, she looked over the edge.

There was a hole in the prairie, a black eye about ten yards across. Steam rose from it in tangled strings. Around the hole the ground was scorched flat and grey; beyond this perimeter the green of the grass blended back in concentric rings. All the grass was flattened though, each stem pointing directly away from the hole as if a giant had dropped a rock on the world.

'What is this place?' she asked. A wind had whipped up and was blowing the steam across her face. It tasted acidic, like lemons soaked in vinegar.

'Oubliette,' said Mister Ren.

'Pardon me?'

'Oubliette. It's a French word.'

'I guessed that. You mind telling me what it means?'

'Oubliettes are popular in medieval times. Every well-to-do castle boasts one. It's a sort of dungeon – or perhaps 'pit' would be a better description. In any case, it's somewhere to put prisoners when you want to just forget about them. So. That's what the words means, you see? A place of forgetting.'

'Oubliette,' repeated Annie. 'Not really in the spirit of Stone. If we're still on Stone that is.'

'Oh, we are, we are! And I have to agree. Amara may look like a gigantic castle wall but it's not a place for an oubliette, oh no, not a place for one of those at all!'

'So what's it doing here?'

'Archan made it.'

Annie considered this. She did not like the turn of the conversation – it felt too much like being on that damned pony and trap again, too much as if she were being steered against her will, out of control.

'It's a place for prisoners, right?' she said at last.

'Correct.'

'And there's only one person I can think of that Archan would want to put behind bars, am I right?'

'Jonah, yes, of course. So.'

'So be damned!' Annie was furious. Furious with Archan and especially furious with this inscrutable character who consistently refused to show all his cards. 'What in hell's name is she playin' at now?'

'Listen and I will tell you.'

'Yes. You will!'

Infuriating to the last, Mister Ren gave her his sweetest smile. 'Archan has deceived Jonah into believing she has changed his past. She has created a stream of false memories – a kind of backwater to the river of time – and thrown him into it. He believes she is tinkering with his memories but she isn't. She's made a pool – a mill-pond if you like – in which she can drown him without actually having to alter the river of time itself.'

Annie's eyes widened. 'She's scared! She really is so goddam scared, ain't she?'

'Yes, Annie! Yes!' Mister Ren was beaming and nodding enthusiastically. 'Archan knows she could change the river itself, just like Jonah. But she's terrified of the consequences!'

'She's already got one twin sister on her back. The last thing she needs is a whole horde of them.' Annie paused and frowned as she realized something else. 'She doesn't know about the turning to stone, does she? Anything she makes by actually changing time wouldn't last anyway, so she's no real need to be scared, but she doesn't know that, does she? She doesn't realize Areken's falling to pieces just like . . . just like poor Malya and that godforsaken wolf-thing.'

'Correct!' cried Mister Ren triumphantly. 'And if we can keep that knowledge from her then we might just stand a chance.'

'So where's Jonah in all this? Where actually is he?'

But of course she knew.

Lying on her belly, staring down into the black well of the oubliette, Annie was reminded of the wells Rance had sunk around their Kansas homestead. Only one had ever yielded water and even that success had been short-lived. Most of the *time they were forced to trek two miles to the stream or go begging to their belligerent neighbour John Clayman. Once Rance had stolen water from Clayman's nearest well but the crime seemed so immense to Annie that she talked him out of any further misdemeanours. The popular epithet 'Drouthy Kansas' certainly held true for the West homestead.*

And now here, on this other prairie, she found herself wondering if there were any water at the bottom of this well. She could hear nothing over the steady hiss of the acid vapour streaming past her face. Moreover she knew this was not really a well, any more than she was really on a prairie.

If Mister Ren were to be believed (and what could she do but believe him?) this prairie was really the meat inside a living sinew of memories. In some other way it was also a river leading to a wide, wide ocean. And this well, this 'oubliette'? The well was a forgotten corner, the useless appendix in Stone's vast and complex anatomy of time. Here was the place where Archan had looped the great river round upon itself, not actually tainting its waters but somehow cutting off an oxbow lake and marooning Jonah inside it.

And I'm the only one who can get him out.

'Just one thing before I go down there.' she said, rolling on to her back and squinting up into the smiling face of her guide. *'Have I always had the power to do this? Have I always been like Jonah, always been an 'adept' as Esh called it?'*

'Think about it, Annie West. I think you know the answer to that already.'

'Infuriating man!' she said under her breath. *'You got a rope?'*

Without a word, without dropping his grin at all, he drew a thick coil of thin twine from behind his back.

'Don't let go,' she said as he paid out sufficient line for her to hold.

'Trust me.'

'Like I got a choice.'

The rope really was little more than twine; she had to grip it so hard she thought it would flay the skin from her palms. She descended slowly and methodically, digging her toes into the soft wall of the well before easing her burning hands down towards her waist. She would drop one foot down, then the other, relying on her hands to hold her weight for the briefest possible time before kicking out footholds again.

In this way she lowered herself in a series of painful, breathless jerks until the circle of daylight above her had dwindled to a disc the size of the moon. Here she paused, breathing hard, feeling the sweat run freely down her sides and gathering in the waistband of the grimy leggings she had been wearing for what felt like years.

All of a sudden she felt like flinging off her clothes and just letting go of the rope, falling free into the cool clear water that must surely lie below. She felt tired, she felt filthy. The clothes she had on were those she had discovered in a Samsonite case ejected from a falling boat . . . oh, so long ago! What had the boat been called? She couldn't remember. It was so many voyages ago and each voyage felt like a lifetime.

'Are you all right down there?' Mister Ren's voice settled like a feather on her ear.

'I'm okay,' she called back. 'I'm goin' on.'

By the time her feet struck solid ground the sky was the tiniest pin-prick of light. She tried to straighten up but failed. Her legs were supporting her weight well enough (and her hands were screaming their gratitude) but her back was bent with cramps. Massaging it with hands rubbed raw and covered with blisters she finally convinced her body it could stand itself upright. Neck popping, every muscle shrieking in protest, she pulled herself erect and looked around.

Blackness, naturally. What else would there be at the bottom of an oubliette? But it was more than just blackness, she decided after taking a series of deep, shuddering breaths. It was emptiness.

Reaching her hand out she discovered the wall down which she had climbed was no longer there. The rope was hanging free, *dangling in empty air. And there was an overwhelming sense of space. Something about the touch of the air on her face, the dead quality of the small sounds she made as her hands rubbed her legs. There was nothing out there, not just no light but nothing at all. If she set off walking she would reach the end of her days before she reached the end of the miles.*

'I know you're down here somewhere, Jonah Lightfoot,' she said, unnerved by the lack of echo, the way her words seemed to die the instant they left her lips. 'Don't think you can hide from old Annie now. Don't you think that for a moment.'

She had a dilemma. She had to start searching, but in all this void what hope was there she would ever find the rope again?

Then take it with you, girl.

It was obvious. But how long was the rope? Wouldn't there come a point where it would just bring her up short? Then she'd have to let it go anyway. Or what if she pulled it right out of the Chinaman's hands? Then she'd be stuck down here for good.

Cursing her indecision she tied the thin rope round her waist, rubbed the sweat from her face with one torn sleeve and set off marching in a direction that felt like north but might have been any point of the compass.

'More likely it ain't on no compass at all. Nor on no map.'

Thinking of maps made her think of old charts on which unexplored lands were marked with images of monsters and mermaids.

Here be dragons, *she thought and shuddered.*

The trek through the darkness was unexpectedly calming. Annie felt her thoughts flee from her mind just as the sound of her footfalls fled from the ground. The emptiness was a sponge, soaking up her presence, leaching away her cares and fears and leaving only the essential Annie, a slender faery-form striding through a sympathetic land. She felt the slowing of her heart and the stilling of her soul. There was peace in the world after all, and she had found it.

Just when she thought she would walk forever (and she

*could, if she chose) she saw a small, squat shape rising out
of the darkness. It was a house with rough sod walls and
little windows. Smoke rose from an iron stack and the door
was ajar.*

*It was her house, the one she had shared with Rance when
they had lived together on the great plain of Kansas, and it
came as no surprise to find it here.*

*Firelight was flickering behind the windows: someone was
home.*

*Annie marched confidently up to the low front door. Why
not confident? This was her house, wasn't it? She had helped
lift these bricks of earth into place, she had laboured beside her
husband to raise this roof towards the sky. Why shouldn't she
feel at home?*

*After a moment's consideration she untied the twine from
about her waist and lashed it to the hitching post. Quietly
she pushed the door fully open. The interior was just as she
remembered: dimly lit, a single large room partitioned with
hanging drapes. Black stove in the corner, leaking smoke. Solid
table foursquare before the bigger of two windows. Her home.*

*Had the room always been this dark? It was as if the blackness
outside was trying to slither inside. She glanced in the mirror
beside the front door but there was no reflection. This didn't
surprise her any more than finding the house here in the
first place.*

*There was a man slumped across the table, snoring loudly.
Rance?*

*She smiled. Of course it wasn't Rance. He was back home in
Kansas – what would Rance be doing here?*

*She touched the man's hair, thick red hair, stroking it. When
he stirred she bent and kissed his cheek.*

'Hello, Jonah,' she said. 'I'm home.'

*Jonah woke up then, rubbed his face slowly and smiled back
at her. 'I did not expect you so soon, my darling,' he said. 'But
I am glad to see you.'*

'Likewise. I've come for you, Jonah. You ready to go?'

The words felt odd on her tongue. Now it was as if the words were dying before they even left her mouth, as if even the thoughts that drove them were starting to decay. She pinched her eyes shut for a moment then opened them again. The room looked brighter. That was better.

'Go?' Jonah was saying. He looked puzzled, dazed even, as if he were trying to remember her name. 'I do not want to go anywhere, Annie. I am perfectly happy here.'

Happy, *she thought.* Here. Yes, we could be, both of us. We could be happy here forever.

Again she pinched her eyes shut. Again opening them brought a little more light into the room. It was harder this time though. Soon even this trick would be beyond her. They had to get out of here.

'I am tired,' said Jonah before she could speak again. 'I think I will rest a little longer. Wake me when . . . when a little more time has passed by.'

His eyelids were drooping as he said this and his head was sagging towards the tabletop. Annie could feel the weight of his head pulling her down too, as if they were connected by invisible strings. It would be so appealing just to lie down next to the man she loved and . . . just let the time go by.

'No!' she screamed, thumping her fist down on the table. Jonah jerked upright, eyes still half-closed with an exaggerated sleepiness that was almost funny. 'Jonah, no! We gotta go and we gotta go right now!'

She grabbed his arm and tugged but he was dead weight, impossible to move. He grunted and tried to push her away, lowering his head yet again into his folded hands.

'Jonah!' she wailed, punching his shoulder in frustration. She cast her eyes wildly about the room, looking for . . . what? A weapon? Did she mean to drive him out on the point of a sword? But there were no swords in here, not even a pitch-fork. It was just her home, her little home, filled with all the homely things she had . . .

But it wasn't exactly her home, was it? There, on the dirt floor beside the stove, was a pyramid of black rocks stacked like miniature cannonballs. And there, hanging on the wall, was a Chinese rug marked with the Mah Jongg symbol for One Circle. There was a heavy metal doorstop she had never seen before in her life; it was shaped like a toad and streaked with blood.

All these things were strange yet she recognized them. But from where?

And here on the table, right beside Jonah, was an open book. Had it been there when she'd come in? She didn't think so.

She reached past him and picked it up. The corner was turned over as if Jonah had marked the place before dozing off, always assuming he'd been reading it in the first place of course.

It was a book of poems and short stories by a guy called Dylan Thomas. Had she heard that name before? Maybe, in a dream . . .

A passage had been circled with blue ink. She read it to herself again but it meant nothing to her. Then a thought came to her. She cleared her throat and read it aloud.

' "There," ' she read, ' "playing Indians in the evening, I was aware of me myself in the exact middle of a living story, and my body was my adventure and my name." '

There was a long, long pause during which his fingers scratched fitfully at the wood of the table. Then he spoke, his words muffled by his hands.

'Between,' he said. 'Stone and sky. Between, Annie. Between.'

Her heart was galloping like the pony now, much louder in her ears than his voice. 'What does it mean, Jonah?'

'Sky above,' he went on, lifting his head up now so that the words were clearer, bigger. 'Stone below. My name is Jonah Lightfoot.'

'I don't understand but I'm here, Jonah. I'm here with you.' She was crying. She felt like a damn fool for doing so but her galloping heart told her it was all right and so she went right ahead and did it.

Jonah was looking at his hands as if he'd never seen hands before. He gawped at Annie, then at the room.

'What on Earth am I doing here?' he said.

'Where did you think you were?'

'I do not . . . there was a storm and I . . . oh dear God, Annie! Archan! She is driving a furrow through the past. She is ploughing up everything, starting with me but she will not stop there, she will never stop! She will . . .'

'Whoa there, hold it! She won't do nothin' of the sort!' She explained about the oubliette, about Archan's reluctance to tinker with the past at all. 'She ain't got no winning hand, Jonah. She just took you out of the game for a while. Everything you saw, all the shit Archan did to your memories, none of it was real, Jonah. It was all a trick to make you believe she was taking you apart. You see that, don't you?'

'Yes,' he said, speaking as if he were testing out words for the first time, 'yes, Annie, I see how that might be so.'

He stood and pressed his hand first against his chest, then against hers. She sighed as the touch lit a thousand tiny flames in her belly. 'Hold me, Annie.'

She held him, entwined her arms behind him and hugged him so close she could hardly breathe, then hugged him closer still. 'You came for me,' he said and she nodded, soaking his hair with her tears. 'You came.'

He said more but they lost the words in kisses. Passion would have led them further but they both knew they had little time. Even here, where the river had muddied and grown stagnant, there was no time to waste.

'It was remarkably convincing.' He trembled in her arms. 'I saw Lily and the mill – there was a dreadful storm, a whirlwind in fact, which tore the mill apart. But it did more than that – it tore my life apart. And there were the dragons . . .'

'Was I there, Jonah?'

'Yes, Annie, you were there. You . . .' Jonah paused, the smile broadening on his face, '. . . you sent me to the moon.'

'I sent you where?'

Something slammed into the window. The impact was huge, the sound reverberating through the little house like artillery *fire. It struck again, then there was a long, keening scream as something sharp etched a jagged line in the glass.*

'The Snallygaster!' Annie cried.

Jonah was already running for the door, throwing his weight against it and slamming it shut. He held it there while she drew the bolts across, then they heaved the table up against it for good measure.

'Archan?' said Annie, fighting to compose herself.

'No doubt.' He was watching the scratched window, waiting for the dragon's next move. Darkness stared back, silent and empty, but there was no doubt she'd been there, no doubt at all.

A snuffling sound came from behind the stove. Something pressed against the wall from the outside, deforming the sods and nudging the stove further into the room. The burning logs jostled, sending a shower of sparks across the floor. Smoke belched up to the ceiling, letting loose a fine rain of soot.

The thing – and they had no doubt it was Archan – padded around to the opposite wall and growled softly. At the same instant Annie saw a white needle rise up outside the little window beside the drape and scratch out a circle on the glass. Not a claw but the dragon's tail, diamond-hard and limber as a rattlesnake, marking them out.

Back at the larger window Archan's head rose slowly into view. Eyeless, it gazed in.

How can she see us? *thought Annie in terrified wonder. But of course she knew: she could feel a thousand tiny worms exploring her guts and her mind, expeditionary charms even now reporting back to their cruel mistress. Annie backed away but they came with her, probing relentlessly, seeking out her weaknesses.*

'Jonah Lightfoot,' said Archan, feigning sadness with theatrical splendour. Her voice carried easily through the wall: another trick of charm. 'You have disappointed me so. I so wanted you to enjoy my hospitality, but now I fear I must cut short your recreation.'

'Is it true Archan?' Jonah demanded. 'Was it all a trick?'

'Tricks are for faeries. I showed you only what was meant to be.'

'You don't scare us, you bitch!' shouted Annie, grasping Jonah's hand for reassurance. 'Scared yourself though, didn't you? Stopped short at doing any real damage, just in case you couldn't take the heat.'

'Oh, Annie,' the dragon crooned, 'do not think I will hesitate to explore your past too. This is merely a – what would you faeries call it? – yes, an aperitif. I have yet to begin the main course.'

'She bluffing,' muttered Annie through the corner of her mouth. 'She's scared all right.'

Archan plunged her tail straight through the smaller window and wrapped it round the stove, uprooting it and hurling it across the room. Fire spilled from the gaping flue, setting light to the drapes. A gout of smoke joined the cloud still roiling against the rafters. Annie fell choking into Jonah's arms.

'Holy cow,' she managed to say.

'We have to get out of here, Annie,' said Jonah. He started to turn her towards the door. 'Can you run?'

'Like the wind.'

'Very well. Are you ready?' He'd pushed the table aside and was now pulling back the bolts one at a time. Behind them the drapes were an inferno – Annie couldn't believe how quickly they'd caught and how fiercely they were burning. 'One, two . . .'

Before he could say 'three' the table began to vibrate. Annie jerked her hand from where it had been resting on the wooden surface and stared at it in amazement.

A dark shape was forming in the exact centre of the tabletop, something vaguely like a face. Hardly daring to hope she reached out her fingers then drew them back sharply as the wood bulged like a bubble about to burst. 'Grandfather . . .' she began.

'. . . Tree!' concluded Jonah as the lesky's head erupted in a spray of splinters. But their joy at seeing their sylvan friend was short-lived when they saw his condition.

His elfin face was blackened and pitted with scars. Most of his beard was gone and the brambles spilling from his mouth were charred and broken. Smoke was rising from his mane of silvery hair and they could feel the heat baking off him. When he moved he winced. Yet his green eyes were alert and alive. There was spirit in the old spirit yet.

'What's happened to you?' blurted Annie.

'Coyote,' said Grandfather Tree. He coughed out a tongue of flame. 'Set the orchard. On fire. All the trees . . . on fire.'

All the trees! thought Annie, picturing the lesky darting from one tree to the next as if each were a stepping stone across treacherous water. But where could he go when the last stone was gone?

'Go back to the Bark,' she said. 'Get out of the orchard, Grandfather Tree. Take cover in the Bark – you can do that, can't you?'

But he was shaking his head, the massive head that was all he was in this strange little dead-end of a world. 'Can't risk it. Lesky jumps the gap, fire jumps the gap. Burning tree, burning lesky, burning Bark. No way back for you then, Annie. No way back for Jonah.'

'But there must be something you can do. You can't just let yourself burn.'

'Called here,' the lesky said, ignoring her. 'Your Mister Ren. Help you need, so he said. So here is lesky, come to help.' He coughed sparks at them. Behind him, in the far corner of the house, the roof was starting to cave in.

'But you're the one who needs help,' said Annie.

'No time.'

As if to prove the lesky right, Archan chose that moment to break through the wall. Sod bricks exploded into clumps of dirt and stone shards; furniture scattered and what was left of the roof gave an immense groan before beginning its final descent to the ground.

379

'Out!' yelled Jonah. Together they pushed through a door in a wall that was collapsing. Jonah shoved Annie out ahead of him then sprinted on her heels as she raced into the blackness. Passing the hitching post she had just enough presence of mind to grab the twine she had tied there. It came loose easily and she thanked the god of knots she had done such a bad job of tying it there in the first place.

Behind them Archan roared. Risking a glance back Annie saw she was boiling inside the remains of the house, a blur of whiplash curves and fire-red light on whirring metal fangs. The walls were almost gone but somehow the windows and doorway remained, brilliant fiery holes in a building that was no longer really there.

Grandfather Tree had remained with her in the house. He had grown tendrils and creepers to match Archan's scaly coils, wrapping up the dragon as he had wrapped her up once before, back at the Aqueduct, but this contest was hopelessly one-sided. Every time he attacked he was beaten back not only by Archan's scythe-like teeth but by the flames in the house, which Archan was directing like a conductor leading an orchestra.

But he was buying them valuable time.

They ran on, hand in hand, stopping only when Annie announced she could see a pin-prick of light high above their heads.

'Here,' she panted. 'God knows how we're meant to climb though.'

'Grandfather Tree,' said Jonah. 'We cannot leave him here.'

'What can we do, Jonah? He came to help us – if we go back for him he'll have come for nothing.'

'But how can we leave him?'

'He got away from Archan once before. He can do it again.' Annie was surprised – not to say a little disturbed – by her coolness. Could he get away? She wasn't so sure. And what about the fire, not the fire down here in the oubliette but the fire in the orchard? Mightn't that finish off the lesky once and for all?

380

'He came down here so we could get away,' she repeated. 'We gotta go, Jonah. We got work to do. If we can deal with Archan we stand a chance of saving Grandfather Tree but only if we go right now! Think about it, Jonah, feel it. It's right, I know it is!'

Is it right, Annie West? Is it?

'All right, Annie. But, as you yourself said, how do we climb?'

Mister Ren's voice, hardly audible, filtered down. 'Make a loop.'

They raised their eyebrows at each other, then Annie shrugged and did as she was told. Embracing each other, with the thin rope trapped between them and their feet notched into the loop she had tied, they allowed Mister Ren to pull them up out of the oubliette.

The ascent was swift. The pin-prick expanded first to become a moon and then a blinding sky. Climbing over the lip of the well was hard and there was an agonizing moment when Jonah nearly fell back into the blackness but at last they were both back on the blighted prairie, regarding solemnly the little man who had somehow pulled them up all that way.

'I wish I'd known you were that strong to start with,' said Annie. 'I'd've let you lower me down instead of scrapin' my hands raw.'

'It took great effort,' said Mister Ren. He was quiet, uncharacteristically subdued. 'Even I was not sure I could bring you out of there.'

'What about Grandfather Tree?' demanded Jonah. He advanced on the Chinaman, who stood his ground wearily. 'Can you bring him out? Or is he not important enough to your precious scheme?'

Mister Ren cocked his head to the side as if listening, then gave a curt nod. 'Your lesky friend has freed himself from the oubliette. And with no help from me, I must confess. As soon as she saw you were gone Archan abandoned the fight and let the lesky go. She's got bigger fish to fry.'

'Like me and Jonah.'

'Among others.'

Jonah was looking at the prairie, paying particular attention to the way the grass had been flattened around the mouth of the well.

'It looks as if something fell out of the sky,' he said. He looked up apprehensively.

'Yes,' agreed Mister Ren. 'Archan.'

'Is it true what Annie says? That Archan has touched no part of the past? No part of *my* past?'

'Not yet. She will, when she's gathered the courage. But . . . no, not yet.'

'Good. Then there is still time. Annie?'

'Yes, Jonah?'

'Grandfather Tree distracted Archan long enough for us to get away. If we go back to Stone do you think you can keep her busy long enough for me to go somewhere else?'

'Sure, I mean, I'll do my best. Where you goin', Jonah?

23

Moon

Jonah perceived space as a tunnel, with the full moon's disc the light at the end. He sped through the black while the cold stars watched, implacable with age. Space too was cold but he was ghost-Jonah and this was just another memory. Atoms sleeted through his body and he felt nothing, for he was hardly here at all.

This memory of the moon was one from aeons past, created long before his world had crystallized. Yet he was able to plot a course to it with hardly a thought. He had been to it before, or close by at least, and perhaps that helped. Twice now he had visited Kythe on the moon, although the second time had been only in Archan's dreams.

But the first visit had been real enough and so was this. While his body lingered between eye-blinks at the tip of Stone, Jonah flew through history and sought out the mother of the dragons.

As he got closer he saw the moon had changed. It looked older and greyer, its craters more rounded than before. Many years must have passed since his last visit. Led by instinct alone, he had not planned this trip but simply allowed his course to unfold before him. Now it seemed fate's great wheel had rolled on in his absence.

'Is Kythe still here, I wonder?' he said. 'Or have too many years gone by? Perhaps the moon is deserted at last. But if so, what am I to do here?'

He smiled as he confessed to himself that he did not know what he was doing here at all, Kythe or no Kythe.

'Onward,' he muttered as the moon filled his vision like a pale, midnight rose.

He came to rest near the spot where Archan's name-rock was destined to be placed. A short walk across the dust led him to the triangle of rocks surrounding that empty space.

The space was not yet filled.

Jonah pursed his lips. What had he expected? If he had found a rock bearing the name Archan would it have made any difference? Of what possible use could such a discovery be?

He felt in his pocket, where a pair of ghost-tiles clacked soundlessly together. His mind felt clogged.

Looking aound he appraised the close and curved horizon. On this airless little world there was no haze to soften the transition between land and sky and so the junction was miraculously sharp. Nor did the stars twinkle: instead they burned with their old, cold fire, changeless except by the longest clocks.

Jonah thought of the words Annie had read from the book, thought of how he had lain naked on the waterwheel staring up into the storm. Though he was only a ghost here he could feel the sunlight filling his eyes like gourds, could feel the tug of this small world's gravity against his bones, could feel its spin within his ears. Though his feet touched nothing but the memory of dust he knew his place on the skin of this tiny, spinning ball, knew his place at the junction between the dust and the sky, knew he had only to reach up his hand and he would bridge the gap between the two.

He reached up his hand and touched the sky, and the sky seemed to touch him back.

It was a moment out of time, soaked with meaning he could not express. It fled like a kiss and lingered like a kiss, old before it was done yet forever young. He dropped his arm and his head, gazing down at the space that was waiting for Archan's name.

'Welcome, Jonah,' Kythe whispered in his ear. 'It is time to say goodbye.'

Jonah stood and turned. Kythe was before him, translucent wings furled loosely on her back, orange scales burning in the sunlight. From her head rose a majestic crown of horns and spines and bony curlicues. She was smiling, showing off teeth of gold.

And behind her was arrayed a race.

There were silver dragons and gold, jade and black and dragons with hides like finest marble. Dragons with scales of ice and frost in their eyes, dragons like autumn leaves, dark and dry. Their wings moved like the sails of a mighty fleet, baffling the light and making wind where there was not even any air. Charm pooled in the dust beneath their claws, in the sky about their tails, making brilliant eddies of magic. Three hundred dragons, the first-born of their race, waiting patiently for their queen to lead them to the world that would be their home.

'We've been waiting for you, Jonah,' said Kythe. She feigned impatience but her smile spoke her real emotion.

'Waiting?'

'Of course. It's time for us to go. The time of the trolls will soon be over – it's time for us to fill up that world down there with dragon charm. Time to make it our world, for a time at least.'

Jonah looked in the direction she was pointing and saw the delicate blue-green shell of Earth. Clouds were knitted protectively across familiar continents, swaddling them with warmth and reflected light. A moan escaped his lips, for it was beautiful.

'Your world,' he said. 'Yes, it will be yours. For a time.'

'For a time. Do you remember the purpose of the rocks?'

'They hold the names of dragons.'

'Of all dragons, yes. These three are Sun, and Moon and Light, and they're with me now.' Kythe beckoned with one gossamer wing. 'Come forward, please, so that Jonah may understand at least a little better.'

Three dragons made their way forwards through the crowd. Jonah did not need to ask who was who.

The first dragon was the yellow of the dawn, a fiery creature with enormous wings that danced like flames. Beside it was a smaller creature, pale and blue, quite humble in comparison to its luminous neighbour. This one had tiny wings but its eyes were large and round, like pools of milk. It smiled shyly and Jonah had to resist the urge to reach out and pet it like a dog.

Third was a dragon made entirely of light, a glowing fire-fly so small it reminded Jonah instantly of Tangent, the Shade who had helped them up the final stretch of Stone's incline.

'Sun, Moon, Light,' he said. 'You suit your names, all of you.'

The three dragons dipped their heads and retreated into the throng.

'Which leaves only Archan,' Jonah went on.

'All the names have arrived except hers,' said Kythe. 'But we cannot wait any longer. Will you wait for it, Jonah?'

Jonah answered without thinking. It seemed the only way to act in this realm of memory. 'Of course,' he said. 'But there is something I do not understand. The fourth name in the litany is not Archan but Name. You told me this yourself, and Annie has heard it in her dreams. It perplexes me, not least because Name seems such a curious name! Yet we know this dragon as Archan! I cannot resolve the puzzle – can you?'

But Kythe was shaking her head. 'Alas, no. Jonah, all I know is this: my job is done here and now it's time for me to lead my dragons down to the world. The world is waiting for them, you see. Their time has come. I also know it's your job to put Archan's name in its place.' She offered a sympathetic shrug. 'Perhaps when the rock finally comes it will all become clear.'

'I hope so, Kythe. I honestly hope so.'

One of the dragons behind Kythe, a pearlescent creature with chameleon eyes and long, slender wings, nudged Kythe and whispered something Jonah could not hear. She whispered something back then addressed Jonah again.

'And now we really must go. Jonah . . . oh my dear friend, this really is goodbye!' Tears rolled across her cheeks. The moon's gentle gravity allowed them to grow huge before they fell and when they splashed into the dust they spilled charm and made rainbows in the grey.

Jonah stepped forward then hesitated, ever mindful of his potential for harm in this fragile memory-world. To his surprise Kythe shouldered her way up to him and embraced him vigorously, making a tent of her wings beneath the cover of which she smothered him with kisses. These dragon kisses, rich with dragon charm, touched Jonah's ghost-face and he too began to cry.

'Don't worry, Jonah,' she whispered beneath the veil of her wings. 'You can do no harm here now. You were always here. Without you the world would not have become the way it is. You are part of the turning world too, Jonah. We all are, in our own small ways. Have no fear, you are safe. And so is the past, so is the world. You, like all of us, were meant to be.'

Spilling ghost-tears into the dust, Jonah watched as she drew away from him. She touched a wingtip against her mouth and threw one final kiss at him. He raised a hand to catch it, just as he had when his mother had blown him kisses from beyond the nursery door. Then, with his arm still raised and his fist clenched on a dragon's kiss, he watched as Kythe rose majestically into the sky and turned to face the Earth.

'Come, dragons!' she boomed, and even at the last, even in her triumph, Jonah could hear the youngster he had met all that time ago in another world. She had been as amazed as he at their first meeting, an awestruck child in the presence of the faeries she had always thought legendary.

'We don't go far,' she had said, summarizing in those four words the malaise of all the dragons of Stone. 'Especially me.'

'Oh Kythe,' sighed Jonah as she led the dragons into the sky, 'you went furthest of all. Bless you, my dear dragon friend. May the world long know your charm.'

The flock, huge at first, soon dwindled. For long minutes the sunlight continued to spark off metallic wings as they beat their way steadily across the gap between the worlds, then even the dragons' light was gone and the sky was dark once more, and all the more empty for it.

Wiping his eyes, Jonah sat beside the rocks and waited.

Opening his hand he saw the skin of his palm was dusted with silvery powder, finer than frost. A dragon's kiss.

24

Archan Rising – 3

The rage had returned. Some small part of her screamed caution, screamed that she must remain calm.

'White ice!' that part wailed. 'White ice and clear sight. Anger is blind. You did not discard your eyes only to make yourself blind. Anger is blind – you are not!'

But the voice was too small and the anger too large. Time, the very enemy she had swallowed and made hers to command, was now trying to gnaw its way through from the inside out. A million years imprisoned in the polar ice. Endless time spent trapped inside ludicrous faery bodies. Immeasurable ages fleeing back through Stone's labyrinthine past. Time was the enemy of all things, even of immortal dragons.

But I can control time! she told herself. *I can change the flow of the river just like the faery! I can!*

But she dared not! Instead she resorted to guiles and glamours, side-tracked the faery into the oubliette in the hope he would believe himself changed. Yet he had escaped even that subtle trap and was free once more.

She looked inside her own mind, looked deep into the mass of Stone memories she had already swallowed, but she found no answers there. She was full of memories, she had gorged herself on them. The memories stretched all the way back into the infinite past but instead of enlightening her they weighed her down.

Is this how the basilisks felt? Is this why they elected to kill themselves? Is this the price of immortality, this . . . this unforgetting?

As rage threatened to spill into panic she clamped down hard claws on her errant thoughts.

Enough, Archan. Rise above your anger. You are immortal and these pathetic creatures are your prey. Treat them as such and all will be well. All will be well.

She did rise then, lifting herself up from the oubliette's lightless pit, leaving behind the shell of the house she had built for Jonah there and which was now nothing but black waste in a black land. Above her floated the world of Stone where her body was waiting for her, frozen between the blinking of the eyes she did not possess.

When she returned to that body she would abandon all her plans to punish the faeries. Now it was enough simply to kill them. This had been her mistake all along, she decided. Young dragons were taught never to play with their prey and, although she had shunned most of the rules of polite dragon society, this was one she had been forced to reappraise. Jonah Lightfoot and Annie West, those most tiresome of all the faeries she had had the grave misfortune to encounter, were even now trapped inside her coils without hope of escape. She needed only to re-enter her body and crush their bones to dust while their flesh spouted blood.

Red faery blood splashed across white dragon scales. It was a pleasing picture.

The rage was subsiding a little now. The promise of murder had always had a cleansing effect and even here, caught between two worlds equally strange, the old magic was working.

Sister Areken would be angry, she thought. *But Archan will be cold, as eternity is cold.*

The image of her twin rose before her, unwelcome in its clarity. Something about it troubled her, some affliction Areken had acquired shortly before she herself had retreated into the memory rod to construct the oubliette. Something shared with . . . faery!

Turning to stone, she thought. *My sister is turning to stone! That wolf-beast too. And the faeries, not all of them though.*

The journey back from the memory rod was nearly complete – she could sense her body waiting just a heartbeat away. Yet she paused, tantalized by the possibility of secret knowledge.

Why are they turning to stone?

The answer was spinning just out of reach but her claws would not close about it. Something to do with the rods, something that might change her perception of her powers over the rods . . .

What does Jonah know about the rods that I do not?

Her claws clutched but retrieved nothing. The rage erupted again, fuelled by her growing frustration.

'What do I care?' she ranted. 'I will kill them all and even when they are long-dead I may still resurrect them into the hells they deserve. Given time I can claim all the answers as my own. And I have all the time there is!'

Driven by this new fury, Archan rose up into her waiting body, felt her flesh grow erect as her spirit drove its way inside. The flesh was hot and vital, a suitable vessel for her wrath.

The faeries were pliant inside her coils. She started to crush the life from them.

25

Name

Jonah emerged from the memory of the moon with his hands plunged deep in his pockets. It was a rebirth, a return to a familiar world – for Stone seemed more familiar to him now than any other place. It felt like home.

Two things struck him at once, neither of them encouraging.

First, the air surrounding the giant statue's fist was blanketed in smoke. The smoke rose in waves while at the same time throwing down dead soot and dying embers. He could hardly breathe.

The second thing was more urgent still – he was being crushed to death. Moreover, with his hands jammed into his pockets his arms were effectively pinned to his sides. He had no hope of freeing himself at all.

Not only am I about to die, he thought calmly, *but I look foolish into the bargain.*

The smoke cleared a little and there was Annie, struggling to escape from Archan's deadly coils. But though she pressed with all her strength against the tight white scales she moved not an inch. She screamed, an exhalation of pain and frustration.

Something moved behind them, something large and grey, a phantom in the smoke. It was Areken, bearing down upon Archan like an express train.

392

The impact was a colossal, soundless bang. Sound-less because Jonah blacked out for precious seconds the instant the two dragons collided. When he came to he was afloat in the smoke; for a moment he thought he was flying. Then the statue's fist punched him in the back and he found himself lying on the ground in the busy shadows of the grappling serpents.

A whip-thin tail slashed downwards, hacking a groove less than a yard from where his feet were splayed. Ignoring the pain in his legs and spine he rolled sideways and kept rolling, only stopping when the grunts and crashes of the battle had diminished a little. Eyes stinging in the sharp, smoke-filled air, he lifted himself to his hands and knees and looked up.

The dragons were invisible behind livid plaits of charm. These blazing ropes lashed and merged and bled raw energy into the heart of the battle, obedient conscripts to the generals within. What the dragons were actually doing to each other behind the lightning Jonah could not guess, but if these exterior fireworks were anything to go by it was death-dealing on an unimaginable scale.

Except there is no death to deal, he thought, pressing his hands into the small of his back, where pain had rooted itself so deep he was not sure it would ever be gone. *What can they achieve when the best they can hope for is stalemate?*

But he knew the answer of course, for only one of these dragons was truly immortal. Archan had only to wait for her sister to turn fully to stone and then . . .

But does Archan know that?

'Jonah!' It was Annie, limping towards him through the murk. She seemed cast from the smoke itself, a faceless shadow with the gait of a woman. A fireball whistled over her head and she ducked. The next few yards she crawled with ungainly haste then, jumping to her feet, she began to run.

A tangle of claws slammed into the ground between

her and Jonah. The shock threw her backwards into a
sudden flare of orange light. A cloud of embers boiled
from nowhere, curling first up and then over with a
snatching motion. Annie ducked again but not before
the base of the cloud had engulfed the top of her head.
She shrieked, the cry like nothing Jonah had heard from
a human mouth before, and when the embers fell back
he saw her hair was on fire.

'Dear God, Annie!' His shriek was no less anguished
than hers. He ran as she stumbled towards him but again
the dragons came between them. Archan's head and neck
crashed to the ground like a felled tree. Areken's fell too
and Jonah saw her entire head had turned to stone. Fire
licked between grey teeth but even that was solidifying,
living flames slowing like cooling magma and losing their
colour, all turning to perpetual grey.

Jonah vaulted Archan's prone neck like a hurdler,
aiming his leap at the most slender part, which was no
thicker than the trunk of a moderate oak. As he jumped
the dragon raised her head. His trailing foot snagged on
her scales and he tumbled head over heels, sprawling on
the hard black stuff from which the statue was made.

Archan continued to rise, casting her long shadow over
him. He ignored her. Now there was pain in his neck to
match that in his back and legs, but he looked up all the
same, expecting to see Annie lying dead before him.

Instead he saw the shadow of a tall, bald man, his
indistinct form thrown into partial relief by flashes of
orange fire. Annie was on her knees before him. He
was holding her head in his hands, almost caressing it.
With each stroke of his large hands the flames from her
hair subsided. There was a final moment when, with the
dreadful fire put out altogether, he simply held her like
a supplicant, hands enclosing her skull completely, face
lowered as if to kiss her poor burned head, lips just inches
from her scalp.

Jonah lay there, watching. His spine felt like a cord of bramble being drawn through his flesh. He could hear Annie biting back the sobs, could smell the awful stench of the smoke and knew that it came not only from the trees below.

Grandfather Tree! he thought in horror.

Then Coyote withdrew his hands. As he did so a pyre erupted behind him and a little to the side, the first actual flames they had seen rise from the orchard burning below. The fire beat away a little of the smoke, which fragmented into dark shapes like birds on the wing, a grim and ghostly flock.

It must be a blaze indeed, thought Jonah, *to reach so high!*

In this new light he saw clearly the stripped and blistered skin of Coyote's hands. His heart went out to the man, who had shared in Annie's pain in order to save her life.

As for Annie herself – her hair was almost gone, but not entirely, and he found room to hope that she was not badly burned. Her breathing was steady, he saw, and her posture composed. He began struggling to his feet, only to collapse again as a fresh bolt of pain seared the space between his shoulder blades. Something cracked lower down in the small of his back and he arched and wriggled like a landed fish, bleating out his discomfort.

In an effort to relieve the pain he rolled on to his side. It did help, more than he had hoped, but now something was digging into his leg, something in his pocket, something hard and angular . . .

The tiles!

Wincing, biting his lip to stop from crying out, he clawed his hand down into his pocket and pulled out the last two tiles of Annie's Mah Jongg set. The Red Dragon and the White.

But which tile is for which? He felt giddy. The cold of

shock was leaching through his body. The black of the smoke was dulled further by the black at the periphery of his vision. The roar of the flames was beginning to sound watery and he knew he was about to pass out.

Still clutching the tiles he rolled deliberately on to his back, expecting the agony but surprised by it all the same. Faintness banished, at least for now, he turned his attention back to the dragons.

Areken, presumably in her last throes, had plunged her stone teeth into her sister's throat. Scarlet blood gushed forth, painting them both.

Jonah began to crawl. Archan was very close to him, turned so that her back was low to the ground. There was a place between her wings correlating almost exactly to the place where his back was protesting most. It was a place he had used before, an empty space into which he had once placed a single, white scale. That scale, retrieved by Jonah from an ancient time, was the talisman by which he had first sent Archan plunging back into Stone's abyss. Now, he saw, the scale was still there.

A place for everything, he thought, *and everything in its place.*

He had been here before, struggling to fit a jigsaw piece into a dragon's hide. That first time had been difficult enough; this task seemed impossible.

Two dragons. Two tiles. One red, one white. But they are really both the same.

'Those symbols are markers,' Annie had said. 'They're . . . I don't know, crossroads or places where weird power's focused . . . And it's up to us to get them working. You gotta set the primer, Jonah. Then we stand back and watch it all blow.'

Watch it blow, he thought dreamily, knowing he was about to faint again. There was a certain peace in the knowledge. Even when the bleeding Archan grinned and bared her steel teeth at him there was no place in his heart for fear. No place at all.

Footsteps and wingbeats. The sounds were unreal, infiltrating not through his ears but through the length of his body where it met with the ground. *Footsteps and wingbeats . . .*

Something had drawn near to him. The dragon, of course.

He looked up into a weather-beaten face. Though blackened by fire it was familiar enough – Thomas Coyote, the man who had saved Annie's life.

'I'll take it, Jonah,' he said, holding out one large, burned hand. The flesh of his palm was red. It looked to Jonah like the surface of a star. 'I'll take it. Just tell me where.'

Trembling, Jonah dropped one of the tiles into Coyote's hand. It landed with the symbol facing down, exposing the painting Annie had made on the blank side: a chrome-eyed dragon made of ice.

'On her back,' he whispered. 'You will know the place when you see it.'

'Is it the right one?' said Coyote.

'It doesn't matter. They're both the same.'

Coyote rose.

Wingbeats.

And Gerent was there, wings striped with red scales like fire and black scales like smoke, wings forming a protective cowl over Jonah's crumpled body. His face, even more begrimed than Coyote's, was both angry and earnest. With one hand he clutched at Jonah's shoulder, in the other he held a naked sword. His lips parted as if he were about to speak, but in the end he simply looked Jonah up and down.

Thus reassured that his friend was still alive, Gerent stood and whirled in a single fluid movement that sent his wings billowing about him like pennants. He spotted

Coyote retreating with the tile held delicately between thumb and forefinger and his brow compressed. Raising his sword, he advanced towards him.

'Gerent, no,' croaked Jonah.

If Gerent heard him he gave no sign. He continued to march resolutely towards Coyote, who was now backing away with increased speed, burned hands imploring. Behind the retreating man, Archan was rising, shaking off her motionless sister like an unwanted blanket. The terrible wounds in her neck were healing already, strings of incandescent charm knitting together the tattered flesh. The blood remained, however, a deep red stain on the white scales.

'Please, Gerent!' Jonah tried to shout but the words failed on his lips. He spat out soot and coughed. Behind the men Archan continued to rise.

Something moved across Thomas Coyote's face. It might have been a change of light or simply a change of expression; whichever it was, when it had passed he looked suddenly at peace. He stopped retreating, lowered his hands and closed his eyes.

Gerent faltered briefly, then stepped cautiously forwards, fearing some trick. Then he stopped too. His head tilted up as he saw Archan for the first time, his eyes at last admitting what had been before him all the time – a massive serpent neck towering like a giant cobra over both him and his prey.

Jonah held his breath, unable to cover his eyes.

Gerent seemed to reach a decision. He drew back his sword and prepared to cut Thomas Coyote out of his path.

A small, pale shape flew through the air and struck Gerent's sword. The object rebounded and thudded to the ground, revealing itself as a miniature skull, human in shape but unrealistically small. Both Gerent and Coyote gaped at this little missile.

Malya strode into Jonah's field of vision. From his low-level vantage, prostrate as he was with his head hardly raised at all from the ground, she looked as tall as the statue they had scaled. Indeed she was statuesque in every way, for now only her face was fully human – the rest of her had fallen prey to the inevitable process of petrifaction. She moved like the crudest of automata, legs jerking in irregular, staccato fashion. Yet there was a dreadful energy about her, an indomitable spirit that would not be quelled.

Gerent was transfixed. His jaw lolled. Above him Archan's jaw opened too, letting loose a spray of glowing spittle that hissed like acid where it struck the ground.

'Malya,' he said, his voice cracking.

'Put down your sword, Gerent.' Malya's voice, by way of contrast, was as unavoidable as her stride; it too simply kept on coming. 'Put down your sword and help Jonah.'

'But . . .' Gerent swung half-heartedly at Coyote, who had opened his eyes now and was turning his attention away from the Neolithics. He too had seen the dragon and his eyes had widened with terror.

Young eyes, Jonah saw. *The eyes of a child in the face of a man.*

'Put it down!' Malya commanded. She was face to face with him now. Her left cheek and the orbit of the eye it underpinned had solidified. Soon she would not be able to speak at all.

Gerent dropped the sword and reached his hand towards her face.

'No time!' she snapped. Then she looked over her shoulder, the movement accompanied by an unspeakable grating sound. 'Jonah, throw it to him!'

Jonah rolled over again, fighting both the fresh wave of pain and the swooning sensation. He lofted the second tile towards Gerent. It landed short but skidded on the smooth ground, fetching up neatly against the Neolithic's feet.

'Where, Jonah?' demanded Malya, her demeanour the very definition of urgency.

'Stone . . .' called Jonah, cursing his weakness. 'Dragon . . .' He could not take his eyes from Archan. The blood-stained dragon had filled her mouth with cold blue fire and was extending her neck over the arena in which they were crowded. It seemed she intended simply to drop a ball of flame on to their heads and consume them all in one final conflagration.

'Help Thomas!' he shouted, summoning all his strength. 'Help him and watch him. Do what he does, Gerent.'

Malya understood. With a single swift command she directed Gerent towards Areken's petrified remains. Then, with a turn of speed unanticipated even by Archan, she impelled her ravaged body forwards and plunged her sword into Archan's exposed belly.

Red blood and blue fire exploded across her but, being made of stone, Malya did not burn. Archan screeched, an appalling banshee sound, and dropped her head towards her attacker. Seizing his chance – and this would surely be his only chance – Thomas Coyote leaped on to the narrow part of her lowered neck, balanced himself on his feet and sprinted without heed for safety up the slope of her spine. Passing into the cleft between her thrashing wings he dropped to his knees and raised the tile above his head like a dagger.

Archan paused. Her whole body froze and despite the orange glare of the orchard fire, despite the red of the blood in which she was soaked, she seemed made entirely of ice. The blood continued to gush from her, forming a lake before which Malya, her movements slowing now, stood like Colossus at the harbour gate.

Then Thomas Coyote slammed the tile into its rightful place.

Jonah gasped. Gerent, who had been watching Coyote's progress closely, opened his wings and flew rapidly to the equivalent spot on the back of the beaten Areken. There he landed, bringing out the tile and pressing it gently into position. This time Jonah saw the briefest flash of light before the tile sank out of view, sucked deep into the dragon's stony flesh by whatever force demanded its presence there.

Will there be fireworks, I wonder?

He let his body fall on to its injured back. The pain there had lessened now; he had no idea if this was a good thing or bad. Archan still dominated the scene, still frozen into place. Ice crystals had clustered beneath her throat, inside her open jaws, expanding in defiance of the heat still pounding up from the burning trees far below.

Fire and ice, he thought. Then he heard a rhythm in the ground. *Footsteps.*

Someone was limping towards him. He craned his neck. No pain at all now.

It was Annie, her mouth a tight line, her eyes creased with both her own pain and concern for his. Her head . . . her hair was reduced to a mess of charred clumps and knots but the scalp beneath did not look badly burned. Miraculously her face, though blackened by soot, was unharmed. She would recover and be well, he could see that, though his heart broke at the thought of the pain she must feel now.

'Have we done it?' he asked, horrified at how weak his voice sounded. Or perhaps his voice was all right and it was his ears that were weak.

'Not quite, Jonah,' she replied. She smiled – her teeth were dazzling against her soot-dusted skin. 'But it's a start.'

She was receding. No – it was he who was being pulled away. A red glaze had washed across his vision; Annie's voice liquefied, her words stretching into indeterminate blobs of sound. Surely this was not death? The red glaze thickened and surrounded him and he was falling into a familiar place.

No, not here! Not now, when there is so little time! I cannot fall into memory now, not when so much hangs in the balance. Annie! Help me, catch me! I'm falling! I'm falling . . .

. . . *into the endless chasm.*

Never before had he been so reluctant to enter the memory rods; never before had they seemed so superfluous. What was this interlude but an unwelcome intrusion into the proper flow of events?

What has summoned me, when I am so unwilling?

The redness abided. He had plunged into a well of blood.

The blood separated into thick ropes, a glutinous web. The web caught him and held him. Phantom spiders inched towards him from places of concealment. As they materialized out of the scarlet fog he saw they were not spiders at all. Sturdy bodies, muscular arms and long prehensile tails. No legs. Faces that were part lizard, part bulldog. The six basilisks, or their ghosts at least.

. . . Send me back! *said Jonah, expelling his demand not through the air – of which there was none down here – but through the fluid fabric of the web.*

. . . Not until you have seen what you need to see, *said the ghost that had once been the basilisk called Ocher.*

. . . Not until you have learned what you need to learn, *echoed the one approximating Geiss.*

. . . No! *replied Jonah* . . . I shall not be manipulated again. I am not here for your sport. Return me at once, I demand it!

. . . Regretfully, Ocher would refuse, *said the first basilisk* . . . Stay and learn.

Jonah was still trying to compose a suitable reply when the web turned him to face a pool of shadow. Shapes swam through the murk; swiftly they resolved themselves into recognizable forms: trees dancing in the wind.

. . . What is . . . began Jonah. Then he saw something that stilled his voice. A small figure was seated at the foot of the largest tree, a little Chinese man with a hat like an upturned bowl.

Jonah fell forwards, slipping through the seam between this memory and the next until he was . . .

. . . floating above Mister Ren in the light of a summer storm. The trees crashed near his head but he was untouchable here, a ghost of a man lingering inside the ghost of a memory.

The little man was moulding something in his hands. Bobbing lower Jonah saw his hands clench tight and then open. Something resembling a swarm of bees flew out, dispersing rapidly into the wind-tossed air. Their buzzing was sweet and clear, so like a memory of his own.

. . . Industry, whispered Ocher in his ear.

Jonah glanced to the side but there was nothing.

. . . Look on, said the basilisk.

Mister Ren was moving his hands again. It looked as if he were snatching up fragments of air and sculpting them into tangible forms. Again the clench came, followed by the sudden release.

This time what emerged was a single white petal, large and round like the petal of a rose. The wind seized it and whisked it into the sky. Mister Ren watched it vanish with a satisfied smile.

. . . Intrigue, said Ocher.

The third creation was a hard jewel. It caught the sunlight like black glass, simultaneously dark and brilliant. This item did not fly; instead it plummeted to the ground, sinking and continuing to sink into the soft, moss-covered soil. The earth shivered, just once, as if it had been touched by a lover, then it was still.

. . . Insecurity.

The little man paused, frowning as if he had heard a sound on the breeze. Jonah had been the eavesdropper often enough to know that his presence here was suspected. He dimmed *himself*, allowed the currents of the air to take him first away from the spot and then back, defining himself not as an intruder but an elemental force. Mister Ren sniffed the air like a dog then, apparently satisfied that he was indeed alone, returned to his labours.

This time – and it was to be the final time – he worked long and hard, pressing and moulding the gathered air over and over. At times he peeked into the secret space between his fingers then, shaking his head, started over again, drawing new filaments from the sky and weaving them afresh.

Time went on. The sun in the sky had reached and surpassed the point of noon when Mister Ren finally opened his hands.

Red light blazed forth, a miniature star. He released it, lifting his hands to shield his face. Jonah allowed the light to pour through him, allowed himself to taste it.

. . . I know what this is, *he said* . . . This is Immortality. Mister Ren told us he created it and it is true – this is that moment. This is the beginning of many things.

. . . Immortality, *agreed Ocher* . . . Look on.

Mister Ren was chasing after the dancing red starlet like a child chasing a butterfly. It was a ludicrous sight: this pastoral scene, this man dressed for the Tibetan wilderness, this firefly light. Finally, cursing the pantomime, Mister Ren stopped to catch his breath. The red star of Immortality stopped too, dipping and rising just out of reach, taunting its maker.

He made a grab for it and it darted away. Mister Ren fell head-first into the moss and rose in a rage.

Snatching at the air as if he were plucking fruit from some huge and invisible vine, he wrestled his hands against each other until a new and somehow gloomy light began to spill from his fists. After a moment's kneading he threw his arms wide and there on the ground before him lay the basilisks, six half-conceived creatures glistening with the afterglow of creation. Charm dripped from their pale green eyes and if their legs had been forgotten in haste then their arms and tails were more than adequate for the job of propulsion.

They gazed like puppies at their master then, instantly understanding their purpose, set off after the mischievous star like those same puppies grown to be hounds. They bayed, expelling clouds of lethal vapour from their blunt jaws, for their maker had so rushed their creation that even their breath was deformed.

But though their bodies and inner workings were ill-conceived, they were perfectly judged to do the task for which they had been made. Too perfectly, as Mister Ren was shortly to discover. As one they fell upon the star, tearing its light into equal pieces and swallowing them equally, as all fair-minded siblings might be expected to do. Their eyes turned instantly to metal; their hasty bodies glowed for a moment, mapping veins and flapping organs through their pallid skin, then they turned and began to chase their creator.

Howling his indignation, Mister Ren fled, abandoning all he had made on this fine summer's day, abandoning both the star of Immortality and the six beasts that had become its vessels. The basilisks continued to chase him for a time then, growing bored with the pursuit, settled down to contemplate what they were, and what they might do with the eternity they had so readily been gifted.

Jonah had seen enough. Defying the pull of this nested memory he hauled himself forcibly back through onion-layers of time and . . .

. . . back into the presence of the six basilisk ghosts.

. . . This corresponds in part with what Mister Ren has claimed for himself, he said slowly. The basilisks regarded him with baleful silver eyes . . . However, the mood of it is very different to what I had imagined. These moments of creation were . . . well, they seemed to me absurd. Forgive me but, you were absurd!

405

. . . Absurd the basilisks were, *agreed Ocher softly* . . . Now they are no more, that fact cannot be disputed.

. . . Can you tell me . . . do you even know . . . who, or what is Mister Ren?

. . . He was not as you see him in this memory. His true form was not possible to comprehend; even basilisk eyes could see only his shade. What the basilisks knew is this: there are two kinds of beasts in all the worlds: those that are *simple* and those that are *complex*. The basilisks would have called them Fools and Kings.

Most beasts – the basilisks, the faeries, the dragons, you yourself, Jonah Lightfoot and all who have travelled with you – are Kings. They are Kings because they have been made that way. Made by the Fools.

. . . Mister Ren was a Fool. He was simple not only in form but also in mind. He was capricious – not malevolent, but neither was he kind. Simple creatures like to play simple games and they like especially to make things. Other than the basilisks, Mister Ren himself made only four things in his life but they were big things. These you have seen. *Industry* was the first, which is in the heart of all the suns and which drives the flow of heat through all the worlds. *Intrigue* was the second, which is most potent when the light of the moon drips it into an open heart. Next came *Insecurity*, which is the force behind all names, for without names we are nothing. The last, of course, was *Immortality*, which is also the light for which all thinking beasts – by which Ocher would mean Kings – strive.

. . . Sun, moon, name, light. These four things.

. . . Of all the four, the last was the one Mister Ren most wanted to keep. Fate decreed it was the one he was least qualified to possess. So he was bound to make the basilisks, whose function was to keep him from owning what he must never be allowed to own. The basilisks succeeded for a long, long time. But their reign is at an end and soon the star of Immortality will be free once again.

. . . And, once again, Mister Ren must be prevented from taking possession of it.

Jonah had lost all sense of where he was, had grown numb to the liquid touch of the web at his back. He weighed the basilisk's words, wanting to trust neither it nor Mister Ren, wanting instead to find his own middle ground of untainted truth.

. . . You speak of Mister Ren in the past tense. You speak of him as if he were dead.

The basilisk glared at him with metal eyes.

. . . He died many aeons ago.

. . . Then how?

The basilisk, which was only a phantom, said nothing and at last Jonah understood.

. . . Mister Ren is a ghost too, *he said slowly* . . . He died and his memory is retained in Stone, just as all memories are retained. He lives here after a fashion, just like you.

. . . A ghost he is. A restless one. He never forgave the basilisks for stealing away his prize. Though he is long dead, his ghost has grown surprisingly powerful. Obsession cannot be denied. Think of Archan, lingering at the pole of your world, growing angry. Mister Ren is little different. Now he has gained sufficient power to challenge she who holds his prize.

. . . Archan herself, *said Jonah.*

. . . Yes, Archan. If Mister Ren can wrest the star of Immortality back from Archan he will be reborn. Then he will live forever.

Jonah thought about this for a moment.

. . . Why must he be prevented from taking what, it might be argued, is rightfully his?

. . . He is a Fool, *said the basilisk as if that were explanation enough* . . . If he lives forever he will grow bored and there is nothing so dangerous as a bored simpleton! He will open all the worlds to the naked teeth of the cosmos!

. . . But what does this mean? *demanded Jonah, frustrated*

. . . I hear these words as I have heard them before and still they mean nothing to me!

. . . Nor did they to the basilisks. *The ghost-voice of the beast that had once been Ocher grew soft* . . . But consider this, faery. The basilisks lived through eternity. Stone, which you have come to know so well, is merely a mirror containing the reflection of all the memories they amassed. It is a duplicate of what they were, what they knew. They saw everything, they knew everything, so that there was nothing in all creation that could surprise them, nothing they could fear, nothing they sought to avoid, except perhaps the abiding doom of their eternal state.

. . . Yet they feared this: that their maker would take back what he had not yet owned and expose the worlds of the Kings to what lies beyond. Whatever lies there, they feared. That fear was real, faery, and it is a fear you must share, if there is to be any hope of triumph.

Abruptly the conversation ended. Without warning the basilisks retreated, fleeing into the depths of the web in grim silence. The individual strands snapped like rubber, flinging Jonah back up through layers of time and . . .

. . . back into the arms of Annie.

'Thought you'd gone for good,' she said, kissing him smartly on the lips. Her eyes were full of love and pain and his heart broke again for her poor, burned skin. 'What'd they say?'

'You saw them?'

'Kind of. You sank, Jonah, like you were droppin' through ice. Saw you swimmin' down there, saw *them* too, all six kind of . . . closin' in on you. I was nearly comin' in after you when you came back to me. You came back to me, Jonah.'

He summarized what he had been told, almost gabbling in his haste. The smoke was still boiling around them and there was so much unresolved. Archan lived still, though she was lying prone and bleeding heavily. And where was Malya? Was she even still alive?

'So,' Annie said, pulling his gaze back to hers, 'our dear Mister Ren ain't quite law-abidin' folk.'

'Who do we believe, Annie? Mister Ren told us he was also Esh, but if that is so then were we fools even to trust Esh? Yet she was so . . . so *good*. Who is left for us to trust now, when everything we see is coloured by the glass through which it is viewed?'

'Us, Jonah. We gotta trust us, that's all there is to it.'

Jonah nodded, aware that his neck and back were not quite as painful as they had been. 'The basilisks fear Mister Ren will return and become immortal. That means it *must* be possible for Archan to lose her immortality. I wonder how . . .'

But he got no further. The statue was trembling beneath them. Yet there was more than that. Something in the depth and frequency of the vibration told Jonah it was not just the statue but all of Stone itself that was on the move. His teeth jangled in his mouth; even the thoughts in his head seemed about to come loose.

'Shit, Jonah! What the hell's goin' on?'

He opened his mind's eye, risking a quick glance down through the hidden system of memory rods. This was after all the very axis about which Stone had been spun; if anything was happening to Stone it would surely show up in the rods.

What he saw made sense of all he had done since they had left Ruane and the upturned ocean behind.

What he saw was every one of the little ivory Mah Jongg tiles he had placed glowing like the light at the beginning of time.

He saw them all: the monolith and the island in the metal sea and the giant orchid-bloom. The Triad, three matched rectangles set into a single rod. Every one of those places was ablaze with the light of charm. They pulsed like hearts.

The pulsing grew more rapid. Little jets of fire began to spurt from each tile; before long the individual jets extended far enough to touch each other, like lovers holding hands across the sea. The jets coalesced into beams, a web of light connecting each tile to every other tile. The pulsing doubled its stroke, pumping waves of charm up, ever up towards the tip of Stone. Stone's interior brightened until Jonah could no longer look at it. He jerked backwards, fending off the light with ineffectual wafts of his hands. Annie caught him before he stumbled.

'What's happening?' she said.

'There is a lot of charm down there,' he replied, 'and most of it appears to be coming our way.'

Then the statue spoke.

'Jonah,' boomed the familiar voice of Esh, their long-dead friend. 'Annie. Hold tight now.'

The whole statue was moving jerkily, like an unoiled machine. The hand holding the cup hove into view through the smoke, which was clearing rapidly.

'Inside,' said Esh.

'Inside?' Jonah threw a wild glance at Annie. His unresponsive legs might as well have turned to stone.

The smoke continued to boil away. Now they could see the statue's face, that unholy alliance of woman and tortoise they had both come to love. The face of Esh.

'Trust me,' said Esh. 'Get inside the cup and hold tight.'

It seemed they had little choice. The cup was bearing down on them at such speed they stood little chance of getting out of its way. At the last moment it slowed and tipped up a little. Jonah jumped inside then helped Annie up and over the lip. Immediately behind them came Thomas Coyote.

'Don't leave me behind,' he called as he threw up his hand to Jonah.

The cup lurched, throwing them in a tangle of limbs about its curved interior. The world was a bright circle of light across which images swept seemingly at random: the sun, blazing still above them; Archan, the white dragon, stemming the wound in her breast with a huge discharge of charm and bearing down on Malya, who was locked in a lake of blood like a statue; wings, beating hard – Gerent swooping in behind Malya and lifting her high. Then came another blur of sunlight and a moving blackness – the side of Esh. A brief sensation of floating then a cruel return of weight as the cup was dropped the last few feet to the ground. It rolled a quarter turn, a chapel-sized drum tossing its weary occupants like marbles, and came to rest.

Jonah peeked outside. The cup brought them to the edge of what had once been a beautiful orchard; now the trees were mostly gone, burned completely away but for a small thicket some distance away. There the fire still raged; everywhere else it had burned itself out.

When they had climbed to this place he had thought of it as the brim of a witch's hat. Now it was simply a circular table-top perched at the very top of Stone.

No, he thought, *not a table-top – a plate balanced precariously on a juggler's finger.*

The gigantic statue of Esh was kneeling like Gulliver in the charcoal. The hand which had held the cup was clearing a shallow pit among the embers. It was very close to the Verge. The other arm came down beside it, muscles bunched and straining beyond measure, and gently spilled the two dragons into the depression. Throughout this procedure the clenched fist never let go of the thread of memory; the sun above was a balloon this child was either unwilling or unable to let go.

Gerent, Malya stiff in his arms, landed gently in the

411

slender shadow of the cup. He laid her down in the ashes and bent his head over her face.

The instant the two dragons – prone, stone Areken and her white sister, who was now gathering her wings behind her in preparation for flight – made contact with the ground they were surrounded by streamers of light. Jonah recognized them at once: this was the web of charm he had seen connecting the tiles down the length and breadth of Stone.

Now the charm was seeking its earth.

Twin streams of brilliant red charm lanced first up then over, spearing the two dragons – one apparently dead, the other alive and most assuredly kicking. Jonah clearly saw the charm first penetrate their spines then burst from their breasts, pinning them to the ground.

There was no blood, only two blinding explosions of light. Both dragons, even the petrified Areken, twitched abominably; it was like watching gods receiving galvanic therapy. The light was clean and white, quite free of fire or smoke, shape or scent. As pure as the light from the sun.

Then, as soon as it had begun, it was over. The charm winked out as if it had never been there, leaving a ferocious afterglow on Jonah's bruised retinas. When this too had died away he saw the stone dragon lying immobile again. Beside her, Archan was clambering to her feet, shaking her head like a beaten dog. But still alive. Still very much alive.

'What in God's name was all that about?' said Annie.

'I do not know,' he murmured.

Archan, eyeless still, inclined her head towards the sun. Using some invisible sense, she was looking up.

The free hand of Esh – the one not holding the thread of the sun-balloon – descended on the stone dragon. Archan flinched as her sister was plucked like a beetle and lofted towards the place where Jonah and the others were cowering. When the dragon was poised over the cup Esh stopped . . . and began to squeeze.

The sound was the worst of it. It was the sound of babies being crushed, of lost souls condemned to torture inside the caves of their minds. From the screams emerged a steady drip-drip-drip. Then, following behind the sound as if the sight were somehow less important, cloudy grey liquid started to leak from Areken's body.

Soon it was not just dripping but flowing, then flooding. It cascaded into the hungry cup, a momentary waterfall in this realm of fire. Then gradually the flood subsided and, after a few final and reluctant drips, Areken ran dry.

Throughout this strange procedure Archan had been struggling into the air. By the time Esh replaced the husk of her sister in the shallow pit she had climbed perhaps forty feet above the smoking ground. But her wing movements were laboured and the charm flowed from her body in spasmodic flashes. When she saw Esh reaching for her she backtracked wildly, flinging her wings forwards in a desperate effort to escape.

But it was to no avail. Esh removed her from the sky and drew her struggling, screaming form into place above the cup. Again she began to squeeze.

This time Jonah had to turn away. He buried his face in Annie's neck; she held him close, stroking his hair as if he were a child. From the set of her body he knew she was watching everything.

The only thing he heard over the appalling sound of Archan's torture was Thomas Coyote saying, just once, 'Holy shit.'

The silence afterwards was more immense and in some ways more awful.

By and by Jonah found the courage to remove himself from Annie's embrace. He was astonished to see Archan not only back in the pit next to her sister, but licking her wounds and looking around. Her eyeless gaze was as alert as ever. There was something different about her however, something . . . *diminished*.

She pointed her head directly at him, opened her jaws to reveal glistening steel teeth and hissed.

He stumbled backwards as she advanced, wondering if she would ever go away. Annie and Thomas both grabbed for him as he fell but they were too late. He dropped heavily on his side, sending fresh jolts of agony through his injured back. Piercing this painful symphony was a new trumpet-call as he crashed on to something hard in his left-hand pocket.

The tiles, he thought stupidly before remembering he had already used them up. *Not that they did any good at all! I might just as well have sat down and started a game of Mah Jongg.*

Pawing uselessly at his back he clawed the object out of his pocket and was about to hurl it away in disgust. It was round and hard, pitted with tiny scars. It felt a little like a skull, a lot like . . .

. . . like a meteorite!

After Kythe had left him on the moon he had waited. A long night had followed, then, at dawn, this rock had fallen from the sky. He had picked it up, put it in his pocket and forgotten about it.

Until now.

He stared at the meteorite. Above him, Annie and Thomas stared at it too. They were bemused, but Jonah felt the beginnings of some deep and abiding comprehension.

Inside his head continents were on the move, pieces of the puzzle locking one by one into place.

'Jonah?' said Annie. Her voice wavered and he fancied there was real fear in her eyes, not at the peril they were in but at the expression on his face.

'Name,' he said and she actually took a step away from him.

The pain in his back had gone. Or perhaps his mind, filled with revelation, had just found better things to concern itself with. He stood up, hefting the rock in his hand like a coconut won at the fair.

'I know you, Archan,' he said, walking to meet her even as she advanced towards him, limbless and undulating. Did she falter? Probably not but it did him no harm to imagine she had. He walked on. 'I know you. And I know your name. Rather, I know your *names*.'

She did hesitate then. A shadow fell across her; it was Esh, a malicious grin on her mobile face.

'Call them, Jonah,' said Esh. 'Call them all.'

Jonah stopped in the smouldering remains of the orchard. A broad puddle of fruit pulp blocked his way, smelling like boiled wine. This was far enough. He twisted his feet, planting them deep in the ground, and let his mind fly up into the sky.

Moon above, earth below. Jonah Lightfoot between.

He was here and he was on the moon, holding the rock and retrieving the rock, now and then. Alive in both the here and there. Making changes, making sure everything remained true and nothing was lost. Binding the threads tight so that no strands went astray. Calling the names, one by one.

'Kythe knew you were special, Archan,' he called and now Archan stopped dead too, held by his words. 'When you came from the egg your father said you might have any name at all. He did not know how true that was. For every dragon, Archan, there is a rock on the moon which bears its name. Its true name, mark you. Most dragons wear their true names with pride, but you . . . you are different. For every list there must be an index; every piece of the arch strives to reach the keystone. You are the index, Archan, the keystone of your race.

'This rock, this name of yours, is the totality of all dragon names. You are Archan, for that is the name your

415

parents chose for you, and a convenient marker it has proved for most of your long life. But a marker is all it ever was. You are more than Archan. So much more.'

He thrust the rock forwards and Archan shuddered. Fire jetted from between her teeth and she growled like a pride of lions. Jonah traced one finger over the pitted surface of the rock, closed his eyes on Stone and . . .

. . . opened them on the moon. The rock remained in his hand and in the airless glare he could see clearly the names traced across its surface. Holding it thus he could see a thousand marks, thus a thousand more. Each turn, each new trick of the light and a new generation of dragons made themselves plain. Here were all their names and Archan was them all, the keystone of her race.

One name appealed to him. He followed its course around the rock with his finger, mouthing the syllables silently in the moon's vacuum shroud.

Then he closed his eyes on the moon and . . .

. . . opened them on Stone.

'You were *destined* to become immortal, Archan. I never realized it until now. *You* never realized it until now, am I not right? One dragon had to remember the names after all the rest were gone. What better way to keep a race alive than to keep its names alive? Stone remembers such things but Kythe knew that even Stone could not be trusted to keep its memories forever. Hence you, Archan, the one immortal dragon, guardian of all.

'But the responsibility proved too great. Even had you understood your role you would still have turned against it, sooner or later. For evil has always been in you, Archan – that is what Kythe could not account for. You were the chosen one but the choice was not made wisely. Such is the folly of the gods, who are simpler beings than we imagine.'

Here Jonah paused. He was breathing hard and fast; his pulse was like a steam-hammer at his temple. Above both him and the dragon, Esh loomed.

'Esh,' he said, more quietly, 'do you wish to tell her or shall I?'

'The pleasure,' replied Esh, 'should be yours, Jonah Lightfoot.'

'Very well. Archan, you are deathless no more.'

Silence like death. Archan's head turned slowly, so slowly, towards the cup. Jonah could not help swivelling his own head in that direction too; he saw Annie and Thomas do the same. A red aura hovered over the cup and there was no doubt as to what was inside.

'Immortality!' growled Archan. 'You dared to take it from me! You dared!'

'All those little tiles,' said Jonah. 'All those little tiles were connection points for the web of charm that was necessary to steal it away. That charm has been in Stone all along but it needed to mature and it needed to be directed. Esh has been preparing for this day for a long, long time, Archan.'

'You dared!'

He thought she would spring then, would leap on him like a cat on a mouse. She was close enough to reach him in a single bound and certainly angry enough to swallow him whole without a care. Yet still something held her back and, during her moment of hesitation, Jonah saw something interesting.

Behind her, one wing of the stone dragon had started to twitch.

Archan had bent her head back and was nuzzling at her tail. At first he could not see what she was doing, then suddenly she closed her jaws with a hard, metallic clack. He heard Annie inhale sharply.

Archan lifted her head. About four feet of her own tail hung bleeding from her jaws. She flung it casually aside then turned again to inspect the stump. For several moments they all watched as the stump bled and bled . . . and quite failed to regenerate.

When Archan turned back to face Jonah the fire inside her mouth had turned pure white; it was so hot that the teeth around which it pulsed began to melt. Gobbets of silver fluid dribbled from her mouth and made mercury pools on the ground.

'Faery,' she said. The words were thick and slurred. 'Oh, faery, what a fate you shall suffer.'

Jonah said nothing, simply lowered the rock and spoke aloud the first of the names he had chosen from its store.

'"Ormungad",' he said. 'You are the Midgard Serpent.'

The name circled the blistered ground, an airborne whisper. From the persistent tendrils of smoke a shape began to form, human in all but its dimensions. It came and went, fighting to substantiate itself, thinning as it grew but growing nonetheless. Becoming, however briefly, real.

'Ormungad,' hissed Thor. His voice was as ghostly as his body. He towered over them all, as tall as Esh. In his hand he swung a hammer the size of an obelisk.

Archan belched fire at Thor but the flames passed through him without leaving so much as a mark. In reply the god swung his hammer, which in turn passed straight through Archan's body. Immediately reversing his grip the god swung again; this time Jonah watched more closely and saw a tell-tale jolt as the hammer encountered Archan's flesh. He had seen such a jolt before, when the god had attacked the Bark.

Already Thor was fading from view. He managed three more strikes before he was gone. Archan spat fire into his wake but now the flames were flecked with charred scale fragments.

Annie's hand closed on Jonah's before he could trace out another name.

'Let me,' she said, 'please.'

He allowed her to take the rock, saw her shut her eyes as her fingers explored its surface, felt the ripple in the air as some inner piece of her reached up for, and touched, the moon.

When she opened her eyes again she was smiling.

'Here,' she said. '"Snallygaster".'

Archan doubled up as if she had been punched. Her white scales paled then turned virtually transparent. They could see her only by glints of sunlight and the refraction patterns she made against the sun and sky. Through her almost invisible body they could clearly see her sister, Areken, heaving her broken stone body into motion.

Annie drew in her breath, held it for a moment, then blew it out.

Glassy scales flew from Archan's body, streaming from her like a blizzard tipped on to its side. Behind her Areken too had turned partially transparent and was losing scraps of stone to Annie's lethal breath.

'Better than the basilisks, eh?' she said, panting. 'One puff and you're dead.'

The twin images of Archan and Areken shimmered back into something resembling reality. Bones showed through tattered hides, revealing ugly flashes of fire deep inside. The fire looked damp and polluted, more smoke than flame.

'Is she really mortal now, Jonah?' said Annie in wonder.

'Let us find out.'

Gently he took the rock from her. There were so many names! Most of them meant nothing to him; he turned the rock this way and that, seeking out a new and final incarnation to force upon the dragon.

Halcyon . . . Scarn . . . Dibilius . . . Quetzalcoatl . . .

This last name he fancied he had heard before but he did not see how he might use it.

Then he remembered Kythe on the moon. Remembered the name that had come to her in a dream.

'Orbos,' she had said, 'or something like that.'

Something like it, yes. Orbos, and a circle of dragons in the air, somehow connected.

At last he had it.

'Though you are mortal, Archan,' he said, 'I will not kill you.'

Then he spoke her name.

'Not "Orbos",' he said. '"Ouroboros".'

Annie frowned at him and was about to question him when he raised his hand. 'Wait,' he said. 'Watch.'

Still Archan had not spotted her sister, so intent was she on crossing the last few yards to where Jonah and Annie stood side by side, facing her. She lumbered, shedding scales not like snowflakes now but like winter leaves that had lingered too long after November's bite. When she was five yards away she snarled at them, opening her jaws to reveal a blistered tongue draped with molten teeth.

'I will burn you both where you stand,' she said. 'Then I will take back what is mine. The power of memory may be yours but you do not know the power of dragon charm. I will take immortality back as I have taken it before. And when that is done I will resurrect you both, as I have long promised to do. I will give you back your lives. Then, and only then, I will start to play with you and . . . oh, I have such games in mind! Do you think all this a puzzle, faeries? It is nothing to the pieces I will make of you!'

She stopped short, head cocked quizzically to one side.

'What the hell is "Ouroboros"?' whispered Annie. She had not flinched at all during Archan's speech, despite being threatened by a creature with a throat like a blast furnace.

420

'A story I remembered from my school days,' he said. 'The "Ouroboros" was a legendary serpent which, if I remember correctly, consumed itself by eating its own tail. It is a Greek name but the serpent is known in Egyptian drawings. It had the ability, to all intents and purposes, to make itself gone.'

'Neat trick.'

Something was pulling Archan backwards. The white dragon started to thrash so violently Jonah thought she was having the dragon equivalent of a seizure; then he realized it was pure anger, long-since boiled to vapour and now inflating her ravaged body like some evil, bloating gas. She whipped round, bending double and clamping her jaws tight shut upon the tail of her attacker.

The attacker was, of course, Areken.

Archan gulped down two-thirds of her sister's cracked stone tail in a single gulp. Areken responded by swallowing a corresponding amount of bloody white flesh. By degrees, they began steadily to eat each other.

Jonah and Annie looked on in horror as the two dragons methodically chewed their way up each others' bodies. Now each pair of jaws was gaping wide across sibling ribcages, now wings were crumpled back by lashing tongues. Flames erupted from behind their collapsing skins, orange turning to yellow as the fire inside was crushed down into itself. Behind the dreadful grinding, sucking undercurrent of sound were their twin screams, high and keening.

'Shit, Jonah,' said Annie. 'This is awful.'

The dragons were glowing white hot now, all their fire, all their charm focusing in and down, in and down. Their rate of consumption was slowing too, either from exhaustion or the simple demands of anatomy. Once he had seen the process begun, Jonah had imagined they might consume each other into some magical oblivion; now, he saw, there was simply nowhere for them to go.

Yet still, incredibly they managed to fight. Jaws locked tight about sibling abdomens, the two dragons started to roll across the steaming soil. There was an awful, beautiful symmetry to their form: white and grey, scale and stone, all glowing with the livid fire of charm.

There was a brief moment when Jonah thought they would crash into the cup holding the precious elixir of Immortality, then their twin coils spun the opposite way and began heading towards the Verge.

We are insects on the edge of a giant's table-top, though Jonah, backing away with Annie's hand in his. *And if we go over we will fall.*

Fused together into an unbroken dragon wheel, brilliant with heat and light and furious passion, the two dragons who had only ever been one, who had once been immortal and now were not, went over the edge.

26

Archan Falling

How could it have turned on something as trivial as a name?

The faery had stood there, daring to speak aloud dragon names, daring to change her from the inside out. How could she not have known? How could she have been so blind?

'We should be dead already, sister,' said Areken, transmitting her thoughts effortlessly into the matched mind of the other dragon. The words were cool, like a breath of winter wind.

'Dead? We shall know nothing of death, sister! Do you not know there is always a way to go on? Do you not know that nothing, in the end, goes?'

'We do, sister. We do.'

As she cursed and swore at the sibling to whom she was locked, Archan grudgingly admitted the truth of what Areken had first said: they should indeed have died already.

'Rejoice, sister,' growled Archan, 'for we are still at large.'

'We fall, Archan.'

'Not for long.'

Archan wrapped talons around the fire erupting from her hot and angry heart and pulled free flames like entrails. This was the fire of remembered charm buried deep inside the recesses of her soul; for, though mortal, she still contained the eternal history of Stone and it was overflowing with charm. Ultimately it would be too much for her finite body to hold back but for now she knew she could contain it, channel it, direct it at her enemies.

'Give it to me, sister,' said Areken. Her voice was still icy, a sharp counterpoint to Archan's fiery rage.

'You have no dominion over me! I will spit you out! You are no kin of mine! You are nothing but a nameless mortal beast with no more right to live than the lowest creature of the deepest, darkest ocean!'

'You cannot kill me, Archan. We are one. We will never be parted.'

Fuelled by her sister's taunts Archan hauled yet more charm out of the furnace. Such reckless expenditure of charm would eventually tear them apart. Having reserved her own energies Areken would be strong enough to fall upon her weakened sister and devour her. Then she would turn her mind back to the lost immortality. Then she would start all over again.

Archan knew this yet still she could not damp her fury. She was ultimately more powerful than Areken, knowing as she did so much of the charm of Stone. As she raged so she also prayed the charm would be enough to tip the balance. She had lost everything; only by risking everything could she hope to win it back.

So Archan raged, her sister fed on her fury and the falling dragon wheel glowed brighter and brighter as it spun headlong into the lightless abyss.

Neither dragon saw the massing cloud of small, bright forms gathering beneath them.

'Fire and ice,' Areken whispered. 'We are both and we are one.'

'You're rambling, sister! Your mind has turned to stone!'

'But charm lives in me, Archan, more than you know.'

424

The firefly lights were clustered now, transformed from a field of stars to an iridescent cushion buoyed miraculously against the falling air. Ripples of agitation passed through the crowd, tremors of anticipation.

'We blaze in the night, sister!'

Archan was trying desperately to ignore the relentless squawk of her sister's thoughts but this last observation sent a chill even through the fire in her heart.

Black world.

She remembered this place now. With all her attention focused inward on the charm she had not thought to consider how they must appear from the point of view of an onlooker.

No need, she scolded herself. *No onlooker can match our presence or challenge our charm.*

A serpentine shape tumbling from the Verge. An unavoidable source of light in a realm where all was in shade.

The Shades!

Too late she sent her senses flying beyond the dragon wheel. Too late she flung her awareness both out and down, turning her inner vision inside out so that she saw herself and her sister from the point of the waiting Shades. The hungry Shades.

They were a blur of light, a curving fish-form falling, falling . . .

The Shades were baying.

Lightfish!

Too late Archan dug deep with her talons. Too late she disembowelled herself of all the charm she held inside, too late she spilled guts and memory over the firefly-cloud below. The wheel was still intact when it struck the Shades, the two dragons were still bound together by force and fate. But it was rapidly becoming a husk as the unimaginable reservoir burst through the dam, flooding the Shades with the charm they craved.

Too late Archan mourned her lost immortality. Too late she vowed to make the faery gone, as he had made her gone.

Too late she said to her sister,

'Areken, help me.'

The end was swift. Well-practised at the long wait and the speedy kill, the Shades tore into the dragons with relish. They rent bone and sinew, lapped blood and bile and raw, pulsating charm.

As for the more exotic contents of the dragons' pulverized remains, they simply let them flow away into the night. The Shades, free as they were to pass between the world of Stone and the world of their birth, were not concerned with the past. As they fed on the flesh and the succulent dragon charm so they let all the knowledge Archan had amassed – all the basilisk charm, all the Stone magic – simply . . . drain away.

The endless history of that most ancient part of Stone, which Archan had devoured so long ago, was in every conceivable sense forgotten.

Had Jonah been witness to this feeding frenzy he would have had time to take just one breath in and let one breath out before the cloud of Shades began to disperse.

All that remained were a few scales spinning downwards on the warm night breeze. These were grey stone, dusted with persistent magic; these were pure white and glowing with their own inner light.

A solitary Shade – had Jonah been there he would have known its name to be Tangent – flew expertly from one scale to the next, ingesting each in turn and leaving nothing in his wake.

In the end only one of each was left: one grey, one white. These he consumed too, leaving nothing.

The dragons were gone.

27

. . . Nothing Goes

They stood for a long time watching the place where the dragons had disappeared over the edge. Even when Annie dropped to her knees and put her face in her hands Jonah could not tear his eyes from the spot. If he turned his back would she not appear? Would not wide white wings rise from beyond the Verge? Would she not return with blank chrome eyes set deep into new white scales, seeking the vengeance she was owed?

Could she really be *gone*?

He could not believe it. One day he might, that much he could allow. But not today, not today.

Annie was crying, raising her hands to her poor, burned scalp and flinching as she touched the charcoal growths bedded there.

'It hurts so much, Jonah,' she sobbed. She was trembling down the length of her body and her skin was ice-cold. With the excitement over she was retreating into herself, giving herself over to shock.

Thomas joined them as Jonah embraced her, rubbed her back, tried everything he could think of to warm her up.

'I put out the flames on her head,' said Thomas. 'I did that much. I wish I could've done more.' His eyes were the eyes of a child seeking reassurance.

'You did well, Tom,' said Jonah.

While his hands continued to rub Annie's back, her arms, her legs and feet, his eyes returned to roaming the battleground. The dragons were gone. Mortal now, they would not survive the fall. That much he told himself, preparing himself for future belief.

But there were other matters not yet resolved, not at all. The fire burned still, steadily reducing the last five trees of the orchard to stumps. There was Esh, as big as Rata Kadul herself, bending over the cup filled with the liquor squeezed from the dragons. Behind her, coming and going through the haze, was the blackened hulk of the Bark. It looked like a chestnut left too long in the pan.

Something was wrong, badly wrong. What was it?

Annie had slipped into something approaching slumber. Instructing Thomas to keep her warm, Jonah picked his way through burned branches to where Gerent was crouched over Malya's body.

He approached slowly, making as much noise as he could so that Gerent was not taken unawares. The Neolithic's red and black wings drooped; his whole posture was one of utter desolation.

Jonah knelt.

Malya was both grey and beautiful. A monument to a Valkyrie, a warrior woman of Stone. His perfect lady knight. The sword she had offered him remained firm in her hand. She was still, at the end, at his service.

He thought he should cry but the tears eluded him. Gerent's face, in contrast, was blotchy; red eyes peered from soot-filled sockets.

It was Gerent who spoke first.

'I did my best,' he said. 'I could do no more for her.'

'No,' said Jonah, 'there was nothing more any of us could have done.'

'Nothing.' Though sad, Gerent's tone was in some way

decisive. Buried behind the words was a devastating acceptance.

A vast shadow darkened Malya's face, turned the two men into shades.

'There can be healing, if you wish it,' said Esh. 'But there is little time.'

Jonah saw Gerent's face move in the darkness with momentary hope, then fall with understanding.

'Annie's head,' said the winged man, 'and Coyote's hands. Jonah, are you all right?'

'My back,' said Jonah, feeling ashamed.

Esh's hand was poised over Jonah, the index finger extended. A dewdrop of clear liquid hung in tantalizing suspension from its tip. The finger moved a little . . . this way . . . then shook the dewdrop free. It fell slowly and struck the nape of Jonah's neck. He felt it course down his back, felt it enter his spine and inflame him. It burned for an instant then was absorbed. A moment later his skin exhaled ice. He turned and examined the ground behind him, expecting to find scattered hoar frost, but there was nothing there.

Slowly Esh moved her hand back to the cup and dipped her finger in. Just as slowly she lowered it over Annie's head. Jonah watched the liquid drain across her scalp, watched it first steam then freeze, saw a momentary haze as it was expelled.

The last droplet was for Thomas Coyote, who raised his burned hands like a supplicant. When the liquid had done its work he pressed his renewed flesh to his face and wept.

'Esh,' said Jonah, rubbing at his back and marvelling. 'Am I right in thinking you have touched us with immortality?'

The giant smiled. 'You have nothing to fear, Jonah. The charm came into you and also left you – you felt it go, yes?'

'Yes.'

'Then all is well. Your body has forgotten it already. You did not drink from the cup, Jonah. Nor would you wish to.'

'No, indeed no!' He shuddered. 'I cannot imagine *anybody* wishing to drink from it! Immortality is a curse best forgotten.'

Esh did not reply, merely broadened her smile.

'Please, you must tell me one thing,' Jonah went on, 'and you must tell me the truth.'

'Anything, Jonah.'

'*Are* you Esh? We saw you die at the Threshold yet . . . here you are. And, if I may say so, rather bigger than when we knew you before! I know it is in the nature of your species to experience rebirth but . . . well, you are not exactly what I had expected to find here at the top of Stone!'

'The answer to your question is simple. I *am* Esh. But I am also more than Esh. I am all the Ypoth, of whom Esh was only a single individual. I am what you might call the collective consciousness of a race which sleeps long and wakes only to do its work, which is to repair damage caused to Amara. I, by way of contrast, never sleep. I am the one who keeps watch and alerts individual Ypoth when they need to be roused. I am the caretaker of caretakers, Jonah, the keeper of all that is below me.'

Jonah let out his breath slowly through pursed lips. 'Then let me say, Esh – for I shall call you by that name – it is good to see you again!'

The giant's mobile lips quivered; tears rimmed her huge green eyes.

'It is good to see you too, Jonah Lightfoot. And I am, as I have always been, your humble servant.'

She bowed low. With one hand at her waist and the other still grasping the thread connected to the sun, she

430

looked both epic and absurd, and Jonah had to stifle a laugh.

'What is so funny . . .' she began haughtily. Then her voice trailed away and she said, 'Oh dear.'

'What?' demanded Jonah. 'What, Esh?'

Gerent had seen it too. Something was rolling towards them through the piles of ash and charred wood. At first Jonah thought it was a ball. Then he saw it was a miniature human skull.

It stopped a few yards away, empty eye sockets profound with shadow. Then it levitated, not stopping until it was floating about five feet above the ground. Charm crackled sporadically inside it, dribbling from its open jaws like shining mucus. It stretched, component bones cracking, until it had enlarged itself to something approaching adult human size. Then a ghost materialized around it.

Jonah's hand went to his mouth. The ghost was Mister Ren.

The little Chinaman rippled in the residual currents rising from the baked soil. Everything about him was the same – his face, his attire, his very posture – yet he was a phantom. Jonah could clearly see the distant and dying fire through the man's clothes, no, through his *body*. Only the skull was opaque, the skull which had once belonged to Malya's father, the shaman, and which had somehow held Mister Ren's spirit safe in its cave until the time came for it to venture forth once more.

That time, it appeared, had come.

'Well done, Jonah,' said the ghost in a voice that was all too real. 'You got rid of her at last. You have determination and even a little bravery. I like that in a faery!'

'You lied to us!' said Jonah. 'All the time you lied to us! You forced your way into Annie's dreams and lied to her there, you sucked us both into Stone's memories and made them lie to us as well! Why should I listen to you now?'

'No reason at all, Jonah. Your work is done. You are therefore inconsequential to me. I am therefore inconsequential to you. And now, if you will excuse me, I'm feeling a little thirsty.'

'Take the immortality, if that is what you have come for. It is of no use to us.'

'Remarkable! The faery offers what is not his to give!'

'It is no more yours than mine.'

'I made it, faery!'

'Some things are too great for any one to possess.'

He had no idea what he was doing. All he could think of was to draw Mister Ren into an argument, allowing time for . . . time for what?

'Reckon we're all played out, Jonah,' said Annie. He looked at her in wonder, his gaze lingering on her clean and hairless scalp. She rolled her eyes upwards and said, 'Looks like the redskins got me!'

Her wit drew no laughter but it did warm his heart.

'Looks like they did, my dear,' was all he could think of to say.

'Annie!' said Mister Ren, drifting towards her on the breeze. 'Let me compliment you on the quality of your dreams!'

'Let me compliment you on being a lousy little lowdown shit,' replied Annie pleasantly. His smile dropped at once; Jonah saw too that he faded, just a little and only for a moment.

You are weaker than you would have us believe.

'Tell me, Mister Ren,' he said. 'You never satisfactorily answered a question of mine.'

'What question might that be, Jonah? Make it quick!'

'Do you deserve to be saved?'

Again that fading, almost too quick to see.

'I am saved already, faery! Now stand aside and let me drink my fill!'

'You are not saved at all, Mister Ren. You died long

ago. You are nothing but a ghost prowling the deepest chasms of Stone, dreaming of a life that can no longer be yours.'

Mister Ren, now at Jonah's shoulder, leered at him with sudden venom.

'It shall be mine,' he spat. 'Life is a commodity like everything else. Immortality is a commodity too. Everything can be traded because everything has a price.'

'If it can be traded it can be stolen too.'

'Damn right, faery! It was stolen from me and now I'm stealing it right back!'

Annie thrust her face into that of the ghost. 'You sure about that?'

Mister Ren looked to where she was pointing. Esh was standing there, arms held out at waist-height, with one hand still holding the thread to the sun and the other holding the cup. He looked first confused and then, to Jonah's chagrin, relieved.

'Oh, don't worry about Esh,' he laughed. 'She's here for me.'

'For you?' Annie looked fearfully at Jonah.

'Oh yes!' He was giggling now, relieved beyond the capacity to control himself. 'You don't think I want to spend eternity down here, do you? All eternity on *Amara*? Oh, you poor simpletons, I see from the looks on your faces that you do! *There* is the true span of infinity, up there! Don't you remember your lesson on the *Beagle*? Don't you remember the blazing truth at the heart of the sun? Don't you remember the ocean where time flows all ways? *That* is where I am bound to go, once I have imbibed the nectar of immortality. And Esh is here to guide me.'

'Esh?' said Annie uncertainly. 'Is this true?'

Esh's face was severe. 'Climb the thread,' she intoned. Her voice was the voice of a god. It was clear she was talking to no one but Mister Ren.

Grinning from one ear to the other, the ghostly form of Mister Ren floated between Jonah and Annie and rose before Esh's face. Her expression was unreadable.

'You must remain in contact with the thread at all times,' she said, her voice still low and thunderous.

'Don't make any sudden moves.'

'Hold on tight,' she replied. 'Trust me.'

Abandoning the aether, Mister Ren pumped enough charm from the skull to permit his body to materialize more fully. It also grew until it was twenty feet tall. Not a Gulliver but a Goliath at least. Then he levitated until he had reached the place where Esh was gripping the thread. He began to climb, hand over hand.

When he was level with her face, Esh lifted the cup towards him. He paused, adjusted his grip then reached for it with a greedy hand. At the last moment Esh stopped. She held it just out of reach. He stretched, nearly fell, clung on.

'What are you doing?' There was a dangerous edge to Mister Ren's voice. 'Do not defy me, Esh! You know the consequences!'

'Yes,' she agreed. 'But do you?'

Esh let the cup fall. It crashed to the ground close beside the cowering humans, though not a drop of the precious elixir was spilled.

'Quickly!' Esh said. 'Who among you has the sharpest sword?'

Jonah knew he ought to reply but held his tongue; he knew also that Gerent would want to take this task – whatever it might be – upon himself.

Please, he thought, *do not let him throw his life away into the bargain.*

But someone else was quicker than Gerent.

'My sword is not sharp,' came a voice from the shadow cast by Esh. 'But my arm is strong and I have sworn it shall do good service.'

And they gasped as Malya rose for the second time from the dead.

She was stone, still stone. But she was no longer grey. Her skin was smooth marble, white shot through with cords of subtle rose; it glowed in the shadow. Her hair was spiked and sulphurous yellow; black obsidian clothes shifted with miraculous fluidity across her pale veined skin; her eyes were fine blue azurite. She moved slowly but there was no stiffness to her gait. Only her sword looked worn, a blade of shale unworthy of this woman of stone.

'Here,' said Gerent. Jonah understood the word *rapture* but had never seen it until now. It was on Gerent's face, it flowed form his every pore. 'Take this. It is the sharpest point I have ever known.'

From beneath his clothes he drew a slim black blade, less a sword than a spike. Jonah recognized it instantly: it was the claw he had seen Gerent retrieve from Esh's corpse. It was Esh's claw.

Malya took it without question, discarding the pale sword. On striking the ground it broke into a thousand pieces.

She marched swiftly then astounded them all by clambering easily up the smooth side of the cup, which Esh, bending low, began swiftly to raise once more.

'I cannot do this myself,' Esh boomed. 'That is why I have waited for you. I need your help. I have always needed your help. I cannot do it alone.'

'Do what alone?' called Annie, but Esh was not listening.

Now the cup, with Malya standing at the ready on its rim, was poised just below the place where Mister Ren was still clinging to the thread. His ghostly body was trembling, weary from the effort of simply holding on.

When he saw the cup his face showed relief. When he saw Malya it contracted in horror.

'No,' he breathed. 'Esh, no. You wouldn't.'

Esh nodded. Malya drew back the claw.

'I trusted you!' screamed Mister Ren, his body flitting wildly between transparency and opacity. The skull within shone like a beacon.

'That shames me,' Esh agreed. 'But I will get over it. Now, Malya.'

It was a smooth, elementary stroke. Perfectly balanced on the lip of the cup, Malya swung the claw in a short, shallow arc. Its tip made contact with the thread from which all Stone hung suspended.

Then it cut through.

'No!' howled Mister Ren, letting go his hold and grabbing for the severed ends. 'Stone will fall!'

'No,' said Esh. 'Stone will be free.'

Somehow Mister Ren managed to coil his hands round the snake-lashing ends. In his right hand he held the thread leading to the sun; in his left he held the thread to which Esh was still attached. His ghostly body, stretched to ghastly extremes by the opposing forces, was shuddering uncontrollably. With the weight of all Stone trying to tear it limb from limb, it was hardly surprising.

'You cannot hold it forever,' said Esh. 'Nobody could, not even I. That is one reason I have done what I have done – I am tired.'

'I'll never let go, never!' screeched the distorted phantom shape of Mister Ren. Then he lost his grip on both ends of the thread.

Several things happened at once. Even later, when he thought back, Jonah could not determine exactly what it was he had seen, nor the sequence in which the events had flowed. He wondered briefly if he should use the memory rods to revisit that moment. But it was a passing fancy, one he buried deep where it might never tempt him again.

The instant Mister Ren let go of the thread the sun

began to accelerate up into the sky like a bubble climbing the ocean. Vast as it was it would take many hours to diminish but flee it did and at ever-increasing speed. At the same moment Jonah and his companions felt a momentary weightlessness, as if the ground had forgotten they were there. Gravity returned after a moment or two but they knew they were falling still and would continue to fall. Perhaps forever.

More immediate was the fate of Mister Ren. As long as he remained in contact with the thread he was owned by the world of Stone. With that contact broken he was flung free of this and all other worlds. He was adrift, a piece of flotsam without even a sea on which to float. He was . . .

'. . . naked,' whispered Jonah in horror. 'Naked before the teeth of the cosmos.'

White muck appeared from nowhere and fell around Mister Ren's grossly elongated body. It was not the whiteness of good light, nor of purity – it was the awful empty whiteness of *nil*. It was a void in which a few rare specimens of consciousness had found sanctuary, not least Archan herself, but they had all been complex creatures, Kings and not Fools. It bore down on him, this whiteness, *bit* down on him. It seemed to make flesh of his spirit before tearing into that flesh, defining its prey before devouring it. He was reborn only in order that he might be sacrificed. He struggled but was engulfed. When he clawed the air the air turned white and clawed him back; when he dislocated his jaw to scream the muck filled his throat and inflated him. It fed him, fattened him, ready for the kill.

Now he was transparent, like glass, a cavity in the sky. White shadows crossed before him, eating him up. Just before he was eclipsed forever something blurred through the air behind him like a bird passing a window.

It was dark and faceless, a blundering shadow with no true dimension. Its mindless screams were deep concussions in the air, fading drumbeats that were quickly gone.

This simple beast whose mind had both conceived and constructed immortality saw white teeth closing finally on his tattered almost-flesh and died hoping he might still live forever. And that hope, as he learned here at the very end, was the deepest pit into which any mind could be cast.

After allowing Malya to climb down to the ground and rejoin her friends, Esh raised the cup and saluted them all.

'May you live long,' she said, 'but not forever.'

Jonah watched as she lifted the cup to her lips.

'What about you, Esh,' he said. 'Surely you do not wish to live forever?'

Esh said nothing. Tipping the cup back she drained it, swallowing down the pure elixir of distilled immortality. That done, she hurled the empty vessel out into the abyss.

Then she turned her back on them, lay down with her head resting on her hands and appeared to sleep.

'I was never dead. I can't explain it . . . it was like a deep, deep sleep. Except I was aware of myself all the time, aware of my body changing around me. I *could* have died, perhaps I even *should* have died. But . . . I decided not to. Not yet, anyway.'

Malya laughed, her smooth marble face creasing into an entirely human expression of joy. Transformed though she was, there was a new lightness about her, a sense of history shrugged away. A feeling of the future.

'Stone lives, you know,' she said, pinching the pliable flesh of her gleaming forearm. 'I am the proof.'

So taken were they with their miraculous friend that it was a while before any of them remembered another still in peril. To his credit it was Gerent, so entranced with his lover that he seemed hardly to have noticed her transformation, who thought of it first.

'The lesky,' he said sharply. 'The trees.'

They raced across the battlefield to where the fire was dying. Here, on the brink of the Verge itself, stood a single tree, its upper branches ablaze, its trunk cracked and blackened. Every other tree in the once-proud orchard was gone; in moments this one would be no more.

Time and time again Jonah tried to get close but each time the flames beat him back. Finally he had to admit it was futile. They had nothing with which they could fight the fire in any case; all they could do was stand and watch.

Under their gaze, perhaps even sensing their gaze, Grandfather Tree emerged from the doomed trunk, his broad, burned face coughing with exaggerated theatre.

It was the last time any of them saw him alive.

'Oh me!' he spluttered. 'Poor trees, poor taiga!'

'Never mind the trees!' cried Annie. 'What about you?'

'Me? No matter. Made it here. Job done well. Time to rest now, time to rest.'

'Why did you not go back to the Bark?' said Jonah, though he already knew the answer. 'It lies intact, though I doubt it will ever move again, not without its pilot. Why did you not take shelter there?'

'Told you . . . fire follows lesky. Lesky jumps, fire jumps. Lesky takes shelter, fire takes shelter. Bark there . . . there because lesky here.'

'But the Bark is no good without you! Grandfather Tree, there must be something we can do!'

'Lesky . . . very old . . . very tired . . .'

Flames were licking at his mane of hair now. Jonah fought the impulse to turn away. He had no desire to see

439

his friend burned alive but nor could he abandon him, here at the end.

'Going now,' said Grandfather Tree quietly. 'Won't burn, fret don't. Into the roots. Fire hates roots. Slow sleep there.'

'There will be new growth,' said Jonah, begging for it to be true.

'New growth, yes, but not . . . not for lesky. Everything changes, Jonah, everything . . .'

The old, elfin face began to melt back into the trunk. There was a sense of slow movement down into the ground, a gradual descent. Then, at the very base of the trunk where the bark met the soil, a mouth moved, just once.

'Farewell . . .'

And Grandfather Tree, too, was gone.

They sat together before the smouldering remains of the last trees. Jonah found his gaze wandering time and again to Annie's unscarred scalp. Without hair she looked younger; she almost looked reborn.

Once she caught him staring at her and swatted his arm. He grabbed her hand before she could pull it back and held on. She leaned against him, her body warm.

Above them the sun was shrinking as Stone plunged away from it. Already it was half the diameter it had been. It was still enormous, filling nearly half the sky, but it would continue to recede and eventually it would be gone.

'Perhaps the basilisks were wrong after all,' said Jonah.

'What?' Annie murmured.

'Nothing.'

Although it was darker than it had been it was still brighter than an English summer's day and the air temperature remained comfortably warm. Jonah leaned against Annie and contemplated the black husk of the tree trunk beneath which Grandfather Tree had laid himself. He felt sad but he was too exhausted to cry. Perhaps grief would come later.

'Look,' said Gerent. He used his wings to help him stand up, an entirely involuntary movement. 'Esh has gone.'

'You must be mistaken,' said Jonah, climbing wearily to his feet. 'How could she just . . . ?'

But Gerent was right. The giant black figure had disappeared. All that remained on the flat, round roof of stone was a broken landscape and, perched at the opposite perimeter, the Bark.

Jonah stared at the empty landscape. Still he felt only weariness.

'Come,' said Gerent, pulling Malya behind him. 'Let us investigate.'

Jonah was the last one to reach the centre point of the orchard, the place where the statue of Esh had once stood. By the time he caught up Malya was kneeling over a coil of thin rope, one end of which was embedded in the ground. The other end was loose, cut clean through. A child's string, its balloon lost.

'Be careful of the cut end,' warned Gerent. 'It looks sharp enough to cut even your new skin, Malya.'

'Don't worry about me,' she replied. 'Jonah? What do you make of this?'

Beating back the fatigue he crouched beside her and examined the thread.

'It is the memory thread, certainly,' he said. 'Esh has drawn it out of her body and abandoned it here.'

'Maybe it was irritating her,' said Annie, throwing herself to the ground. 'How are your hands, Tom?'

'Fine, ma'am,' he replied. The sight of a full-grown man shuffling his feet in the soil like an embarrassed child was endearing.

'Tell me, Tom,' said Jonah. 'How much of your life do you remember.'

The tall man's expression changed instantly. Instead of bashful it was now haunted and much, much too old. 'Everything, Jonah. I remember it all.'

There was a sudden draught of cool air. Then, from behind a black and fallen tree, rose Esh. No giant this but the Esh they remembered from before, taller and thinner than a man, a gleaming ebony figure with luminous green eyes and a tortoise carapace. Long insect limbs folded into complex patterns as she crossed her claws before her face and bowed.

'Hello, Esh,' said Jonah. Surprise, like grief, eluded him.

'Forgive my brief absence,' Esh replied, 'but I was tired of that guise. Now my hardest work is done I prefer a less imposing form.'

'It's good to see you,' said Annie. 'I mean it's good to see *you*, like this!'

Esh's approach had been hesitant, humble even, but now her face broke into a vast grin and she stumbled forwards to return the embrace Annie was offering. 'I am very tired,' she said, winking at Jonah over Annie's shoulder.

'That makes two of us,' he said.

'Sit with me a while,' said Esh, patting Annie's arm as they pulled apart. 'It will do us all good to rest.'

'Can we afford to?' said Annie. 'What I mean is, there ain't no more nasty surprises, are there?'

'Surprises I cannot vouch for. As for nastiness . . . I think we can put that from our minds for a long, long time.'

They formed a loose circle around the cut and coiled thread, Jonah holding hands with Annie. Gerent and Malya sat close beside each other, Tom Coyote fidgeted by himself and Esh was resplendent and somehow at the head of it all.

'Now,' she said when they had settled themselves.

'Before we start I wish to present some gifts. Or rewards, if you prefer.'

While the others exchanged mystified looks she rummaged beneath her shell with one skeletal arm. After a prolonged search and a muffled apology she brought out five loops of thin rope.

Not rope, thought Jonah as the receding sunlight danced along the dense black threads.

'This is for you,' she said, standing and dropping the first loop over Tom's head. It fell across his shoulders, the necklace reduced to its most primitive form. He mouthed a soundless 'thank you' and Esh proceeded round the group, ending with Jonah.

'No,' she said softly as he started to get up. 'There is no need to stand.'

As the necklace brushed the skin of his throat he felt the touch of the memory rods. For him the contact was familiar, welcome even; he wondered how the others would react.

Looking into their eyes in turn he saw there was no reason for alarm. They were all regarding their gifts in wonder. There was no fear in their eyes, only delight.

'They are safe to touch,' confirmed Esh, seating herself once more. 'Amara is open to all now.'

'What happened here, Esh?' said Jonah. 'We saw so much and understood so little.'

'You understood more than you realize,' she replied. 'The rest I will tell. First of all, be assured that Archan is gone. The great task is done and the power of immortality has found rest at last.

'Immortality – you will have learned by now that it is not a clever thing. This is to be expected, since it was created by a Fool. Like most Fools, Mister Ren was dangerous. Now he too is gone. The immortality he created – and which I now possess – is nothing less and nothing more than the ability to regenerate. It is not a shield against death but a cure for it. The basilisks understood this for the curse it surely is, for they died and died again throughout eternity. For them, the price of eternity was life without escape.

'In some ways Archan was stronger. Had she lived she would have torn down everything in her vision, including Amara. Eventually she might have accepted her mistake and made new company for herself. I could never have allowed that to happen, for while I am Esh I am also Amara. I am Stone. And I will always protect myself. Have you not heard it said that the memory rods are alive, that Amara itself is alive? It is so, and so the memories are me and Amara is me. I am all you survey.'

'Gee,' said Annie. 'That's quite a thought.'

'Yes. But always remember that, when I am with you, I am especially Esh.'

'All right,' Annie went on. 'So let me get this straight. Mister Ren helped you steal the immortality from Archan. He brought the tiles here – or got me to bring them here since he couldn't himself – and the tiles were what triggered off the whole thing, the transfer of power, or whatever you want to call it. But why did he trust you – come to that, why did you trust him? The way things turned out it's pretty clear you each had your own games to play.'

'Trust was never an issue. Fools neither trust nor love. They scarcely even think. They have clever ways but simple minds. He was playing a game, certainly, but with no concept of the rules. We each moved our pieces and I, in the end, outplayed him.'

'Did you always know you were going to win?'

'Until the moment when Malya cut the thread I was convinced I was going to lose.'

They regarded her silently. Jonah tried to imagine this elegant ebony creature as the tip of the iceberg of Stone and failed. At the end of it all she was simply Esh.

'So what was his real identity?' said Jonah. 'He presented himself as a man from China, and he claimed also to be *you*, Esh. But there was always a sense that these were only masks, that there was something more mysterious underneath.'

'I can assure you he was never *me*,' chuckled Esh. Her laughter was delightful, like spring rain. 'As for his name, well, *Tai Yi Huang Ren* is the name of a Chinese mountain god but even that, as you rightly say, was only a mask. It suited his game so he stole it. But he was no god, only a Fool, though many gods are fools too, it must be said. As for what lay underneath, I cannot say. I think we may have seen a glimpse of it at the end but . . . perhaps some things are best left beyond our ken.'

Jonah raised his hand to suppress a yawn.

'Forgive me,' he said. 'Esh, why did you cut the thread? What have you done to the flow of time? And what can be done to stop Stone falling to its doom?'

'Nothing can be done.' He stared at her open-mouthed. 'Nothing *needs* to be done, Jonah. Amara is not falling – it is free! The void through which Amara moves is infinite. Amara will never come to rest, it will never strike the bottom of the well. It is not falling: it has just embarked on the greatest journey of its life.'

'But what if it hits something on the way down?' said Annie.

Again that delicious chuckle. 'Then won't *that* be an adventure!' Then she frowned. 'Jonah, you look so sad.'

'Yes, well I was thinking about all that has been lost. The basilisks said that nothing goes but they were wrong. So much *has* gone. I doubt I will miss Archan or her sister or that cursed trickster Mister Ren but . . . oh Esh, all those memories! All those memories from the deep past which Archan consumed and which must now surely be lost forever. And all those future memories contained within the sun's ocean. Forgive me but *you* have cut away those future memories, Esh. Stone may live but it is crippled. It is a mere shadow of what the basilisks made.'

To his astonishment Esh was laughing yet again. 'Oh, Jonah! You still have no comprehension of what you have done!'

Jonah's fatigue was rapidly transforming into anger. He had no desire to lose his temper with Esh and was grateful when Annie, sensing his deteriorating mood, intervened.

'Look, Esh,' she said, standing and taking centre-stage, 'are we safe for now? I know without the Bark we're stuck up here, probably forever, but we're safe, right?'

'Safe for a long time, Annie.'

'Okay. Then let's leave this for now. The sun's goin' down – well, okay the sun's goin' *up* but all the same it's getting' dark. I vote we take us some shelter and maybe get a little sleep. Night's fallin' and even if there's no dawn to come we'll all think better after we've rested properly.'

Though the sun dwindled to a tiny star in the otherwise empty sky its light continued to fall upon the little disc of land at the summit of Stone. The night, though inevitable, was less anxious to descend than they had predicted.

Inside the Bark it was a different matter. With all its charm drained and Grandfather Tree gone the vessel was lifeless. No light penetrated the broken interior beyond the first few corridors and Gerent's attempt to salvage some wood to build a shelter had to be aborted when an entire stack of decks collapsed under its own weight. He barely escaped with his life, sprinting from an expanding cloud of sawdust and splinter, his wings momentarily forgotten.

The expedition was not entirely without success, however. Before the collapse Annie had found her way to

446

her cabin and retrieved her painting box. Now, as Bark dust settled over orchard ash, she opened it and picked her way through the contents. Empty tubes of paint, colour-soaked rags and a sheaf of brushes cleansed and maintained with painstaking care. No tiles, of course, not a single one. The inside of the box looked huge and abandoned.

'It served its purpose well,' said Jonah. He closed the lid of the box and latched the little brass clasp. The dark wood was stained even darker by time and travel. Annie traced her finger across the marquetry: here was a scorch mark, there a gouge from some weapon or other, there a faint white stain – the tidemark of an Earthly ocean.

'Salt from the Java seas,' she said. She touched her fingertip to Jonah's lips, let him taste it with his tongue. He closed his eyes as a sensory flood threatened to overwhelm him. 'You okay, Jonah?'

'Yes . . . yes, I . . .'

'What?'

'Now . . . I think that now we can never go home, Annie. I do not know if we ever really had the choice but . . . well, Stone has suffered so much. So much is gone from both the future and the past. Perhaps the connections with our world have gone too. Everything goes, Annie, in time.'

They slept beside the ruined Bark. A flat dusk had come, slowing their thoughts one by one. It was quiet and both the air and ground were warm. There seemed nothing else to do.

When Jonah woke the dusk had deepened only a little. The sun was still centred above them, no bigger than Sirius now; its light was only a little stronger than moonlight.

Easing Annie's head from his lap he stood and stretched.

This miniature world at the tip of Stone was sketched in shades of blue. The sky was nearly black at the close, curved horizon, paling to indigo near the watching star. Features on the ground – broken branches, upsurged roots – were limned with cobalt. Absently he fiddled with the loop of thread about his neck, for it had begun to chafe.

He squinted in the curious half-light. Two figures were moving at the centre of the little disc of soil, their identities lost in the partial light. He walked towards them. Halfway there he stumbled on a jutting root; when he looked up again the figures had squatted, face to face. A pow-wow. He was close enough to recognize them now: they were Esh.

Both of them.

'Jonah,' Esh's voice called. 'Come. Tread carefully. And be quiet.'

'Esh,' he stammered, looking helplessly from one to the other, uncertain of which to address. Then he saw that one of the figures was only partly there, a phantom presence. Trembling, he raised his hand and passed it through the empty space where this ghost-Esh appeared to be.

The other Esh – *his* Esh – spoke again.

'Look around, Jonah. See the world you made.'

He looked and saw a ghost-orchard; leaves like veils danced in an invisible breeze. From the ground rose a ghost-thread, rising into the sky to meet a ghost-sun. Ghost-light wafted down. His fingers worked the necklace like a string of worry-beads and for a while he did not understand.

'You do understand,' whispered Esh, reading not his thoughts but his face. 'Here at Sunlight Pass you can see across to the other Amara, the second Amara you made when you split the river of time. Before me is my twin, who is also called Esh. Behind her is the twin of the orchard we watched burn. Between Amara and sun is the twin of the memory thread. The memories are still there, Jonah. All of them.'

The green eyes of ghost-Esh blinked. Suddenly Jonah saw the differences. The green of her eyes was the green of jade. Her black shell was basalt. The red Mah Jongg mark on her shell was cut from brightest garnet. Mineral hues, rock tones, the colours of stone.

'Your twin is made of stone,' he said and then he *did* understand. The ghost-orchard: granite trunks and leaves of quartz. The spindly line of the thread: obsidian. Even the sun: a vast disc of brightest opal. 'It is all made of stone, all of it.'

'Now do you see, Jonah?'

'Of course – it has all turned to stone! Like Malya, like Areken . . . like Darwin's book! I made it and it has turned into this. An entire world made of stone! But why has it not crumbled like the book, and the wolf-creature? And Areken?'

'They did not crumble, Jonah, they were broken. You dropped the book and broke it. Tom Coyote tore the White Wolf to pieces and I myself crushed Mister Ren's stone-body, the one stolen by Frey, between my fingers. As for Areken – she fell, and was consumed. The intermediate stage is fragile – once broken, these things cannot be mended.'

'Intermediate stage?'

'Malya has passed through that stage into what lies beyond. So has the other Amara. They alone have survived the great change. They are now both made from living stone.'

Jonah stared at the ghostly trees. They were superimposed over the solid reality of the burned orchard like a photographic effect. He was seeing Stone as it had once been: an infinite spiral of memory hanging from a burning sun.

'It is all still there, Esh,' he said. 'This is Stone as it was before Archan ravaged it. Esh, it is intact!'

'Everything changes,' agreed Esh. 'Nothing goes. *Nothing*.'

Jonah pressed both hands to his face. When he looked again the curious double-world had started to fade. Ghost-Esh raised her hand in salute, then she was gone. The orchard and the sun vanished too.

Jonah stood in the darkness, contemplating what he had learned. He brought his hand up to the necklace again, touched it gently. The other Amara returned. When he took his hand away it disappeared.

'The necklaces give us the power to see,' he said.

'Why else do you think I gave them to you?' replied Esh.

Jonah took a deep breath.

'Do they give us the power to travel there too? Can we visit this other Stone?'

'Of course.'

'And we can explore its memories?'

'Yes.'

'Then I am afraid I cannot accept your gift.'

He removed the necklace and held it out to her. She took a step backwards.

'Jonah, no. I cannot take it back.'

'But I have had enough, Esh! Oh, at first it seemed a miracle, this ability to travel through time. But you know as well as I that it is a curse! I cannot so much as breathe inside the rods without wreaking change there. History should not be at the mercy of people such as myself. I have seen . . . I have seen too much, Esh. I choose not to see any more. I choose not to. Please. Take it back.'

'Jonah,' she said softly. 'Jonah, do you think I would have given you all such a gift if I believed there was any danger?'

'But how can there be no danger? You said . . .'

'Jonah, the other Amara is immutable.'

'What?'

'It is immutable. It cannot ever be changed. You can visit it as often as you like. You can interact with whomsoever you choose and change nothing. In that other Amara, time is no longer a river: it is an orchard, an orchard of memories. You can taste its fruit as often as you wish and always there will be more to take its place. Go there, Jonah Lightfoot, go there and walk barefoot through the gardens of time.'

Jonah fingered the necklace. 'Will we meet ourselves there? Will we meet Archan?'

Esh laughed. 'Only if you choose to do so.'

'And the paradoxes that may arise?'

'As I said, the memories are immutable. This is not time travel, Jonah. Now it is reminiscence, pure and simple. The only changes you make will be inside your own hearts.'

Jonah gazed into that other world. He felt the pull of the memories, the safe embrace of the living stone in which they were cradled. Soon he would go there to explore, soon . . .

'What about the sun?' he said, letting go of the necklace again. 'If we ever journey back down Stone's face we will do so in darkness. Is that not so? All the suns in all the worlds we passed on our journey up the Helix, were they not all just reflections of that one, great sun, the one from which you have cast us adrift?'

'"Projections" may be a more accurate term. But yes, Amara had only one sun.'

'And now that sun is gone . . . our Stone will be dark forever.'

He thought of the other Stone, where an opal sun still shone from an azure sky, and envied the people who lived there.

Esh frowned. Her claws clicked together like knitting needles. Then she smiled.

'Perhaps there is something I can do.'

*   *   *

He returned to his friends in a daze.

Whenever he touched the necklace he saw the strange dual landscape: the other world's ghostly trees rising from this world's burned roots, charcoal and granite performing impossible sleights of hand. He saw one world and walked through another. The only things he could be sure of were his feet so these were what he focused on as they raced each other through the orchards.

Squeals of laughter speared him and he looked up into blazing light and a wall of greenery.

Jade, he thought. *Light from a stone world.*

Light, it was light. Dawn had come. A new sun was in the sky.

Annie and Thomas were whooping and dancing before them; Malya and Gerent were grinning from ear to ear, quite dwarfed by this unexpected mass of foliage. Malya had just finished arranging a circlet of woven grass stems about her lover's head; it looked charming, a festive daisy chain picked from a riotous meadow. She plucked an errant petal from his brow and kissed the place where it had clung. Her stone touch was as delicate as a child's.

'You look every inch a king, Gerent,' Jonah said.

'Did you not know, Jonah?' the Neolithic man replied, wafting his wings enthusiastically. 'We are all kings.'

'What d'you think?' yelled Annie, rushing up to hug her man.

'Esh has certainly increased my understanding of the situation,' Jonah said lamely.

'Stuffed shirt!' she said. 'Anyhow, you don't know what you're talkin' about. I mean what d'you think of *this*!'

She turned him towards the Bark. He drank it in.

Green creepers as thick as his waist; a skirt of green ferns; green leaves of every shape and size bursting from the spherical hull. Purple flowers bloomed about its waist like a braid on a May queen. Jonah knew them: they were *amaranthus*, Prince's Feather. The flowers that, according to legend, lived forever. The entire vessel was engulfed in vegetation. The time of hibernation was over. Spring had come to the Bark.

'It is a miracle,' he said, squeezing Annie's hand in his.

'It's Bud!' she said. 'He's brought the Bark back to life! Oh – what did Esh want?'

Jonah looked up at the new sun, trying to understand where it had come from. 'I will tell you later.'

Something burst through the ferns at the base of the ship, something disc-shaped. It swung on a vine like a large wooden medallion. Pressed into one side like a living wax seal was a young elfin face. A lesky face.

'Bud up now! Shine and rise! Come aboard! Bud going, you come? Don't know way, mind! Still. Now Bark is awake. Now he go anywhere!'

Two huge clusters of palm-fronds drew aside, exposing a phosphorescent doorway. The Neolithics ran in, giggling like children and closely followed by Jonah and Annie.

At the threshold Annie paused and turned. Thomas Coyote was fidgeting outside, hands shoved deep into his pockets.

'You comin', Tom?' she said.

'Don't know, ma'am,' he replied. The words of a child lost in the voice of a man.

'You must come with us,' said Jonah. 'There is nothing for you here.'

'She healed my hands.'

Jonah and Annie exchanged a glance.

'The rest is up to you, Tom,' said Jonah. 'But we will help, if you will let us.'

Thomas Coyote stared at the trees in the orchard for a long, long time. Then he ran up to the nearest of them and plucked a transparent peach from the lowest branch.

'Catch!' he shouted, tossing it aboard.

Annie snatched it from the air and bit into the soft and barely visible flesh. She gasped. 'Sweet as honey!'

'Tom Coyote comin' aboard with a pocketful of fruit!'

He burst between them, pockets bulging, and disappeared into the green cave of the Bark. Annie touched Jonah with a sudden angel's kiss.

'We'd better get goin', Jonah Lightfoot!'

'Oh, Annie! Must we rush everywhere? With Archan gone we have all the time in the world.'

'You know what's so great?' She laughed as she bit into the peach, relishing the flood of juice down her chin. 'We don't.'

28

Stone

Jonah saw Esh once more before the Bark began the long descent. The departure was delayed a little once Bud realized that the riot of vegetation he had released was something less than aerodynamic. The passengers looked on as Bud detached roots from the hull and cast countless vines and shrubs and saplings and creepers to the ground.

'They grow here maybe,' he said. The mournful expression with which he had begun the task transformed slowly into one of enthusiasm. 'Orchard becomes garden. Let's hope.'

While Bud worked Jonah wandered across to the burnt stump where Grandfather Tree had died. Esh was there, gazing up at the new sun burning like a huge gem in the sky.

'How did you do it, Esh?' he said, shielding his eyes from the glare. 'Where did it come from?'

Instead of replying, Esh smiled her strange tortoise-smile. She took Jonah's hands in her gentle claws and kissed his fingertips.

'Thank you, Jonah,' she said softly. 'Thank you for everything.'

'You're . . . you are very welcome.'

'However – no riddles,' she went on. 'Come with me now, I will show you how it is.'

She led him to the edge of the orchard, to the very lip of the Verge itself. Fighting vertigo, Jonah permitted her to hold his waist and tilt him forward, ever so slightly, so that he was peering right over the edge of this gigantic table-top, looking down to where Stone lay.

'What do you see?'

'The upper reaches of Stone, such as they are,' he said. 'I see the realm of the Shades. But it is all dark.'

'Even the light of the new sun cannot reach that part of Amara. Theirs is a world that was always meant to be black. But look further, down beyond the world of the Shades. What do you see?'

Jonah strained his eyes but there was nothing. Below the Verge there was only blackness, fading to blue as he raised his eyes back up towards the sun.

'It is dark,' he repeated.

Esh nodded. 'Now look with my eyes.'

Jonah felt the lightest of touches against the back of his head. Another kiss. He felt the warm buzz of charm crawl across his scalp from back to front, felt it tingle across his temples and over his brow. He blinked rapidly and as he blinked he shed tears. The tears dropped into the abyss and when his vision cleared again he understood how, just occasionally, a man could feel that scales had been lifted from his eyes.

Is this how Esh sees things all the time? My God!

Now he could see far beyond the black world of the Shades. Now he could see *everything*.

Beneath the blackness was the thin spiral line of the Helix, clearly visible as a glowing white thread wrapped around Stone's conical form. Below that was a vast curved wall cut from great blocks of grey stone and etched with unfathomable patterns. It was glowing in the light of the new sun. Stone, in all its glory.

The lower part of this wall was bounded by another turn of the Helix. Below that on Stone's ever-widening cone was another stretch of wall. Here, Stone had a greenish tinge and seemed to sparkle as if studded with emeralds. Vast shapes moved across it, giant travellers made tiny by distance.

Further down: the Helix again, the next turn of the spiral, then another world. Then another world, and another. All the worlds through which they had passed on their journey up here, all laid below for him to gaze down upon, on they went, down and down and down. This was Stone as Jonah had never seen it before, this was the overview he had never experienced through all his voyages.

Here, at last, he had all Stone at his feet.

He feasted on it. For a time it looked like an enormous map, an ever-widening, ever-descending spiral of pages on which were painted the most extraordinary lands. Then the immensity of the drop returned to him and he felt giddy. He clung to Esh, more terrified than ever that he would fall and never stop.

'Trust me,' she whispered. 'I won't let go.'

Then she was holding him more tightly, and his feet were lifting from the ground. Turning his head he saw that her smooth black shell had spilt down the middle and opened to reveal four shining wings that shimmered like a beetle's. Tucking him close against her breast she lifted him clear of the ground and carried him out over the edge, out into clear, spice-filled air, out into the raw glow of the sunlight until they had left the Verge and the orchard and the Bark and his friends far behind and there was only him and Esh flying with the sky around them and the sun above and Stone below. They flew in a great circle, circumnavigating the tip of Stone and all the while looking down, surveying their world and contemplating all the worlds it contained, and all the worlds to which it was connected, and all the worlds it was and would ever be. Far, far below, almost at the limit of Esh's extraordinary vision, they saw the very lowest extremity of Stone, the ragged edge where Archan had once bitten it through. They mourned the infinite reaches of Stone which had once existed below that scar and which were now lost. And they rejoiced, for the memories of those lands were not lost at all but existed still in the sister world, the Stone of stone, and they could walk through those lands whenever they chose.

And after a time Esh brought Jonah back to the Verge and placed his feet back on to the soil. They stood close together for a while and instead of looking down they turned their gazes up to look at the sun.

'It's just a trick,' said Esh. 'But a good one. The new sun you see in this sky is simply the sun from the other Amara, mirrored in this world. Another projection, if you like. There is magic between me and my sister – our kinship both spans and joins the worlds. This new sun is our gift to Amara.'

'I had guessed something of the sort,' said Jonah. 'I may not think as fast as my Neolithic friends, but I arrive at the answers eventually.' He thought for a moment, then went on, 'But tell me this: if our Stone is falling, why has it not fallen out of reach of its twin?'

'No matter how far Amara falls it will always be within reach of its sister world,' said Esh. 'It is simply the way of things. You are far from home, Jonah Lightfoot, but your memories of it are still inside your heart. All the same, you dwell on the fall. Does it bother you, that the thread has been cut?'

'Bother me?' Jonah laughed. 'Well, yes, I should say it does rather bother me! Here we are on a broken world, plummeting into the depths of heaven-knows-what with no idea of what we shall strike should we ever reach the bottom! I trust you, Esh, and love you, but I suspect this knowledge may rather keep me awake at night.'

He watched as Esh folded her beetle-wings back inside her shell. The carapace closed with the softest of clicks.

'All worlds fall, Jonah. Even your home-world. The Earth falls around its parent sun and will never come to rest, not during the age of man at least. Whenever you take a step you fall and it is only by taking another step that you break that fall. So on you walk, one step at a time, each step its own adventure and its own name. We fall, Jonah, every one of us, and Amara is no different. Like Stone, we fall. And no matter how far we fall, our memories fall with us. Remember this each morning, when you see the new sun rise. Remember how far away that sun really is, how with every day that passes it grows further still. Then remember how close it is too, all the time, how it will always be near you, inside you.'

The Bark hovered over the Verge. Jonah was standing with Annie on the outermost deck; Esh was standing at the edge of the orchard. They extended their arms, touching finger to claw, their collective reach spanning this narrow place in the sky.

'Goodbye,' said Esh. Her smile was dazzling. 'Look after him, Annie. He is precious to me.'

'Me too,' said Annie, squeezing Jonah's waist.

'Will we see you again?' said Jonah.

'Look for the thresholds,' Esh replied. 'There you may see the Ypoth, and in the Ypoth you may see me, from time to time. Other than that . . . I will be here in the garden. Come and see me. I will be waiting for you.'

'Goodbye, Esh,' said Jonah.

The Bark pulled gently away and they were no longer touching each other. As they sank into the dense air of the Verge they saw Esh wave once, then turn away to walk back across the orchard. Then she was gone.

Blackness came. Annie's voice floated out of it towards Jonah.

'Feels like comin' home.'

'I am tired of travelling, Annie. When I sat in my parlour in London, I used to explore the world by browsing through the *National Geographic*. That was adventure enough for me. I should like to make myself a parlour here, on Stone. Esh said that falling was like walking. Well, I have walked far and fallen further. I should like to stop for a while and simply take in the view.'

'And when you get bored?'

'There are always memories.'

'Kiss me, Jonah Lightfoot.'

Falling stars streaked the sky, but they were only lightfish. The Bark scattered a flock of feeding Shades and by the time it crossed over the Helix and descended into the next world Jonah and Annie had found themselves a place inside its hull, a dark space in which they could be close and quiet, while all around them flowed the charmed and scented air of Stone. After a while, when their pulses had slowed, they asked Bud to make them a window.

They sat before it, arm in arm, and watched the worlds go by.

Epilogue

Jonah takes him to the edge of the clearing. The stone redwoods are just as big as he remembers.

Tom hesitates. In the clearing there's woodsmoke and there are familiar faces. He's anxious now. He tries to turn back but Jonah stops him, his hand gentle on the boy's shoulder.

'This is where you have to start it, Tom,' he says gently. 'I do not imagine the rest of it will be easy but . . . every journey must start with the first step.'

'I'm scared, Jonah.'

It's not only the redwoods that are made of stone. The campfire is an exotic ruby phoenix, precious flames cutting sharp red light through graphite undergrowth. The sky is made from quartz.

Tom's father and sister are both sculpted from marble, perfect Greek statues embraced by sylvan stone. They are waiting for him to join them.

'What will I say to the others? The ones I k-killed?'

'Was it really you who killed them, Tom?'

'I d-don't know. The White Wolf was there. Jonah, is the White Wolf here?'

'Everything is here, Tom. But everything changes. Never forget that. Now go – they are waiting for you.'

Crying just a little, Tom Coyote crosses the clearing. As soon as she sees the boy his sister leaps up and rushes into his arms.

He spins her – the same airplane spin that thrilled her when she was only three.

'Tom!' she squeals in delight.

'Hi, Ellie,' he says. He ruffles her hair which, even though it's made of stone, feels like the purest silk. He looks deep into her stone eyes and all his doubts melt. She's in there, little Eleanor, his baby sister. Everything has changed and nothing has changed. What counts is that they're here together, now.

His father calls his name. He's a dim shape, partly obscured by the smoke from the ruby fire. He calls his name and Tom decides that although it's that same liquor-mean voice maybe it isn't so bad after all, maybe this whole place isn't so bad. There's other places he can go – other places he must go – but this is the first step along the road and maybe that's okay too. What counts is this: whatever happens, even after he's gone, he can always come back. As often as he likes, he can always come back.

He glances back over his shoulder, meaning to say good-bye, but the Englishman from the last century has already gone.

Annie has still not emerged from the house.

It seemed like a good idea, for him to accompany Tom at the start of his odyssey, giving Annie the time she needed. Now he is not so sure.

Stone smoke is rising from the house, which is built from stone sods. Surrounding Jonah is a limestone prairie, an immense crop of stone shining beneath the light of an opal sun. Kansas carved, a living still-life cut from bedrock.

Does she mean to spend the night here? Or worse, does she mean to stay?

Jonah tries to imagine what it would mean to remain in the garden of memory forever and fails. It means either nothing or everything; he cannot decide which. Simpler to sit and watch and wait.

When the sun has reached the horizon and the shadow of the stone crop is hard on the wall of the house, the door opens.

462

Annie emerges. In the shadows, doubled by the glossed marble mirror, stands a tall man of stone. She kisses him lightly on the cheek then walks to where Jonah is waiting without once looking back.

'You can come here as often as you like.' The words sting his mouth but he says them all the same. To his shameful relief she shakes her head.

'No, that's all I wanted, just to see him again.' She searches his eyes. 'I never said good-bye 'til now, Jonah. Not to his face.'

'So, where d'you want to go now?'

Jonah looks out across the orchard.

'There is so much to choose from.'

'You could see your father again. Or Lily. Bet you'd like to, don't deny it!'

He blushes. 'Annie, my darling, you know you are . . .'

'The only gal for you, yeah, I've heard it all before, you sweet-talker! So where? You want a rest? The Bark'll be back at our old ocean again soon. We could catch some sleep before trackin' down Ruane.'

'No, I am not tired.'

She shrugs, plucks a malachite apple from a nearby tree, tosses it in her hand.

'I got another idea.'

'Where?'

'You trust me?'

'To the ends of the Earth.'

'Save that for another day. Hold my hand. Trust me.'

She bites into the apple.

'Karak-at! Karak-at!' shout the parrots as they burst from the forest, rehearsing their names in a carnival of colour. The forest is green and upright, rooted deep in the sheer slopes of the volcano. The parrots are jewels — emeralds and sapphires and fine diamonds set in a silver sky. Elsewhere lies black

lava and edgy pumice. The volcano is itself, comfortable in the garden.

In the stone sea swim two people. Only their heads are visible above the waves. The touch of the water is strange against their skins.

'Feels like tar,' says the woman.

'It is basalt, I think,' says the man, allowing the liquid stone to dribble between his fingers. Though dark, it runs through the light like quicksilver.

'You remember where you left it?'

'It was further back than this. Beyond the fallen tree.'

'There?'

He climbs up the beach. Liquid stone pours from his naked body.

On the sand is a pile of clothes. They too are made of stone. Buried beneath them is a bag and inside the bag is a book.

'I have it, Annie!'

'That's great! Bring it over and we'll finish our swim.'

He lets his fingers trail down the spine of the book. Closing his eyes he imagines the touch not of stone but of leather. He holds it against his chest for a moment, breathes deeply, then replaces it in the bag and returns to the water.

'Jonah, you forgot your book.'

'I know where to find it.'

'Yeah, I guess you do. So, you think that ol' mountain's gonna blow its top?'

'No question.'

'But not today, huh?'

'No. Not today.'

Between the sea and the sky they swim, and the sea is stone and the sky is stone and the light of the sun above them is stone. They are within it and between it all and they are their own adventures, and they know their names.

Author's Note

It's been a long climb. Thanks for staying with me.

I remember vivdly the eruption of Mount St Helens in 1980. It was the first time I understood such things really do happen. Sometimes mountains just blow up. I used the January 1981 edition of National Geographic to help fill in the details. The pyroclastic flow raced a lot of people down the mountain, just like Tom Coyote. Not all of them made it.

All the gods alluded to in these books have some basis in legend. Some of them may even be real.

Thanks to Joy and Sarah at Voyager, and special thanks to Andy for another close read.

And thanks first and last to Helen, for reminding me why.

Graham Edwards
July 2001

Visit the official Graham Edwards website at
http://members.tripod.co.uk/amara